THE LAST MOMENTS OF LOVE . . .

Cole put his cup down and turned to Iris suddenly. "Ah, Posey," he said, grabbing her hand, "this is the way we're meant to be. Together. Always."

She couldn't bear to look at his eyes, fearful he would read the pain welling up within her, so she looked at their hands, his large strong fingers clasped protectively over hers.

"We'll be married before the year is out, I promise," he said. "But now come on back to bed with your poet. We have almost two more days before I have to report back to the base. I don't want to waste a second of them with you out of my arms."

They spent that night and the next day and night together, laughing and rejoicing in each other, tumbling at will into each other's arms. When they made love, Iris clung to Cole, taking in his love as if to store it in her very bones. At rest she watched him, memorizing his every line, absorbing his presence, his tenderness into her very soul. For on Sunday she must tell him she was leaving. . . .

FLOWER OF THE PACIFIC

FLOWER
OF THE
PACIFIC

Lana McGraw Boldt

BANTAM BOOKS
TORONTO · NEW YORK · LONDON · SYDNEY · AUCKLAND

FLOWER OF THE PACIFIC
A Bantam Book / June 1984

ISBN 0-553-22848-X

Published simultaneously in the United States and Canada

Bantam Books are published by Bantam Books, Inc. Its trademark, consisting of the words "Bantam Books" and the portrayal
of a rooster, is Registered in U.S. Patent and Trademark Office
and in other countries. Marca Registrada. Bantam Books, Inc.,
666 Fifth Avenue, New York, New York 10103.

PRINTED IN THE UNITED STATES OF AMERICA

H   0 9 8 7 6 5 4 3 2 1

*This is for Darrell
and because of Darrell
with love*

ACKNOWLEDGMENTS

It is with grateful appreciation that I recognize the gifts of time and experience that others have contributed to this novel.

I have had welcome access to the files, libraries, and collections of several institutions. In particular, Southern Oregon State College Library was most helpful with its microfilms of *The New York Times* and the *Nippon Times* and its general collection. The Graduate Library Special Collections Department at the University of California at Davis was useful, and the department head, Donald Kunitz, gave of his time and enthusiasm. The Smithsonian Institution's National Air and Space Museum was a source of vast information and they graciously opened their doors and files to me. The University of California at Berkeley has a useful collection of maps and the facilities for reproducing them as well as an extensive Graduate Library. Finally, the National Archives in Washington, D.C., gave me access to their recordings of the original "Tokyo Rose" broadcasts of World War II.

However, my greatest gratitude is to the individuals who gave so much in time, information, and caring.

Virginia Adams spent countless hours in the National Archives, recording tapes for my use.

Antonio Jose Belo and his mother, Matilde Belo, helped me find wonderful Filipino resource people.

A Major General and his wife who wish to remain anonymous were most kind in answering questions and sharing their remembrances of World War II in the Pacific Theater.

Noie Koehler gave of her hospitality and unbounded enthusiasm while I was doing research at UC Davis.

Don Lopez (Colonel, USAF, ret., now of the Smithsonian NASM) took time out from his busy schedule and through his recollections allowed me to soar in the World War II skies with him in his fighter planes.

Lawrence C. Lott patiently gave of his time in research and encouragement.

Kiyoko Matsunaga gave what I thought was unobtainable. She opened her heart and unstintingly shared her painful memories of the war in Japan. With her stories she helped me to see what it was like to live in Japan during World War II. Unknown to her, she also gave me a most beautiful name for a beautiful fictional character.

Dr. John Mauer, with good humor and understanding, patiently answered my morbid questions about accidental deaths.

Merle E. McGraw carefully checked for accuracy all aviation material, took me for single-engine "flying lessons," answered countless questions, and ultimately gave days in proofing a manuscript he had never quite believed would come to fruition under his daughter's hand.

Mike McGraw gave unwavering encouragement and days at the typewriter preparing the final manuscript, an effort above and beyond brotherly duty.

Wendy McGraw gave time at the typewriter, editing prowess, boundless encouragement, and the unfaltering faith of a little sister.

Chiyoko Nozaki patiently helped give accuracy and grace to her native language, which I had used so clumsily.

Rogy Panganiban answered countless questions and found countless answers concerning the Philippines, all with good grace and humor.

Ted Reyes (Theodore Dime MacArthur) most graciously received me into his home and unstintingly gave of his time, telling of his experiences as a Filipino guerrilla in World War II on Leyte.

A.M. Sebastian likewise generously answered my questions, reliving some of the most painful times in his life by recounting the fall of Manila, the fall of Bataan, the Death March, and POW camp.

Dr. William Sammons answered my unusual health questions with understanding.

Con Sellers generously gave of his time, his library, and his encouragement.

Benjamin F. Sparks answered questions about the Pacific

Theater of World War II, good-naturedly taking my calls and telling anecdotes to help me envision everything from the terrain to the battles and conditions of that unfortunate time in his life.

Toshiko Vaughan with great trust and generosity gave of her time, helping me, through her vivid recollections, to walk with her in war-torn Japan, baring her childhood terrors and, like Kiyoko Matsunaga, unknowingly loaning her most beautiful name to a most beautiful fictional character.

Akiko Watanabe (along with Chiyoko Nozaki) spent long hours taking apart my stumbling Japanese and making it accurate within the context of the story.

Ed Winegrad helped greatly in finding material, making maps, and helping me find my way around the Berkeley Graduate Library.

Marilyn Yarnell graciously typed part of the final manuscript.

Finally, no acknowledgment could be written without including those loved ones who gave the intangible and perhaps the most important help. Darrell Boldt, who is my sounding board, my encouragement, and my first editor as well as my husband; Katrina and Kirsten Boldt, who have undying faith in and patience with their mother; and Jessie McGraw, who has encouraged and guided her daughter throughout her lifetime, all deserve special recognition and thanks.

CHAPTER I

When fate strikes, it strikes without warning, even though when looking back we can see the signs. For some it comes with sharpened talons, suddenly from a sunlit sky, reaching for them alone. For others, it arrives in a thunderclap, washing civilization in its indiscriminate flood. Such was the year 1941.

Hawaii thrummed with anticipation. The military buildup of the American fortress of the Pacific filled the streets with brash, confident young men in uniform. Fringed by swaying palms, barracks lined up like glistening white dominoes beside clipped green parade grounds, while sleek ships rode at anchor on the gleaming waters of Pearl Harbor. Airfields reverberated under the roaring engines of bright new warplanes crisscrossing the skies with their maneuvers and acrobatics. The military and civilian contractors alike pleaded for workers. And they came, high in hopes, eager to be part of the stirring parade.

Two young women had joined this cavalcade early in 1940. When Iris Hashimoto and Eva Nakamuro finished their freshman year at San Francisco State, they took their remaining savings and bought third-class tickets to Hawaii, hoping to earn enough money to finish school while fulfilling their search for adventure. They spent their days on ship eagerly pacing the bow, the wind whipping their thin cotton dresses around their slender legs, as they scanned the horizon, never looking back at the anxious families they had left behind.

They had allayed their parents' fears by arranging to be met at the dock by a distant cousin of Eva's father, a man who courteously took them to dinner, left them at the YWCA, and left on the morning clipper for Vancouver. That night they laughed at the turn of events. Their parents were saved many a sleepless night by never learning that their daughters were alone without kin in strange, exotic Hawaii.

They had become secretaries at Hickam Field and had soon worked their way up in pay and responsibility. That was not the adventure; that was what comes naturally, for they were bright and hard-working. The adventure came from living on a lovely island where orchids grew wild, an island filled with hopes and energy; the adventure came from meeting two handsome Army Air Corps men, from laughing together and walking white beaches under a star-shimmering sky, discovering the enchantment that is love.

Iris had grown up in the past year. She was no longer the naïve coed who had left San Francisco. She'd learned to rely on herself instead of the watchful protective parents she'd left behind. When she fell in love with Cole Tennyson, she found the courage to brave the censure a mixed couple faced even in Hawaii.

Now, on the eve of 1941, she stood on the tiny porch of the house she and Eva rented, brushing her dark hair to the rhythm of the rain pattering heavily on the tin roof. The tropical shower quickly built to a crescendo, then faded, leaving the late afternoon sun to angle warmly through the mist. Putting down her brush, she gazed at the rain-washed garden below her. Silvered streams of water ran down the large leaves of the banana tree and weighted its crimson flower cone, and the plumeria spread its branches in a near-bonsai form, its pink flowers fragrant in the new-washed air.

The string hammock between the acacia and palm trees was a dripping crescent, but in Iris's eyes it was still a warm envelope where she had lain in Cole's arms last night.

Over the rainy afternoon sounds, she heard a low steady drone, like that of a lazy fly. As the sound gradually grew louder, Iris stepped to the edge of the porch and looked up. A tight V formation of P-35 fighter planes came into view, growing larger and louder with each minute. It was an impressive sight, one that brought a sweet pang of pride to her heart and goose bumps to her skin. As they passed over, the lead plane waggled its wings rakishly. Even though she knew she couldn't be seen, she waved back enthusiastically. Cole was the leader of the flight and the instructor for most of the fighter pilots now coming into Pearl.

The drone of the planes faded into silence. She shuddered,

2

thinking of the letter she had to write. She had not yet worked up enough courage to write about Cole to her parents, who were hidebound in old Japanese custom and pride, despite their enthusiastic embrace of their adopted country.

Iris remembered the time she'd wanted to go to the junior prom with a Caucasian boy named Alex. "When two rivers from different mountains come together, they make only muddy waters and uncertain banks. Muddy swirling water is dangerous," her father had declared ominously. Iris had stayed home, listening to records alone in her room.

"Iris!" Eva called from the bedroom. "Iris, where are you?"

"Out here—on the porch."

"Oh . . . listen, Sparky's turning in the drive." On cue came the squeaking of brakes and the honking of a horn. "I've got to run. How do I look?"

Where Iris in repose was like an ivory rosebud, Eva was like a porcelain doll, her round face framed by a shiny dark pageboy. When animated, Iris's beauty was full-blown in dancing almond-shaped eyes, a quick wit, and delicate features. Eva's beauty was reflected with a dimpled charm and a shy smile. Ever since they were Girl Scouts together in San Francisco, Eva's quiet grace had always complemented Iris's impetuous energy, the kind of balance that creates mutual admiration.

Iris scrutinized her friend. Her New Year's Eve dress was red silk, bias-cut to reveal her soft curves. Her tiny black pumps with the bow over the open toe completed the doll-like impression.

"Great!" Iris said. "But wait." She reached over the porch rail, plucked a red hibiscus, and tucked it behind Eva's ear. "There. Now you're perfect."

Eva blushed, touching the flower with her fingertip. "Thanks. See you guys later?"

"That was Cole flying over just now, so it looks like we'll be late again. We'll try to catch up with you later, though."

"Okay." Eva waved and ran out the door to meet Sparky. As they drove off down the hill, Iris looked at her watch and sighed. It would be at least another hour before Cole would arrive.

The early evening breeze rustled through the leaves of the hibiscus. Iris couldn't resist the temptation to walk in the garden, cooling her bare toes in the wet grass, protected from

3

prying eyes by the overgrown trees and vines. A Hawaiian ring-necked dove cooed from the top of the acacia tree, a forlorn sound. Iris waited for its mate to answer. Silence.

She wandered over to the gardenia bush under the bedroom window and picked three creamy white blooms, capturing the rich fragrance in her hands. As she started up the porch steps with the gardenias, the dove cooed once more. Still no answer. It made her feel a little sad.

She slipped into her teal blue jersey dress, bought especially for tonight. Then, imitating the style she'd seen Dorothy Lamour wearing in the last *Collier's* magazine, she pinned her thick black hair to the top of her head and arranged the three gardenias on one side. Viewing the results, she smiled. Cole would like it.

She began filing her nails, a familiar tightening in her throat at the thought of Cole. It had been seven months. The first flush of love should be gone—but it just seemed to grow more intense. Of course, tonight was special, New Year's Eve. A trip not to Pearl City as usual, but to Honolulu for a night of fancy restaurants and dancing. An exciting beginning to 1941. Iris ignored the nagging worry about the ominous troop buildup and the war in Europe. After all, this New Year she had Cole. . . .

Gravel crunched and brakes squeaked in the driveway. Iris ran to the window and watched him climb out of the jeep, a grin lighting his rectangular face as he saw her.

A bubble of joy rose in her throat as he ran his hand through his sun-streaked hair and started up the path, carrying a beribboned package. She opened the door before he had time to knock.

"Hi." She smiled, suddenly shy at seeming so eager.

"Hi." He grinned. "Gosh, you're beautiful." He pulled her tightly to him, his kiss taking her breath away. She felt engulfed in his arms, fearful of the feeling surging through her, yet wanting only him.

"Ah, Posey," he whispered in her ear, "I love you more each day."

"Me too," she whispered, nuzzling his neck.

"Did you see me wag my wings?" he asked, kissing her forehead.

4

"Sure. Did you see me wave back? I was the dot behind the mango tree."

He chuckled and pulled her to the sofa. "Sit down. I have something for you before we go."

He set his package down on the coffee table and glanced at the envelope lying there. "You got a letter from your folks. What did they say?"

A shadow passed briefly over Iris's face. "Nothing much. They heard from Aunt Suki in Japan. Her diabetes is worse and Mom is worried she isn't getting the proper medical treatment. And Papa worries about his mother because she's very old. Other than that, the folks are fine. Business at the store is heavy this time of year. Stuff like that."

Cole grinned knowingly. "Still didn't tell them about us, huh?" As she smiled sheepishly, he added gently, "You'll have to, you know." Then he shoved the package toward her.

Iris instantly knew it was a book, and she grinned as she tore away the paper. "*Sonnets From the Portuguese . . .* my favorite." She kissed him. "You remembered."

"There's a book marker . . . of sorts," he said awkwardly, pointing to a bulge in the center of the book. "It tells you everything."

The book fell open to a pink ribbon looped through a hole punched in the top of the page. It held a gold ring centered with a small diamond. Iris's eyes filled as she read the poem beneath it.

> *How do I love thee?*
> *Let me count the ways. . .*

"Oh, Cole," she whispered.

"I want you to marry me, Posey, but—" he put his fingers to her lips, "no, don't answer until I explain something." His blue eyes seemed more flecked with green, as they always did when he was intense.

He stood up and walked to the window. "You know flying is my life right now," he said over his shoulder. "I'm only a second lieutenant, but I'll be promoted within a year or so. It would mean two hundred dollars a month. We could get married then." He paused, looking down at the floor. "Posey, I know it won't be much of a life, moving from base to base—not for a while anyway—but we'd be together. That's what's important to me. I'm nothing unless I'm flying, but

5

flying is nothing without you." He turned and looked at her questioningly, pleadingly.

Iris knew that Cole's drive for advancement was based on something much deeper than the salary that came with it. His father, a decorated ace during World War I, had been forced to leave his beloved airplanes and return to the family farm to support his mother and younger sisters. His dreams of glory and flying free into the sun were shelved, dusted off only when he marched at the head of the Fourth of July Parade or when he enchanted his two sons, John and Cole, with tales of bravery and soaring flight. Both John and Cole had grown up dreaming their father's dream: they would become flyers. It was their father's wish. Because they loved and revered him, it was also theirs.

But John, the stunning athlete and brilliant student, had been killed on the eve of his high school graduation, by a swerving car on a dark country road, and all the winter and springtime dreams had suddenly dropped onto Cole's grieving shoulders.

He had vowed somehow to make up to his father for the loss of his elder brother, somehow to redeem that lost promise. All his athletic training and skill, all his studies—even his major in aeronautical engineering—all were aimed at achieving this one goal.

Iris knew all this and loved him for it. Though their backgrounds were so different, in this way they thought as one—to fulfill their filial birthright, the solemn obligation to honor their parents with their lives.

She walked over to him. "Cole, you don't have to explain. I want to share my life with you. I know that means sharing your career." She held out her left hand with the ring in it. "I'll wait . . . however long it takes."

Cole's hand was shaking as he slipped the ring onto her finger. "And I trust my life to you, too, Posey." He wrapped his arms around her and they stood together, looking out the window as the lights began twinkling on the waters of Pearl Harbor.

"Doll, I tell you," Sparky said with a grin as the rickety truck sped between two fields of pineapple, "Cole has it bad. Something big is up between him and Iris." They had passed Cole on his way to pick up Iris about five miles back, and it

6

had taken Sparky that long to come out with what was on his mind.

Eva smiled and nodded. They made a strange pair, the quiet Japanese-American girl and the short, muscular boy from New York who wore his sergeant's cap tipped jauntily over his dark curly hair. Yet, under Sergeant Irwin Sparks's cocky bravado and Eva's shyness there was a strong bond of affection. Neither of them doubted that someday there would be "something big" between them, too.

Sparky abruptly pulled the truck onto a dirt road bordered by sugar cane fields. "What are you doing?" Eva asked, grabbing the dashboard for support.

He grinned. "I thought we needed something special tonight." He came to a halt before a tiny cane-worker's shack.

Eva stayed in the truck, surrounded by the sweet scent of sugar cane, listening to the leaves whisper in the breeze, a counterrhythm to the distant, upbeat chatter between Sparky and a large Hawaiian man. The conversation ended in hearty laughter as Sparky handed some keys to the man, then gestured for Eva to wait as he disappeared into the cane behind the shack.

Suddenly the evening quiet was broken by the rumble of an engine. To the cheers of five half-naked children, Sparky drove from behind the shack in a bright red fire truck, complete with flashing light and bell. It looked ancient—1920s vintage, Eva judged.

"How about it?" Sparky crowed proudly as he came to get her from the truck. "Somethin' special, huh?" He held out his hand.

"Sparky, what on earth . . . ?" She laughed. "We're going in. . . .?"

"You bet, Doll. We'll show those navvies in Honolulu what real style is. Here," he said, handing her the rope attached to the bell on the hood of the truck. "Give those kids a bell-ringing good-bye." Giggling, she tugged the rope all the way down the road.

As they drove back onto the highway to Honolulu, she tied the rope on its hook and said, "I'll never understand how you do these things."

"It's just a matter of knowing what someone else wants and using it to get what you want. See, that guy won this old fire engine in a card game, but he needed a flatbed truck to haul

7

something on a night when things weren't going to be watched too careful. And on New Year's Eve no one else in camp wanted an old truck from the motor pool. So I made an 'arrangement.' Simple," he concluded with a wink.

The Dancing Pele Grill was one of the old Hawaiian establishments reaping the benefits of the military-base buildup. The bar was topped by a thatched roof and flanked by booths upholstered in a dark orange material that scratched Eva's legs as she sat down. She was uncomfortably aware of the three sailors staring at her from the bar. They had obviously lost their inhibitions several drinks ago, so she kept her eyes averted.

"Hey, flyboy!" the tallest of the sailors called to Sparky.

Sparky caught Eva's eye reassuringly before turning to answer, "You talking to me?"

"Yeah. That your fire engine out there?" He swaggered to their table, supported by the snickers of his mates.

"Yeah, what about it?"

"I guess you might need it later when you light a fire between your Jap's legs tonight," he drawled, as he stood weaving over Sparky.

Eva gasped and Sparky clenched his teeth. "Button up and go back to your bilge buddies," he said, turning his back on him.

"You tell 'im, Tex," said one of the other sailors, giggling drunkenly.

"Yeah, flyboy," Tex continued, "we understand. You flyboys need some now and then, just like a real man. You just can't get a real woman. You have to settle for a Jap—"

His words became a startled cry as Sparky jumped up and pulled Tex's right arm behind his back, throwing his own arm across Tex's throat as he spun him around. The sailor's eyes bulged and his hands clawed uselessly at Sparky's arms.

Eva saw the two other sailors suddenly move toward them. "Come on, Sparky," she said, tugging at his shirt. "Let's leave."

"No. This rotten piece of—"

"What's the matter, son?" A strong hand rested on Sparky's shoulder from behind.

Sparky turned and saw his commanding officer, Colonel Hughes. He took his hand from Tex's throat, allowing some of the color to return to the sailor's face. "Not much, sir," Sparky said, saluting quickly. "The navy just has trouble tolerating air superiority."

"I see. Well, I imagine the shore patrol doesn't like to have to pick up their men with their necks and arms all bent out of shape. Maybe if you let this sailor go back to his mates, they'll leave in good enough shape so I won't have to call the SP."

Sparky released Tex and shoved him back against his two friends. The three staggered into a barstool, then stood up, bristling for a fight, considered the colonel and his companion, another colonel, and decided against it. They turned and headed for the door.

"Jap lover," Tex hissed over his shoulder.

Sparky looked at Eva, who was quietly wiping tears from her cheeks. He turned to Colonel Hughes. "Thank you, sir."

"There are many ways to avoid trouble, Sergeant. One of them is not to walk into a bull's pasture waving a red flag." He glanced pointedly at Eva, then returned Sparky's salute halfheartedly. "Have a happy New Year," he said as he turned toward the door.

"Hey, honey," Sparky pleaded, handing Eva his handkerchief. "Don't let it get to you. Creeps like that aren't worth it."

She sobbed quietly. "It's just that . . . I've never caused trouble like that."

A Hawaiian boy in a brightly flowered shirt appeared at their table. "Sir, the management regrets the trouble and would like to buy you and your wahine a drink before you order." He glanced compassionately at Eva and shrugged, as if to say, "Such is the trouble of our skin."

She smiled shyly as Sparky said, "She'll have a rum and Coke and I'll have a Manhattan. Somethin' from home." He winked. "And while you're at it, hold out two of your best mahi mahi steaks. We want the works—you know, the sauce and fruit and stuff."

"Yes, sir. Two Pele specials." The waiter's white teeth flashed his approval.

"There," Sparky said with his old cheer, "you see, it's gonna be a great New Year's. We'll meet Cole and Iris later and take a ride to the beach. Did you bring your swimsuit like I told you?"

Eva nodded. "I'm wearing it under my dress."

"To 1941," Sparky said, raising his glass, "and to my Doll."

Jake Devon's face was a contradiction. Its craggy structure was young and strong, yet his hazel eyes flashed with the cynicism of age. With his characteristic half-smile, he leaned his six-foot frame against the bar of the Black Orchid and listened to Marta Rothboeck. She was above average height, with blond hair falling past her broad cheekbones to rest seductively on her square shoulders. In fact, everything about Marta was seductive, especially the clinging, low-cut black satin dress she'd worn for their New Year's celebration. A striking woman, and not dumb, either, he thought, focusing his attention back on her.

"Roosevelt is just too smart to go in against the Germans," she said, emphasizing her point with the red paper straw from her drink. "He knows they'll win. Look—right now, France is German territory and England is on her knees. You're a fool to count on getting a transfer to a European war that we won't join. You might as well sit back and enjoy yourself here," she added, with sly meaning.

"You've been reading too much of that Hitler drivel your German relatives have been sending you," Jake commented coolly. "If you keep reading those pamphlets, you'll actually begin believing all that crap."

"Don't be a fool, Jake. I was born and raised in the United States. I can see who runs things—and they certainly aren't black, yellow, or Jew. They're like you . . . and my father."

Jake raised his dark eyebrows. He could imagine Marta's father, a real Prussian ass, sure of his superiority and making everyone jump because of it. It must have been tough for Marta, growing up trying to please a father like that, but that was probably why she was so good at pleasing men now. That was one reason why Jake put up with her. Her voluptuous body was made for pleasure and she constantly found new ways of pleasing with it. Still, he wouldn't stick it out through these Aryan-superiority tirades if it weren't for some other attraction. He sipped his Scotch thoughtfully and pretended to listen to her. What really kept him coming back for more was her wonderful sense of adventure. She was like an unfettered bird, soaring to new horizons, a kindred spirit to his own restlessness.

"Roosevelt knows," she was saying intently. "You'll see. Hitler is right. The Aryan race is destined to lead the world. . . . Take you, for instance," she added provocatively, "you could lead anyone into anything."

Jake gave a short laugh. "Just how far will you follow me?"

Her throaty laugh left him little doubt. That was another thing: it appealed to his sense of irony that she was eagerly bedding down with the kid whose boyhood nickname was Chief. It would have appealed to his Cherokee grandmother, too, he thought.

He leaned forward, suddenly serious. "Just remember that we'll be with my buddy Cole and his girl, Iris, tonight, and his ideas don't fit in with yours. Iris is Japanese-American—"

"Wait a minute," Marta interrupted indignantly. "I'm not palling around with any Jappo."

"—she's bright, pretty, and very nice. And she makes Cole happy," Jake finished, eyeing Marta calmly.

"Oh, come on," she cooed, leaning her breasts against his arm, "wouldn't you rather find a deserted beach? The motion of the waves can give me marvelous ideas."

"Maybe later. I told Cole I'd welcome in the New Year with him and Iris. You can come along. But keep your Nazi ideas to yourself—or leave now. It's up to you."

Marta looked at him, calculatingly, then smiled. "You'd better be worth it."

Jake met her challenge with a sardonic grin. "And so had you." He glanced at his watch, then continued in a bitter tone, "Cole was probably late getting his flight in. You know, some of these shavetail lieutenants out here have been waiting ten years for a promotion, but I'd take a demotion just to do what they do every day—fly. The only thing they let me pilot regularly is a radio mike. . . . Can you imagine the army insisting on their own radio to keep up the morale of the men on the bases?"

"What do you expect, Jake? You were a star in Seattle before you enlisted. They'd be fools not to use you."

"If I hadn't joined up, I'd be with a network in New York right now. They offered it to me, but—"

"But you had to turn it down for the hope of flying," Marta finished. "I know. Everybody still thinks you were crazy . . . but I understand."

Her pale blue eyes flashed as she leaned forward, suddenly

11

intense. "At least you get to keep up your hours by flying in your free time. . . . Jake, I'll never forget that ride today. I've just got to learn to fly. Will you teach me?"

He shook his head, but she persisted. "Jake, please? We both need to run free, a challenge, something to conquer. We can do that in the sky. Please."

Her childlike pleading was more suggestive than Jake wanted to resist. "If we can hire a plane again, I'll get you started on some of the basics. But—" he held up a finger to stop her from kissing him, "you'll need to have your final lessons and checkouts with someone like Cole. He's the best birdman in the whole Pacific. He was the one who finally qualified me . . . whatever good my wings do me."

He paused and looked at her appraisingly. "But for tonight, let's keep our explorations closer to home—" Someone coming in the door caught his eye and he grimaced, "Oh, Christ, that's all I need. Don't look. It's Colonel Hughes and his buddy Mason. They always have some 'swell' ideas for a radio show." He leaned his head on his hand and stared down at his drink, hoping they wouldn't see him.

"They're coming this way," Marta whispered.

"Shit." He glanced between his fingers and saw the two colonels order drinks sent over to the table behind him and Marta.

"Sparks will never go past sergeant if he keeps fraternizing," Colonel Hughes was saying.

"Should we leave?" Marta whispered.

"Shh," Jake hissed sharply.

"Can't say I disagree," Colonel Mason drawled. "How can you promote someone who might have to fly missions against his in-laws?"

"I'm going to use the phone," Jake whispered to Marta. "Go wait outside the door and catch Cole and Iris. You'll recognize them."

Marta was chatting with Cole and Iris when Jake came up from the alley behind the restaurant. "I see you've already met. Hey, Iris, you look terrific!" he said, putting one arm around her and the other around Marta and starting down the street.

"Jake, what's going on?" Cole demanded.

"I'll tell you later," he said quickly. "I just thought you

should celebrate New Year's in real style. Sparky says Pele's serves the best mahi mahi steaks you'll ever sink your teeth into."

"Listen, Jake," Cole said, pulling his arm, "Iris and I have something to celebrate. We were looking forward to—"

"You'll love it! The dancing is terrific. I just called and made reservations." He kept up the chatter as he led the way down the street toward the flashing neon sign of the Dancing Pele Grill.

Trying to ease what she sensed was a tense situation, Iris exclaimed suddenly, "Look at that old fire engine!"

"See? Real local color here, not stuffy like the Black Orchid. We don't want 1941 to be a dull year, do we?" Jake continued his sales pitch as they filed into the restaurant. "We've both got enough jinxes on it already," he muttered as Cole went by him. Cole shot him a curious glance and Jake smiled sweetly at Iris.

"There's Sparky and Eva," Iris said, waving.

"Let's join them," Jake said quickly, giving Marta a warning glance.

Cole surprised everyone by ordering a bottle of champagne immediately, then proposing a toast. "To the woman who has promised me a life of happiness," he said, smiling at Iris, "as my wife. I love you, Posey."

Iris blushed and laughed as Eva hugged her and Sparky cheered. Yet she couldn't help noticing that Marta's smile was forced, and that behind his smile, Jake's dark eyes were troubled.

Even though the meal was filled with jokes, gossip, and optimistic analysis of the "war situation" in Europe, Iris was uneasy. There was something in the air, palpable and ominous. She tried to bury it in the gaiety of the champagne toasts and the warmth of good friends. Yet still it stayed, lying on the edge of their laughter, like a knife blade that had missed the first time but was sure of its target on the next thrust. Whatever it was, she told herself, it was her fate and she couldn't change it. She smiled as Cole reached under the table and squeezed her hand.

He had been watching her steadily, as if sensing her unease. "Do you think the band will play 'Careless'?" he asked. The song had been playing when they'd had their first misunderstanding; since then it had come to be a code word for something wrong.

Iris smiled ruefully. "I don't know." She leaned her head against his shoulder.

When the band began to play and people started to dance, Cole pulled Iris to her feet.

"What's the matter?" he asked as soon as they were on the dance floor.

"I don't know. But something's wrong. It could be Marta. . . . She doesn't seem to like me."

Cole frowned. "Ah, ignore her. Jake says her parents came from Germany and she really believes that Aryan-race stuff. Maybe she doesn't like meeting a Japanese-American who's smarter and prettier than her. So don't let her spoil your evening. She's not worth it."

"I suppose you're right. But don't you think it was kind of funny, Jake changing our reservations like that?"

"He had his reasons, I guess."

"And then Eva said Sparky almost got into a fight tonight with some sailors who were making remarks about him being with her."

"There are always going to be creeps around, Iris—no matter where you are. Don't let it bother you. We're supposed to be happy tonight."

"I am," she said as she leaned her head against his chest. She could hear his heart beat almost in rhythm with the band. It was comforting. He seemed so strong and steady.

The band began a jitterbug version of "I'm Nobody's Baby" and Cole and Iris sat down as Jake and Marta got up to dance. Marta's uninhibited movements, emphasized by her shimmering black dress, caused appreciative cheers from the crowd. When the vocalist with the band asked her to join him in a hula to the next song, Marta kicked off her shoes and began to undulate to the throbbing music, capturing the full sensuality of the dance.

Sparky whistled under his breath, glancing at Jake, who was watching the performance through half-shuttered eyes.

"She knows how to move," Jake said simply, then added, "You don't mind how many people have admired the merchandise in the window, as long as you're the one who takes it home."

The crowd applauded as the dance ended and Marta came

back. Looking at Jake, she said huskily, "Did that give you any ideas for the rest of the night?"

"Sure did!" Sparky cut in. "I've got a ride to the beach for us all . . . in a fire engine."

"That thing outside is yours?" Iris said incredulously. Cole and Jake guffawed.

"Sure is. Ready to go?"

"I have to powder my nose first," Marta said. "Anyone else?"

"I'll come with you." Iris got up.

There was a subtle change in Marta's attitude once they were in the restroom. She looked smug as she straightened the seam of her stocking. "Have you set the date yet?" she asked, arching an eyebrow.

"Not yet, but we hope to get married before the year is out."

"That's good. Just as long as you're not going to wait for Cole's promotion."

Iris put the top back on her lipstick and watched Marta carefully in the mirror. "Why do you say that?"

"Well, he's just not about to get one, now or in the future."

"Why do you say that?" Iris said sharply, turning around to face Marta. "Jake is one of Cole's best friends and I'm sure he's told you that Cole is an excellent officer."

"Sure he has. But he knows Cole won't make it. I guess Cole just won't accept it."

"Accept what?"

"The fact that they'll never promote someone married to a Jap."

Iris gasped as if she'd been slapped, but she kept her anger in control, refusing to let Marta see how badly her vicious words had hurt. "I'm an American, born and raised in the States, the same as you," she said evenly. "Your parents came from a foreign country the same as mine, but we're both Americans."

Marta shrugged. "If you really love Cole, you're not going to want to be a stone around his neck, holding him down all his life. You're right—according to Jake, he could become a leader in military aviation. But he'll never make it married to you." As Iris started to protest, she added quickly, "Jake and I overheard a conversation between Hughes and Mason in the Black Orchid. Hughes said he couldn't promote someone who might someday have to fly missions against his in-laws. Those were his exact words. That's why Jake insisted we not eat there—he didn't want the colonel to see Cole with you." Then she added lightly, "Life is hard. I should know. Take what you can get from him and then move on. What a man has to offer in bed is sometimes enough." She looked Iris over as if calculating how far she'd gone with Cole. "Besides, in the long run, you'll be better off with one of your own kind." She turned to leave. "Ready? They'll be wondering what happened to us."

Iris shook her head no and turned on the water faucet. When the door closed behind Marta, she slumped against the basin, numbly watching the running water trickle down the drain. She felt as if she'd been raped, as if something irreplaceable had been cruelly ripped from her. She looked at her engagement ring, and a tear slipped down her cheek and fell into the basin with the rest of the escaping water.

CHAPTER II

Iris would have robbed or killed for Cole. She would have cut off her arm for him. But she couldn't change the color of her skin or the shape of her eyes.

Marta's words had left her numb. Like a wounded doe, she ran blindly, hoping that somehow the pain would go away. She went to work the day after New Year's, going through the familiar motions while her mind was reeling, seeking denial of that bitter accusation.

Perhaps it wasn't true. Maybe it was just Marta's vicious bigotry. Then again, there could be some truth in what Marta had said. There had been incidents that demonstrating that a Japanese person was considered a second-class citizen in this army.

There was one thin hope left for her to cling to. The

January promotions were coming out; surely Cole, the top-rated pilot on the islands, would be promoted. That would prove Marta's words a lie. That would prove that a Japanese fiancée couldn't keep Cole from achieving his life's dream. Iris was in agony waiting for Friday's list and Cole's phone call.

When she finally heard his strong voice on the other end of the line, she blurted, "Did you hear what promotions were posted?" She'd wanted her voice to sound light, but it was tight and harsh.

"Oh, that. Hey, you didn't expect me to get anything right away, did you? I'll probably make the list before the end of the year, though. How about a movie tonight?"

So it was true. Her mind swirled. She needed time to think. "I'm not feeling well . . . sort of sick to my stomach," she said truthfully. "If you don't mind, I'd better just go to bed."

"Sure, honey." His voice was tender. "I'll stay in the BOQ and read some of these new manuals they're putting out. Get some rest—I'll call you tomorrow."

She replaced the receiver and stared down at the phone. Eva was out with Sparky. The house was oppressively silent. She went into the bedroom and crawled stiffly between the sheets, and lay there, staring at the ceiling. She was overcome with bitterness, but she was realistic enough to admit that no matter how cruel were Marta's intentions, what she'd said was true. Iris was plunged into despair.

The following day Cole came, bearing flowers and concern. She feigned sleep, not trusting herself to see him or talk to him.

She stoically accepted Eva's nursing, until Sunday afternoon, when Eva said she was going to call the doctor.

Iris wearily shook her head. "No one can do anything," she whispered.

Eva sat on the edge of the bed and stared at her. "You aren't really sick, are you?" she asked softly. "I mean, not physically."

She reached out and rested her hand on her friend's shoulder. At her touch, Iris could hold back no longer. She turned and sobbed into Eva's lap.

Tears now filled Eva's eyes. "I've never seen you like this," she murmured. "It can't be all that bad, can it? It's not Cole—he's been calling almost every hour. So, what is it?"

Iris reached for a handkerchief and told her about Marta, her fears and anger tumbling out in a confused torrent. "And she said she'd overheard Colonel Hughes say that he couldn't promote someone who might have to fly against his in-laws someday," she finished.

"And you believed her?" Eva asked.

Iris blew her nose and nodded. "Why would she make up something like that?"

"Because she's probably jealous that Cole wants to marry you and the only thing Jake wants is what she's giving away." Eva got up and opened the bedroom curtain, filling the room with the apricot glow of the sunset. "Besides," she continued, "what makes Marta so sure her German parentage won't be a strike against Jake ever getting to fly? It's not the Japanese who've bombed and destroyed all Europe."

Iris sighed. "It doesn't work that way. She's white. Why do you think Cole doesn't take me to the officers' club? It's that 'No Coloreds' sign. Besides, later that night I asked Jake if he thought we might run into Colonel Hughes. He looked at me sort of funny and said, 'No, he's at the Black Orchid.' His look said even more than his answer. I knew then that Marta hadn't lied about overhearing the colonel. And that would also explain why Jake changed our reservations so suddenly."

"If what you say is true, then I'm the same kind of albatross to Sparky. What does Cole think of all this?"

"I haven't told him," Iris said, fighting back the tears again. "I can't. He'd say he loves me and would give up flying for me. I wouldn't consider doing that to him. Even if he meant it now, can you imagine what our life would be if every time he looked at me or one of our children he would see the reason he lost the one big dream of his lifetime?" Her voice faltered. "He'd grow to hate me. I love him too much to let that happen."

"I can't see what else you can do," Eva said, her voice trembling.

"Just before you came in I got an idea," Iris said softly. "In that last letter I got from my folks, they asked me again to go to Japan to meet my grandmother and my uncles, and to check on Aunt Suki and take her some insulin. My parents are too ill to travel now, and they're anxious for me to fulfill their family duties before Grandmother dies. Papa says they'll have settled the China issue by the time we get there."

Eva shrugged disconsolately. "So? It's the same story my father has been giving me. I should go to Japan and meet my dying grandparents." She paused and looked at Iris. "But how does that solve the problem with Cole?"

"I will go. It's the only way he won't think that something's wrong—won't feel he has to be noble. With me gone, he'll get his promotion. Eventually, he'll maybe even forget . . . forget about me." She closed her eyes against the pain of that thought. "He'll think there's an insurmountable cultural gap between us. He'll be upset for a while, but he won't feel obligated to protect me or be loyal to our engagement. Don't you see? The distance and time will ease the pain . . . maybe for both of us. I'll use Japan to try to forget him. I'll learn about my heritage . . . prepare myself for a Japanese husband, maybe," she added, her lips quivering.

As Iris spoke, Eva had sat staring out the window, calm and still, as if she were meditating. Now she broke her silence. "It means, of course, that I will go with you."

"Why?"

"Two reasons. One, my father will naturally assume that I am going if you are going. He would be shamed if I let you go alone. I don't want to upset him now—you know he hasn't been well since Mother died. Besides, I can't let you do this by yourself." She paused. "Most of all, if the conversation Marta and Jake heard between the colonels was true, it means that I'm holding Sparky back, too. If I leave, it will give him a chance. The military is his only way of getting away from a dead-end life in New York. I can't keep him back any more than you can hold Cole down."

Eva was right, of course. Iris could see not only the pattern of their lives woven together thus far, but the inevitable extension of that pattern into their future. She took Eva's hand in hers. "Thanks. Somehow, it'll be easier to do this, knowing that we carry the same load, that we have the same hurt."

Once their decision was made, they found new energy. Still, their departure was fraught with difficulties from the very beginning. It should have served as a warning.

Bureaucratic red tape erected seemingly impossible obstacles.

They needed their passports before they could apply to the Japanese consulate for their visas. In order to get the passports, they needed their birth certificates, which meant another long wait while their fathers in California sent for copies from the state capital.

"It all takes so long!" Iris lamented to Eva.

"I know." Eva gnawed at her thumbnail. "What about the guys?"

Iris walked to the window, folded her arms, and looked out over the Hawaiian night. "I don't think we should tell them until right before we leave," she said finally. "If we tell them now, we'll have to put up with weeks of them trying to talk us out of it. There would be arguments. Maybe it's selfish of me, but I want to leave with good memories."

"Me too," Eva said glumly.

They had hoped to book passage on the Japanese ship leaving Honolulu the week of January 16, but with all the delays, they had to wait for the next freighter, the *Arabia Maru*, which was scheduled to leave Honolulu February 18—a date on the downhill side of Valentine's Day, Iris noted unhappily. They made their reservations and then settled down to wait. It was going to be a painful month.

That Friday, Iris realized just how painful. Cole called just as she got home from work. "Hey, Posey! Put on your party clothes. Our gang is going to have something to celebrate tonight. Sparky and I'll pick you two up at 1900 hours."

His enthusiasm was contagious; she couldn't help laughing, though she had been dreading their usual weekend date, worrying about keeping up the pretense. "At least tell me what we're going to do."

"We'll hit the dinner club and then take a ride to the beach. Jake got a squadron assignment and he's flying high."

"Oh." She tried to keep her tone casual. "Marta will be along, then?"

"Guess so. Listen, gotta go. I've got a bunch of green recruits to chew out. See you later. I've missed you, Posey. A week is too long."

"For me too, Cole," she whispered before he hung up.

"I don't think I can face that woman again," Iris said bitterly when she told Eva the plans.

"Are you going to let her know how her words hurt you?"

Iris lifted her chin. "You're right. She's going to have to suffer through an evening with the devoted engaged couple."

Eva smiled mischievously. "That ought to do it. She'll be green."

An hour later Sparky and Cole picked them up in the fire engine and took them to Alvarito's, a pleasant little restaurant in Pearl City. It was run by a gloriously fat Filipino-Portuguese woman and her Italian broomstick of a husband, and its spaghetti and veal scallopini were renowned.

When they arrived, Iris gave Jake a congratulatory hug, and couldn't help feeling smug as Marta's forced smile conceded her a minor victory. As the meal progressed with a bottle of red wine to toast Jake, even Marta became almost tolerable.

As they finally headed out the door toward the fire engine, Jake asked what Sparky had brought along for refreshments. When he learned it was only beer, he said, "Hell, for an occasion like this, we need champagne!" Jake ran back into Alvarito's, while Cole went to buy cigarettes. Sparky went to get a couple of newspapers from the corner stand, so they would have something to sit on.

Eva looked at Iris with a sad smile, then as she turned back to watch Sparky, her smile suddenly faded, and Iris heard her quick intake of breath.

Following Eva's gaze, Iris saw two sailors coming down the sidewalk. The shorter one stopped, looked at the fire truck, then poked his mate in the ribs and pointed.

"Are they the same ones?" Iris whispered. "The ones from New Year's?"

Eva nodded silently, then murmured to herself, "A red flag in front of a bull . . ."

"What are you talking about?" Marta interrupted.

"You wouldn't understand," Iris said, never taking her eyes off the sailors. They had spotted Sparky and were coming up behind him.

"Sparky . . ." Eva called tentatively, trying to keep her voice low enough not to be heard by the sailors but loud enough to warn Sparky.

Sparky turned just as they were upon him. "Well, if it isn't old Tex," he drawled, trying to brazen it out.

The news boy looked frightened as the tall sailor shoved Sparky back toward the darkened alley. His mate followed menacingly. The wind carried the words *score to settle* before they disappeared from view.

Iris ran back to the restaurant for Jake. She could hear the sickening sound of flesh hitting flesh and pained grunts—then suddenly the air was filled with a clanging alarm. Eva was ringing the fire bell for all she was worth.

The two sailors bolted from the alley. Simultaneously, Jake and Cole appeared from opposite directions—just as Sparky, his nose bleeding and his uniform torn, jumped Tex from behind. Jake helped with a left hook to the sailor's chin, while Cole sent his mate reeling with a solid punch in the stomach. Pulling him up by the hair, he turned him around, and with a well-aimed kick, sent him staggering down the sidewalk, followed by Tex, who had to hold on to the side of the building.

"Think twice before you take on the air corps," Jake called after them.

Cole smoothed his shirt and took Iris's arm to help her back in the truck. "Well, they sure as hell didn't check out their flanks."

"Those gobs sure never learned the basics of attack, either, did they?" Sparky laughed as he dabbed at his nose with his handkerchief. "All I want to know is, what took you guys so long?"

Jake rolled his eyes. "That's gratitude for you, flyboy!" he said, mimicking the sailors. "Where to now?"

"Manamanalimi Beach," Sparky announced as he pulled out onto Hoolehua Street. "Heard about it from a Hawaiian. It'll take about forty-five minutes, so sit back and enjoy the ride."

Cole settled down with his arm around Iris as the lights of Pearl City faded, giving way to lantern-lit cameos of island shanties and roadway stops. Finally, Sparky turned down an unpaved road, and the tropical dark surrounded them. Iris leaned back, watching the headlights catch the tops of drooping palms in flashes of gray-green light. She nestled her head on Cole's shoulder, enjoying his warmth and pushing all thoughts of the future into the dark corridors of her mind. Live for now, she told herself. It has to last a lifetime.

Two days later Iris still smiled to herself as she remembered their interlude on the warm sands of the purpled

Manamanalimi Beach. Marta and Jake had disappeared immediately, leaving the others by the flickering light of a bonfire. Eventually she and Cole had taken a walk along the beach alone, finding time to be in each other's arms, time to savor their precious moments together.

Now, as Iris arranged gardenias for the table centerpiece, she wondered if she would ever again be able to smell those sweet, creamy blossoms without the painful memory of the love she must leave behind.

Eva and Sparky had gone to the store to pick up some last-minute groceries for their Sunday dinner. Cole would be late because he was spending extra time taking Jake through maneuvers to boost his rating up to the level of the more experienced pilots in his squadron. It was quiet moments like this, alone with her thoughts and memories, that Iris dreaded the most. She mustn't think about what must come. . . .

She heard the crunch of gravel in the drive and ran to let Eva and Sparky in, grateful that her solitude was ended.

She opened the door and gasped. Cole stood in the doorway, his face chalk-colored under streaks of dirt and grease, his shirt bloodstained. "Darling, what's the matter?" she cried, pulling him in. "Are you all right?"

"It's Jake," he said flatly. "He was caught on takeoff. Didn't compensate for the torque in a crosswind. Plane flipped over. He's in the hospital. The doctors are working on him now. I don't know how bad it is. I couldn't stand to wait alone. Come back with me."

He had come because he needed her. "Of course," she said. Her hand was shaking as she scrawled a note for Eva and Sparky.

"How bad is it?" she asked as they got into the jeep. "Were you with him? Are you sure you're all right?"

"I was in the plane behind him, waiting for takeoff. He just didn't compensate. Flipped right into another plane." He sighed and rubbed his eyes. "I was the first one to the wreckage. I pulled him out. God, he looked awful, blood all over his head and face. I don't know if he'll ever fly again. That would kill him, you know."

Iris put her hand on his knee. Despite her anxiety about Jake, she was warmed by Cole's need to lean on her in this crisis. How could she leave him? Then, a dark, chilling voice answered from the relentlessly logical part of her mind: *Because to stay would destroy him.*

When they reached the hospital, the nurse at the station looked up at their anxious faces and shook her head. "The doctor is still with him, Lieutenant. You can wait over there and we'll let you know as soon as he comes out."

Iris sat on the couch, but Cole couldn't stop pacing and smoking. "The CO will have to order a routine investigation, you know. It'll just kill Jake if they don't give him flight clearance. He's bound to ask about it every day. How can we . . ." he broke off with a sheepish shrug. "I'll bet this is just the beginning. As a career air-corps couple, we'll have to plan all sorts of strategies."

Iris nodded bravely, fighting back the carefully masked hurt. "Remember that story Jake told about the colonel and his wife at that party? The colonel must have said something, because suddenly his wife diverted the whole conversation to another topic." She smiled wistfully. "It must have been some kind of signal they'd worked out."

"Say—that's what we need!" Cole said with new enthusiasm. "A set of signals like the colonel and his wife. Like the way we use the song 'Careless' to show something's wrong. We can start now, and by the time we're married, we'll have a whole system all ready to go."

"Cole, I don't think . . ."

"We'll have to keep this investigation secret from Jake until he's stronger, Posey. Besides, it makes us sort of special— closer than other couples."

Iris was torn between laughter and tears.

He looked over his shoulder at the nurse, who was busy at her station. "I mean something simple," he said more softly. "Like if I'm not able to say what I really mean, I could say the opposite. You know, everything's just great, when it's really not—that kind of thing. You'll know it's not true if you hear a special signal . . . I'd say something's 'inside out' or 'don't twist yourself inside out.' 'Inside out' will let you know I mean the opposite."

Iris laughed at his enthusiasm for the new game. "But how will I know when you stop lying and start telling the truth?"

"I'll say something else, like—'Okay, now.' That's it— the simpler the better."

Iris turned as Sparky and Eva came running in.

"How bad is it?" Sparky asked anxiously.

"Still waiting," Cole said, and then briefly explained what had happened. "He just didn't compensate enough for that left pulling torque. Flipped right over at the end of the runway. Clipped that old biplane parked at the end there. Right after I pulled him out, the gas tank blew. Some sight," he finished.

Sparky whistled. "Too close. And that's the second time in the past three months that's happened. It's not smart to train stateside in twin engines and then switch to single engines without some special instructions."

Cole agreed, and added, "We're going to have to keep his mind off it for now. Let's plan on meeting here for our evenings. We can bring a deck of cards, or chess or checkers when just one of us can come. I just hope he's well enough to . . ." Cole stopped as the doctor came in.

"I was worried about a fractured skull," he reported, "but that boy has entirely too hard a head. And it looks like that eye will be okay, too." He smiled wearily. "He's all stitched up now. He does, however, have a fairly serious concussion and a broken leg. He'll have to remain hospitalized for at least a week, maybe two. He's conscious now, so you can see him, but don't stay long. Just go in and let him know you care. By tomorrow night he shouldn't be so sleepy." He nodded to Eva and Iris. "His recovery will be aided by you young folks keeping his spirits up."

Jake was too groggy to say much that night, but the following night, all four of them saw the wisdom of the doctor's words. Jake was not only in pain but depressed and self-abusive, afraid that he'd lose his chance to fly again. It took all their efforts before he finally began to respond.

Iris and Eva smuggled in their record player and all the latest records. Between the music and games and their constant banter, he slowly began to cheer up. Grateful that Marta visited Jake in the afternoons, Iris and Eva spent the rest of January patterning their lives around their work and nightly visits to the hospital. It was therapeutic: their tight schedule pushed the pain of impending separation into the secret chambers of their minds.

Thus, the month passed quickly. When February began and they still hadn't received their passport papers from their fathers, Iris reluctantly placed another transpacific call to her parents.

Her father's voice, thousands of miles away and distorted by radio static, was still an echo of her childhood. Chosu, or Joe, as he was called in America, had been the final voice of authority in her life. Although it was always from her tiny, soft-spoken mother that she got her orders, Iris had always known the directives originated with the remote, aloof man with the gentle smile, the man she'd reverently called Papa-san. All her life she'd endeavored to please him, savoring the moments when her mother would come to her and announce that "we are pleased with your school report" or "your election to the student council brings us honor."

Now, her father patiently explained in his familiar accent, "Your papers have arrived for the passport. It will arrive in your mail within the week. You must take your papers to the Japanese consulate there and get the visa."

"But, Papa-san," Iris protested, trying to picture his face, trying to make him understand the urgency, "I won't have time for the processing."

"I have talked to the authorities here. They say for you to take a statement to Japan with you if that is the case. The American consulate in Japan will clear everything. For now, you must go to visit the country of your heritage."

"Yes, Papa-san, if you are sure it is safe."

"There is nothing to fear in Japan," he said confidently. "You will have your family there."

"I will write to you. Give Mama-san my love. Please try to come join me soon."

"If the fates will it, Iris, my child. Good-bye."

His words haunted her as she hung up the phone. Everything seemed so uncertain, so unsettled. Yet, she had no choice. She was determined to leave for Cole's sake.

That night Iris was quiet, unable to shake her depression. Even Jake noticed.

"Say, Cole," he said over the Monopoly board, "I think coming here every night is getting Iris down. You ought to take her out. Tomorrow they're taking off my bandages, and she might not be up to the scare."

"Nah, we can't miss the unveiling," Cole said. "Besides, I'm saving my dough for the Valentine's Day bash. We're gonna make it a big night—dinner and dancing, right, Posey?"

"I have a better idea," she countered, smiling at the warm idea she'd had for their last bittersweet weekend together. "Sparky and Eva are going to take that interisland cruise then. Why don't I fix dinner for the two of us?"

Jake laughed. "You'd better not pass that one up, buddy. It's the only way you'll find out if she can cook without Eva to bail her out." He looked at Iris appraisingly and suddenly she felt as if she might have met Jake's criteria for Cole's wife if only she were Caucasian. *And what about Marta's German blood?* she thought in response. *Isn't hers just as tainted?*

Almost as if hearing her thoughts, Jake suddenly changed the subject. "You know, Marta has hardly missed an afternoon coming up to see me, but she's seldom here at night. Is she seeing another guy?"

"The only time I've seen Marta is when I've been with you," Iris said simply. "Our paths don't cross."

"Marta's been using her time after work to study for a pilot's license," Cole said casually. "Wants to surprise you, I guess. Least, that's what she said when I saw her on the base the other day." Something in his tone made Iris glance at him curiously. He grinned and picked up the Monopoly dice. "Let's play—and if you get careless, Posey, I'm gonna get Park Place away from you."

"Careless" . . . something *was* wrong. To hide her confusion, she laughed and pretended to concentrate on the game.

However, Jake wasn't through. "What's gone on with the accident inquiry, buddy? They must have come up with something by now."

"Don't twist yourself inside out on that one, Jake," he said casually. "From all I've heard, everything's going just fine. You just have to get out of here and prove to them that you're well enough to get behind a stick again. Okay now, if you aren't going to roll those dice, you lose your turn," he added with a laugh.

Iris had almost forgotten their code until now. Cole had just used it twice: once to tell her all was not what it should be between Marta and Jake, and once to tell her he was lying when he assured Jake that the accident inquiry was going along fine. She smiled quickly, taking the dice and joking with Jake.

Later, as they were walking out to the jeep, Cole said thoughtfully, "You were great in there, Posey. For a minute there I was afraid you were going to say something, like maybe you'd forgotten the code."

"Well, you did take me by surprise. What's going on?"

"It doesn't look good. The inquiry board questioned me yesterday. Maybe after what I said they'll just settle for requiring him to take a special single-engine fighter course. It'd mean they'd send him stateside for six weeks. It'd be a blow to his ego, but at least he won't be taken out of the flight program. But as long as he's still in the hospital, I don't see any need in worrying him."

Iris agreed, then asked, "What's the story on Marta?"

"Oh. She's something," Cole said, seeming almost embarrassed. "She really does want to learn to fly. She told me if I would teach her, she'd be happy to teach me other things in return—in a horizontal position, I assume." Iris looked at him wide-eyed, and he laughed, adding, "I told her I had other plans and she could find another teacher."

"Oh, Cole," Iris giggled, "I do love you."

"Well, I'd certainly hate to be spending the rest of my life with a woman who doesn't," he said flippantly. Iris said a silent prayer that he never would—that whatever woman he ended up spending his life with would love him at least half as much as she did.

Iris and Eva had decided to quit their jobs the Wednesday before Valentine's Day. That would give them one day to make final arrangements for their voyage. On Friday, Eva would leave with Sparky on the interisland cruise. By Sunday, when she returned, both men would know of their plans. Iris didn't know which would be worse, the telling or the leaving.

The Japanese immigration officials told them that their visas would not be ready in time for their Tuesday departure but that they could make out notarized certificates of identification stating that they were entering the country to visit relatives. Grateful to avoid more red tape, they took care of that formality and arranged for a moving company to pack their belongings for storage the day before their departure. They spent Thursday packing the gifts for their Japanese relatives that their parents had sent to them, plus a year's supply of insulin for Iris to take to her aunt Suki in Shizuoka. Sunday and Monday would be time enough for packing their personal belongings.

Eva left with Sparky early Friday morning and Iris spent the afternoon of Valentine's Day getting ready for Cole. It had to be perfect . . . it must last her a lifetime. The end had begun.

Cole arrived as she was putting the chicken in the oven. "Hey, Posey!" He laughed. "You're still in your robe. Did I come too early?"

"Not really," she said, going to him. "I just didn't want to get my new dress dirty while I was fixing dinner."

"Smells great . . . mmm, and so do you," he said, burrowing his nose in her hair. "What's the schedule? Do we have time for a drink and a cuddle on the couch?"

"We have all the time in the world," she murmured as he squeezed her tightly to him. "Dinner's in the oven and it can keep. The house is ours for the whole weekend if we want it. Now, if you'll let me go for just a minute, I'll fix that drink."

She filled two tumblers with ice. Her pulse racing, she poured Scotch into one glass and quickly downed half of it with a shudder. She wasn't much of a drinker, but she needed something to keep her from shaking so obviously. Closing her eyes, she willed herself to forget everything but Cole, everything but now.

As Cole sipped his drink, she put on a stack of records. Bing Crosby's "Pennies from Heaven" filled the room and she sank down next to Cole, nestling under his arm, feeling the warmth of him spread through her.

As they sat silently watching a column of afternoon sun give way to dusk, Iris raised her face and pulled Cole to her in an eager embrace. In his arms, all doubts and fears were forgotten. Breathless, she trembled slightly as he slowly caressed her back, her side, and then gently cupped her breast. Instinctively, she arched her back, urging his exploring lips and hands to fulfill the aching need surging through her. Her robe slipped over her bare shoulder as he tenderly kissed her neck.

"Cole," she whispered hoarsely, "take me into the bedroom."

He pulled back for only an instant, his eyes questioning. "Now, Cole," she murmured, "now."

He swiftly lifted her in his arms, his eyes drinking the very liquid of her soul. She clung to his neck, kissing the well at the base of his throat where the golden hair curled.

As he set her down, she loosened her robe and it fell around her feet. She watched him as he undressed, feeling his hungry gaze burning her naked body in the dusky light.

When he lifted her gently to the bed, the air was still and warm, as if the tropical evening were holding its breath. An electric shiver of excitement ran through her as his mouth explored and claimed her face, throat, and shoulders. A breath of desire escaped from inside her as his mouth caressed her breast and enveloped its rigid tip. She trembled with newly released passion as he stroked her thigh, then explored the depths between her legs. Eagerly, she returned the pleasure, running her hands down through the soft hairs of his muscled stomach to his hard swollen manhood. She moaned, lost in his sweet breath, giving way to his weight as he came down on her, penetrating her with his hardness. As she cried out, receiving his heat, a torrent of rain poured savagely on the roof, pounding a rhythm through their passion, washing the air with its perfume. The gentleness was gone as she cried, eagerly raising her hips to meet his urgent thrusts, blending her body with his until, like the rain, they slowly quieted, sated and washed by their passion, cleansed by their love.

He turned to his side, still holding her to him, reluctant to let her go. "Posey . . ." he murmured, his voice filled with wonder.

She put her finger to his lips. "I can love only you. It's good that we have each other this way . . . forever."

He tasted her lips, slowly drinking in her breath, then laid his head back on the pillow. She could tell from his even breathing that he'd fallen asleep in her arms. She closed her eyes and floated in a dream of warmth and love, pushing away the dark emptiness lurking beyond the edge of her happiness. She savored the moment, burning into her memory the feel, the sounds, the very smells of this moment.

The deep darkness of the night surrounded them when Cole awakened her with teasing kisses. "Hey, Posey," he whispered, "I'm hungry. How about you?"

"Hungry?" she murmured sleepily. "Hungry! Our dinner . . . what time is it?" She dashed out of bed and into the kitchen. The chicken was a burnt offering, a dry black block at the bottom of the pan. The rolls were small chunks of charcoal. She put it all on the counter and stared at it tearfully.

"That bad?" Cole asked, coming into the kitchen, then as he saw the pan he laughed.

"Oh, Cole, I wanted to give you a good dinner. . . ."

"Hey, Posey, it's all right. I'd go through a month without dinners just to have what we had tonight," he said, taking her in his arms. "We'll fix something else."

When a search of the cupboards yielded nothing but a can of broth, Cole announced, with firm dignity, unabashed by the fact that he was standing in the middle of the kitchen stark naked, "We are forced to live on love and broth. And I sincerely believe," he said, raising his eyebrows in imitation of a lecherous Groucho Marx, "we shall make medical history by finding the former more sustaining than the latter."

"Oh," Iris exclaimed through her laughter, "I forgot the coleslaw that's in the refrigerator."

"Well, get it. We need everything we can find, unless you want me to nibble your ear for real."

As they sat down to their dinner of broth and cabbage salad, Cole said, "You know, I remember reading about the Great War and the starving children who had nothing to eat but some kind of gruel and cabbage."

She looked at him across the table. He was somehow vulnerable, like a small boy cheerfully sitting on a limb munching stolen apples, unaware that the branch was about to break. "Some kind of a poet you are, Lord Tennyson," she said, bringing up an old teasing reference to his name. "Just pretend that we're making history."

He put his cup down suddenly. "Ah, Posey," he said, grabbing her hand, "this is the way we're meant to be. Together. Always. I can't wait until we get married. I'm going in to the colonel tomorrow and ask him if he thinks my chances of advancement would be improved if I asked for a transfer." She couldn't bear to look at his eyes, fearful he would read the pain welling up within her, so she looked at their hands, his large strong fingers clasped protectively over hers. "We'll be married before the year is out, I promise," he said. "But now come on back to bed with your poet. We have almost two more days before I have to report back to the base. I don't want to waste a second of them with you out of my arms."

They spent that night and the next day and night together, laughing and rejoicing in each other, tumbling at will into

31

each other's arms. When they made love, Iris clung to him, taking in his love as if to store it in her very bones. At rest, she watched him, memorizing his every line, absorbing his presence, his tenderness into her very soul. For on Sunday she must tell him she was leaving.

CHAPTER III

"What the hell are you talking about?" Cole's eyes flashed with anger.

Iris sat quietly beside him on the sofa, her hands folded, her face composed. It had been over an hour since she'd told him and still he raged.

"It's not stupid, Cole," she repeated quietly. "My parents want me to visit their relatives in Japan. Mother and Father can't travel now. I'm the only one in the family who can fulfill that duty."

"A visit, okay—but for a *year?*"

"Father said he will join me in December if he can. I must at least stay until then."

"Haven't you been reading the papers?" he asked, trying a new argument. "Things aren't too friendly between America and Japan. It isn't safe for you to go."

"Oh, Cole, things aren't that bad," Iris countered. "The United States is too powerful. We're shipping tons of weapons and equipment to England to use fighting Hitler and we're keeping our own fences strong, building up bases like the one here at Pearl. No nation would be foolish enough to attack us, much less a small country like Japan. If we're pulled into war, it will be in Europe, not out here."

"But how can you possibly go for so long?" Cole persisted. "It kills me to think of you away from me for even a day. And you've had this planned for weeks and haven't told me. What's going on with you, anyway?"

Cole couldn't know that his every word cut like a burning sword through her heart. "I didn't want to listen to you talking like this for a full month. I figured it would be easier for both of us this way."

"Easier? I can't figure you out, Iris. How can it be easy to just up and leave someone you say you love without even a consultation? Don't I have any say in this?"

"You don't understand, Cole. This is between my parents and me. I'm the bridge between their culture and yours. I have to fulfill my duties to them. If you can't understand, then you can't understand half of me. Perhaps it's best we find this out now, before it's too late."

There was a long silence, then Cole got up and walked to the window, his back to her. Iris counted each second with a heavy heart. She willed her hands still, fearful that she would crack, that she would run to him.

"What about us?" he finally asked in a hoarse whisper, still looking out the window.

"I won't hold you to our engagement." Iris swallowed hard, painfully. "Perhaps my life is too different from yours after all. You may find a Caucasian woman who would make you a better wife. If you want, I'll return your ring before I leave."

"Return it?" Cole spun around and faced her. He was trembling, and his eyes blazed with anger. "Hell! If you want out that easy, go ahead." Then he added more bitterly, "Are you trying to tell me that all this weekend was an act on your part? Was it all that bad?"

Iris looked down, trying to hide her face, and shook her head slowly.

"Look at me!" he shouted. "Dammit! Look at me. Hand me back my ring. Tell me you don't love me. Say it to my face."

Iris slowly took off her ring and handed it to Cole, not daring to look at him towering over her.

"Look at me and say you don't love me."

Tears streaming down her cheeks, Iris looked up. The misted vision of the man who was her life was more than she could deny. Sobbing, she held out her hand with her engagement ring in it. The words would not come.

He slapped the ring from her hand, then roughly took her in his arms, crushing her to him. Helplessly, she clung to him, crying uncontrollably.

"You can't deny me any more than I can deny you," he said huskily. "You're part of me." Iris buried her face in his chest, and when tears began to slow, he murmured, "Posey, I don't know what's going on, but I'm trying to understand. Keep the ring, will you?"

Iris nodded, another sob catching in her throat.

"A year is a long time. There's no guarantee it won't ruin us," Cole said quietly. "I can't help being angry with you. I'm hurt. But—you mean too much to me. Keep the ring: it's a promise, one we will try to keep. Maybe you'll come back early. Meanwhile, we will write to each other."

"Here's my uncle's address," she said quietly, taking a slip of paper from the coffee table.

"I have to go out on a training mission. I can't even see you off. But I wouldn't want to anyway. I don't think I could stand the pain. I'll say good-bye now. I love you, Posey. I damn well wish I didn't, but I do." He kissed her deeply, desperately, holding the length of her against him possessively. "If it's through hell, you come back to me," he commanded hoarsely.

Then he quickly turned and went out the door, letting it slam behind him.

Iris fell to the floor, searching desperately through her tears to find the ring. Her fingers grasped it and she put it back on, then collapsed on the floor frantically sobbing in soul-wrenching tears.

By the time Eva returned, Iris had calmed down. Eva had told Sparky of their plans, and while he'd not been as explosive as Cole, he clearly wasn't happy. Eva and Iris consoled each other that it was all for the best in the long run.

Although he was hurt, Sparky at least helped them get their baggage to the boat. However, the freighter left on the early-morning tide, and since they spent the night aboard, there was no one to see them off when they raised anchor in the predawn light.

If the seemingly interminable voyage was any indication, Iris and Eva were sure that they were going to hate Japan. The crew on the scrap-iron ship was distant and aloof and the food was dreadful. They didn't even like rice. However, misery shared is more easily borne. They leaned on each other for strength and tried to mend their shattered spirits with shared laughter and tears.

When the boat docked in Japan, Iris had a brief flash of joy. She thought she saw her father standing there waiting for her. However, as she ran toward him, she realized it wasn't her father, but a man who seemed a cold and aged statue of him. His brother, Anami, lacked the animation and the indulgent smile that she could expect from her father. She approached her uncle expecting a welcoming embrace. Instead, she got a formal bow.

"Iris, daughter of my brother, Chosu. I trust your voyage was comfortable," he said with a heavy accent. He actually seemed afraid that she might touch him.

"Yes, and you must be Uncle Anami." She smiled. "For a moment I thought my father was standing here."

"I see," he said, with no trace of a smile. "If you come this way, we get baggage."

"But my friend Eva is waiting for her family. I can't just leave her." Iris turned and pulled Eva forward, saying with more enthusiasm than she felt, "Eva, this is my uncle Anami."

Again there was a formal bow from the waist, his face a mask. "I hope you enjoy your visit, Miss Eva. Now we must go."

"But—"

"It's okay, Iris," Eva said hastily. "I think I see my cousin coming through that corridor."

"But when can we get together?"

"I don't know. Just call me."

"Where do your family live, Miss Eva?" Uncle Anami asked.

"Yokohama."

"Ah . . . forty-minute train ride. You will write my niece. Here is my card." He pulled a small white business card from his pocket; it was covered with Japanese characters. Without waiting for a response, he turned and walked briskly toward customs, forcing Iris to follow lest she get left behind. She glanced over her shoulder and Eva waved bravely, pointing to a man beside her, presumably her cousin.

The ancient taxi, with her trunk and suitcases precariously strapped to the roof, cut an erratic path through the teeming throngs of bicycles, carts, cars, and buses, seemingly bent on collision and leaving Iris breathless with fear. She could not tear her eyes from what she was certain was her impending doom any more than she could force herself to make polite conversation with her silent uncle.

The silence was finally broken when Uncle Anami said reproachfully, "Your father's mother has been waiting for your arrival for three days."

Iris gasped as the taxi nearly grazed a bicyclist. Everyone seemed oblivious to the driver's reckless path except herself. Tearing her eyes from the road, she said, "I'm sorry if she was worried," then added irritably, "Of course, I had no way of urging the freighter to go any faster."

She turned back to the window. They were now scattering pedestrians on the small winding streets of the outskirts of what Iris assumed was Tokyo. Everything was so different, she thought, wondering how she would ever adjust to such a strange land.

Exhausted, she sighed with relief when they finally careened to a stop in front of a walled entry on a narrow back street of the city. Behind the gate was a graceful garden with a winding rock path leading to a small timbered house with an arched front entrance of faded red.

No one greeted them at the door, and Iris followed her uncle down a narrow corridor to a small room at the end of the house. A small, rotund woman, wearing a pale blue kimono with delicate pink and orange flowers printed on it, and a wide, dark blue obi, stood up as they entered the bare room. Uncle Anami introduced her as his wife, Iris's aunt Toshiko. She bowed politely and Iris politely said something about how nice it was to meet her. Uncle Anami said, "She doesn't speak English," then turned and left the room, leaving Iris standing awkwardly facing her aunt. She smiled at her and Aunt Toshiko solemnly bowed again.

As she straightened from her bow, she glanced at Iris's shoes and began chattering in Japanese and pointing at Iris's feet. Iris looked down at her stylish high-heeled pumps and smiled at the assumed compliment.

Seemingly exasperated, Aunt Toshiko bent down and took off Iris's shoes, replacing them with soft silk slippers.

"Oh. Thanks." Iris smiled, feeling awkward and somehow reprimanded. Aunt Toshiko took Iris's shoes and placed them outside her sliding door, pointed to them, and said something in Japanese.

That taken care of, she walked to a washbowl and pitcher

on a low stand in the corner of the room. She pointed to it, then took a small white towel from a bamboo peg and hung it over her arm. Iris nodded to show that she understood. Aunt Toshiko pointed again, then pantomimed that Iris should wash her face.

Iris nodded. "Yes, that will be fine when I want to wash up."

Aunt Toshiko again pantomimed washing and gestured for Iris to come over to the bowl, once more speaking in Japanese.

"Oh. Now?" Iris said with a half-smile. "Well, if you think I need it." She went to the bowl and started to reach in to splash her face with water, but Aunt Toshiko stopped her. Taking the lid from a brown pottery bowl with enameled white and blue flowers on it, Aunt Toshiko reached in with bamboo tongs and pulled out a steaming hot towel and held it out to Iris.

"What'll I do with that?" Iris asked.

Aunt Toshiko pushed it toward her again, so she took it, bouncing the hot damp cloth from one hand to the other so as not to burn herself. Aunt Toshiko seemed to be trying not to smile. She placed her hands on her face and indicated that Iris was to wash with the hot towel. Obediently, Iris patted her face. It was amazingly refreshing. She scrubbed, wiped her neck and hands, and smiled at Aunt Toshiko.

"Thanks," she said, and nodded in response to Aunt Toshiko's bow. Then as she turned from the bowl, Aunt Toshiko touched her arm, said something in Japanese, and pointed to the unused water in the washbowl.

Iris looked at her. "I'm not done?" Aunt Toshiko pantomimed that now Iris was to splash her face with the cool water. Obediently, Iris turned back to the bowl. "All right, if it'll make you happy." She splashed her face with the lemon-scented water and realized that the combination of the heat and then the cool scented water was cleansing and refreshing.

Aunt Toshiko handed her the towel. "Thanks," Iris said, patting her face dry. "Am I finished now?" Aunt Toshiko bowed in response and Iris nodded again.

Gesturing and speaking in Japanese, Aunt Toshiko indicated that Iris was to follow her. Dutifully, Iris walked behind her aunt down the corridor, feeling clumsy and awkward, like a child in a stranger's home, out of place and frightened of breaking something precious.

The only light in the narrow hallway was filtered through the white screened wall along one side. The woven mat on the floor rustled under her slippered feet and the air had a musky smell reminiscent of incense. At the end of the hall, Aunt Toshiko knelt and slid back a paper screen door, and gestured for Iris to enter.

Iris stepped in and saw that she was in a clean, expansive room that opened onto a wooden deck and a lovely garden. The walls were of thick white paper checkered with dark wood lath strips. The floors were covered with light tan woven mats. Pillows were placed on the floor. In one corner was a single curved branch of plum blossoms. Uncle Anami and her grandmother were waiting for her.

Iris's grandmother was a wizened old woman with graying hair pulled tightly back into a bun. She was wearing an elaborate kimono of navy silk printed with bright red chrysanthemums. Her wide red obi emphasized her round shape. Despite what Iris's parents had said about the old woman's health and despite her obvious age, she appeared far from dying. In fact, she had a regal air, and Iris had no doubt that she ruled the household. Her two sons, Uncle Anami, who had met Iris at the boat, and Uncle Kuni, a slender, bespectacled man, and their wives and five children all lived under Grandmother's roof. Uncle Anami was the eldest son and consequently the head of the household now that his father was dead. However, even he deferred to Grandmother.

"This is your honorable grandmother," Uncle Anami said, taking Iris to his mother. Iris started forward to kiss her grandmother, but her uncle touched her arm and said harshly, "You must bow to her."

"What?"

"Bow. Like so," he explained, barely concealing his disdain while demonstrating.

Iris followed suit, chagrined by her sudden lack of social graces and sensing that this was only the beginning. These people looked like her parents, but they were not at all like them. Their faces were masks, not given to ready American smiles, their actions were formal and studied, and their eyes were shuttered, closed off from laughter and open expression. How would she be able to fit in with them for a whole year?

Only Uncle Anami spoke understandable English. Uncle Kuni professed to know some words, but his accent was so heavy that Iris found even these unintelligible. She took to simply nodding and smiling when he spoke to her.

Presently, her aunts slid back the screen at the end of the room, creating a much larger room, with a small table at the far end, laden with steaming dishes. Iris inwardly flinched as she saw the strange foods that she would be expected to eat.

Japanese food had rarely appeared on Iris's mother's table. "You must eat American," she had always told Iris. "We are American now. There is very few ingredient for Japanese." Their enthusiasm for their new country had dictated their decision to speak only English in their home and to cook only American foods. The few times her mother, in an uncharacteristic fit of homesickness, had tried to serve Japanese food, Iris had been revolted by the array of vegetables and fish. Now, she thought morosely, it would be all she had to eat. Her heart sank at the thought and at the sight of the steaming mound of white rice.

Her aunts brought out a long low table of black lacquered wood and began setting dishes on dark bamboo mats. Exhausted, Iris could barely look at the artistically arranged dishes proffered to her. They all seemed equally unpalatable.

She answered each question about her mother and father and sat quietly while her answers were carefully translated by Uncle Anami for the benefit of Grandmother, Uncle Kuni, and her two aunts, all of whom listened politely and made approving and animated comments in Japanese with each translation. It was a tedious process. However, it allowed her time to fumble with her chopsticks. They politely averted their eyes as she repeatedly dropped her food. Iris was almost ill with the strain before she was allowed to retire, still hungry, to her small room at the end of the long, darkened hallway.

She was shocked to find that her aunts had unpacked her belongings. Her trunk sat empty in a corner of the small room, and her clothes, cosmetics, and other possessions were in incongruous piles in a strange cabinet against the wall. It may have been just a helpful gesture, but to Iris it felt like a blatant invasion of privacy.

She quietly pushed aside the paper screen door and sat on the *tatami*, the mat of woven dried grass that covered the floors. She let the cool spring air wash over her face as she looked out at the garden, fragrant with early flowers and graceful budding trees, lit by the amber light of a hanging lantern. Admiring the view, Iris pushed back her anger and indignation.

Finally, she rose and began rearranging her things, disturbed to think that each item had been examined by her aunts. When her room was reordered in her own way, she was able to calm herself enough to lie down on the thick comforter her aunts had placed on the floor to serve as her bed. When sleep finally came in the dark quiet of the night, she still seemed to be rocked by the ghost movements of the ship, suspended in a cradle stitched with the chirrup of midnight crickets.

It was not many days before she realized that the meal she could hardly touch upon her arrival had been a sumptuous feast by all comparisons. Through questioning her uncle and observing in the marketplace, she found that Japan had been at war with China for four years and the populace was suffering from the privations of such a prolonged military adventure. Her presence was obviously a huge burden on the family. She felt she must somehow contribute to the household expenses or they would all pay dearly in the months to come.

Her father had written that he would arrive in Japan early in December. Yet, he'd given her no money to live on while she waited. She had only her small savings, which she was determined to save for a return ticket in case of emergency. No, she wouldn't touch that. Her only hope was a job of some sort. But what could she do in a land where she didn't understand a word, let alone the strange customs?

She spent two weeks trying to find a job. Then, when she inquired at the home of the Swedish chargé d'affaires, she was informed by his wife that they didn't need her but perhaps her background could be used at the embassy. She applied for and got an afternoon job as a typist. It paid enough to help her family's expenses with enough left over for her to take language lessons in the mornings. She was amazed to find that the monthly amount equaled only $9.37 in American money. However, in Japan it was just enough.

This ultimately brought a solution to another of her problems: eating. She was trying, without success, to eat the strange food served to her. She abhorred the omnipresent steamed rice and was revolted by thinly sliced raw fish, which they considered a delicacy. The tiny, salty pickled plums were strange, and the seaweed wrapped around vinegary rice and eels was repugnant. The clear soups had unidentifiable objects floating around in them, and even when they contained noodles, she couldn't dip them out because she was inept at using chopsticks. In fact, she viewed most of the items in her dinner bowl with nothing more than suspicion. Only the few recognizable vegetables, steamed and still crisp, sustained her. Her weight had dropped to ninety-five pounds before she hit on the idea of eating lunch away from home, claiming she couldn't take the time to return to the house between her lessons and her job. At the marketplace she bought bread and hard-cooked eggs, and she found a small grocery catering to the foreign community. It was expensive and had mostly German and English foods, but the tinned treasures were worth saving up for. As a result, she brought her weight back up to one hundred pounds, still five pounds lighter than she'd been in Hawaii.

She'd had no trouble writing Eva in Yokohama. Her uncles had willingly addressed her envelopes with Japanese characters and told her how to post local mail. From Eva's quick responses, Iris knew that their situations were similar. Despite the fact that Eva spoke Japanese well, she also felt isolated and strange. However, Iris determined she must learn the language before she could get through the other walls dividing her from her relatives. She threw herself more energetically into learning Japanese.

On the other hand, her uncles seemed peculiarly obtuse when she wanted to mail a letter to Cole. She'd planned to write just one letter, to let him know she'd arrived safely. Her question was greeted with strange ignorance on the part of her uncles, especially considering that they had been able to write to her father in America several times a year, and in fact had told her that they'd already written to him of her safe arrival. Her aunts conveyed a sense of fear through their tight-lipped silence while the matter was being discussed. When she repeated her request, the aunts took the small children out of the room.

Her grandmother sat silently in the corner, and her uncles remained sitting silently on their pillows. Grandmother seemed to be concentrating on her view of the garden. It was as if Iris had not asked the question.

There was a soft rustle behind the white paper screen wall. Silhouetted by the morning sunlight, her uncle's youngest son crouched on the floor behind the paper wall. His chubby finger, wet with spit, wiped a spot on the treated paper. With the moisture, the paper became translucent and her little cousin's eye appeared at the resultant peephole. As his view faded with the drying of the paper, he moistened his finger and again began making a peephole. Only this time the process was stopped by a slap on his hand and a harsh word from his mother behind the wall.

Finally, Uncle Anami broke the silence. "My niece," he said carefully, his eyes conveying genuine concern, "there is much you have to learn about your native country. In the Nippon ways there is much that is seen and remembered." Both he and his brother seemed to feel that was a sufficient answer, for they got up, bowed to Grandmother, and left.

Confused and still carrying the unmailed letter, Iris went to work, where she asked Inga, her newfound friend at the Swedish Embassy, about her family's strange response.

Inga carefully looked around the empty office. Assured that they were alone, she said flatly, "It's the *Kampetei*. The Thought Police. Everyone is afraid of them. They have great powers. You see, it is a crime to be disloyal to the Emperor, even in your thoughts."

"Your thoughts?" Iris echoed in amazement.

"Shhh! You will have to watch what you say. The walls have ears." She smiled grimly. "These police try to make sure that the crime of illegal thoughts, and all else that goes with them, is not committed. They have their own interpretations of what constitutes disloyalty, so the people are very cautious not to do something that might make the police take them down to the station for questioning. It can be expensive for the whole family, not to mention painful . . . even fatal."

Iris was incredulous. "But a letter home? I'm an American. What kind of country is this?"

"Your country is not on the friendliest terms with the Emperor's Japan. For several years now America has limited immigration of Japanese citizens. That is an insult. They have lost face—the worst thing to happen in their society. To lose face is to be avoided at all costs. Why, even prisoners are allowed to wear a kind of basket hat that covers their faces.

"And now your president is threatening an embargo against Japan, unless Japan stops its aggression in China. He would allow only cotton and foodstuffs, cutting off Japan's supplies for hard industrial production, like the scrap iron on that ship you said you arrived on."

"And for war materiel . . ." Iris added, catching on.

Inga nodded. "There is much propaganda against the Western nations. Japan wants all Orientals to unite in a Co-Prosperity Sphere, under Japan's leadership, of course. Your family is simply concerned that your letters might be interpreted as spy letters, which could bring great harm to all the family. After all, you did say your fiancé was in the military."

"Yes, but he isn't—"

"The Japanese take no chances."

"But what about my letter?"

"The American Embassy will send it out for you. All you have to do is be the courier for us to the Americans once a week or so. Then there isn't such a risk for your family. But even that mail will be read, so be circumspect in what you say, and leave off your fiancé's rank. Have him send his letters to us . . . in care of me," she added generously.

Iris destroyed the letter she had written and carefully rewrote it that evening. She hoped Cole would remember all the little things she was referring to, like Aaron Liebold, the snoop in the finance office at the base, and their special songs, and the code they'd set up when Jake was in the hospital, their signal of "inside out" meaning that everything following was the opposite in truth. The letter was certain to confuse any Japanese censor, she thought, and that made her smile as she reread it:

Dear Cole,

I have arrived safely in Japan. Since my arrival, I have often been reminded of Aaron Liebold in the finance office. There are many here with his same traits. I have also often found myself humming one of our favorite songs, "Careless."

I could just turn myself inside out telling you of everything that has happened since I've arrived. My family is so easy to get along with. Their customs are so much like what I grew up with. I am free to do whatever I wish and to write to you. Okay now. I have a job

*at the Swedish Embassy, typing in the afternoons. You
may write to me there in care of Inga Andersen. You
needn't include your business address on the envelope,
unless it changes, because I already know how to write
to you. Write only if you feel like it.*

Love,
Iris

Iris gave the letter to the American Embassy and spent two
months worrying about the results. Finally, her fears were
eased. Cole wrote, in care of Inga at the Swedish Embassy,
clearly avoiding any reference to his military assignment in
the return address. It even had a civilian postmark. Her
hands were shaking as she read:

Dearest Iris,
*I received your letter last night and have finally
figured out how to answer. You will be relieved to hear
that Aaron Liebold is still the same as you remember
him. I also have been singing "Careless" daily since you
left. Once I understand the desertion I will probably
get it out of my head. I seem to get the words inside
out.*

*Things have been just as happy around here since
you left. You needn't hurry back. Everyone seems to
feel that Japan and the United States will soon be
having a peaceful and profitable relationship.*

*Okay now, I should let you know that I've asked my
"boss" for the chance to work at another location. I will
let you know if I have another address. Perhaps it will
keep me busy until you return and will be more
profitable. I miss you.*

Love,
Cole

Iris hadn't expected to react with tears, but she was so
relieved to hear from him, and devastated by his simple
statement of missing her. He'd obviously understood most of
her letter, although he still sounded hurt in his reference to
her "desertion." She wiped away her tears and decided that it

44

was best not to write back right away. Did he really think Japan and the U.S. would soon be at war?

A month later, she received a short letter from Cole, telling her he "had business" in the Philippines. He gave no address. It seemed as if he'd already begun to put her aside. It was what she'd said she wanted, what she thought was best, yet she ached at the thought. The spring and early summer were dull and miserable for her.

Iris wilted in the Tokyo summer. The heat was heavy, turning clothing to limp rags, filling each breath with debilitating lassitude. The heavy humidity hung in the hot air like dank cobwebs, irritating her skin with constant perspiration. Only by remembering that her father would arrive in December and she would leave with him in January was she able to endure it. The part-time job at the embassy kept intact her precious money for the return trip and emergencies. She couldn't lose that.

Now, she wiped her hands on her cotton skirt and began typing a memo to the American Ambassador, Joseph C. Grew. Then she remembered her previous conversation with Inga about Japanese foreign policy. She looked up as she finished and asked Inga, "Do you really think the Japanese have started invading Indo-China?"

"Of course. What does the message say? Our sources don't lie."

"It talks about an Imperial Conference on July second."

"That was when the Japanese said they would 'negotiate' in the southern regions and 'promote other necessary measures.' "

"Does that all have to do with that Co-Prosperity idea?" Iris asked. "Will other countries buy it, realizing Japan would be in the driver's seat?"

Inga got up and closed their office door, then sat on the corner of Iris's desk.

"The Western nations have colonized the East for centuries," she explained quietly. "They've taken the natural resources and used the people for cheap labor. Many Asians feel they'd be better off under an Asian master. Indo-China is now as good as Japanese. You can see that the tripartite treaty with Germany has nothing to do with the European war as far as Japan is concerned, unless you consider the golden opportunity it offers to move into Asia while the Europeans are busy fighting in Europe.

"Now, write a letter to your boyfriend," she said, pointing to the letter Iris had received that day with Cole's Philippine address. "I have a packet for the American Embassy to be taken over tonight."

Iris dreaded delivering the packet after five o'clock, so she hurried through her letter to Cole, keeping it brief and noncommittal. If she arrived at the embassy after five, that patronizing Irving Lasher would be at the desk. He never remembered that she wasn't Japanese and spoke loudly and slowly to her, as if she had difficulty understanding English, her native tongue. How he had gotten into the diplomatic corps, Iris could never understand.

As she crossed the street, she told herself that her tension was due to the heat. The wilting temperature was what made her so impatient with the heavy traffic. When she was caught behind an ambling grandmother in a kimono and clogs, she chafed at the delay. It seemed deliberate that a rash bicyclist cut her off from her streetcar. Dripping with perspiration, she raced to catch it, but ended up waving down a jinriksha. In broken Japanese, she urged the sweating driver to pedal the cart faster. Still, when she arrived at the American Embassy, Irving Lasher was just sitting down at the desk, coming on duty.

He nodded with exaggeration and took out the envelopes. "Ah," he said too loudly as he spotted her letter, "I see you are determined to make East meet West." He gave a high-pitched laugh.

Iris didn't smile. "West meets West," she said evenly. "You must be forgetting again, Mr. Lasher, both my fiancé and myself are American citizens . . . native-born American citizens."

His smile cooled noticeably.

It was ridiculous to let such a petty minor official upset her so. Yet, he was her countryman and was showing a small-mindedness she'd never encountered at home. It must be the heat, she told herself again, unable to ease her tension as she approached her grandmother's house.

Entering the small front garden, she closed the gate, leaving the noisy bustle of the street beyond the wall. She hurried up the curving rock pathway, kicked off her shoes, and went to her tiny room. She splashed her face with the tepid water her aunts had put in the washbowl and tucked a stray strand of hair back into her bun. It was customary for her, like the rest of the family, to make a polite report to her grandmother each evening when she returned. Tonight she'd stopped at one of the market stalls on the way home and purchased some of the tiny oranges from the southern regions. She was sure her grandmother would approve. Iris stepped out of her street clothes and donned a kimono. Again, *Oba-a-san*, Grandmother, should approve. Anything to make things go more smoothly . . . to ease the tension that was tightening her stomach. It must be the heat.

It was strangely quiet as Iris hurried down the short corridor to the main room where her grandmother presided. She kneeled and quietly pushed aside the paper screen, the way she'd been taught. An ominously silent gathering greeted her as she bowed her head.

Grandmother was seated on her customary cushion. Sitting to her right was a guest, dressed immaculately in an olive green uniform and a soft-billed cap with a leather chin strap. Sitting stiffly in the place of honor, he seemed filled with an importance out of proportion to his slight stature. He was flanked by her two uncles, their faces masks of indifference. The children sat strangely quiet at the back of the room with their mothers. Even the baby, little Kibo, normally quite active, was sitting quietly on a pillow, seriously gumming a knotted cloth.

Iris hesitated, then moved toward her grandmother. "I brought you some oranges from the market, Honored Grandmother," she said in her halting Japanese.

She glanced at the stranger and thought she saw a glimmer of approval in the tiny eyes set in his masklike face. Something was wrong, and she sensed that somehow she'd just made it a little bit better. Her grandmother's eyes remained cold. Iris finally remembered to bow low to her grandmother, to each of her uncles, and then to the stranger. Uncle Anami almost smiled. Grandmother noticeably softened.

"Our guest has come to talk to you," Uncle Anami said slowly, so that she could understand. He turned to the officious man. "Sergeant Ito, may I present the daughter of my brother, Chosu." Iris chafed at the idea that she was so insignificant that he didn't deign even to mention her name. However, she bowed politely.

Sergeant Ito merely nodded. He did not waste his time

47

with the customary Japanese formalities. "I understand you were born in the United States?" he asked, with her uncle translating.

"Yes, Sergeant Ito," Iris answered politely. Who was this man, she wondered, and why was there such an aura of fear throughout the household?

"However, your father and mother were born in Japan?"

"Yes, that is correct."

He relaxed, becoming almost congenial. "Very good. I have come to help you."

"Help me?" Iris was puzzled. As her uncle had translated that last line, he had smiled gratefully at Sergeant Ito.

"Yes, it must be of great concern to you that you are not a Japanese citizen."

Iris proceeded with caution. There was something about this man, a moral stench, which warned her, made her search her mind for past information. She looked at his small cruel eyes, his too-full mouth and flattened nose. Suddenly she remembered what Inga had told her. *Kampetei!* The Thought Police. "A Japanese citizen?" she asked, stalling, trying to think what Inga would have her say. "I am pleased that my father sent me to learn about his native land. I would want my own children to understand their heritage and be proud."

Sergeant Ito beamed with approval. As her uncle translated, the family looked relieved. Reaching into his pocket, the sergeant pulled out an American passport. Hers! It must be, but how? She carefully composed her face, while her mind raced.

"This is how I can help," the sergeant said. "I will take your useless passport, and we will go down this evening and register you properly in the family registry. You are by inheritance a Japanese citizen. Just this simple formality is keeping our records from showing it to be so. Shall we go now? Perhaps one of your uncles would like to accompany us?" Uncle Anami translated rapidly, his eyes urging her to comply.

Iris suddenly reached out and snatched her passport from the sergeant's hand. "I'm afraid you don't understand, Sergeant Ito. I am of Japanese descent, but I was born in the United States, I grew up, went to school there, and I intend to live there. I am an American." She kept her voice low, but her posture was defiant. She knew they couldn't touch her as long as she had her passport. She also knew that never again would she be without it, even when she was sleeping.

"Iris!" Uncle Anami exclaimed.

"Please translate," she said stubbornly. Uncle Anami bowed and apologized as he translated.

A sudden, chilling gasp swept the room as he did so. From the droop of her grandmother's shoulders, Iris felt she'd dealt the family a cruel blow. Yet, she had no choice.

Sergeant Ito measured her coldly, then suddenly stood and nodded briefly to Grandmother. "Very well. However, there may come a time in the near future when you will wish to change your mind. It is a simple matter. Your uncle will bring you to me." His last statement came out as an order. He waited while Uncle Anami translated, then abruptly turned and left without a bow.

"That was not wise," Uncle Anami said fiercely.

"I'm sorry, but I had no choice," Iris murmured, frightened by the shock in her grandmother's eyes.

Chilling fear crept into the room, borne on the heavy silence of the family. Iris quickly excused herself and went to her room, declining supper.

Each night since the second week after she'd arrived, she'd had a headache. Tonight it was worse than ever. She'd always thought it was caused by the fumes from the charcoal brazier, but now she knew it was also due to the constant pressure under which she was living.

She thought of the dimpled charm of baby Kibo as he played under the flowering plum tree, of the easy laughter of Matsuko and Massaki as they flew their brightly colored kites with little-boy enthusiasm, of the musical laughter of Mieko and Hanako as they picked flowers for their mother in the summer evenings. She'd always attributed the aloofness of her uncles and aunts, even her grandmother, to their customs and disdain for her personally, but now she realized that it was a part of their real fear of her presence in their midst.

Yet, they would lose face if they sent her away. She could no longer endanger them. She would go to Yokohama this weekend and talk to Eva. In the meantime, she had much business to tend to in Tokyo. Inga would again be of help.

She slid back the paper door that opened onto the back garden, then sat down and looked around her tiny room, grateful for the light breeze. There was a strange wardrobe-

49

type cabinet that held her *futon*, the thick comforter that served as a Japanese bed, and the clothes she could fit on the shelves. The rest of the room was empty, save for her trunk, which she'd covered with a light blanket and used as a dressing table. It hit her with cold realization. They'd known where to find her passport. They'd obviously searched all her possessions. She shuddered, feeling exposed and vulnerable.

Never again. She closed the screen and took out a needle and thread. From some underwear, she fashioned a soft packet with a thin elastic belt, in which she would carry her passport next to her—at all times. She slipped her passport into the cloth envelope, then reached inside her kimono and pulled out the chain she always wore around her neck. She unfastened it and slid Cole's engagement ring off the chain; she'd worn it next to her heart ever since she'd boarded the freighter. The small diamond glittered like a piece of shining hope as she slipped it on her finger one last time. Reluctantly, with tears in her eyes, she took it off and dropped it into the packet with her passport. From now on, all her connections with America must be hidden.

She adjusted the slim pocket to fit at the small of her back, then rolled out the *futon*. As she lay there, trying to clear her muddled mind and chase away her throbbing headache, she thought of Cole. He was in the Philippines now. Closer. Somehow, the thought cheered her.

CHAPTER IV

Cole leaned his head against the metal brace of the troop plane and looked out the window. Predawn was still more a feeling than a light as they raced the rising sun toward the Philippines. The engines hummed steadily, lulling some of the men to a restless sleep. There was a smoky poker game going on at the back of the plane; other men were sprawled against their barracks bags, writing or quietly talking. Beside him, Jake slept, his snores masked by the steady sound of the two big engines of the C-47. Jake's transfer had been both a surprise and a delight to Cole.

It was over three months since Iris had left Honolulu, but still he couldn't keep her from his mind. It seemed as if she haunted his every step, visited his every dream. Maybe someday when they were together again he would understand what had made her leave. On impulse he had put in for a transfer. Whether it was running away from his hurt or a realistic attempt to advance more rapidly and perhaps win Iris back, he didn't know. He knew only that he was now winging his way to some distant tropical islands, the last American outpost in the Pacific; islands that were hidden in the clouds of vague information and rumor.

In front of him, Captain Dick McDuff leaned against the bare sidewall, his chin resting on his chest, his eyes covered with his tipped cap. He was a tight-lipped, square-rigged man, with short-cropped sandy hair and a big grin that belied his G-2 rating for the Corps of Intelligence Police in the Army Air Corps in the Philippines. Even Captain Dick McDuff didn't seem to know much about the Philippine situation. Or else he was keeping it to himself.

Jake opened his eyes and yawned. "What's it look like out there?" he asked. "Are we getting near landing?"

"Too dark to tell," Cole answered, having to raise his voice above the sound of the engines. "We should be approaching soon, though, judging from the time since we left Guam."

"Wonder what kind of planes they have," Jake said.

"Don't expect much. Especially since Hawaii just got their first P-40s. Don't know how I can train men to fly them if we don't have them to fly." Cole tried not to sound bitter. Then suddenly he asked, "Were you sorry to leave Marta?"

Jake shrugged. "In a way. She was good in bed. Full of life. Had exciting, daring ideas. In her own way, she seemed to care for me. But I knew it wasn't a permanent kind of thing. Not like the way you feel for Iris."

Cole grunted and turned his head back to the window to hide the pain he felt at the mention of her name. "Looks like we're over land now." He leaned forward as he pointed out the window.

A dark mound of land rose below them. A scatter of lights

spilled over hillsides, indicating a city. To the side and beyond were the lights indicating a landing field. "If that's Clark," Cole said, "it sure is easy enough to spot from the air."

Dick McDuff stirred and looked out the window. "That's going to be a familiar sight from now on," he said dryly.

The sun was just beginning to pipe an outline around Mt. Arayat as their C-47 came down to Clark Field. Still, the steamy heat of the Philippines penetrated the morning mists and wilted them as they stepped from the plane. As the sun began its fiery climb in the sky, they stood in a weary group along the turf surface of Clark Field, waiting for a transport to adjoining Fort Stotsenburg.

Cole stared in amazement at the planes around him. This was an American stronghold? Where was the strength? The bombers were not the modern Flying Fortresses, the B-17s, which wasn't surprising since they were still a rarity in Hawaii. Nor were they even the outdated, unsatisfactory, two-engined B-18s. They were the utterly obsolete, unarmored, and practically unarmed B-10s, which were both slow and vulnerable in the air. And there were no sleek P-40s to strengthen the ranks of the fighter planes. No P-39s. Among the few P-35s were several ancient P-26s, almost museum pieces. Cole's heart sank at the sight. No wonder the Japanese were so arrogant in their negotiations.

"Welcome to the Philippines," Dick McDuff said sardonically. "Not much besides the sun to warm your heart. Come on, Tennyson. Quit staring. We'd better get in the jeeps or we'll have to hitch a ride on a pony cart."

As they were soon to find out, the lack of planes was just the beginning of the problems. The list of things they didn't have or couldn't do so far outdistanced the list of things they could do, that they soon gave up listing.

However, it was the general torpor of the military personnel that sent Cole, Jake, and Dick into frequent rages during their indoctrination to the islands. The lassitude that weighted down any action or decision seemed to be found not in any one segment of the military community, but generally throughout. However, there were some men who were frantically trying to rouse the installations to readiness. General Grunert, who had arrived nearly a year earlier, was trying in his way to make strong defense plans. Colonel George, of the Army Air Corps, had arrived a couple of weeks earlier; he was a known scrapper, a man who would work long and hard to stir up military defenses. Still, the tropic indolence was going to be hard to fight.

Orders had been sent giving Cole a promotion to first lieutenant after his arrival in the Philippines. He was to be in charge of training the new pilots scheduled to come in. It was a bitter celebration he had with Dick and Jake that evening. He couldn't help but wonder what would have become of him and Iris if the promotion had come earlier, when they were together.

"You never know," Jake countered. "Take Marta, for instance," he said as he sipped his beer. "Got a letter from her yesterday that didn't sound like her, not all of it anyway. She said that maybe Hitler was going too far, and that she's learning to see a lot of people in a different light—whatever that means. Then the rest was pretty much like her. She's learning to fly. Quite a daredevil, I guess." He put down his beer. "What I'm saying is, people grow and change. Maybe Iris needed this time to find out about herself before she settled down. Maybe this is all for the better."

Cole scowled.

Because his assignment took him between airfields, from Clark and Del Carmen north of Manila to Nichols just to the south, Cole was frequently in transit. Dick was stationed in Manila and had a house of his own. By arrangement, Cole helped out with expenses and used the house for his headquarters when he wasn't staying in the bachelor officers' quarters at the bases. Inevitably, Jake managed to spend a good part of his time there as well.

It was the first week of June when word came that an RAF captain was going to speak to a group of officers at Fort Santiago. Cole went with Dick to hear what the Royal Air Force had to say about their allies, the Americans.

The fort was a centuries-old relic of Spanish rule. Its potbellied, mossy walls contained the musty air of old age and the headquarters of the Philippine Department, United States Army. Settling into his chair in the room with the other officers, Cole could see the quiet boats gliding up and down the Pasig River in the growing darkness.

Group Captain C. Darval of the RAF had made a survey of the defenses of the Philippines. The British were desperately fighting the Germans in Europe and expected soon to be fighting the Japanese, German allies, in the Pacific. The RAF had a vested interest in the defense of the Philippines, a strategic outpost between the Japanese and the rich British colonies in southeast Asia. What Captain Darval had to say was not heartening.

Standing ramrod straight in front of the room, he used a pointer to tap each location on the map. He stunned his audience by saying first that in his opinion a sudden air attack would practically wipe out the air force on Luzon, the main Philippine island. Cole felt his heart sink in a strange way. Was it fear? The thrill of battle calling? He exchanged glances with Dick, who smiled tightly.

The RAF captain went on to say that lack of dispersal was one of the Americans' greatest weaknesses: the bases provided too big and too inviting a target. The airstrips were too close to beaches, and there were no camouflage or dummy strips or protection against parachute attacks. Clear to the end, he pulled no punches, for in the Americans' weakness he saw his own doom. He covered the dubious state of Nichols Field and ended by pointing out that all air supply was openly concentrated in the Philippine Air Depot, where all buildings offered easy, obvious, and flammable targets.

During the question-and-answer period, Cole asked him to rank in order of importance the areas needing correction.

Captain Darval smiled disarmingly and said, "They must all be corrected if we are to survive." When the murmur died down, he continued, "However, I would recommend that you look to your airfields first." He went on and listed not only the problems he'd already covered but new areas of concern, such as the lack of antiaircraft protection and foxholes around the fields.

On their way out of the lecture, a bird colonel remarked to his companion, "He sure makes it sound like the Brits are going to pull us into this after all. They're counting on our fire power to cover their back door in the Pacific, protect their colonies while they fight Hitler. You'd think our military presence was enough."

Cole didn't have to hear his companion's reply to know that the RAF captain had possibly done them all a favor—if it wasn't too late. He grimly followed Dick to the jeep.

They were silent for the first part of the ride back to

Manila. Finally, Cole said, "They could be trying to make it sound worse than it is, just to get us in gear against the Germans."

"I wouldn't bet on it," Dick said flatly.

Cole was silent once more. If the Japanese attacked the Philippines, what would that mean for Iris, behind enemy lines? How would he feel conducting an air attack against Tokyo, knowing she was there?

A week later, Cole was still talking about the RAF group captain's analysis. He still wasn't sure how Jake had managed a transfer to the same post, but he was pleased to have him with him. His presence on these quiet evenings before dinner and his incisive comments were both reassuring and amusing.

Cole leaned back in his rattan chair and sipped his Scotch. The large paddles of an old ceiling fan slowly stirred the heavy tropical air. From the window he could see the lights of Manila spreading down the hill to the purpling waters of the harbor. A bougainvillaea vine stirred in a soft breeze beside the screen door. In the background were the soft strains of Glen Miller's dance music on Honolulu Station KGBM, picked up by the shortwave radio Jake had hooked up.

"You can't blame those guys for thinking this is just a tropical country club with the inconvenience of reveille," Jake said. Then he gestured at their surroundings. "Look at this. A great house with an ocean view, walled garden, cook and housekeeper, and all for one-tenth of our monthly paycheck. Who in their right mind would want to screw up such a paradise by insisting that it might be overrun tomorrow with enemy troops?"

Dick came in, poured himself a bourbon over ice, and asked Cole why he looked so grim.

Cole shook his head. "It's so goddamned frustrating. Our squadron spotted some more unidentified craft off Luzon again today. I reported it—told the major that it had to be Japs and that it meant trouble. He just shrugged and said, 'You're getting paranoid, Tennyson. Soon you'll be seeing Japs behind every tree.' I asked him if that meant he wouldn't put it on the report. He just said, 'It's for your own good. You're good officer material. You might even be up for another promotion soon. What will you accomplish with all this? They'll just write you off as a fanatic up in headquarters. No Jap in his right mind will be trying anything with the U.S. Army down here.' Can you imagine?" Cole refilled his glass. "Tell him what you were saying, Jake."

Jake rattled the ice in his glass and gave a short laugh. "I was monitoring the radio frequencies last night. There was some real funny stuff going on. Couldn't understand it at first. Then the houseboy at the radio shack said it sounded like Japanese. I tried to get a fix on it and had it narrowed down to the Iba area when they shut down. Can you imagine? That's right where the new radar is being set up—right under our noses! I reported what I had to the major and got pretty much the same story as Cole got."

"Do you think we're overreacting to this, Dick?" Cole asked.

Dick ran his fingers through his thick, sandy hair and sighed. "All I know is that there's a hell of a lot of espionage and potential sabotage going on for some comic little nation with no serious intentions."

"Have you been able to pass on your information?"

"There're believers and nonbelievers in every department," he said noncommittally.

"Well, we can't wear ourselves out trying to save the world," Jake said flatly.

Cole was silent. It had been over four months since he'd said good-bye to Iris. In that time he'd been filled with a growing, inexplicable fear that something was going to happen, something beyond his control, which would trap her in Tokyo, away from him forever.

Another of her strange letters had been forwarded to him in Manila in the second week of June. His depression grew as he read it. She still seemed to think that her mail was being read. It didn't make any sense, until Dick explained what he knew about the fanaticism of the Japanese Thought Police and suggested that Iris was trying to get past the ever-present censor. Then Cole suddenly understood, and was gripped with fear for her safety.

When he answered, with proper circumspection, he ached to tell her his feelings and fears. He prayed that his last letter had been cautious enough, and at that point decided to work in every way he could think of to help prevent a collision between the two countries—a collision that he believed could be avoided only through preparedness, not by tempting aggression with foolish weakness. He also vowed that somehow he would convince her to leave Japan as soon as possible, autumn at the latest, whether her father was there or not.

"If we don't try," Cole said finally, going back to their conversation, "just try to pass on these warning signs that we should shape up, who will?" He sat up and gestured with his cigarette. "Look what we have right here. I'll bet no officer in the islands has the pool of knowledge that we have—at least not all in one easy place where it can be evaluated in relationship to all the other pieces. We have Dick's CIP stuff, Jake's radio, and my flying."

"So what do we do, invite General Grunert over for drinks and a chat?" Jake countered.

General Grunert, the army commander in the Philippines, was a good man, but none of them felt that he had full control of all the defenses on the islands. Douglas MacArthur, retired from the United States Army, was now Field Marshal of the Philippine army and had long been a hero to both Cole and Dick. They all believed that any successful defense of the islands must ultimately rest on his genius.

"What about MacArthur?" Cole asked tentatively.

Dick slapped a mosquito on his arm and said flatly, "Well, you have as much chance as anyone. Seems your questions made an impression on some of the brass the other night when that RAF captain was spelling out our doom. Colonel George is calling a staff meeting so he can pass on his conclusions to Grunert, who is meeting with MacArthur next week. You're invited to the colonel's staff meeting." He paused and looked out the window. "It's a long shot, but if even a few of our reports can get through, it might stir things up a bit." He turned back to Cole. "You'll get the orders from Colonel George tomorrow."

Colonel George, a lively man with snappy brown eyes, had won their admiration immediately through his emphasis on intelligence and support for the air defense system. During the staff meeting, he received Cole's input with interest, impressed with the carefully compiled documentation Cole presented.

Cole was elated when, after the meeting, Colonel George took him aside and told him he appreciated such a well-informed officer. He intended to continue calling on him. From that time on, Cole, Dick, and Jake maintained an ongoing file of all they experienced. At least they felt they had a pipeline.

Almost three weeks later, on July 27, Jake brought news to Cole and Dick over dinner: Roosevelt had not only frozen all Japanese funds held in the United States and its territories, which included the Philippines, but had recalled MacArthur to the United States Army, making him Supreme Commander of the Philippine and American armies in the Far East, which he'd merged into one entity. He'd also made MacArthur a lieutenant general.

In the same swift stroke, FDR had closed the Panama Canal to Japanese shipping. All oil, iron, and rubber were forbidden shipment to Japan, a sharp blow because forty percent of Japan's iron ore the previous month had come from the Philippines. At his request, Britain and Holland declared similar embargoes. The sudden Japanese moves into Indo-China and their seizure of every port on the Chinese coast except Hong Kong had met with swift action.

That night Cole composed a letter to Iris, using their code, urging her to leave Japan immediately.

At Cole's third staff meeting with Colonel George, in early August, he meticulously listed the problems of getting the men to practice dispersed parking of the planes. He also told of further radio transmissions monitored by Jake. After the meeting, Colonel George took Cole aside and told him that he appreciated his input into the meetings, but that it had become apparent that he should have someone of captain's rank providing him with such information.

"Yes, sir," Cole said, his heart sinking. *Here goes our pipeline,* he thought. "I hope you find one soon."

"I already have. You'll have your promotion in your next envelope." The colonel laughed and slapped him on the back. "Just make sure you work much harder with another bar on your shoulder."

"Yes, sir. Thank you, sir!" Cole said, saluting.

It seemed a hollow achievement, without Iris to share it. He still hadn't heard from her and was becoming increasingly anxious. Perhaps his letters were not getting through. Perhaps because the writing was English the letters were suspect, even though he sent them to the neutral Swedish Embassy.

He paced the floor of his bedroom, considering all the possible problems that could have befallen his letters. Finally, he headed out the door. If he could find someone who could help him address a letter in Japanese . . .

He went to the area of Manila where many of the Japanese nationals resided. After driving around the district for half an hour, he went into the Nisikawa Hotel, where he was greeted with bows from the couple who owned it. However, they understood little English. Cole showed them an envelope and pantomimed that it was a letter to his girlfriend. The wife giggled behind her hand and led him to the desk clerk, a tall, handsome young Japanese man with high cheekbones and neatly combed dark hair.

"May I help you?" he asked in perfect American English.

Surprised, Cole said, "I have a letter I'd like to send to my fiancée in Tokyo." The desk clerk glanced at Cole's uniform. "She's there visiting her relatives," Cole explained. "She's an American, and I'm afraid that my letters haven't been reaching her because they're addressed in English. Could you help me put a Japanese address on the envelope?"

"Oh. I see." He turned and spoke rapidly in Japanese to the hotel owners. The woman giggled and said something to Cole.

"Mrs. Fujiama says that you must have very high standards to have chosen a Japanese woman for your love. She says I am to help you."

He led Cole to a table in the corner. Mrs. Fujiama followed, carrying a pot of tea and two small, handleless cups.

"You speak very good English," Cole commented when Mrs. Fujiama left them alone.

"I'm American. My name is William Maresuke Ando, from Hood River, Oregon," he said amiably. "But call me Bill, Lieutenant."

"I'm Cole Tennyson. I'm out of Streator, LaSalle County, Illinois. Please call me Cole. I'm only 'Lieutenant' to my squad," he said, laughing.

"You're a flyer, then?" His eyes flitted quickly around the room as Cole nodded. "Hand me your envelope. Do you have any contact with the intelligence people?"

Cole was suddenly on guard. "In my duties I meet all types of army personnel. Why?"

"I can't talk here, but I'd like to pass information on. I'm worried about some things I see happening around here and I'd like to be of help. Could you pick me up by the old cemetery, Juan Paco, in two hours?"

"Tonight?"

"Yeah. Now, let's see to that address." He quickly wrote Japanese characters on the envelope, then offered to mail it with the other hotel mail. "It might have a better chance getting through in with a group of legitimate Japanese letters."

"It might be worth a try," Cole said. "Thanks."

Two hours later, he pulled up to the main entrance to the cemetery. Tall trees drooped in the moonlight and there was the sound of distant music as some lonely Filipino played his guitar and sang of lost love. Bill stepped out from behind the tall stone wall surrounding the parklike churchyard and quickly climbed into the car. "Drive to the outskirts, toward the farmland," he ordered. "Farmers go to bed early and there are no eyes there at this time of night."

As they drove through the darkened streets, Bill quickly unfolded his story. He had signed on at an early age to a ship, seeking adventure. However, when his duties took him to the Philippines, he fell in love with the country and jumped ship. Alone in a foreign country illegally, he used his knowledge of Japanese, which he'd learned from his parents, to find a job. The Fujiamas had taken him under their wing, and had even expressed an interest in adopting him, because their own son had been killed in the China wars. He was accepted by the Japanese and soon became their confidant. They trusted his generous offers of help in interpreting official documents, making personal decisions, and all other matters of importance in dealing with the Americans and the Japanese homeland. In the process, he'd learned that there was much Japanese espionage going on in the Philippines. His loyalties were firmly tied to the United States. He wanted to use his unique position to act as a self-appointed spy for army intelligence, but he needed a pipeline to the proper authorities. It was imperative that his identity be concealed.

"I can't promise anything, Bill," Cole said, "but I will pass the information on to a friend of mine in intelligence."

"That's all I ask. I think there's going to be a big war with the Japanese, and every guy with my skin and eyes is going to have to fight like hell to prove he's a red-blooded American. I'm just getting a head start." He reached into his pocket and pulled out a sheet of paper. "Here's a list of information that should help prove my credibility. Give it to your friend. Pull over here," he said, indicating a darkened street corner as they approached the edge of town. "Remember," he said just before opening the door, "my identity must be protected if I'm to live to help you further. You mustn't come to the hotel again. Send a young Filipino you can trust with a pack of American cigarettes to sell me on the black market, Lucky Strikes. I'll know then that I'm to meet you in the same place at 10 P.M."

Cole went back to the house and awakened Dick. After telling him the incredible story, he concluded, "I can't believe it. It sounds like something from a Bogart movie. Do you think it's for real?"

"Well," Dick said, perusing the list Cole had given him, "this stuff he gave you looks genuine enough. Keep up the contact—you know, keep regular appointments and see what else he comes up with. In the meantime, I'll send back to the States and check his records. And," he said, leaning forward to look more closely at the paper in his hand, "let's test him, to see if he's going to give us the good stuff or just lead us down the primrose path."

"You mean he might be working for the Japs?"

"We'll never know unless we test him, will we?"

Cole felt chagrined at his own naïveté. "What do you propose doing?"

"Nothing too complicated. We have the name of an old Jap down at the hotel who's been taking some interesting walks. We know he's pretty high military, but we aren't too sure what and how. Let's ask about him. If your contact says he's clean, to protect him, or tells about him and the old guy disappears, having been forewarned . . ." He shrugged. "But if we've got a good spy on our hands, he'll give us the full scoop and the old boy will continue his walks, thinking he's as safe as ever."

When they met, Bill had another paper prepared for Cole. As Cole took it, he asked Bill to find out about the old Japanese man at the hotel.

"You've got it right there," Bill said, lighting a cigarette. "I've been working on that one for a couple of weeks now. Finally got all the pieces put together. I think your men will be able to put his long walks to a good use. Maybe he'll have an accident or something."

Bill was for real. His records confirmed he was American. The old man was a Japanese admiral and had sent out some pretty crucial information. He continued his long walks, oblivious that his disguise as a simple merchant had been exposed. Bill's other information about Japanese coming into the islands as bicycle repairmen, salesmen, and the like revealed engineers, cartographers, and military personnel of all types—all spies.

From August through November Cole met with Bill at their secret rendezvous. His information was useful, accurate, and increasingly alarming. Dick was elated. He provided Cole with cars from the intelligence section for the meetings, preferring to have Bill deal exclusively with Cole. Reluctantly, Bill had met Cole once when Jake was along, so that Jake could be his backup contact in case Cole was ever unavailable.

By late November, their meetings were more frequent; by the first of December, they met every other night. Bill said the Fujiamas were beginning to tease him about having a girlfriend. He had feigned embarrassment at being found out.

On December 4, Cole was pacing his bedroom. The French doors to his balcony were open not only to let in the warm evening breeze but so that he could hear. He'd sent a messenger to Bill earlier in the day and it was time to leave.

He heard the faint squeak of a car's brakes and looked out. Through the bougainvillaea he saw a dark sedan parked in the dim light of a street lamp. The driver got out and walked away.

Dick had come through again. Cole closed the doors to the balcony, slipped on a civilian shirt, and quickly went down the stairs.

The key to the car was under the mat. He started the engine and eased down the darkened, quiet street.

Pulling up in front of the block wall surrounding the cemetery, he lit a cigarette, flicking the lighter three times to do so. The door on the passenger side opened and Bill slid in.

"How's everything?" Cole asked, pulling back into the street.

"Tense. I'm going to have to make some pretty big decisions in the next two days. All hell is going to break loose. I'd say by the tenth of December we'll be at war. If I stay where I am, I'll be rounded up and probably shot by the Filipinos.

If I go to Mindanao like the CIP wants me to, I'll still probably be shot by the Japanese down there."

"You think it will be that soon? Most of the brass think it will come after the monsoon season."

"I *know* it will be that soon."

"What do you have?"

"There's an ancient shoeshine boy, been working outside the hotel. He's really a Japanese general. He's been taking long walks, sending interesting radio signals late at night. He just disappeared. The word is that he was picked up by a sub the other night so that he can come back in three days, riding in glory."

"Do you think it's true?"

"No doubt about it." He paused and looked at the sugar cane waving in the headlights as the car slowly drove through the countryside. "You remember that headline in the *Honolulu Advertiser* saying that the Japanese would attack on Thanksgiving?"

"Yeah, like the little boy who cried wolf."

"Well, I don't know who their source is, but now they're saying that the Japanese fleet is moving south. They're right, from what I'm hearing. In fact, they were almost right the first time, except for a quick diplomatic feat."

"It couldn't be right. The Japs won't hit Hawaii."

"I didn't say that. I think they might try to hit the whole damn Pacific."

Cole laughed uncomfortably. "That's ridiculous. They aren't that big."

"Like hell they aren't. Besides, we aren't that prepared."

Cole was grimly silent. Bill was right on that count.

"Listen," Bill continued, "if you really are getting this stuff through, make sure that all regular-schedule business is stopped right now. All these seemingly innocent little bicycle repairmen and shoeshine boys are really military. They've started dribbling away, leaving in the dark of the night. They have us down pat. They know whenever we take a leak and where. We've got to change everything if we're even to stand a chance. We can't be on the ground sitting at our dinner tables as usual when they expect us to be."

"I'll send the word on."

"We don't have enough fighters, either. They're putting a lot of confidence in their fighter planes, especially those little

63

Mitsubishi jobs. Sounds like they're pretty hot stuff with them, from what one air-force guy was describing over his sake one night. I'm not sure I understand their reasoning, but it seems that we should have some of the same up there to counter it."

"Anything else?"

"Yeah. I've decided not to go to Mindanao. The Corps of Intelligence Police is going to need some help from the inside, so I'm going to call on some of my 'friends' and get myself shipped to Japan. Pretend that I'm seeking asylum in the fatherland. I'll try to get something out. I'll use the code name 'Flower of the Pacific.' "

Cole couldn't help laughing. "I think you've seen too many movies."

Bill grinned. "There's got to be some entertainment in all this. Look, I like excitement. I don't have any family left, and I love this kind of intrigue. I think I can really be of some help. Even if I do have a corny streak. How else can I guarantee my hamburger supply?" Then he was suddenly sober. "Besides, as a Japanese-American, my life isn't going to be worth a damn back in the States when the Japs hit with their sneak attacks. I'd like to earn my way back home."

Cole was silent for a moment, weighing the chances he was taking, thinking of the full meaning of Bill's words. "If that's what you're going to do," he said finally, "there's something I want you to know. Remember my fiancée and those letters I sent?"

"Yeah, did she ever get them?"

"I think so. I've gotten two letters since then. I'm afraid she's going to be caught in Tokyo. If you can, get her out. If you can't find her, or can't get her out without jeopardizing your position, I'll understand." He pulled the car over to the side of the road under a breadfruit tree and quickly wrote on a piece of paper. "This is her name and the last address I had for where she's staying—her grandmother's house. And, uh, if you find her, tell her I love her. And that I'm still waiting for her."

Bill took the paper and studied it quietly for a moment. When he spoke, his voice was unusually soft. "Why the hell does it have to be this way?" he said more to himself than to Cole. Then he put the paper in the ashtray and lit it.

"You can't do it, huh?" Cole asked, his heart sinking.

"Of course, I'll try. I've memorized it. I can't endanger her or me by carrying it."

"I should have thought of that." Cole turned the car around and headed back towards Manila. They had just reached the outskirts of the Tondo district when Bill told him to stop the car. He got out and melted into the darkness. Cole never knew where Bill would get out; he had many ways to cover his tracks. Cole drove on to his house, trying to push the nagging fear about Iris to the back of his mind. It looked as if he'd soon be needing all his concentration just to save his own neck.

Cole and Dick spent most of the night putting together the information he had received from Bill in order to be ready for the staff meeting in the morning. Cole had arranged for a private conference with Colonel George prior to the meeting.

Cole's anxiety didn't allow him to sleep much. At 6:00 A.M. he made his way to Military Plaza.

"Sorry it had to be so early, son," Colonel George said as Cole came into his office. "Have a cup of coffee and tell me what you've got."

"Thanks, sir. My information indicates that the Japanese forces are mounting for an attack before December tenth."

The colonel set down his coffee cup. The silver eagle on his uniform caught the morning sunlight and gleamed. "That's four days away, Captain. What makes you think it'll be so soon?"

"The flyers have spotted Japanese reconnaissance planes in the early morning off the west coast. One unidentified craft on the second of this month. On the third and fourth we picked up craft maneuvering off the west coast, again in the early-morning hours. Sort of like they're getting their bearings and distances just right. And you know of the two high-altitude flights we've had over our bases by single craft. That would give them photo reconnaissance."

The colonel nodded. "We had planes waiting for the next high-altitude flight, but they haven't come back."

"They probably don't have to. Already got what they wanted. Actually, right now, they probably have all they need to make a very good attack."

The little colonel nodded solemnly. "You're talking pretty much known information. Do you have anything else?"

Cole drew a deep breath and explained all that Bill had told him in the car the previous night, adding, "We've asked a

Japanese-speaking interpreter to listen in on the radio broadcasts Jake has been picking up. They're definitely from the Japanese fleet and part of them are not far from the Philippines."

"There's pretty reliable information reporting that most of the fleet is on leave in Tokyo."

"With all due respect, sir, if I were planning an attack that's exactly what I'd want you to believe."

The colonel walked over to the window and looked out, his hands in his pockets. "Over half of the Flying Fortresses have been sent far south to Del Monte Field on Mindanao. They're out of reach. We're working night and day trying to get the defenses built up. Don't know what else can be done. We've been on full war alert since Thanksgiving now."

"I only wanted you to have the information that was given to me. All our schedules are known, all our standard operating procedures. If we want to avoid being caught with our pants down, we should shake things up a bit, sir. You know, start acting like we believe it really is a full war alert."

"There've been orders cut by MacArthur for some time now, putting everything on full alert and canceling regular leaves and schedules. We'll have to see what we can do about getting them all released and implemented in full."

"Yes, sir. And we need to get our shipments of supplies. We don't have enough P-40s yet to train the men for them. That shipment in July came without any Prestone. Apparently some yahoo stateside can't see the need for engine coolant in the tropics. The crews are still working on getting the bugs out of the last shipments. We have a whole squadron trained for those A-24 dive bombers that are sitting on some dock somewhere. Do you know that up to seventy percent of our ammunition is a dud when we practice fire?"

The colonel turned, his eyes widening optimistically. "There's relief from that, at least. New shipments have just arrived and there're more coming. The *Pensacola* is right now escorting eight troop and supply ships to us." He glanced at his watch, then clapped Cole on the shoulder. "Now, let's get on down to the staff room before they eat all the doughnuts I've ordered."

Cole paused as the colonel picked up his papers and headed for the door. Beyond the balcony doors of the office was a view of Manila, bustling with morning sights and sounds. The city seemed to have the gay appearance of a lovely Spanish dancer laughing over her castanets, unaware of the vicious rapist waiting just behind the curtain. He turned and followed the colonel down the corridor, right past a "V for Victory" sign.

CHAPTER V

Iris stood on the steps of the Swedish Embassy shivering in the October rain. Early evening darkened the sky. The lights of cars and neon signs reflected on the wet pavement. Hunched against the chill rain, pedestrians darted in and out of the traffic, their wooden clogs clacking a hollow rhythm against the street sounds. Reluctantly, Iris raised her umbrella and hastened down through the crowds to catch the electric car for the short ride to the Azabu-ku district of Tokyo.

Abhorrence for everything Japanese still seeped from her very bones. However, life was much easier now that she'd moved closer to her job and was rooming with Eva. Iris's relatives had been abashed but relieved at her sudden decision and had helped her move. Eva said the plan had received much the same reaction from her relatives in Yokohama.

With Inga's help, they'd been able to rent the small gardener's house on the grounds of the Swiss undersecretary's estate. It was much closer to work and school and even had room for a small vegetable garden in the back, where they'd enthusiastically grown familiar vegetables last summer. After Eva had gotten her job translating English shortwave broadcasts for the Domei News Agency, on nearby Atago Hill, it had been harder to keep the garden weeded, but the money she earned more than compensated for their smaller crop.

However, best of all was the fact that they could go home and speak English and eat recognizable food with a fork and knife and not worry about offending someone by forgetting some mindless custom. Frightening as the move to live on their own had been, they knew now that it had been the right decision for everyone concerned.

The electric tram started to pull out and Iris dashed through a puddle to catch it. The car was crowded but she felt the crush of time more than the crush of strangers. She and Eva must come to a decision tonight. As the car clicked along, her mind circled around and around the events of the last few days.

Her father had written that he was booking passage to Japan and would bring their return tickets with him. But was there time? Then, when he arrived, would they have time to wait until January, when he'd completed his nostalgic visit?

To leave now, spending all their savings, seemed childish paranoia. Papa said he saw little sign of war or danger in the American press. However, she could hear the clock ticking with each warlike harangue against the U.S. in the *Nippon Times*. Time was running out with each report of Japanese advances in Southeast Asia, with each proclamation of Japan's destiny in the Greater East Asia Coprosperity Sphere. Who could she believe?

When Iris left Hawaii, she had promised herself only one letter to Cole to let him know of her safe arrival. When he'd not only answered but written one after another pleading letter, she could not help but write back. Slowly, with each letter, with each heart-turning answer, she admitted that she could never stop loving him, nor even pretend to forget him.

The fact that Cole still wrote and his love still was strong kept an ember of hope burning. It colored her decisions. It fired her fears. She had so much to lose if she were caught in Japan by war. Fate had given her a second chance; surely she would never have another. Could she afford the gamble of waiting for her father? Cole's latest letter had arrived at the embassy today. Its coded message seemed to be burning in her pocket.

The car stopped and she jumped from the steps and hurried down her street, turned up the darkened alley, and went in the side gate of the massive wall surrounding the estate.

The Japanese insistence on natural beauty and grace in their surroundings was one quality Iris admired. There was a charming front garden for their tiny three-room house, and even in her hurry tonight the rubied leaves of the maple tree lifted her spirits. The path was cleverly devised to turn just enough to catch the slanted rectangle of warm light spilling from the long window of the house, thereby making a welcoming pattern on winter evenings. Eva was home already. Iris left her wet shoes in the stone entryway and went inside.

From the smell, she knew that Eva had dinner on the *konro*, the charcoal cooking brazier. With luck, she would have a pot of tea waiting as well. Iris had volunteered to wash the dishes in order to avoid having to cook in this impossible Japanese way.

"Hi. You look beat," Eva said as Iris slid open the *karakami* screen that separated their eating and living areas. "Want some tea?"

"Love it. Do we have time to sit down and talk before dinner? We've got to get this thing settled. I can't stand it any longer."

"Sure. Do you want me to light the *kotatsu*?" she asked, referring to the sunken charcoal fireplace.

"No, we'd better save the charcoal. I'll just put on some dry clothes and wrap up."

"Did you see the paper tonight?" Eva called as Iris changed.

"No, what now?"

"It says there are three ships taking Americans back to the States and returning Japanese from America."

Iris whistled softly. "Do they give a reason?" she asked as she came back into the living room, rubbing her wet hair with a towel.

"A lot of ranting and raving about unfair tactics when the Americans froze all the Japanese money last July. What do you think?"

"I got a letter from Cole today. Translated, he insists I leave Japan immediately, without waiting for my father or anything. He can see nothing but war coming, and soon."

"The broadcasts I've been translating at Domei sound pretty threatening. What about our savings?"

Iris paused, biting her lower lip. "Better our savings than our lives," she said finally. "What does the paper say about departure dates?"

"We don't have much time," Eva said, referring back to the *Nippon Times*. "Next week, October fifteenth, the *Tatuta Maru* leaves Yokohama, the *Mitta Maru* leaves on October twentieth, and the *Taiyo Maru* leaves on the twenty-second and," she said, her voice rising in interest, "arrives in Honolulu on the first of November. Gee, wouldn't that be great?"

Iris knew Eva was thinking of Sparky. It would also mean that she could once more write freely to Cole. Maybe even see him. After all, he had gotten two promotions. . . . Her heart lifted with hope. "Let's go down to the American Embassy and see if we can get on."

Eva laughed. "Imagine, home! Turkey for Thanksgiving!"

They went to the embassy first thing the next morning and breathlessly asked the man behind the desk if they could get on board any of the ships returning Americans to the States.

"Yes," he replied cautiously, blinking behind his wire-rimmed glasses. "There is a possibility. Are you American citizens?" There was dandruff on the collar of his outdated black suit, and he twiddled irritably with a corner of the form he was working on.

"Of course," Iris smiled, "born and raised in California."

He looked at them coolly before answering. "I see. We will need proof of citizenship. Bring in your passport and visa tomorrow morning and we'll begin trying to process it. You must realize that there are many diplomatic and press people applying as well."

Eva looked worried. "What if we don't have our visas, just the passports?"

"How could you have a passport without a visa and still be in Japan legally?"

"Well, the consulate in Honolulu didn't have time to process the visa before our boat sailed, so they told us to just write a notarized statement of our intent to leave the country and that would suffice," Iris explained, trying to hide her rising fear with a mask of calm efficiency. "We brought it here and were told you would file it and we wouldn't have to worry about it until time to leave, because they gave us a temporary visitor's permit at the boat."

"I don't know who told you that, but it's time for you to start worrying," the embassy official said blandly. "We'll just hope something really is filed here and will turn up in time. Write down your names and I'll give you a file number. We can't do anything until you bring in your passports tomorrow morning, though."

"I have mine with me right now," Iris volunteered.

"Well, that doesn't help your little friend, does it?" He put their names in a file folder. "Just bring them both in tomorrow morning," he said, dismissing them as he would bothersome schoolgirls.

"They couldn't have lost those letters, could they?" Eva asked anxiously as they left.

"I'm just wondering if they'll do any good even if they find them." Iris's mouth was dry with a deep foreboding.

They had less than two weeks before the last boat left. A seemingly endless round of trips to the American Embassy began. After four days, the embassy found their letters of intent to leave the country. Eva and Iris would have to take them to the Japanese authorities and get a confirming visa permit before the embassy could continue processing of their papers.

On Tuesday, October 14, the day before the first boat was to leave, they went to the Japanese officials, requesting a visa permit. The Japanese would not give it to them unless they had proof that they were American citizens. They took a taxi back to the American Embassy, got their passports, and dashed back to the Japanese office. The uniformed Japanese official smiled tersely at them and took their passports, examined them, then turned and walked toward another office.

"Wait a minute!" Iris called. He stopped and looked at her. "Where are you going with our passports?"

"My supervisor must approve them as authentic."

"Then I will accompany you," Iris said, ignoring the nudge from Eva. "I have been taught that I must remain with my passport at all times."

"It was not on your person earlier this morning."

She didn't want to chance losing their one official piece of identification, yet she was afraid of offending the Japanese officials. Just how much should she gamble her safety? She explained with a forced calm, "That was because the American Embassy assured us of our safety while it was in their hands. Since we are not Japanese citizens, but American citizens, I can understand that you are not able to give me the same assurance."

"Very well," he said, "you may keep your passports and wait until my supervisor is able to come out here."

After an hour of waiting nervously, Eva decided she would have to call in sick for work. When she came back, she resumed the whispered argument that had been going since they had sat down.

"You insulted them. They're going to ignore us," she said accusingly, "never even give us our papers or anything, just because you got jumpy."

"*You* didn't have them try to take away your citizenship when you were in Yokohama," Iris whispered back sharply.

Just then a heavyset, officious-looking man came from the back office. He bowed in their direction and they got up and bowed respectfully in return.

"Are you the supervisor who must approve the authenticity of our passports?" Eva asked politely in Japanese.

"*Hai*," he nodded, "I am the supervisor. You wish papers to allow you to return to the United States?"

"Yes," Eva said, holding out their passports. "You see, our parents are not able to travel and we must take greetings from our grandparents back to them. It will bring great ease to their old age to know that their honored parents send their blessings."

"I see." He glanced through their passports, rubbing the pages between his finger and thumb. "Your papers seem authentic," he said finally. He signed the form, then looked up. "However, you must bring us proof that you actually were students while you were in Japan."

Eva stiffened in fear. "And if we can't produce that proof?"

"What reason would you have put on your visa permit if you had filled out one at the proper time?"

"I came to visit my relatives."

"Ah, then you are a Japanese citizen?"

"No, I was born in the United States. I came here as a visiting American citizen," she replied, paling visibly.

"But you could become a Japanese citizen through your family register?" he asked ominously, his dark, bushy eyebrows bristling.

Iris had been following their Japanese conversation with difficulty. She could see that Eva was not going to hold up much longer. "Why do you ask these questions?" Iris demanded, trying to sound sure of herself.

He paused, briefly considering Iris, then turned to Eva. "You will need to bring a written statement from your relatives that your reason for coming to Japan was strictly per-

72

sonal and due to familial duties." He turned and started to go, their passports still in his hand.

"We will take our passports with us," Iris called quickly after him.

He stopped and turned back. "If you wish," he said simply, placing them in Iris's outstretched hand.

Iris hid her feelings by politely bowing her thanks as he turned and left the room. She then took Eva's icy hand and walked to the door. By the time they reached the sidewalk, Eva's face was bathed in tears. They crossed the street to a small park and sat down on a bench.

"I'm not going to be able to go home," Eva whispered, as Iris handed her a handkerchief.

"Don't be foolish," Iris snapped, hiding her fear in anger. "They were just trying to break us down, make us think we should stop trying to get out. We just have to prove that we intend to stand up for our rights. We can't let them bully us. It was just like that Sergeant Ito trying to make me renounce my citizenship. He came back to my grandmother's time after time, but I stood up to him and he eventually stopped harassing me. He even started acting friendly."

"Changed his tactics, you mean," Eva sniffed.

"Eva, will you snap out of it!"

She blew her nose and nodded. "You're right. I'll take the train to Yokohama and be back tonight. I've already called in sick at work. We'll just have to come back tomorrow with the statement he wants. Do you think your language classes qualify you as a student?"

Iris shrugged. "I'll try it. If not, I'll get a note from my grandmother, I guess," she said with a wry smile. "Whatever, we'd better get busy. That *densha* should take you to the station," she said, pointing at the approaching streetcar. "I'll walk to school from here. Will you be all right?"

Eva managed a smile. "Sure, just a temporary case of the shakes. See you tonight."

Iris went directly to the office of the Nihongo Bunka Gakkō, where she took her language lessons, and requested a paper confirming that she was a student. The secretary looked up her file and quickly filled out the proper form. Enormously relieved, Iris went on to her class.

She was in high spirits by the time she got to work, barely able to contain herself until she could talk to Inga privately and tell her that she was on her way back home, back to Cole.

Inga listened calmly to Iris's enthusiastic announcement, then shook her blond head with Nordic woe. "Don't you realize that every journalist, businessman, and minor embassy employee is applying for the limited space on those three ships?"

Iris's smile faded. "Surely they won't take up three full ships. . . ."

Inga put her arm around Iris's shoulder. "Your papers are not in order," she began listing. "There are businessmen, the diplomatic corps. There are, according to our embassy's estimates, over ten thousand Japanese-American students here in Japan right now. If even one-tenth of those want to go home . . ."

Iris's knees felt weak. She sank down in her chair, stunned. "What can I do?" she whispered.

"Pull out all the stops you can," Inga replied matter-of-factly. "You have proof of student status. Now get your relatives' statement that you're an American citizen and came over for a visit at their request. If you think that boyfriend of yours could have any influence at all, send a wire. Request that he send confirmation to the American Embassy that you are an American citizen and should be given priority rating for return to the U.S."

"How do I send a wire?"

"Unfortunately," she said with a shrug, "we're all dependent on the Japanese government dispatchers to get our communications out. They're not supposed to hold things up, by international law, but they do. Sending something to the Philippines, a strategic American territory in Asia, would probably only have a fifty-percent chance of getting through, at best, especially considering the contents. It's worth a try, though. I'll see if we can get one sent out of here."

Unfortunately, the liaison officer at the Swedish Embassy was afraid that Iris's telegram would compromise the neutral status of the embassy. She would have to try to send it through regular channels. With Inga's help, she wrote a cryptically worded message, then left work half an hour early and dashed down to the telegraph office.

The clerk at the station looked at Iris through thick-lensed glasses as she handed him her message. He read it laboriously, then called over a superior, who also read it slowly. They both looked at Iris, nodded, and went into a back room. Within a few minutes a tall, uniformed man came out.

"Are you the American?" he asked in Japanese.

"*Hai*," Iris replied in halting Japanese. "I wish my wire to go quickly. How much do I pay?"

"Standard fee. You know there may be problems telegraphing to the Philippines. We are not responsible if your wire does not get through."

Iris's heart sank as she realized he was telling her it would probably be stopped by censors. "Please try," she said. "It's very important I get back to my parents, who are old and sick," she added, trying to play upon his sympathy. She handed him her precious yen currency. He nodded and took it without a word.

She went outside and gloomily looked for the *densha* that would take her to the suburbs where her grandmother's house was. But first, a small gift to take to help smooth the way. She stopped at a nearby *panya* and bought some sweetbean cakes from the baker.

Her packet of cakes safely tucked in the *furoshiki*, the cloth shopping bag she'd learned always to carry in her purse, she ran across the street to catch the *densha*. It was early, so she was able to find a seat and settle back for the half-hour ride. A mother with a baby strapped to her back sat next to her, staring ahead. She looked around at the closed faces in the streetcar.

The same old feelings of dread crept into her stomach each time she approached her grandmother's gate. Although she made a duty call at least once a month, she still had the feeling that she was inadvertently going to offend each time she visited. She rang the bell at the gate, opened it, and walked slowly up the path, allowing someone in the house time to go to the door. Aunt Toshiko greeted her with a bow. Iris bowed, took off her shoes, and went in.

Luckily, not only her grandmother was there but Uncle Anami, who would be able to augment Iris's limited Japanese. "*Konnichi wa, Oba-a-san*," she said, bowing low from her pillow as she greeted her grandmother. "It has been a long time since I have seen you. I hope you are well." She then turned and bowed to Uncle Anami, repeating the prescribed greetings.

75

Grandmother accepted the sweet cakes with a smile. "*Arigato,*" she said, thanking Iris. "Your Japanese is improving. It has served you well to attend the school. But I worry that you live away from your family. You are living safe and well?"

"I came to you today for help," Iris answered, thankful for her grandmother's concern and the opportunity to ask gracefully. "You see, there are three boats leaving Japan to carry American citizens home . . ." she paused to ask her uncle for help with a word, "due to difficult times between our countries. I need to have a paper from you stating that I am an American-born citizen and that I came here to visit you at your invitation."

Uncle Anami helped her with the last word and then asked in Japanese, "Why would anyone want to know if we asked you here?"

"I don't know. Maybe they want to be sure that I did not come here as an agent of the American government. That is all I can think of. Your statement that I am actually an American citizen would be most helpful because I did not get a visa, just a visitor's permit."

He corrected some of Iris's Japanese for his mother, who leaned forward in response and said reasonably, "But you could become a Japanese citizen very easily." She waited, and when Iris didn't say anything, she added, "And you could live with your grandmother and make her very happy with your presence." Iris was torn by this, the first open expression of affection she had received, yet she remained silent. Finally, Grandmother leaned back and went on, "But then, you choose to remain in America and take care of your parents in California. That is your duty."

"*Hai, Oba-a-san,*" she agreed politely.

Grandmother turned to Uncle Anami and nodded. He frowned and hesitated. Grandmother looked at him sternly. "She suffered through a long journey to our country in order to pay her respects and lighten the heart of an old woman. We must give her the papers she needs." Uncle Anami bowed and left the room.

Within minutes he returned with a paper, carefully filled with Japanese characters. Iris knew he had obeyed his mother and written exactly what she had requested even though he disagreed. She bowed her thanks, then turned and bowed good-bye to her grandmother, backing respectfully toward the door. "I will come back and tell you of my departure," she said.

As she paused at the entryway to put on her shoes, Aunt Toshiko came to say good-bye. But first she asked with genuine concern, "Are you well, my niece? It is not good to be so far away from your family. Do you have enough to eat? I noticed that you did not eat much rice." Aunt Toshiko took a packet from the shelf over the shoes. "I have some potatoes for you. Perhaps this will make you and your friend a nice American meal."

"*Arigato gozaimasu*," she said, bowing deeply to her aunt. "You are most kind to me. I thank you also for Eva. Oh, I almost forgot," she said suddenly, straightening up and reaching into her purse. "I brought some rice candy for the children. Will you please give it to them for me?"

Aunt Toshiko took it with a smile. "They will be happy to have the treat. Thank you, my niece," she said, speaking slowly so Iris could understand her.

Iris bowed once more and took her leave. Her aunt stood at the doorway, watching her until she was out of sight. Iris sensed that despite all she had thought before, her family here really did care about her. It was all a matter of trying to learn their ways, trying to learn how not to be rude in Japan. Once she understood that, once she understood the real terror under which they lived, then she could finally break through that invisible barrier and tie the cord of affection that was rightfully hers. And now that she'd learned that, she must leave them. It seemed a sad condition, for her and for the whole world.

That night over their meal of real potatoes and charcoaled fish, Iris and Eva decided that they would not be able to make the October 15 ship. However, they figured they could make it in time for either of the boats leaving the following week. Nevertheless, it seemed ominous that the next day the Japanese official refused to give them a formal visa. He insisted that a "letter of fact," as he called it, would have to suffice for the American Embassy. Besides, it was a matter of fact that they were already here in Japan; the purpose of a visa was to admit them, not release them. It was with growing doubts that Iris and Eva took their increasingly larger pile of documents back to the aloof man at the American Embassy desk.

"It says here," he said, looking at Eva's papers, "that you

were not a student. You just hopped aboard the first boat for a visit?"

Eva flushed at his implication. "I came to meet my grandparents. My mother is dead and my father is too ill to travel here. They wanted to see me."

"Yes," he mused almost to himself, "you Japanese are quite tied up into this duty to your relatives."

"I am an American," Eva said with controlled calm. "As an American and a human being, I wish to make my sick father happy."

His thinning brown hair fell over his forehead, almost touching his glass frames as he leaned over and picked up Iris's file. "It says here that you actually were a student of some sort," he said, looking up at her myopically. She nodded yes. "I'll take these forms back and they'll go over them," he said vaguely.

"The next boat leaves the twentieth," Iris said firmly. "Since we'll have only four days to get ready, we will return first thing in the morning to pick up our clearance."

"If it's ready," he said, turning back to the file cabinets.

Eva waited until they got to the door. "What now?" she asked.

"What else?" Iris replied with a tense smile. "Go home, pack, and pray." The door swung noisily shut behind them.

They were waiting at the door when the embassy opened the next morning. A different official was at the desk, a young man with pale cheeks, fine blond hair, and a tendency to talk down his nose as if he were standing high above them. It took him an hour to find their files. In the meantime, they sat and watched the line of applicants for the remaining boat spaces. Rumpled journalists, frightened missionaries, fat businessmen, all Caucasian—all had tickets handed them as a matter of course. The Japanese-American students were another matter. They came with petitions and thick file folders. Only a few of these were handed clearance.

"A decision will be made by this evening," the young official finally told them. "Come back around five o'clock."

They had walked down the street several blocks before Iris said glumly, "I know who will be on the desk this evening: that Irving Lasher, who insists I'm Japanese every time I deliver the Swedish packet."

The wait that afternoon was unbearable. However, at three

o'clock, Inga brought in some relief, a letter from Cole. There was naturally no mention of her wire, because the letter had been mailed three weeks earlier. However, he again emphatically insisted that she leave immediately. She shook her head as she read the letter. If only he knew how hard she was trying.

Irving Lasher seemed surprised to see that Iris was the face belonging to the file in his hand that night. "Is this really your passport?" he asked.

"Of course," she said, barely controlling her irritation. "Can you tell me whether we've been cleared to go home?"

He shrugged. "It isn't all clear yet. But the boat that's leaving day after tomorrow is filled beyond capacity. I'm going out on it. Ambassador Grew himself has sent word that no one else is to be admitted on the passenger list. It's mostly been Americans with a real reason for being here, like businessmen, missionaries, and such, who have been let aboard," he added pointedly.

"Our reasons for being here are clearly justified as well," Iris said. "What about the last boat, at the end of the week?"

"There are still a lot of natural-born Americans waiting. You'll just have to come back and find out after they're processed."

"But we are natural-born Americans!" Eva objected. "Just look at our passports."

He smiled ingratiatingly. "Well, you know what I mean. Try again tomorrow or the next day."

They stayed away from their jobs, claiming sickness, and spent the next three days haunting the American Embassy. They were there first thing in the morning; they were the last ones out the door at night. There was a multitude of people coming in, most of whom wanted clearance to go back to the States. Sitting on the hard bench against the wall, walking the open corridors, they watched missionaries scurrying out the door with their approved papers, businessmen striding up to the desk demanding better accommodations on the ship, and embassy staff glibly talking about which ship they chose to ride on. Still, Iris and Eva did not get their clearance.

On Monday, October 20, Iris began pleading with whichever embassy personnel she could corner. Some pretended not to hear. Some rebuffed her. A few were sympathetic but not encouraging. Their one chance was the ship leaving the morning of Wednesday, October 22. The pale blond man came on the desk at five o'clock that night and Iris immediately cornered him. Surprisingly, he quickly looked up their files.

"It seems that you, Iris, were actually a student," he said to Iris. "They are giving most careful consideration to those who came here to study. However, your friend Eva only came here for a visit. Her request will not have the same priority of processing. Do you wish to go without her?"

"Without Eva?" Iris asked incredulously. "I don't see how—"

"She will go without me," Eva interrupted.

"What are you talking about?" Iris asked in a harsh whisper, taking her aside.

"I'd rather know that you were in the United States battling the government from that side than have us both here alone and helpless," Eva reasoned. "I'll have a better chance of going home that way than if you stay here out of some false sense of loyalty."

Iris looked at her friend, biting her lip to keep from crying. "All right," she said. It felt as if there were a lump of cold oatmeal in her throat. She turned back to the clerk. "I'll go without her."

"Fine. Be here first thing in the morning."

Tuesday morning, October 21, Iris and Eva again approached the embassy. Eva was told that they were still processing her papers. Iris was told to come back that evening.

Eva had resolved herself to the disappointment. She was now pinning all her hopes on Iris's efforts on her behalf once she got back to the States. Iris vowed to do everything in her power to bring her friend home from Japan.

Iris spent the afternoon packing. Eva quietly wrote letters for Iris to take to her parents and Sparky and one statement of fact, pleading for help in leaving Japan, for Iris to take to their state senator. Deciding to be cautious in all matters, Iris slit the lining of her trunk and hid the letters.

Eva went with Iris to the embassy late that afternoon to pick up her clearance papers. The pale clerk was again on the desk. He picked up a notice from a pile on his desk and handed it to Iris, saying, "Don't be too disappointed. They say there will be other ways of returning. Besides, you'll be able to blend in here. Not like the rest of us."

Her clearance was rejected.

Tears burned Iris's eyes as she turned wordlessly and walked to the door. Her whole world was crumbling in around her.

Almost a month later, on Friday, November 28, Inga came excitedly into Iris's office and said, "I just heard that the Swiss Red Cross is going to send a ship out leaving Yokohama for the U.S. next Tuesday."

"It's just another rumor," Iris said wearily.

"No. The name of the ship is the *Tatsuta Maru*," Inga insisted. "If you get going, maybe you can get on this one. You've got three days to get things in order. I'll cover for you if you want to leave now."

Iris hardly dared to hope. But once more she began the rounds, haunting the steps of every embassy official she could find. This time it got results. On Saturday morning, November 29, she got a conditional clearance from the embassy. She dashed to the ticket agency for the ship line.

The ticket agent looked at her papers carefully, and slowly Iris began counting out her precious savings on the counter. "One minute, Miss Hashimoto," the agent said. "You don't have a clearance from the Japanese finance office. It must be signed by them, and that statement of finances must be cleared by the American Embassy."

Iris took the electric car line to the finance office. There she learned that it would take at least three or four days before they could clear her.

"But I don't have four days. The boat leaves on Tuesday. What do you have to know? What is so important you can't clear me right now?"

"We have to confirm your statement of the amount of money you brought into Japan and that you aren't taking more out of Japan."

"When I pay for my liner ticket, I won't have anything left! Surely you can see that."

"Come back Monday afternoon. There seems to be a complication because you have not only been a student, but you have been employed here as well."

"I had to pay my tuition . . . what else could I do?"

"If you will come back Monday afternoon," he repeated.

Once again Iris and Eva started packing Iris's few belongings. Eva had to go to work on Monday, but Iris stayed home, pacing and worrying until it was time to go to the finance office. It was so close now. What if it was taken away this last time? she agonized. Twelve more hours until the boat left Yokohama . . .

She waited impatiently for half an hour while the official at the Japanese finance office found her papers. "You have been granted approval to leave," he said, offering no explanation for the delay.

Luckily, she was able to get to the American Embassy before it closed. A young secretary took her papers back for final clearance. She returned momentarily, beaming. "All cleared. Are you going down to the ticket agency now?"

"You bet." Iris grinned, hardly daring to believe that she was finally cleared to go home.

She raced back to the ticket agency, gleefully handed over her papers, and began counting out her money on the counter.

"Where are your reservations?" the ticket agent asked.

"I don't have any."

"All the tickets are reserved."

"You mean I can't buy a ticket to go—"

"No."

Stunned to find the door shut so abruptly, so cruelly in her face, Iris turned to go.

"You might go down to the dock tomorrow morning anyway," the agent added, apparently taking pity on her. "Sometimes at the last minute people don't show up to take their place on the boat. When that happens, sometimes you can get a ticket right there on the dock and get on."

"Do you really think there's a chance?" Iris asked, forbidding her hopes to rise.

"Well, it's better than not trying at all."

Iris nodded and tried to smile.

It was impossible to sleep that night. She packed and repacked one small bag that she could carry on the ship, limiting the contents to important papers and essential items. Eva stayed up and shared her anxiety, planning, hoping, and exchanging promises. Shortly after midnight they were on their way to the station to catch the train to Yokohama. Before the night thinned to morning they were on their way to the docks.

The sight greeting them at the pier caused Iris's heart to sink. There were at least two hundred other young Japanese-

Americans waiting before the ticket office. Despair swelled inside her throat.

A group of Roman Catholic nuns filed in and waited in the confirmed passenger section. The group next to them was obviously Protestant missionaries. Bristling with self-importance, a group of dark-suited businessmen stood farther on, smoking cigarettes and drinking coffee from thermoses.

A low murmur of expectancy rustled through the crowd of students waiting before the ticket office as a light went on behind the window. Shamelessly, frantically, Iris tried to shove her way to the front. She was crushed, pushed, and finally pinned against the wall of the ticket office. It was four-thirty, she could see on the terminal clock: half an hour before the ship pulled anchor and sailed. Suddenly the window opened and a man quickly placed a sign over the counter. A rumble of disgust rose from the students. There were no more tickets available. All passengers had checked in.

"No!" Iris cried.

"I don't know what you're upset about," a young man standing behind her said bitterly. "At least you won't have to fight in the Japanese army. I will." He turned and walked away.

Eva was still waiting for her by the wall. Iris couldn't talk. She just took some paper from her purse and began tearfully writing.

"What are you doing?" Eva asked. "Aren't they going to sell any tickets?"

Iris shook her head, sealed two envelopes, and addressed them. "No," she said flatly. "Just a minute." She turned and ran after the departing nuns starting up the gangplank. "Sisters!" she called. "Sisters!"

The last nun turned. "Sister," Iris said breathlessly, "I am desperate, trapped. Would you please mail these letters as soon as you get back home? One is to my parents and one is to my fiancé. I want them to know I love them and that I have tried to come home to them."

The nun looked at her benignly, her wrinkled face pinched by the starched white wimple of her habit. "I will be glad to, my child," she said, smiling. "Be brave and God bless you." She slipped the envelopes into her pocket and turned to go.

Iris turned and walked back down the pier. A long hollow

blast from the ship's horn echoed mournfully across the harbor. The oily waters churned and the black boat slipped away from the dock.

Iris and Eva stood arm in arm, tearfully watching their last chance of escape leave without them.

They slowly turned and walked to the station to catch the morning train to Tokyo.

"We must learn to endure," Eva said prophetically.

CHAPTER VI

Sparky lay on his bunk at Wheeler Air Force Base and watched the early-morning sun lighten the eastern Hawaiian sky. Following Cole's example after Eva and Iris left, he'd put in for a transfer, never thinking that they'd just send him a few miles inland. But the brass needed a plane mechanic who was also a pilot to take care of the increasing number of P-40 fighters they were bringing into Wheeler. He'd accepted the move philosophically after his initial raging and had plowed all his energies into making his crew one of the most efficient in the air corps. However, that hadn't helped his moments alone. He'd written numerous letters to Eva and had received damned few in return. But that last one . . . he just couldn't figure it. He pulled it out to reread it for the hundredth time.

It was dated June 11, 1941. He'd received it right after the Fourth of July. Today was December 7 and he hadn't heard any more from her since. Six months. It didn't even sound like her. The words were obviously hers, but the message sounded like something from another world.

Dear Sparky,
I am so far all right. Things are so different in Japan that it is more than I would expect anyone who had not

84

*seen it to understand. I have enjoyed hearing from you,
but I'm afraid that I will have to ask you to stop writing
to me. The situation is such that your letters are a great
embarrassment and cause of worry to my grandfather.
He has asked me to tell you not to write to me here
again. It is also most difficult to send letters from Japan
at this time. I am afraid that we have both lost several
in the process. Don't worry about me, and take care of
yourself. I am sure that you will go far. I will write if
and when I can.*

> *Love,*
> *Eva*

It sounded like a good-bye letter, yet she had signed it
"love." He just couldn't understand it. He'd written to Cole
and had just received a letter this past week telling him about
Iris's strange letters.

He couldn't help getting a funny cold feeling in the pit of
his stomach every time he read a headline about the trouble
brewing between Japan and the United States. For a while
he'd thought Eva had found some rich Japanese man who
interested her more than a poor kid from Brooklyn. Now he
was crazed with worry.

He glanced at his watch: 7:15 A.M. Time to go down to the
mess before they closed. He wasn't on duty today, but he
planned to hang around this morning and check out the flight
line. He'd heard that a big flight of those new B-17s was
coming in from the Coast this morning. It might be worth it
to talk someone into riding over to Hickam later and looking
at the big bombers—Flying Fortresses they were calling them.

Hardly anyone made it up in time for the Sunday breakfast
so there was no chow line and plenty of food. After eating,
he ambled out to the field. It was going to be another nice
day, he mused, glancing at the high thin haze in the blue
sky—warm, too, just like the tourists liked. In the distance
he could hear a radio playing Tommy Dorsey's "Chattanooga
Choo-Choo."

The fighters were lined up in neat rows in response to the
general order to be prepared for sabotage from fifth columnists.
The hangars sat empty. Dispersed among the parked planes
were men, guarding the planes with their rifles.

Must have just begun their watch, Sparky figured, judging from the time. He spotted Second Lieutenant Lester Murray standing in front of one of the hangars, talking to Staff Sergeant Joe Reese. He walked over to join them.

Lieutenant Murray, fresh from the military academy, was one of the "chinless wonders," very proud of his textbook expertise. It was always entertaining to listen to him speak so pompously to Sergeant Reese, who, in his down-home way, always managed to reduce everything to its most elementary level, as if cutting through the lieutenant's fancy education like a hot knife through butter.

As Sparky walked toward them, he saw a line of six to ten planes coming through Kole Kole Pass to the west. He glanced at his watch: 8:02. Early for a flight to have made a foray on a Sunday morning. He shrugged and kept walking toward the hangar. The planes circled back, joined some others coming in from the northwest, and suddenly charged down the field.

"Hey! Look out!" Sparky called to the lieutenant and the sergeant. A dive bomber peeled off and came straight down the field. "What the hell?" It dropped a bomb on the first line of fighters, followed by three more dive bombers who appeared to have every intention of doing the same.

"Navy's going to get hell for that," Reese commented as three planes caught fire from the first bomb.

"Navy, shit!" Sparky shouted, shoving the other two men back against the wall of the hangar. "Look at that red ball on their wings. It's the Japs!"

Lieutenant Murray watched as a plane dropped three more bombs, like a bird laying eggs. "That would certainly be in keeping with the Japanese history of surprise attacks," he mused as black smoke boiled overhead.

The guards were scattering, frantically trying to hide under jeeps, behind burning debris, anything that might offer protection from the bombs and strafer bullets. One dropped to his knees beside his plane and tried to fire at the attackers with his rifle. Within seconds he was dead, a crumpled mass beside the flaming wreck of the plane he had been guarding. The air throbbed with the noise of more planes coming in. The thick black smoke from the burning field darkened the morning sky and painted the field with strange curling shadows.

"Hell," Reese said with a shocked look, "I didn't even know they were sore at us."

"Do you believe it?" Sparky said to Reese, stunned by the blazing inferno in front of him.

Just then a plane with fixed landing gear roared down the runway, strafing all in sight. A soldier running for cover was left writhing in his path, clutching a red gaping hole in his side.

"Hey! Look out!" Sparky yelled, and dove behind the heavy sliding door of the hangar. The other two piled on top of him.

To their amazement, the Zero came right through the hangar opening, guns blazing. Bullets whined overhead. Deadly red and white streaks of tracers crossed the air. Impending death nudged Sparky closer to the concrete floor. Then the plane crashed through the other side of the hangar and burst into flames. Reese crawled off Sparky's legs and reached down to help Lieutenant Murray up. "Can you believe that?" His face was white with fear. He kept shaking his head and looking at the burning plane. "He did that on purpose," he muttered finally.

Sudden, blind anger swept through Sparky. He was helpless. Here they were on the ground like sitting ducks, not even fighting back. "Those sons of bitches can't get away with this!" he raged. "Come on. Why doesn't somebody do something?" He looked around. Planes were still coming in. Would they never stop? The sitting P-40s were ablaze. Lieutenant Murray seemed to be stunned into inaction.

"Fighters!" Sparky declared. "Reese, run over to the guardhouse. The brawlers—those are the kind to deal with bastards. Let them all loose and send them to the antiaircraft batteries. There's a machine gun on top of that guardhouse. Have a couple of the prisoners man that, too. Maybe they can get a couple that way. Hey! Murray! Snap out of it and give Reese the keys to the guardhouse. You have them."

Murray looked at Sparky, his eyes glazed with shock. "Okay," he said, handing the keys over to Reese. "What else?"

"Put out the fires on those planes. Save some parts at least. Maybe we can build us some new ones and chase after the bastards."

"Head up the detail," Murray said, his voice becoming stronger. He'd caught some of Sparky's anger and was beginning to take command. "I'll go find out who's the officer on duty. The armament shack is locked. I'll unlock it on the way. Pick up a sidearm for yourself. No telling where they'll be landing."

As they ran across the field toward the shack, dirt suddenly began spewing up in fountains around them. Sparky glanced over his shoulder. A Zero was closing in, shooting at them like clay ducks at Coney Island. "That SOB is trying to kill me!" he yelled incredulously. He could see the grim face of the pilot behind the goggles. Sparky shook his fist as the plane roared overhead, pulling up at the end of the runway. "I'll get you sons of bitches!" he yelled over exploding bombs, the clatter of the plane's machine guns, and sporadic rifle fire.

The air-raid siren suddenly howled, mingling in the cacophony of the reverberating bomb blasts and death screams. Reaching the shack, they were surrounded by men caught dressed and undressed by the attack. They'd been hiding in the bushes. Everyone wanted something to fight back with, anything they could use to defend themselves. Two men had been easing their frustration by throwing rocks at the planes and were now anxious for something more effective.

Sparky grabbed a sidearm and a tommy gun. Running to jump on the running board of the fire truck racing across the field, he yelled, "Get the ones blocking the runway first."

Cole found that the round of parties and dinners given by their Filipino hosts gave the place the aura of a gentlemen's club, indolent in a jasmine-scented Southern afternoon. However, when he sat down to dinner with Jake and Dick in the house off Dewey Boulevard, his fears and anxieties were reaffirmed with each day's reports.

However, his added concern, the gnawing fear about Iris's safety, was uniquely his own. Her last letter had been written just before Thanksgiving. She'd said that her father was going to meet her in Tokyo and they would come back to the United States in January. Cole had immediately written in their code that it was imperative that she leave on the next ship, regardless of her father. He met each mail call, but he did not hear from her again.

Hoping desperately that she'd already returned to Hawaii, Cole allowed himself the luxury of picturing her back in the little bungalow on Halawa Heights, all snuggled down in her bed, her dark hair a fragrant tangle on the pillow. He smiled at the thought. Because of the international date line, the Philippines were a day ahead of Hawaii. It was still December 6 in Pearl Harbor. All Sunday afternoon in Manila, Cole consoled himself, pretending he knew Iris was sleeping away her Saturday night in Hawaii's safe, star-gentled warmth. Yet, as he began getting ready for the party that Sunday night in Manila, his growing uneasiness made his fantasy dissipate into the familiar tense reality of his fears.

The 27th Bombardment Group was putting on a big party in the hotel ballroom that night, December 7. Dick, Cole, and Jake agreed that they would feel much better when it was over. The B-17s had been ordered to Mindanao, six hundred miles to the south and out of range of the Japanese base on Formosa. Half of the Flying Fortresses had already dispersed. However, the remaining seventeen bombers and their crews had remained in Manila, finding flimsy excuses to stay on. Their eyes were on this last big bash, set up to give General Brereton, the air commander, a big send-off for his trip to Java. Once this night was over, the B-17s would all be safely parked on a rough, unsheltered strip far to the south.

"You know, I'd give anything, to be able to go there tonight and enjoy myself," Jake mumbled as they walked to the hotel. They were all spit and polish, properly attired to meet all the brass, and to smile at and dance with Philippine society's lovely wives and daughters with their flashing dark Spanish eyes and graceful embroidered gowns.

Cole shook his head with a cynical grin, one that all too often these days echoed Jake's bitter cynicism. He was particularly edgy tonight. They'd had a scramble early yesterday. It had turned out to be a false alarm and the squadron had returned to base, but still it had left him tense and nervous, on top of his worries about Iris.

Suddenly Dick stopped and stared at the bay. "Look at that," he hissed. There was the usual scattering of freighters anchored in the magnificent harbor. To the south were the familiar shapes of Admiral Hart's Asiatic squadron, the *Houston*, the *Marblehead*, a flock of old "four-stacker" destroyers, some oilers, and, most likely, hidden in the depths, some submarines. In the sultry distance were the purplish masses of Bataan

Peninsula and the fortified rock island, Corregidor, barely visible in the fading evening light.

Cole studied the familiar scene for a moment. "What's the matter?"

"There's not a single Red Ball freighter out there," Dick muttered, tersely referring to the Japanese flag depicting the rising sun with a single red circle on a white background. "If that isn't something for intelligence to pick up on, I don't know what is."

"Yeah," Jake cut in, "maybe we should go right into the ballroom, stop the band, and announce that we, three junior officers, have deduced that the Japanese will attack within the next eighteen hours. At that startling revelation the band will pack up and go home, the refreshments will be dispersed to the poor, and all the crews will immediately report to battle stations."

"Come on, you two." Cole sighed. "We're only making it worse on ourselves. We've done all we can. The only reason we're going tonight, you may remember, is to see if we can pick up any more rumors." He paused, then said to Jake, "Dick has to go up to Clark to check out a report of sabotage on the generator of a B-17. I got permission to tag along and put in with the squadron up there for a checkout. Want to make it a threesome?"

"Can't. I've got a program to do tomorrow night. Got to keep the morale up, you know," he said bitterly. He still had a squadron assignment, but personnel had asked him to be "temporarily" assigned to the base radio station. "Besides, I want to put in some hours monitoring the radio reports. Sometimes stateside knows more about what's going on out here than we do. Maybe I'll hear an amusing anecdote that'll serve to put someone on their toes. Who knows?"

If the success of a party could be determined by the intensity of the hangovers the following day, Cole was sure that this one for General Brereton was one of the all-time greats. The food was plentiful, a bounteous mixture of American and Filipino tastes. They danced to the happy strains of Terso's band, and the liquor flowed as if from some bacchanalian fountain.

By nine o'clock, Jake was deep in conversation with a beautiful young woman named Maria. Cole wandered to the balcony and stood in lonely isolation, his solitude magnified by the sounds of merriment inside. He wondered what Iris was doing in Tokyo, how all this massing of forces was going to affect her, whether she had received his letter and had managed to leave yet. As he stared across the lights to the dark hillsides, he felt an emptiness that seemed to plumb the depths of the sea and sky. He ached to hold her once more.

"Ready to go?" Dick's deep voice startled Cole from his reverie.

"Clear to Tokyo," he said, putting his glass on the railing. They turned and made their way through the crowd.

Cole was sleeping fitfully when the phone awakened him at 3:00 A.M.

"It's happened! They've hit Pearl Harbor!" Jake shouted over the line.

"Pearl? How do you know? When? What happened?" Cole was instantly awake. "Where are you?"

"I'm at the radio shack. I thought I'd show Maria and her father the facilities and we just happened to pick up a San Francisco station. They said the Japanese have bombed Pearl Harbor. The reports are still confusing, but it was bad. They're having to explain where Pearl is, even. Caught them on Sunday morning . . . asleep."

"My God!" Cole was stunned. Then he grasped the magnitude of the news. "We're next."

"They're probably on their way now. I'm having a hell of a time raising anyone in Manila. Get your pants on." The line was dead. Cole hung up. Dick was behind him, already half-dressed.

"They hit Pearl first." Dick's words were a statement, not a question. "How bad?"

"Not clear, but it sounds pretty bad."

"Now maybe they'll believe us. You'll get a call to scramble next. I'll go ahead on up to Clark as planned. Maybe I can be of more use up there."

The phone rang again before Cole had finished dressing. He spoke briefly, then ran back into his bedroom. "The P-40s are going aloft," he confirmed over his shoulder.

"If I get that generator working, I'm going to make them test it out by heading south," Dick called after him. "Maybe you'll give me some fighter protection."

It was five-thirty before the engines of the fighters pounded the humid tropical darkness. Cole knew that most of the pilots must find the pulsing noise excruciating to their tender heads. Once aloft, the usual radio chatter was less than normal, whether due to the hangovers or the possibility of coming face-to-face with the enemy, Cole couldn't tell. He just knew that finally he could do something. The stick felt good in his hand. He watched the green dials and felt the sure response of the plane. He scanned the horizon, sighting on a bright star in the thin darkness of the early morning. They banked and headed north in formation.

By mid-morning the comments over the radio had changed from tense and short to a steady grumble. Flying without breakfast, looking for what they considered an imagined foe, on low fuel tanks and even emptier stomachs was more than they wanted to endure. Cole tried to keep their spirits up, but even he couldn't argue with the needle on the fuel gauge, which hovered dangerously close to empty. As squadron leader, he had no choice but to order them down to Clark Field for refueling.

As he climbed out of his cockpit, he glanced at his watch and his heart sank: eleven-thirty, the time they usually landed for lunch break. The B-17s were also on the ground. He was horrified to see that each pilot had followed the old habit of neatly parking wing tip to wing tip in protection against ground sabotage from fifth columnists, but perfect targets for air attack. It was just like Bill had said. He dashed to the crew chief and ordered the P-40s immediately refueled.

"My men are going to lunch," the sergeant said amiably. "We'll get right on it when they get back." He turned and sauntered toward the mess hall.

Something in Cole snapped. The sergeant was only one of many who didn't see the urgency in the situation or the impending danger, only one of many who felt America was invincible, but it was the sergeant Cole could reach out and grab by the shirt. He shoved the startled man against the wall. "Listen you son of a bitch," he growled, "you'll refuel those planes now or the only thing you'll be eating for the rest of this war is bread and water. Now get your crew and hop to it!"

"Yes, Captain," the sergeant said, wide-eyed, as he scurried after his crew.

Cole hurried toward the mess hall, dripping in the pounding midday sun. He had to hurry the pilots and get those planes back off the ground. Stopping momentarily at the control tower, he found that Dick had checked in. The men thought it highly amusing that Dick had insisted they take the B-17 up when all the others were coming in for lunch. Well, Cole thought, at least one plane was safe.

A radio operator in the corner seemed to be having trouble with his set. "What is it?" Cole asked.

"Don't know, sir." The operator was young and intense. "Something coming in from up north, but it's full of static."

"Keep trying," Cole encouraged. "It could mean our lives."

He looked at his watch as he walked into the mess hall: eleven-fifty. The men were all sitting around the tables, eating. "We're taking off in ten minutes," he announced.

"What's the matter, Tennyson," asked one of the bomber pilots, "you think that oxygen's going to help your hangover?"

"Nah," countered the copilot, "Tennyson's been riding a burr because he left his girl back home and he hasn't been getting any."

Cole ignored their jibes, made a sandwich of a couple of slabs of Spam and bread, and headed toward the door. "Pearl Harbor wasn't a drill and we're sure to be next. They've almost finished refueling. Let's go!" He turned to the B-17 pilot and added, "Those Fortresses of yours are going to make a pretty neat target all lined up like that."

"Come on, Cole," one of his squadron pleaded, "at least let me get a cigarette with my cup of coffee."

Three of his younger, more serious pilots caught his concern and followed him, grabbing their flight jackets as they headed out the door. The others slowly got up, coffee cups in hand, and meandered outside. He was halfway across the field when he noticed them still standing in the shade, stalling over their cigarettes. "Move it!" he shouted.

A low moaning sound slowly grew from the north, building in volume as the planes approached.

"Hey! Here comes the navy!" someone shouted. "We can't take off now."

Cole looked up and saw a dark cloud of planes approaching on the far horizon. "Navy, hell!" he shouted. "It's the Japs! Get those planes up!"

He climbed into his plane and slid back the canopy. The other three pilots soon had their engines pounding the superheated air on the landing strip. Ahead, Cole saw a dark V formation, headed for the field, growing larger with each second. They taxied down the runway. As he lifted off, he saw the men below starting to scatter into disorganized action. Some of his crew were throwing their cups to the ground and scrambling for their planes. Others were scurrying around, looking for the newly dug and far too few foxholes. One man was running toward the antiaircraft battery. Three of his squadron made it off the ground and quickly grouped on him. It was clear that the others weren't going to make it, because the men were still running toward the planes. Only three of the others even had their engines beginning to turn over.

The radio crackled in his ear. Dick's B-17 was heading south, looking for Japanese carriers on the way. They needed fighter cover. "Riley, you and Marshall head south and provide cover for that B-17," Cole ordered into the radio. "Craig and I will hold them off here and then follow." He could see his left wingman give him the high sign as the other two P-40s peeled off and headed after the only bomber the Americans had in the sky.

He didn't have time to see if they made it. Glancing over his shoulder, he saw the first wave of Japanese planes sweep down over the field. Two P-40s were taxiing. One burst into flame; the other veered to avoid hitting it and ran drunkenly off the strip, crashed into a B-17, and exploded.

"Zero at two o'clock!" Craig shouted into the radio.

One of the lead Japanese fighters had spotted them and broken out of the formation that was attacking Clark Field. Cole caught sight of the red circle on his wing as the Zero maneuvered past him, guns shooting flames. Cole's heart stopped with the sudden first horror of realizing that someone was actually trying to kill him personally. The P-40 shuddered and Cole knew he had taken a hit. His hands were shaking as he gripped the stick. How could they maneuver so fast?

From the corner of his eye he saw two others converging on Craig. Now, overriding his intense terror, came the results of all those hours of training and practice maneuvers. Despite the cold sweat dripping under his flight jacket, despite his shaking hands, he knew what to do. He shouted into the radio, "Craig! Above you!" He tried to bank and come up under the enemy plane. His P-40 couldn't respond as quickly as the Zero and the Japanese was soon around on top of him once more. In frustration, he tried to bank again to avoid the fire. The air was thick with black smoke from the devastation below. His plane was repeatedly buffeted from explosions all around.

Craig's voice screamed over the radio, "I'm hit! My God, I'm hit!"

Cole looked to his left and saw Craig's plane in flames. The cockpit was red with splattered blood.

He tried to ignore his shaking hands and banked to the left, trying desperately to outrun the Zeros on his tail. He pushed the engine until it screamed. When he was over Subic Bay, far from Clark Field, he turned and looked behind him. A spurt of fire from the guns of the lead plane shot past Cole's right wing. A wave of nausea swept through him as he saw a small hole open on the tip of his wing.

He banked quickly, caught the lead Zero by surprise, and fired at it. A trail of black smoke came from the Zero's engine. A whoop of victory escaped his lips as he saw the plane start a slow spiral toward the water. "That's one for Craig, you son of a bitch!" he shouted.

Fear gripped him as he remembered his other two pursuers and automatically started evasive maneuvers. How could the Jap planes be faster and more nimble than the P-40? It wasn't like his officers had told him it would be. It was a stinking, unfair match and it was terrifying. He couldn't see one of them and the other was fast on his tail again. He banked and saw the second plane come up from under him. He opened fire, but it easily avoided his shots, banked, and came back down on him amid streaks of tracer bullets. He felt his plane shudder.

Help, he was thinking. *Why doesn't someone help me?* He tried to bank, but the left rudder was gone. Another burst of fire and his engine exploded in flames. The cockpit filled with smoke. He tried hopelessly to control the sudden plummeting dive, his head thrown back against the seat by the force of gravity. He was coughing, caught in a spiraling death plunge.

Anger filled him. He pulled the release lever and jettisoned the canopy, then jumped. The plane slipped away from him as his stomach flipped over with the feel of free fall. He pulled the ripcord and his body snapped as the parachute opened. He was floating above his plane as it burst into flames and crashed into the bay in a spume of oily water.

He glanced frantically around, his eyes stinging with smoke, fearful that the Zeros would be back in to finish him off as he dangled helplessly from his parachute. However, they had quickly turned tail and headed back to the main battle.

He floated down through the smoke toward the blue of Subic Bay. *I'm probably the first American shot down in battle,* he thought with disgust. Then, strangely, his thoughts were no longer of the battle, nor of his own safety, once he hit the shark-infested waters. *Iris,* he thought as he hung suspended over the water covering his lost plane. *What will happen to Iris?*

CHAPTER VII

By the first week of December, Iris and Eva were very concerned. The last letter Iris had received from her father had been mailed from San Francisco in early September. He said he would arrive in Yokohama on December 15 and they would depart from Japan on January 21, 1942. He said he could not detect in the American press any of the frightening indications of war Iris had mentioned.

They hoped against hope that it was just diplomatic maneuvering and somehow it would come out all right. In any case, the dates sounded real and reassuring. They chose to believe that he was still coming. On that thin piece of information, Iris and Eva had hung all their hopes.

Yet each day had fed their rising apprehension until their fears had grown close to panic. There was a harsh military atmosphere growing in the city. Daily as they went to work they had noticed fewer and fewer able-bodied civilian men, and more and more soldiers. The radio blared with military marches. Slogans and paintings of planes and tanks appeared on walls. It was hard to nurture optimism in such surroundings. Each evening they shared their fears and marked off one more day on a homemade calendar, counting the remaining days until January 21, 1942, when they would finally depart Japan.

Iris was concerned that her father, accustomed to the moderate climate of central California, was going to find the Tokyo winter intolerable. She was suffering miserably herself. Their house, as all Japanese homes, had no insulation; the only source of heat was the charcoal brazier. She and Eva had learned quickly to bundle up in several layers of clothing, as the Japanese did.

When the sky was a brittle blue, the wind whipped in off Tokyo Bay, cutting through her thin coat like thousands of icy needles. When dark clouds rolled in and weighed heavily over the city, there was a dreary cold, wrapped in sheets of rain, sleet, and snow.

Monday morning, December 8, the clouds were black and gloomy. Ice dulled the surface of puddles as Iris ran to catch the *densha*. Once on the streetcar, out of the cutting wind, she mused that most likely the clouds would be blown away by evening, leaving the bitter cold to sting her ears. She felt in her coat pocket to make sure she'd brought her scarf.

Tension was in the air. She tried unsuccessfully to ignore it by reminding herself that there were only seven more days until her father would arrive. From then it would only be thirty-seven more days before their escape. Forty-three days in all. She glanced out the window of the streetcar and saw a military truck cut through the traffic. It carried several soldiers in the rear, with guns slung over their straight backs and arrogance written on their young faces. Forty-three days suddenly seemed an eternity. The *densha* stopped and she climbed down the steps and walked rapidly up the street toward the Matsumiyo Nihongo Bunka Gakkō, the Japanese Language Culture School, in the Shiba-Ku district, where she took her language lessons.

The class was gloomy and chill and the lesson was boring. Precisely at eleven o'clock Iris walked briskly up the street. It was a long walk to the Swedish Embassy and her job, but perhaps the exercise would release the tension and ease the depression she was feeling. She had gone less than a block when she began noticing the unusual activity on the streets.

People were talking excitedly. Some carried Japanese flags. Radio speakers were blaring martial music on every corner. There were newspapers out in special editions. Since the papers were all in Japanese characters, she couldn't tell what was going on. She stopped a newsboy and asked him if there were any English editions. To her bewilderment, he looked at her strangely, then spat on her shoe. Startled and suddenly frightened, she turned and quickly lost herself in the gathering crowd.

What is it? What has happened? Her mind probed the possibilities as she hurried breathlessly down the street.

The Swedish Embassy was a block away. Iris pushed her way through the jubilant crowds. Then an army truck swung around the corner in front of her. It was immediately surrounded with cheering people throwing flowers to the soldiers in back, who were waving triumphantly. Had the war in China been won? Perhaps that was it. She reassured herself, pushing down the growing fear, trying desperately to deny her worst suspicions. Just then one of the young soldiers jumped down from the truck and landed directly in front of her. She stopped, holding her breath. Could he tell she was American?

Boldly holding out a flower just thrown to him, he smiled at her and said something in rapid Japanese. Her comprehension of the language was halting when she concentrated. Now, in her confusion, she could only pick out the words *beautiful, victory,* and *Emperor's glory.* Then he waited for her answer. The crowd quieted, seeming also to wait for her response.

They're smiling, she thought; *they must not know that I'm American. Perhaps they think I'm Japanese. Yet, if I speak, they're sure to tell from my accent.* She forced a smile, took the flower, bowed, and murmured one word: *"Hai."*

Perhaps simply saying yes would satisfy them. The soldier beamed and bowed and the crowd cheered. Iris turned and ran the remaining block to the embassy.

Breathlessly, she climbed the stairs to her office. Her throat was dry with dread. The office was empty. Typewriters were silent. Phones didn't ring. Where was everyone?

Exhausted, Iris sat down at her desk and tried to catch her breath. She was shaking as if desperately cold, yet perspiration dripped from her forehead. She felt dizzy and slightly nauseated. Could it be that Cole was right? Had it happened? Was she trapped in Japan?

"Iris! You're here, thank God! I was afraid you'd be caught in the streets." Inga was flushed as she bustled in the door. "Did you have any problem getting here? Have you heard?" she asked rapidly.

"Inga!" Iris cried, holding back her tears. "What has happened? I saw the newspapers and the crowds and heard the loudspeakers with the marching music, but I couldn't understand any of it."

"The Emperor issued an imperial rescript. I was there in the translating room with the rest of the office staff. Japan has declared war on Great Britain and the United States. They attacked Pearl Harbor today, and from all they say there's not an American soldier, ship, or plane left in all Hawaii."

"It can't be . . ." Iris whispered.

"Well, the military has a tendency to exaggerate, but there's more evidence coming in which seems to back it up. I'm sorry," she added sympathetically. "My country has tried to protect itself by declaring neutrality throughout all this. Yet, we too have suffered much."

Iris tried to clear the clouds of fear from her mind. "I'm an enemy alien, Inga," she said slowly. "What should I do?"

"I'll try to find out. In the meantime, go home and stay there. Don't open the door to anyone but me. I'll find out and get to you as soon as I can. If they're going to put you in prison camp . . ."

"Prison camp!"

"Don't get excited," she cautioned, looking over her shoulder. "Yes, prison camp. They often do that during wartime, you know. I will find out, and then, if necessary, we'll find a way . . . maybe make you a Japanese citizen or something."

"No! I will not give up my citizenship. I can't. Someday this war will be over, and I will have given away any chance I have of ever going home again, of ever seeing Cole again. He'd hate me if I gave up my citizenship. I'd rather die." She began to sob. "I'm not Japanese. I'm American."

Inga put her arm around Iris's heaving shoulders. "There, don't cry. I know you're American. I'll talk to the ambassador. Maybe he can even talk to Ambassador Grew at the American Embassy. Maybe something can still be done."

"Don't forget Eva. She's here too. Do you really think you can help?"

"I don't know," Inga said with blunt honesty. "There are many more important people than you who will want to leave Japan. But we'll think of some way for you to make do. Perhaps you'll have to pretend to be Japanese for a few years. Now go home. Remember what I said. Don't talk to anyone on the streets; they will know you're not Japanese if you open your mouth. Lock your door. And don't worry about Eva. She will be better off than you because she can pretend to be Japanese and sound like one. When I come, I'll shout so you'll hear my voice and know it's me. Don't answer to anyone else."

Iris nodded. "Will I still be able to work here?"

"I don't know. Now go."

If anything, the streets were more crowded and noisy. The people seemed intoxicated with victory and war and military invincibility. Iris raced to the corner where she normally caught a streetcar to her neighborhood, but apparently they were not running on schedule.

She stood waiting on the sidewalk, trying to be inconspicuous while standing still and fighting back tears in the middle of a shouting, laughing crowd. When the *densha* finally came, she saw why it was late. Every block it was stopped by groups of teen-age boys waving Japanese flags. They would jump on the steps, cling to the rails of the car, and shout what must have been military slogans while the passengers cheered.

Iris jumped on board quickly and moved to the back, hopefully out of the way of the demonstrators. The car started up with a jerk, only to be stopped at the next street corner by a gang of youths waving flags. The ride seemed interminable. What usually took twenty minutes took an hour.

When the car stopped, she jumped to the ground and scurried to the safety of their little house, unable to overcome the feeling that she was being chased, of someone behind her. She didn't even take time to remove her shoes before going in. She closed the door, then pushed shut the *amado*, the heavy night door. Breathless, she leaned against the solid wood and tried to calm her panic.

War! What of Papa? How could they have gotten away with bombing Pearl? It must be a lie. But why all the celebration? Could they get away with lying to a whole nation? Pearl

Harbor destroyed? What of Sparky? She remembered Inga's words: "Not an American soldier, ship, or plane left in all Hawaii." What of dear Sparky? *How can I tell Eva?* Tears were flowing down her cheeks and sobs caught in her throat. *Does this mean Cole is at war? Will he be flying over Tokyo, dropping bombs on me?* She felt as if she were fighting her way out of a confused, raging nightmare. Rubbing her eyes with the palms of her hands, her knees crumpled and she fell to the floor, crying hysterically.

"No!" she screamed, pounding the floor. "No! No! No!"

Slowly, her weeping calmed, her tears dried. Exhaustion took over and she fell asleep. It was a sleep haunted with the ghosts of Sparky and a gallant Cole sweeping down out of the sky and picking her up on the wing of his plane while Eva cried her name from below. But she was slipping. No matter how hard she tried, she couldn't hold on to the wing of Cole's plane.

"Iris!" Eva called. "Iris, are you all right?"

Iris turned her head and saw Eva's anxious face leaning over her. "Yes, I'm okay," she said with a sheepish smile. "I had the most vivid dream. It was terrifying. Japan had wiped out Pearl Harbor and Cole flew over . . . well, never mind."

"Pearl Harbor wasn't a dream, Iris," Eva said grimly. "I've been listening to the Allied broadcasts all day. They say Pearl was bombed. It really is war." She began to cry. "Everyone in the station was clapping one another on the back and cheering. They're even saying that everyone on Pearl was . . . killed."

Iris put her arms around Eva and said consolingly, "Sparky's okay. He just has to be. Don't worry."

"It's Cole, too."

"What do you mean? He's in the Philippines."

"They hit the Philippines, too." She turned her tear-stained face to Iris. "I'm sorry. They said they took out all the installations there as well. Shot down all the planes either in the air or on the ground."

"No! Eva, no!"

They looked at each other in horror. "I feel so helpless," Iris whispered.

"Me too."

"Inga said she'd find out what's happened and what we

should do. Let's make a cup of tea and sit down and piece things together as best we can."

Eva wiped away her tears and headed toward the low-roofed cooking room that leaned like a porch on the side of their house. She went outside to start the charcoal burning in the *konro*, put the water in the teapot, then called to Iris, "There's some rice cookies in the cupboard and some cheese. Why don't you get them out?"

Iris smiled wanly. "Those are rare treats. When did you get them?"

"I found them in the market yesterday. It was going to be a surprise. I thought it would be nice to . . ." She stopped, covering her face with her hands, her shoulders shaking with silent sobs.

"Eva," Iris said. "Don't! You mustn't!" She put her arms around Eva.

"I got it for . . . for when your father came . . . a celebration. And now . . ."

"And now," Iris finished for her, "we don't know if we'll ever see him again, or Sparky or Cole or anyone we really love. . . ." For some reason, Eva's tears made Iris stronger. She cried, but she was also able to think. She had to in order to survive. "Listen," she said, "let's put all this together. Maybe there's something we're missing."

Eva took her cue from Iris and dried her tears, then poured the tea. "First things first," she said deliberately. "The reports I translated today came from Australia and San Francisco. They said it was too early to report damage, but some of the . . ." She began to shake all over, then pulled herself together and continued, "Some of the broadcasts, although they didn't say how much damage had been done, referred to the many American lives lost due to the sneak attack by the unscrupulous Japanese." Her lower lip began to quiver.

"No indications of where and how hard they hit?"

"No, they just referred to American bases in and around Pearl Harbor."

"What about the Philippines?" Iris persisted.

"Not much other than what I told you. The Japanese were attacking all of the main island of Luzon. American bases reported that they were rallying, but other reports said that almost all the air defenses had been wiped out."

Iris was still for a moment. Then, taking a slow breath, she said softly, "There's no way we can know for sure. We'll just have to pray that they're still alive and live for that. America certainly won't take this sitting down. Japan will be squashed soon; American soldiers will land in Tokyo in no time. We'll just wait until then."

"Other reports said the American territories of Wake Island and Guam are also under attack. The British and the French are fighting off invasions and attacks throughout Southeast Asia, and the Dutch are expecting the same thing anytime. Even Singapore is ready for the worst."

"Surely that can't all be right!" Iris cried. "How could the Japanese have that many troops? What are they going to do? Take on the whole world?"

Eva shrugged. "They have an agreement with Germany. Sounds like they plan on splitting the world between them." She passed Iris some cheese and they sat eating in silence. Suddenly Eva asked, "Do you think Inga will come tonight? It's late."

"I don't know. I'm tired, though. Let's go to bed; we'll wake up if she calls at the gate."

They unrolled their *futons* and quickly climbed under the padded blankets to keep from getting chilled. Soon Iris could hear Eva's even breathing; exhaustion had taken over and she slept peacefully.

The pale moonlight filtered through their window, spilling a crosshatched light on the smooth wooden floor. Outside, the wind soughed through the pine needles of the gnarled old tree at the side of their house, a deceptively peaceful sound that was periodically shattered by the distant crack of firecrackers in celebration of Japan's victories. The patch of moonlight had grown long and thin before Iris was finally able to drop off to sleep.

The next day they decided that Eva should continue with her job. It seemed safe enough for her because of her facility in the language. Besides, they would desperately need the money, especially if Iris lost her job at the embassy. Because of the possible danger for Iris, she was to stay locked in the house until they heard from Inga.

The day was intolerably long. Iris's mind crawled with fears. She tried to read. She'd brought along the poems of Elizabeth Barrett Browning, which Cole had given her the night he proposed. But she couldn't concentrate. She cried over the poems and her own lost love.

By early afternoon the garden behind the house beckoned in the winter sun. Skeletons of fruit trees caught the sunlight and bent in empty promise under the wind. The barren grass and fallow flower beds were empty and solemn, matching Iris's mood. She slid the shoji screen door and stepped out on the worn stepping stones. As she sat down on the small bench at the side of the garden, she tried to collect her thoughts.

She had no doubt that the American army would soon be occupying Japan. However, she was not so foolish as to believe that their bombs would be selective enough to fall only on Japanese citizens. She and Eva were in great danger of being killed by their own rescuers. Would it be best to try to go to the countryside? There was her aunt Suki, who lived in Shizuoka, the one to whom Iris had sent insulin upon her arrival in Japan. But what would make her presence less of a threat to Aunt Suki than it was to her other relatives here in Tokyo? Besides, she couldn't afford the trip, especially if she lost her job at the embassy. It would be difficult enough just to buy food and pay the rent on Eva's small salary. And why hadn't Inga come?

"Pardon, miss."

Iris jumped and turned, gripping the bench tightly. To her amazement, she saw standing in her garden a woman somewhere between the ages of forty and seventy, dressed completely in black and carrying a basket. It might have been an apparition out of a fairy tale. Iris blinked and tried to still the beating of her heart. "Who . . . who are you?"

"You call me Kiyoko." She smiled and bowed politely. Her accent was difficult, one that wrapped the *l*'s in an *r* sound and tended to forget the endings of verbs. "I work in Big House, there," she said, pointing over the hedge to the Swiss undersecretary's residence. "Be no 'fraid," she said, moving toward Iris. "I come talk friendly. Big-house people say you not Nippon."

Iris shook her head, knowing that she could be putting herself into the hands of a spy, yet somehow doubting it. "Yes, I am an American."

"I have brother he fight in Manchuria. He say it big place. Bigger than Nippon. American big too?"

Iris nodded. This strange little woman was sitting down on

a nearby rock and chatting as if she were talking over tea. It seemed only natural for Iris to ask, "Would you like to come in and have some tea?"

She bowed sweetly and said, "Thank you. That is honor."

It was only then that Iris remembered that lighting the charcoal was an almost impossible task for her and she had gotten herself into a very awkward situation. She dropped a few pieces of charcoal in the *konro*, reached for the matches, and prayed. She succeeded only in burning her fingers. She tried several more times, managing to get a blister on her forefinger, black smudges on her hands, one arm, and the sleeve of her dress, and still the charcoal refused to burn. Iris looked helplessly at Kiyoko. "I'm sorry, but could you—"

Kiyoko picked up the matches, deftly rearranged and lighted the charcoal, and said, "I teach." She pointed to the neat stack of glowing charcoal. "Must put close yet allow to breathe."

"Thank you." Iris smiled.

Kiyoko sat respectfully silent while Iris poured tea, accepting her cup with a polite bow. She then continued her questions as if there had been no interruption. "American is bigger than Japan?"

"Yes, much bigger. If I can find a map, I will show it to you," Iris said casually.

"Good." There was a long, expectant pause. Finally, Kiyoko broke the silence by saying, "I wait while you look."

Surprised that this persistent little woman expected her to stop right now and give her a geography lesson, Iris got up and went into the other room. Slightly irritated, she sorted through her belongings and found a small history book with a map of the world.

"Here," she said, shoving the map in front of Kiyoko. "That yellow area, here, is Japan. This big green area over here is America."

Kiyoko studied the map for a long time. She was obviously genuinely interested in this new information. Iris felt a little twinge of guilt for her impatience.

"Thank you very much," Kiyoko said, handing the book back to Iris. "I have much to learn." She sipped her tea. "I am very sorry our countries fight. People like us, we don't fight. Just countries."

Iris was taken aback by her simple gesture of friendship.

"Yes," she said quietly, "I am sorry too. It is too bad people like us don't decide about fighting."

"*Hai*. So good idea," Kiyoko exclaimed, covering her mouth and only partially hiding a lovely, melodic laugh. She seemed to enjoy the idea immensely. "Women decide when to fight. So good idea!"

Iris could not help but join in the spontaneous joke. Kiyoko's laughter was contagious and a welcome relief.

When their laughing died away, Iris poured another cup of tea for them both.

Kiyoko watched her carefully. "You work?"

Iris nodded. "Yes."

"Why not work today? You 'fraid?"

"Yes. I cannot speak Japanese very well and I would be recognized in the street as an American."

"Ah. You need work?"

"Yes. I hope I can keep on at the Swedish Embassy. I don't know where else I can find a job."

"Don't work in place make bullets and guns."

"A munitions factory? I certainly would rather not, but why do you say I shouldn't, Kiyoko?"

"What you called?"

"I'm sorry. I forgot. I'm Iris Hashimoto."

"Ah." She bowed politely. "Iris, you not work in that place. When people work there, they get much sick, die."

"Why do you tell me this?"

"People say *gaijin* . . . what you call it?"

"*Gaijin?* Uh, foreigner."

"Yes, foreigner make work there."

"But how can I keep them from making me work there?" she asked somehow believing Kiyoko's warning.

"You make important work other place."

"Where?"

The woman was quiet for a moment. "I find out."

"Thank you, Kiyoko," Iris said. This lady was particularly talkative for a Japanese. Yet, strangely, Iris trusted her. She wondered if it was because she was so frightened and needed someone or if Kiyoko really was the friend she appeared to be. "Why did you come here?" she couldn't help but ask.

Kiyoko smiled slightly at the abruptness of Iris's question. "I see you long time in garden. You much like my daughter. This is bad time."

"Where is your daughter now?"

"She die."

"Oh, I'm sorry." Iris didn't have the courage to ask how so young a woman had come to die. Something in the air said it was tragic.

"You have a mother and father?"

"Yes, in America."

"Husband?"

"I was engaged to be married. He is in—America too." It seemed best not to trust anyone with the information that she was engaged to a military man, one who wasn't even of her race. "I'm worried about them. I'm afraid I will never see them again."

"Ah, so you need letter?"

"Something, desperately, to let me know how they are."

"You try Swiss Red Cross. They get much news. You want I ask for you?"

"Of course!" Iris cried with delight. "The Red Cross through the Swiss Embassy. Why didn't I think of that?"

"I think for you," Kiyoko said beaming. "It be so good. I find out for you. You give name of father and love."

Iris paused in her rising hopes. Should she give Cole's name and rank, thereby letting on that he was with the military, to this woman? Could she even trust the Red Cross with that information? Have they been infiltrated by the Kampetei? Maybe it was best to go slowly. "My fiancé will be harder to find," she said, then added awkwardly, "He was just sent somewhere else on business."

Kiyoko nodded wisely. "Ah, then you make name and place of father on paper. I take to Swiss Cross."

"Yes, yes, of course," Iris said, quickly writing down her father's name and address. "If the Red Cross can, tell them that I want my parents to know that I'm all right. Tell them I love them and . . . and that I want to come home." She looked down at the paper, trying to hide the tears that had filled her eyes so quickly.

Kiyoko reached out to take the paper, then Iris suddenly remembered Eva. "Oh! Wait. Give them the name of my friend's father as well."

"Ah, yes. Your friend. She live here also." As Iris wrote down Eva's father's name and address, Kiyoko added, "Good friend. I hear laughter come from house when I walk other side of garden."

Iris smiled and handed her the paper. "You must have known we were here for a long time."

"Yes," she smiled sweetly, "I know you come. Then I hear voices. Sounds much like my daughter. I walk to hear. Make me happy."

The wistful smile, filled with sad memories, touched Iris. She wanted to reach out to this gentle woman who had brought friendship to her when she felt most alone. Then she remembered that Japanese seldom touch one another. Iris bowed deeply. "I am honored that you came to talk to me," she said sincerely. "I want you to come again. I was very worried and frightened when you came. Now I feel better. Thank you."

Kiyoko returned her bow, then turned to go. As she reached the door she turned and put on her shoes. "Oh," she said suddenly, reaching into a fold of her dress, "I forget. Have paper for you now."

Iris took the envelope and used the Japanese phrase she liked best. "*Arigato gozaimasu*," she said, thanking her.

Kiyoko looked surprised. "Ah, you learn talk Nippon. You want I come help?"

"Yes," Iris said, surprised at the sensible offer. "Come very often so I can learn quickly."

"I come tomorrow."

Iris brightened at the thought of another visit. "Yes, please come tomorrow." Then she paused. "But what if I have to go back to work tomorrow?"

"I will know. You no worry." She bowed, turned, and walked out.

Iris glanced at the envelope in her hand. It was addressed in Inga's slanting European handwriting. Quickly she tore it open and read the note inside.

Dear Iris,

I'm sorry I couldn't come to your home but it didn't seem wise for either of us. I have asked the Swiss undersecretary's assistant to arrange for this to be delivered to you.

As you might guess, things are in quite an uproar and it is hard to tell what is going to happen. For now, it is best that you remain in your house. Don't come to work. They will consider whether your employment at the embassy will be an embarrassment or compromising to our neutral status within the next two weeks. In the meantime, wait there to hear from me. There is a possibility I will be shipped back home to Sweden.

Keep courageous and use your head throughout the war. Don't let your heart be the cause of your death.

> With best regards,
> Inga

Startled by the ominous sound of the letter, Iris stepped out to the garden to see if she could catch Kiyoko and find out how she could write back and ask Inga for more information. Kiyoko had already left.

A shadow passed over the garden as clouds covered the sun. There was a small opening in the corner of the hedge; that must have been where Kiyoko went, Iris thought, yet it seemed hidden and too small to admit such a welcome friend. Iris shivered in the chill air and went back into the house. She would wait.

CHAPTER VIII

Cole opened his eyes. Everything was white and blurry. Where was he? He was going to be late. Iris was waiting. He started to get on his feet but a sharp pain in his ankle threw him back down. His head throbbed as his memory returned. He closed his eyes, and behind them he could see the Zeros closing in on him.

He opened his eyes again and concentrated on focusing. It was a white ceiling above him. He strained and then with sickening clarity remembered the plummeting dive of his plane, his dreamlike fall under the cloud of parachute, and the salty taste as the waters of Subic Bay filled his mouth. Something had hit his head at that point, and now things returned to him only in disjointed, hazy remembrances, a picture puzzle with missing pieces. He could see the worried eyes of a Filipino and the tangled fishing nets he was lying on as the smoky blue sky skirted behind a sail. He remembered parts of a painful journey in the back of a cart pulled by a lumbering carabao, sleeping in a nipa hut, and then an even more uncomfortable, jolting journey in the back of a truck. He must have been rescued, but where was he now? He turned and looked around the room, despite the pain the motion caused him. Was he with Americans or Japanese?

"It's about time you woke up, you lazy dog."

Cole turned entirely too quickly toward the familiar voice. He winced and said, "Hey, what happened?"

Jake stretched out his long legs and grinned. "Seems you weren't satisfied to let the Nips shoot out all our planes. You had to take one up and break it yourself. You're just lucky someone is sticking up for you and claiming you accidentally shot down a couple of Nips in the process. They even want to call you a hero of some sort."

"God, I was scared," he murmured in response.

"I'll bet," Jake said softly. He leaned forward with his arms resting on his knees. "Tell me—are they as good as they're saying?"

"I don't understand it," Cole said, strangely choked up. "Our planes don't stand a chance against them. They're faster and they maneuver quicker than a cat in a fight. It's going to take retraining to get our pilots ready to handle them. They must not have any weight in those machines. I've got to get out of here. What day is it? How bad am I hurt?"

"Don't worry. You're not too bad off. Seems you got a sprained ankle and hit your head on the rudder of your own plane. Least, that's what we gather from the fisherman who pulled you out. Said he was right there and saw everything. Thought you were going to drop it right on his boat for a while there. Whatever, you got a mild concussion."

"But how long have I been here? What about the Japs?"

Jake shook his head. "It's going to take a long time to beat those bastards off, buddy. They took out almost all our airfields and the planes with them. We're going to have to fight them off with broomsticks until they can get us some more supplies out of the States."

Cole closed his eyes. "Oh, God."

"Yeah. Hey, you get some rest now. The doc says you can get out as soon as your head stops hurting, so try to sleep it off. If you don't mind, I'll bring a visitor when I come in this afternoon."

"Sure, that'd be great." Cole managed a grin. He was tired. It must be the bump on the head . . . he was asleep before Jake reached the hallway.

He awoke to see an army nurse beside his bed. "Your friend was glad to see you wake up," she said with a smile when he opened his eyes. "Want some lunch? If you're not too dizzy, you can sit up and eat from the tray."

"Thanks," Cole said, sitting up despite the throbbing of his head. His ankle didn't hurt as much to move it now. He'd not noticed the cast before. "Hey, what's with the cast? I've got to get out of here."

"It's just a sprain, Captain. You'll be able to hobble along with some crutches in a day or so."

"That's just great," he said bitterly. "Pilots who hobble don't pilot. What's today, anyway?"

"December tenth. You've only been here overnight. A Filipino family took care of you until the medics got you. I thought your friend told you all this before he left. He spent the whole night sleeping in that chair beside your bed. I couldn't drive him out. He doesn't seem to have much respect for army regulations."

Cole could tell from the look in her eye that the cavalier approach Jake had to life was both an irritation and attraction to her, as it was to so many women. He grinned, and she added as she turned to leave, "I'll bring you your shaving things so you can spruce up after lunch."

He was sipping his second cup of coffee when his mind momentarily wandered back to the battle. He still could hear the drone of the planes and the nearby dull thud of bombs. He turned and looked out the window. It was no dream.

An ominous black cloud of smoke was drifting over the rooftops, boiling with malice and death. The drone continued high above, and the steady whump of explosions was pierced by the staccato of ack-ack fire. Manila was under attack.

He lay in bed, listening to the noise of battle. In an unreal, detached manner he found himself analyzing the sounds. They were bombers. Must be at least fifteen thousand feet high. *The little bit of antiaircraft fire we can put up would never touch them.* Now he could see the white puffs of useless AA bursts superimposed over the black burning clouds, like dandelions gone to seed.

We've got to figure out a way of hitting them when they're so high, he mused. Those high-level bombers could go much higher, even higher than his P-40 could go. *We're helpless against them now.*

He was still turning the problem over in his mind when Jake came in later in the afternoon.

"Can you get me out of here?" Cole asked. "I've got to get back to work. Those bastards are still coming in. Where were you at noon?"

"Standing on the roof of the house, watching their flight pattern. They know what they're doing. Their formation is precision work. They're hitting us as calmly as if they were swatting flies."

"Have you talked to a doc? I've got to get out of this place."

Jake nodded. "Dick said he'd have dinner for you tonight. I'll bring a car around this afternoon and pick you up. Military commandeered everything that moves. Civilians have to take horse-drawn calesas. Dick said he'd finagle a ride for you as soon as you started getting cranky with the easy life. Why don't you just leave Doc a note? They need the beds for the real wounded."

Cole leaped at the idea of escape. "I'll be ready." Then he realized that Jake seemed more alert, even happy. "What have you been doing with your time?"

"Mostly watching you sleep. But that can get pretty dull, so I went out and made some new friends. Want to meet them?"

Cole was more than interested. "Sure. Bring them over to the house tonight?"

"Well, they're here right now. Seems they want to meet my friend, the hero. Sit up and straighten that pajama collar. I'll go get them."

Cole was puzzled by the sudden tension in Jake, then understood as Jake's new friends came into the ward—a slender, dignified Filipino man of about forty-five, followed by a lovely young Filipino woman. She was the woman who had caught

112

Jake's eye at the reception the night before the attack. She was even more lovely than before, with a simple white cotton dress covering her slender figure and her long black hair pulled back from her face, emphasizing her fine facial structure and large dark eyes. So, after all his warnings to Cole about getting trapped in the web of a woman, Jake himself had finally succumbed. Cole could tell by the look on Jake's face that he was torn between being defensive about his "fall" and being openly proud of his new love.

"Cole, I'd like you to meet my friend, Rodrigues Sebastian and his daughter, Maria."

"You don't know how delighted I am to meet you." Cole couldn't help beaming.

"It is our pleasure." Rodrigues smiled. "The people of the Philippines are grateful that you have fought in our defense."

"Well, I have to say that when I looked out my cockpit and saw those Zeros coming in on me, I wasn't thinking about saving the Philippines. I was more concerned with saving my own skin."

"Yes, that is the way of battle." Rodrigues nodded with understanding. "Still, your efforts have made you a hero. Jake says you are planning on leaving the hospital to go back to fighting. That is not the action of a coward. That is bravery. Now you know what you are returning to."

"You were one of the few who were able to shoot down the Japanese," Maria added. "Are you going to train the other pilots? There are many Filipino pilots who would welcome your experience. Jesus Villamoor is a family friend."

"Is that right?" Cole recognized the name of the already outstanding Filipino pilot. "I'd love a chance to sit down and talk with him. He can make a P-26 fly almost like my P-40."

"Perhaps you will accompany Jake to our home for dinner one of these evenings?" Rodrigues asked. "We live in Lubao, a small town to the north of Manila."

"Rodrigues is the mayor of the town," Jake put in.

"That would be an honor, thank you."

"I'm glad I had a chance to meet you," Maria said. "Jake speaks highly of you. Perhaps you will become our friend as well."

"Yes, you will . . . uh, thanks for coming in," Cole said, suddenly awkward as they turned to go.

"Well, what do you think?" Jake asked, barely able to wait until they were out of hearing.

"You're a damned lucky bastard and you'll have a beautiful family."

"Yeah. Now I know how you feel about Iris," he admitted almost apologetically. "Maybe it's in my blood after all. You know, my mother was half-Cherokee. I always thought she was the most beautiful one in the family. Well!" he said, suddenly changing his tone, as if to cover an indiscreet revelation. "How's your head?"

"Fine."

"Liar." He grinned. "Get up and get dressed. Your clothes are in that bag and I have a military vehicle illegally parked for nonmilitary use downstairs. I'll go get some crutches for you."

Cole wrote a note telling the doctor to release one Captain Cole Tennyson whenever he felt like doing the paperwork. Then Jake came back in with a set of crutches, gathered Cole's things, and followed his thumping progress down the corridor.

War had come to Manila. As they drove, Cole saw charred skeletons of bombed buildings grotesquely interspersed among blocks of undisturbed shops and offices. Pup-tent encampments and military patrols were springing up around the city and sandbagged emplacements of machine guns were bristling incongruously near the Old Manila walls.

Cole ate dinner with Jake and Dick in a house darkened by strict blackout regulations. Their meal was lit only by the brilliance of the Philippine sunset, now made a more virulent red by the lingering smoke of burning buildings. Jake excused himself early, explaining that he wanted to check in with Rodrigues before they left for Lubao in the morning.

Cole smiled. "Tell Maria hello for me."

Jake grinned at being so transparent and waved good-bye. Dick laughed and helped Cole up the stairs. "I go to Mindanao with a B-17, you take a swim in Subic Bay, and our friend there rides over the rainbow."

When morning came, Cole was anxious to get going. He'd lain in bed since the first olive hint of dawn, thinking about Iris. He'd not heard from her and couldn't expect to now. He could only pray that she was all right. The only thing he could do for now was his job—fly and fight. He rode down to Colonel George's office with Dick.

The colonel was in a meeting but sent out word that he was pleased with Cole's recovery and proud of his victories over the Japanese. Cole's orders were cut and waiting for him. He was to be assigned temporarily to G-2, the intelligence section. He and Dick were to gather as much as possible on the Zero, including everything from personal interviews and reports to collecting pieces from the seven reported shot down during the December 8 attack. They set out immediately for Clark Field. Jake stayed on in Manila.

They could spot Clark Field by the still-smoldering ruins. They were stunned not only by the devastation all around but by the low morale of the men. Nothing in their experience had prepared them for the violence of the Japanese attacks. In one day they suddenly found themselves, citizens of the world's wealthiest nation, trying to care for their wounded, bury their dead, and defend themselves with whatever they could scrape together from the burned-out rubble. Their machine shops were black and crumbled. Hangars were useless, gaping maws. They became scavengers just to keep the few remaining planes operating. The Japanese attacks were so frequent that any effort to rebuild was pointless without proper antiaircraft defense. There was a general, overwhelming fear of an impending paratroop attack.

Cole and Dick began collecting data and testimony from the pilots. One young lieutenant was recounting the Japanese strafing approach for them, when suddenly, without warning, they were provided with a live demonstration. Dick pulled Cole down into a foxhole as the air-raid siren screamed belatedly over the howl of the approaching planes. They watched their efficient approach, attack, and return with morbid fascination. Even before the drone of their engines had faded, Cole was out making notes and asking pilots coughing in the smoke-filled air how they thought the P-40s and P-39s might possibly counter the Japanese methods and lighter machines. He hobbled through the debris, listening to theory after theory and writing each one down.

Word was that there was a downed Zero to the north of the field, possibly the one that Cole had shot down. Taking an army jeep, they searched the area for most of the afternoon.

Just as they were about to give up and return to Clark, they were approached by a Filipino farmer.

"What are you looking for?" he asked, having observed the last hour of their crisscrossing search.

"We need to find a Japanese plane so we can study it," Cole explained. Dick glared at him. They'd had several long discussions during the day about the reports of fifth-column activities. Cole maintained that it was probably the result of Japanese who had long ago infiltrated the islands. Dick insisted that there were some Filipinos who helped them.

The farmer nodded. "I can help. Follow me."

Several hundred yards ahead was a burned-out section. There obviously had been a crash there. The farmer stopped and pointed to the black patch. There was a cleared field beyond it. "That was where my house was. It crashed into my house and my wife and two daughters were killed. When I found you, I was beginning to walk to find army. I want to fight."

Cole stared at the charred ruins, horrified. The same thing could happen to Iris, he thought. He shuddered and turned to the farmer. "I'm sorry," he said softly. "You can ride back with us."

Unfortunately, the only part of the plane that survived the fiery crash intact was the tail section, which was badly twisted. Nevertheless, it might prove useful. With the mourning farmer's help, they picked up some scattered pieces of metal and marked the tail section as army property so a truck would come and pick it up. They carried what they could back to the jeep, past the three newly dug graves marked with lovingly handcarved, whitewashed wooden crosses.

The farmer sat beside the fragments of the Zero that had killed his family, silently watching the changing landscape as they neared the base. "We're going back to Manila tomorrow," Cole offered as they stopped outside the gates. "If you want to ride with us in the morning, you can."

"I will be here." He nodded his thanks and disappeared into the gathering dusk.

Clark Field was ghostly in the night. Their few planes were now widely dispersed, as they should have been three days ago. Small lights moved around the silver bodies of the planes in silence. Men with hooded flashlights were at work, fueling and servicing them. Along the runway, bodies of dead men still lay, awaiting burial. The sweetish smell of death permeated the air. Mount Arayat's great cone towered above the field in the night sky, reminding them of times unchanging, of a world that once was.

Cole was anxious to put into action some of his theories of how to maneuver the P-40 against the agile Zero. If he was correct, he would not only become a more effective pilot himself, but he could teach other pilots how to win. A week later, he insisted the doctor cut off his cast. He had thrown away the crutches the first day and had limped with his weight on his ankle from then on. He was convinced that he could strengthen the sprain by pure willpower and exercise. The doctor gave in, maintaining that he had more important things to do than argue with a fool. By December 19, Cole was walking with a limp, but he was walking. By December 20, he was sure he'd be able to fly a plane in no time and began badgering for permission to do so.

There was more and more confusion at HQ. No one seemed to know what anyone else was doing. The Japanese were landing to the north and southeast. Squadron assignments for pilots were rare because the planes were few and far between and the pilots clamoring for them were many. Most pilots were getting assigned to ground duty, digging trenches, learning to man artillery, everything but flying. By December 22, Cole had concluded that no one would notice if he managed to have his own orders cut. A pursuit group was being set up in a small, hidden field outside Lubao. Cole knew about it because Jake, like many of the other pilots, was doing the ground work. Jake had comforted himself by managing to get assigned to Lubao to build the airstrip. The fact that it was Maria's hometown helped him forget to mourn his loss of flight time.

On December 23, Cole shook hands with Dick, who was the only other one to know of his "assignment," and commandeered a jeep ride to Lubao, north of Manila Bay. Had his driver not known where he was going, Cole would never have found it on his own. It was a shining example of the kind of fields that should have been constructed before the war, instead of in a flurry of almost inhuman activity after the Japanese had already struck and were on their way to complete invasion.

The runway was cut out of a plantation of sugar cane. Half

of it was covered with windrows of dead canes to look from the air as if the field were being harvested. When the planes took off, they scattered these windrows and the Filipinos quickly rushed out and swept them back into place.

The other half of the strip was left bare, as if it were a new planting. Parking strips ran at right angles from the runway into the sandbagged revetments dug deep into the ground. Each revetment was covered with chicken wire held up with bamboo poles. Short sections of notched cane were carefully fitted into the chicken wire to match the height of the surrounding living growth of cane. These had to be changed every two or three days to appear fresh. In front of each revetment bamboo cups were placed in the soil two feet apart to hold full-length canes. The result was that even a low-flying pilot couldn't see the field. Cole was even more amazed to find that it took only a moment for the wall of cane to be removed and the planes to run out onto the field. It was a delightful testimony to combined Filipino and American ingenuity.

On December 24, Christmas Eve Day, Cole wanted to take up a plane with two wing men and challenge some of the Zeros that would be covering the milk-run bombing the Japanese put in over Manila daily around noon. He'd asked for volunteers and the whole squadron had come forward. They'd cast lots and two of the best were chosen, Tex and Arnie. There was no time for a practice run. Cole spent the night before briefing them on his plans. The rest of the pilots had listened in approvingly. Although they agreed that it was dangerous, they believed Cole's theories would hold up in combat.

The trio left amid cheers of encouragement. They pulled their sticks and climbed into the clear blue sky. They would have to go to fifteen thousand feet and they didn't have any oxygen. Cole hoped the Japanese were on schedule. They didn't want to hold that altitude for long because it could severely affect their judgment and reflexes.

As usual, the Japs were on schedule. Cole hadn't quite reached altitude when Tex signaled. Below them was a precise formation of fifteen Japanese bombers droning toward Manila. They were flanked by about twenty-five Zeros, their silver bodies flashing arrogant challenges in the sunlight. Cole whistled under his breath. It was suicide to take on the whole formation. But they could hit the tail end of the formation as planned and maybe bring no more than ten or so down on themselves. More than three against one. Should he risk his and the other two pilots' lives on his unproved theories? He glanced to his left. Tex waggled his wings, indicating his itch to get some victories under his belt. On his right, cocky little Arnie waved eagerly.

"Smash the tail first, then take out the stinger," Cole said, breaking radio silence with their prearranged signal. He nosed his plane into a dive.

Part of Cole's theory depended on all three planes working in close partnership, almost as one plane, for mutual protection. He was pleased to see that they were diving as planned, their wing tips making a precise V with each other. He put the last bomber in his sights and squeezed the trigger as he commanded the others, "Now!" Tex and Arnie filled the air with their tracers almost simultaneously with Cole's. The bomber's engine caught fire and exploded.

His headphones were filled with Tex's yelp of victory. They didn't have time for anything else. The Zeros had spotted them and nine peeled off formation. Three to one. The P-40s held their dive, using their heavier weight and gravity to build up speed.

Not until five hundred feet did the P-40s begin leveling off. Looking back, they could see the Zeros do a wing over and begin following. As Cole had predicted, the P-40s were faster in a dive and at very low altitudes. However, the Japanese didn't know this, and the nine Zeros were hot on their tails, filling the air with burning tracers from above. By now they were just barely clearing the fringed treetops of a coconut plantation.

The Zeros were still going wide open behind them. They weren't going to be shaken off. Cole's engine was screaming with the strain of the wide-open throttle. He looked at his wingmen and called over the radio, "Now!"

Simultaneously, all three planes suddenly throttled back. Nine astonished enemy planes flashed over their heads while the three P-40s poured their machine guns into their tails. Before they could think of an evasive maneuver, four more Zeros flamed and crashed. Another pulled up sharply, then spiraled down, penciling a smokeline to its fiery crash. This left them with four very angry Japanese pilots and no more tricks in their bag.

"Hedgehop to Nichols," Cole ordered.

They banked and opened throttle once more, heading straight over the single antiaircraft battery to the northeast corner of Nichols Field. With luck, the crew manning it could tell the difference between American and Japanese planes.

Cole felt his P-40 shudder as the Japanese began firing again. His stick was sloppy but he could hold course. The nest of antiaircraft gunners was scrambling for their gun. They turned it behind him as he buzzed over their heads. The concussion of their firing made the plane lurch. He looked behind in time to see two Zeros disintegrate. The other two turned tail after an impotent blast from their guns.

"Check in," he said over the shouts of victory ringing in his earphones. "I've got a sloppy stick, but think I can make it. What about you two?"

"Your stabilizer looks like Swiss cheese," Arnie said. "I've got a hit in the leg, but it's just a flesh wound. We sure showed those sons of bitches!"

"You can coach me anytime, big boy," Tex chimed in. "I'd fly into hell following you."

Cole had Arnie land first because he was losing blood. Cole came in second, barely able to keep his right wing tip from catching the ground before he rolled to a tipsy stop. Tex entertained the ground crews while waiting for the other two to land by doing a double loop in the air, proclaiming their victories.

"How many victories do we claim?" Tex asked.

Cole thought for a moment. "We got five out of nine, plus that bomber. No telling who was the one responsible for each kill. Do you think they'd let us each take two?"

"Sounds pretty damn good to me," Arnie said, as a medic wrapped his leg.

"Not a bad beginning for a poor boy with shit still on his boots." Tex grinned.

"All right then. I'll report it that way at HQ," Cole said, shaking their hands. "I've got to get back there and let as many as I can know about what we found out today. When I take off next time, I hope you two are on my wings."

"You got the pull, put in for it!" Arnie commanded.

Cole climbed into a jeep. As he drove away, he saw the Filipinos raking the windrows back into line. He couldn't even find where his own plane had been pulled.

The traffic into Manila was confused and jammed. When he reached the city, the streets were so congested that he had to park the jeep on a sidewalk and walk a quarter of a mile to headquarters. In the gathering darkness, troops, trucks, cars, bicycles, and other vehicles crammed every street. It was confused, slow-moving panic.

"What's happening?" Cole asked Jake as he ran into him on the steps of headquarters.

"We're evacuating to Bataan Peninsula. The Japs are closing in. I've got to warn Rodrigues and Maria. They'll be safer in the hills. We've talked about it before and already decided where they'll go."

"There's a jeep I left on the sidewalk just off Orani Street." He handed Jake the keys. "Make it fast. You might get caught and you can't speak Japanese."

"There's only one road to Bataan and it goes over Calumpit Bridge. I intend to be across it before the engineers blow it up. See you there."

Cole watched his friend disappear in the crowd. How long would that be? he wondered with a sense of foreboding.

Dick greeted him as he came into the office. "Gather your stuff up. I got your clothes and kit from the house . . . and your letters. We've got half an hour to get down to the dock. MacArthur's setting up HQ in Malinta Tunnel on Corregidor. Take only the important stuff. We'll burn the rest."

Twenty minutes later, still wondering what his assignment was and why he wasn't going to Bataan, Cole was stuffing reports, maps, and huge amounts of paperwork into an incinerator at the back of the building. When Dick called to him, he raced out to the waiting jeep.

The trip to the dock, perched on top of papers and commandeered supplies, took them past frightened, running Filipinos, shouting soldiers, burning supply depots, and on to the confusion of a hundred milling people loading a small ship. In the light from the burning buildings and supplies, Cole read the name of the small interisland steamer: *Don Esteban*. Finally, they all filed on board. The slim woman with the small child was Mrs. MacArthur and her son, Arthur. The last on board was General MacArthur himself.

Then a convoy of heavily guarded trucks appeared on the pier, halting their departure. Heavy crates were soon loaded onto the ship. "What's all that?" Cole murmured to Dick.

"Considering that the Japanese will probably have Manila under their thumb tomorrow morning, and considering the fact that President Quezon is on board, I would guess that's the treasury of the Philippines. Probably full of gold and silver."

Cole whistled softly.

At last they cast off, leaving the chaos of Manila behind them. The moon was bright, shimmering on the water in the tropical night. Manila lay behind them, dark and brooding except for the fires. The normally fragrant night air was filled with the acrid scent of cordite and burning petroleum. Cole leaned on the rail. Some Christmas Eve. Across the port bow, the naval oil reserves in Cavite were blazing, fired by the Americans to keep the Japanese from using American resources against them. Blacked-out Corregidor Island lay ahead of them, the bone in the throat of Manila Bay, an invisible dark presence.

It was three days later, after the Japanese had taken Manila and discovered that their prize, MacArthur, had escaped to Corregidor, after they had sent eighteen white, twin-engined Mitsubishis over to Corregidor for a vindictive three-hour-and-forty-seven-minute bombing raid, after the Calumpit Bridge had been blown up by the American engineers, after all that, that Cole and Dick managed to get radio contact with the air force camp on Bataan and find out that Jake had not made it.

CHAPTER IX

Iris pulled the blanket more tightly around her shoulders. The gray light of late morning dimly lit the room, creeping over the *tatami* floors and up the thin white walls. Outside the window, a pine bough drooped mournfully under the weight of cold raindrops. The silence of the empty house seemed to make the winter air more chill, the faint traffic sounds from behind the garden wall more haunting.

December 13. It had been five days since they'd heard the devastating news of Pearl Harbor, four days since the note from Inga. And still, everything Eva learned from the foreign broadcasts at the listening station indicated that the Americans were staggering under the blows. The Japanese were not claiming false victories.

Iris and Eva knew that they must pull out of their shock and concentrate their energy on survival. Eva's small salary wouldn't be enough; Iris must find work. But Inga hadn't written further instructions, so she didn't dare leave the house, didn't dare speak her heavily accented Japanese outside. She got up and restlessly paced into the other room, moving to keep warm. How long could she go on waiting?

Kiyoko had faithfully come to give her language lessons each afternoon. That was probably the only thing that kept Iris sane between the time Eva left each morning for work and returned in the evening with the few parcels of food she'd been able to buy for their evening meal.

To save food and money, Iris made only a pot of tea for lunch, carefully burning only three pieces of charcoal the way Kiyoko had taught her. It was still a few minutes before noon, so she forced herself to go slowly as she placed the charcoal in the *konro*. It began burning on the second match. Rubbing her hands together for warmth, she watched the coals begin to glow. The three lead balls in the bottom of the teakettle gave a tentative pop as the temperature rose, then were silent. Iris hovered over the brazier, mindful not to breathe the charcoal fumes but desperate for the small warmth it provided.

She went into the bedroom and put the blanket back around her shoulders, then returned to the kitchen to sit in front of the *konro*, trying to hold the weak heat in the folds of the blanket.

Everything had collapsed. Everything they'd ever depended on had been either destroyed or ripped from their grasp.

Why, Cole, she thought, *why was I such a fool? Why did I run away? I'd rather be dead in Hawaii from Japanese bombs than alive here without you. I should have trusted our love to see us through. I should have had more faith in you than that. Now I don't even know if you're dead or alive. If I believed you were dead, I couldn't go on.* She tried to chase the thoughts from her mind. It was enough that her nights were tortured by fear; she couldn't let it creep into her days as well.

Watching the rain drip down the windows, she knew she didn't believe Cole was dead. She knew he was alive and was just as determined to reach her as she was to reach him. He was out there fighting . . . fighting for her. Maybe believing it was just her way of surviving, but she didn't think so. The bond they had couldn't be broken by time or distance.

The garden bell tinkled faintly behind the house, interrupting her reverie. Kiyoko was coming down the path, the rain dripping from her black umbrella in steady rivulets. She wore a dark bulky coat over heavy loose pants and clopping wooden *geta* with their unique heel and toe platforms to keep her feet well above the water. It was an infinitely practical outfit, but it made Kiyoko look like some rounded little creature from a fantasy world, bearing mystical secrets. Iris smiled as she watched Kiyoko's cheery, splashing approach up the winding rock path.

"*Konnichi wa, Kiyoko-san,*" Iris said, opening the door.

"*Ah, Iris-san, konnichi wa,*" Kiyoko replied, bowing politely.

"*Go-kigen yo?*" Iris said, suddenly remembering her bow as she asked Kiyoko how she was.

"Cold and wet, like all the rest," Kiyoko said, breaking off the formalized greeting and speaking English. "Okay, I leave *kasa* here?" she asked, placing her umbrella near the smooth rock platform where she was leaving her *geta*.

"Of course. Come in. I've just started the tea."

"Oh, you cold," she said, noting Iris's blanket around her shoulders. "You need me make *kotatsu* burn?" she asked, referring to the large charcoal heater in the center of the main room. "Rain begins to be snow. Look at window."

Iris glanced out the window. The ground would be covered by evening. "No, thank you, Kiyoko. We must save the charcoal. We have so little money since I don't have a job."

"Ah," Kiyoko nodded, "maybe this help." She reached into the depths of her coat and pulled out a white envelope. "Come from Swedish man today."

"From Inga . . . Thank you, Kiyoko. *Arigato gozaimasu*."

"You read now," Kiyoko said. As Iris began reading silently, she added petulantly, "I listen, if you want."

Aloud, Iris read:

Dear Iris,
    This will not be of much help to you, I'm afraid. The Swedish Embassy is going to try to act as a liaison for the foreign nationals caught by the war in Japan. For that reason, they cannot jeopardize their neutral position by continuing your employment. They assure me that they will try to help you if you get in serious trouble. However, for now, they advise you to try to get a job and blend in with the rest of the country. That is the advantage of your race. Your citizenship is your disadvantage. Try to hide it when possible.
    I will not be staying here, even though the embassy is not cutting back their staff. My family back in Sweden require my immediate departure. I wish you Godspeed and safety in returning to your home.
    If you need help, talk to Mr. Kinnmark at the embassy. I've told him of you. Burn this letter for your own safety.

                With best regards,
                Inga

Iris was silent after reading the letter.

"Maybe best you be Nippon now," Kiyoko volunteered.

Iris began making their tea. "That's the problem, Kiyoko,"

she said finally, deciding to put her trust in this woman who seemed to be a gift dropped in her lap. "I refused to give up my American citizenship when the *Kampetei* asked me to register my name in the family registry."

"Ah," Kiyoko said quietly. "What they say when you say no?"

Iris shrugged. "Just that when I change my mind it will be a simple thing. However, my family was so upset with me, I knew it could be bad for them. That's when I talked to Eva and we got this place. I didn't want to bring any harm to them or the children. . . ." Her voice trailed off as she realized the full implications of her past decisions, how right they had been, how real the danger actually had been, and still was.

"Kampetei no talk you more?"

"No."

They sipped their tea. Only the soft whisper of the wet snow against the window broke the silence.

"You no want to be Nippon," Kiyoko said finally, "but now you must learn talk Nippon, act Nippon." She smiled proudly at her idea. "I help. You no more talk English. You talk Nippon always to me. When no understand, ask and I will find English. But always talk Nippon. You talk only Nippon with Eva also. Too cold live without heat. I talk to people for job. Soon you have to go out and be Nippon. Now, all talk Nippon," she commanded.

Iris nodded, seeing the wisdom in her words. Kiyoko immediately switched to Japanese, speaking slowly and simply so Iris could understand.

"Your first test in getting along outside will be in three days," she said in Japanese. "There is going to be a *tonarigumi* meeting in the evening. Everyone must go. You will go, listen, and learn. Let Eva do any talking that is necessary."

"What's that, *tonarigumi*?"

"The neighborhood association," she said in English, then reverted to Japanese. "Every few houses, maybe ten or fifteen, form the *tonarigumi*. They elect a *kumicho*, the head of the group. It is through these small groups that everyone receives their instructions from the government. We get our ration cards, our instructions for drills during war time, those kinds of things. It is a very good thing. You will find that we work together and help one another and are stronger as a unit than as a single thing, like many threads together make a strong rope, but alone will break when pulled."

"What I do?"

"You listen, learn from watching, keep quiet as possible. That will not be hard because a good Japanese woman is expected to be quiet. The meetings are held in different houses each time. For each meeting the host provides tea and a small treat for his neighbors. Your turn will not come for several weeks. Perhaps you will have a job by then," she added, seeing Iris's distress at the possibility of having to entertain the whole neighborhood.

"The meeting is at seven o'clock. I will come and get you and we will go together. Now," she said, putting down her cup, "you must also begin learning more of the Japanese customs. We have something to say for all situations. That way there is no offense given by accident, and everyone knows who they are and what they must do. We are comfortable with our lives ordered by custom." She paused, and Iris nodded her understanding.

"First, that means yes in your country," she said, referring to Iris's nod. "In our country it means no. To indicate yes, most often you must say *hai*. If you nod, it is the other way, from side to side."

Iris started to nod again, then caught herself and said, "*Hai*."

"Good. Now, I tell you the tea was very good. You say it is not so good, you are so sorry you couldn't have given me better."

"That's silly. It's the only thing I could have given you," she blurted out in English.

"That may be, but it is the custom that we say these things. That way both people feel that they have the most face, the most respect."

"I understand. Then what?"

"You go with me to the door and thank me for coming and bow to me. I will bow back and say it was an honor for you to have me. Then you say the honor is yours, bow, and bid me a good day. I will bow and bid you a good day and turn to leave. You wait in the doorway until I have gone down path. If I am a very honored guest, you must walk all the way through your gate with me."

"I understand."

"Another thing. About the bows. You and I are friends. We are equal, *neh?*"

"*Hai, Kiyoko-san.*"

"Then when we bow, it is just the same. But when you bow to someone who is not your equal, you don't go as low as they do. When you bow to your superior, you bow lower."

"Like when I greeted Grandmother, Uncle taught me to kneel down on the pillow and touch my head to the floor?"

"Yes, or to a high official. Most especially when the Emperor drives by or any of the royal family. You must never look up, but keep your head to the ground until he is past."

"I don't know how I can remember all these things."

"You must. You must look and act Japanese at all times. You must not attract attention when you are outside. Your language is accented, but if you act Japanese, people might assume you are from a province or were raised in one of our posts in China or another country."

"I will try very hard," she promised.

Kiyoko got up from the mat. The charcoal in the *konro* was burnt down and the ashes were cold. "Your tea was very good."

"Oh, thank you. I mean, it was not so good. So sorry I could not give you better."

"Just the same it was very good."

Iris followed Kiyoko to the door and remembered to bow and say, "Thank you for coming. It is an honor to have you in my house."

Kiyoko smiled approvingly. "It was an honor for you to have me," she said, bowing back equally.

"Oh no, the honor was mine." She bowed again.

"Thank you, just the same," Kiyoko said, returning the bow.

"I think this is so silly between friends," Iris confided as Kiyoko turned to go down the walk.

"Even so," Kiyoko said firmly, "it is the custom of the country in which you must live."

"I am grateful I have you to help me." For the first time, Iris bowed and really meant it.

That evening Eva's face was long as she came in the door. She went straight to the kitchen with her small bag of food.

"What's the bad news today?" Iris asked, starting the *kotatsu* so they could warm themselves and cook the meal at the

128

same time. "We might as well see who can come up with the worst."

"Guam fell to the Japanese. And the Philippines doesn't look too strong. The American reports are all vague, full of promise but no statistics, no numbers killed, just points where the Japanese are landing."

Iris sat on the floor, unable to speak, her heart beating in slow, heavy thuds. Cole was in the Philippines.

"I know what you're thinking," Eva said quietly, sitting down beside her. "But apparently it's true. I've been listening to the American radio stations coming in from stateside all day."

Iris nodded numbly. Eva got up and emptied the grocery bag: a tiny red fish, some green beans, a small onion, and one potato were the contents. "I'm sorry, but that's all I had money for. I thought we could make a kind of fish soup. There's some of that bread left in the cupboard; it's hard and we could soften it by dipping it in the broth."

Iris smiled and put her arm around Eva's shoulder. "It ought to be pretty good. Shall I put a pot of water over the coals?"

"Yeah. And tell me your bad news. We might as well get it all out at once."

Iris put on the teakettle as she briefly told of Inga's letter and ended with Kiyoko's instructions. "She even said that we should always speak Japanese when we're alone together. It makes a lot of sense, but it sure does limit what I can say. What do you think?"

"It's a good idea, but I'd hate to have all our conversations limited to what was in your vocabulary. Let's say all the time we're around the *kotatsu*, eating and keeping warm, which is really a pretty long time each night, we speak Japanese. But you can ask in English how to say words you haven't learned yet."

Surprisingly, Iris was able to carry on a fairly extended conversation in Japanese. Eva corrected her pronunciation a few times and added a few words to her vocabulary, but the rest was all on her own ability. Kiyoko was right: she was gaining the confidence she would need to go out into the streets and speak Japanese. What had been a convenience to know before was now imperative. She learned quickly under pressure.

Three days later, on Monday evening, Kiyoko came by after dinner, carrying a *chochin*, a lantern made of a candle inside a white paper globe hanging from a short stick. With the *chochin* lighting their way, they went to the neighbor's house for the *tonarigumi* meeting. It was only about a block, but to Iris's beating heart it was the last mile. She knew it was important to get along with her neighbors. It was necessary to work together in this society. But as she silently followed Kiyoko through the swirling snow, she wondered how they would treat a foreigner. Would they be suspicious, reporting to the Kampetei her every move as if it were subterfuge? Eva must have sensed her fears, for she reached over and squeezed Iris's hand as they approached the house. She would have to rely on Eva and Kiyoko to cover her poor Japanese, her "foreignness."

Three other people were filing into the small wooden house on the corner, bowing as they entered. Warm yellow light streamed across the snow from the open doorway as they went up the path. Leaving their shoes in the tiny stone entryway, they bowed to their hostess, repeating the formalized greetings as they filed into the crowded main room with their neighbors. They were the last to arrive and took a place along the far wall, shadowed from the lantern light.

The windows were covered with blackout curtains as required since December 8. There was a small lantern in the center of the room, its faint yellow light casting most of the faces into shadows along the wall. Iris began worrying that she would never be able to recognize her neighbors on the street in the daytime, but then she realized that they would never recognize her either, at least for a while. That would give her time to work on her Japanese. With that thought, she was able to relax somewhat and concentrate on what they were saying. Mr. Ikuzu was the head of the neighborhood association, the *kumicho*. He would be the one to receive the government directives and pass them on to his neighbors. He had already been given several important matters to discuss.

Each house was to keep a bucket of water and a huge flyswatter type of apparatus by the door for fire fighting. They would have a fire-brigade practice the following afternoon for the whole neighborhood. It was forbidden for anyone to wear white or light-colored clothing, because it would be too visible from the air. Each backyard was to have a bomb shelter.

In areas where there was no room to dig a shelter in individual yards, there was to be a large one for the whole neighborhood. A survey was taken within the group. Each household had room for a six-foot-square bomb shelter in their garden. They were to have their shelters dug by the following week, at which time there would be an inspection. They were to keep emergency food rations and bottled water in the bomb shelter.

Iris listened to the list of instructions with a sinking heart. Clearly, the government was preparing for an attack by the Americans. Shocked at the immensity of the situation, she sat silently, forcing her mind to concentrate on the words, trying to decipher the meanings from the quietly spoken questions and directions.

"The ration lines are too long for each household to stand waiting," said an older man. "Because of them, some families go without food. Perhaps we should take turns waiting in the lines."

There was a consensus that this was a good idea. "Is there anyone who will take the morning lines?" asked Mr. Ikuzu. "The men work, and most of the women have children and elders to care for. Perhaps there is someone who is not employed during those hours."

Iris tensed. She knew it was logical that she be the one to volunteer. They must know that she didn't work.

"I am not working in the mornings now. I will stand in the lines until I begin working again," she said, choosing her words carefully and speaking slowly.

"Ah, Miss Hashimoto, that will be most convenient." She was surprised that he knew her name. "If each house will bring their ration booklet and their order each morning to your home, will that be convenient?"

"*Hai*," she said, with a slight bow of respect. "I will leave by the eighth hour for the lines."

"So," said Mr. Ikuzu, "if we have no further business, my wife would like you to honor us by sharing some tea and shaped sweetcakes."

She must have been working all afternoon making them, Iris thought, not to mention the many stops and lines she must have braved just to find the precious sugar. Everyone complimented her work. Iris savored each tender bite of the moist cake. It had no real flavor other than the sweetness and a faintly musty taste, yet it was a great treat because sugar was so rare, having long been rationed because of the war with China.

As they left the meeting, the family groups slowly walking in separate directions, their *chochins* now properly shuttered with black paper provided by Mr. Ikuzu, Kiyoko spoke quietly so as not to be overheard. "You were very wise to volunteer to help. Your language was simple, well phrased, and didn't sound too accented. I'm proud of you. When your neighbors entrust their precious ration cards to you and you faithfully carry out your duties, you will have built up a feeling of trust and belonging. That is very good."

"Thank you, Kiyoko-san," Iris said, bowing her farewell at the gate. "You have given me much. I only hope that someday I may serve you as faithfully."

"Ah, you are becoming more and more Japanese every day," she said, bowing. Then to Eva: "We have a good pupil. Keep her faithful to our teaching. Good night." She bowed and walked the long way down the street, choosing not to reveal to any observing eyes the private passage between Iris and Eva's little house and the Big House. Iris and Eva stood watching the swirling snow for a moment, then went inside and closed the heavy wooden *amado*, the night door with which they locked out the world.

Iris's standing in long lines for the rationed food items underlined their own severe situation. Each week they had to turn to their meager savings, taking out a small amount in order to eat until Eva's next paycheck. They would soon have no money to buy a return ticket even if one was available. Iris was desperate for a job. They'd both lost weight and looked gaunt and emaciated.

Iris's afternoons were spent digging a deep shelter in the space where they had grown their summer vegetables. In the bitter cold afternoons, she forced her sore muscles to push the shovel ever deeper into the rocky, icy soil. Her hands were covered with blisters; she wrapped them in rags and continued digging. Frequently she was so weak that she almost fainted. If she were going to work physically, she needed to eat a noon meal, but they couldn't afford it.

The only good that came from the long, aching waits in the ration lines was that Iris's Japanese improved. She listened to conversations, pretending not to overhear, and learned new words, phrases, and slang expressions, which made her Japanese more authentic. The long waits also meant that she no longer had to pace alone in the empty house, waiting for Eva to return. It gave her something to do. It kept her sane.

Christmas wasn't celebrated in Japan. However, Iris and Eva were very much aware of its fast approach and had promised to save what precious food they could for a small Christmas dinner. However, Kiyoko inadvertently provided a real gift for them both when she visited Iris on the morning of Christmas Eve.

"Do you know how to make the typewriter machine work and how to order papers in cabinets?" she asked Iris over their customary cup of tea.

"File?" Iris asked, using the English word. "Yes, I did that in my jobs."

"Very good. I have heard of a job that is for you. Here is the address." She reached into her pocket and pulled out a paper. "A man at the Big House said they want someone who speaks very good English, who makes the typewriter work, and makes what you call 'file.' I told them you would come down this afternoon. They will ask for a recommendation from the Swedish Embassy."

"Oh, Kiyoko, what should I say? What should I wear? Do you think my Japanese is good enough? Will they ask about my citizenship?"

"They have great trouble finding someone with good English. I think they will be happy to find you. It is in the radio station, NHK. Wear what you have on, it is simple and dark, like a good Japanese," she said. Over her American slacks Iris wore *monpe,* the bulky, coarse overpants that tied around the waist and had drawstrings around the ankles. It was capacious enough to hold whatever she wore underneath in its full legs, keeping her warm and making her look like all other Japanese women. It was considered patriotic to wear them; in fact, it was an implied order.

She would never have had the nerve to go through with the job interview had she had time to change clothes or to think about what she was doing. Still, her heart was racing by the time she got to the NHK Building in downtown Tokyo, at Uchi-sai-wai-cho. The office manager asked if she could type, file, and correct the English on scripts for radio broadcasts so that it would sound proper to an American ear. The job was initially for half a day, but she would have to work longer hours if requested. The interview was most notable for what he didn't ask. They were eager for a qualified person. He didn't ask for Iris's citizenship papers.

At dinner that evening, Iris presented her Christmas present to Eva: her job as a typist, file clerk, and editor for the Japanese radio station NHK. They celebrated, and went to sleep for the first time without worrying if they would be able to keep from starving before the Americans invaded Japan.

Iris felt that she was closely watched on her first day at the job, but she was too pleased to be working to let that bother her. Her behavior was without reproach. She began to feel confident for the first time since she had left Hawaii. All she had to do was tread softly until the Americans landed. It couldn't be much longer.

It was late by the time she got home. She'd stopped at the market and splurged on two eggs and a loaf of bread for their Christmas dinner. She was surprised to see the house still dark as she hurried up the path. The thin layer of snow had begun melting during the day but now it crunched under her feet. Why wasn't Eva home? she wondered as she took off her boots and went in.

The house was silent and dark. She went into the kitchen area, set down her package, then turned to light the lantern and the *kotatsu*. She was stopped by a shadowed movement in the corner.

"Eva? Is that you?" she said softly, cautiously.

"Yes."

"What are you doing? What's the matter?" In the early moonlight, Iris could see Eva's expressionless face washed with quiet tears.

Eva shook her head slowly. "I just can't take anymore. It's too much," she said flatly. "We're going to have to stay here forever. I'd rather die."

"Eva, for the first time we have hope. I have a job now; we'll start eating better and your spirits will pick up. Come on, I've got a surprise for Christmas dinner," she added, gently tugging at Eva's arms. She stopped when Eva withdrew even more into her corner and fresh tears spilled down her cheeks. "Eva, has something happened? It's not like you to do this."

"It's the news," she whispered. "I can't stand it anymore.

134

Every day I have to translate more and more defeats for the Americans; each time, I feel as if the words are ripping my heart out, but each time, everyone I work with cheers and sings patriotic songs. They celebrate what I mourn."

"Eva, I know it's hard. We can do it. The Americans are going to win."

"No, they aren't," Eva said dully, turning her tearstained face to Iris for the first time. Her soft round features were twisted with bitter anger and fear. "It was confirmed today. Wake Island is Japanese. It was taken two days ago. Today Hong Kong fell to the Japanese troops. The British conceded defeat." She listed the other Allied defeats mechanically as the tears continued flowing down her cheeks. "Look at the map. It's almost all Japanese now. The Philippines aren't going to hold up. MacArthur declared Manila an open city, which is supposed to make it neutral, but the Japanese are bombing it anyway. The Japanese have control of the rest of Luzon, the main island. They're landing pretty much unopposed all over the Philippines. There's no one who can stop them. The Americans have retreated to a peninsula called Bataan."

"It sounds like a trap—they'll be trapped on a tiny bit of land, surrounded by the Japanese . . ." Iris said, suddenly sitting down beside Eva, stunned. "Cole . . . I wonder . . . what if . . ." Silent tears bathed her cheeks.

"They say on station KGBM out of Honolulu that they'll hold out on Bataan until the Americans bring a convoy of reinforcements," Eva continued listlessly. "But there's not much area on the Pacific map that isn't held by the Japanese. I don't see how a convoy can get there to rescue them . . . not if the Japanese are as strong as their victories indicate." She reached over and took Iris's hand.

"They must have a plan in Washington," Iris insisted. "They wouldn't just let a whole army of Americans slowly die in a death trap. . . . They won't leave Americans to be starved and captured by the enemy without rescuing them. There's got to be a plan," she said, echoing the reasoning of a hundred thousand troops digging in on the jungled peninsula of Bataan. "We'll just have to wait," she whispered.

They were quiet then, lonely in their silence and fears. The two young friends sat huddled in the dark, long into the cold Christmas night, afraid to turn on the light, afraid to eat, afraid of each other's eyes and what they would discover if they should look there.

CHAPTER X

Now there were two: two whose faces haunted his dreams, whose imagined voices startled him into painful remembrances of laughter and love. Jake and Iris: were they dead? Or, worse, were they alive and suffering the nameless Oriental tortures already being whispered about in terrified gossip from front-line encounters? It was 9:30 A.M. and the Philippine sun was already like a heated blanket on Cole's bare back as he and Dick sauntered toward a grove of trees for a cigarette break. Still, Cole shivered, chilled by the horror of his recurring thoughts.

Dick seemed not to notice. "You know," he said with a tight grin, "it's quite a view. Too bad we can't enjoy it."

Cole lit a cigarette and sat down on a rock. Beyond the protective clump of trees on Corregidor, Manila Bay gleamed like crystal and sapphires in the morning sun. The emerald green of Bataan Peninsula lay beyond. Rising above the coastline were the Mariveles Mountains, their graceful silhouette forming what the natives said was the outline of a reclining woman. But, beneath the serene facade it was festering with war, blemished by the deadly white puffs of artillery fire floating above the land and the muffled whomps that followed. The "view" was of death, slowly reaching over Bataan and across to Corregidor.

"Listen," Dick said, holding his cigarette in mid-air. Cole froze with his head half-tilted to pick up any sound. The low drone of an airplane slowly grew in volume, like a determined, prowling wasp. In the past two months their ears had become finely tuned to the sounds of airplane engines. All too infrequently, the steady buzz of the P-40s' in-line Alison engines meant some vengeance was being carried out in their behalf, and each American within hearing cheered it onward. More often, the irregular rachet sound of the Japanese Zero brought death.

"It must be 'Photo Charley,'" Cole murmured as the altitude and patter of the single-engine plane became apparent. "We'd best go back in."

Every morning an enemy photo-reconnaissance plane flew over the Philippines, taking pictures so the Japanese could assess the accuracy of their early-morning shelling. Every afternoon and evening, their guns adjusted accordingly, the Japanese renewed the shelling and bombing with deadly precision. Every night the Americans would repair, move, and replace, and the whole procedure would start all over again the next morning.

Reluctantly, Dick and Cole returned to their work in the stale air of the tunnel. Photo Charley would have to get their picture another day. They spent most of their time in Lateral No. 3, MacArthur's command headquarters thrust deeply into the heart of Corregidor Island. After two and a half weeks of living like moles in the laterals of Malinta Tunnel, Cole and Dick had decided they couldn't stand it any longer. In defiance of regulations, they slipped out each night to sleep under a tarp they kept hidden in the grove where they had just been smoking. They wanted to feel free as long as possible. There was an unspoken fear between them that the time might soon come when they would be irretrievably locked behind Japanese prison walls. They were stuck on an island, encircled by the enemy; for now, at least, they still could have the fresh air and stars at night.

Corregidor was about the size of Manhattan. When they had first arrived it was like a tropical garden, with monkeys, brightly colored birds, and small deer playing in the jungles. Fort Mills had sat in neat military dignity on the highest point of land. But now the monkeys and deer were almost all gone, consumed by half-starved troops. The graceful terrace of the jungled hills had been bombed and strafed by Japanese planes and artillery. The ordered parade ground and white buildings of Fort Mills were twisted and blackened. The chatter of birds was silenced by death.

It was at lunchtime, when Cole and Dick had taken their canned peaches and thin gravy over hard biscuits back to their grove, that the sirens began. Cole looked longingly at his plate, having had only two hardtack crackers for breakfast. "There's a foxhole just beyond the trees," he said, as the sirens persisted. "I suppose we can just as well polish this off there."

They ran to the foxhole, clambered in, hunched down below the sandbags, and began shoveling food into their mouths as the roar of the bombers grew closer. Heavy explosions reverberated throughout Corregidor, The Rock. The bass voice of American guns responded.

Finally, the bombing stopped as the Betties flew beyond their target. Cole set down his emptied mess kit, waiting for the inevitable. It came. The high-pitched scream of fighter planes coming in low on a strafing run. This time, they came right for the tunnel entrance, for the trees, for Cole. Dirt and rocks exploded all around him. Someone was screaming. He huddled helplessly in the hole. Pieces of metal and limbs of trees whistled above. Dust and smoke clouded the air. Cole looked up and counted fifteen Zeros, barely clearing the treetops, filling their world with fiery death. The circle on their white wings was obscenely red. Cole trembled with impotent anger.

They banked and came back, again and again, firing their destruction. With each blast, with each cry of death, the walls of the foxhole closed in on Cole. It was slowly growing tighter, smaller, covering him, cutting off all air. He choked back the screams, feeling each dust-filled breath scrape his raw throat. It was thirty minutes, a lifetime, before the bombing stopped.

Cole stood staring at his mess kit, shaking, unable to comprehend. The metal plate was bent in half. He knew he must have done it in his claustrophobic fear, but he didn't remember how, and somehow that seemed important now.

Dick was shaking. "We've got to get some planes in the air," he finally murmured through clenched teeth.

"There aren't any," Cole said hoarsely. All that remained of the Fil-American Air Corps on both Bataan and Corregidor was a handful of dilapidated fighter planes, each one on its last leg, held together with hope and grim determination.

It was a sultry January day following the attack, when a

radiogram arrived from Chief of Staff George C. Marshall, in Washington, D.C. From the crumbs of hope offered in that transmission, the whole staff built a feast of promises as it passed from hand to eager hand. In it Marshall assured General MacArthur that

> . . . A stream of four-engine bombers, previously delayed by foul weather, is en route. . . . Another stream of similar bombers started today from Hawaii staging at new island fields. Two groups of powerful medium bombers of long range and heavy bomb-load capacity leave next week. Pursuit planes are coming on every ship we can use. Our definitely allocated air reinforcements together with the British should give us an early superiority in the Southwest Pacific.

Strangely, no one questioned the exact destination of these lifesaving planes. No one wondered where they could land on the beleaguered and encircled Philippines. No one checked the maps for any possible islands not now held by the triumphant Japanese, where new fields possibly could have been built. No one considered exactly what was included in "Southwest Pacific."

Cole was in the radio room when MacArthur's message to the men on Bataan was sent. It was stirring to hear the reassurances of their leader broadcast all over the islands. He memorized the text so he could repeat it to Dick that evening:

> Help is on the way from the United States. Thousands of troops, hundreds of planes are being dispatched. The exact time of arrival of reinforcements is unknown, as they will have to fight their way through Japanese. . . . It is imperative that our troops hold until these reinforcements arrive.

A month later, they had heard no further mention of reinforcements. The daily messages contained no progress reports of the convoy. Privately, Dick and Cole dubbed the promised reinforcements the "Phantom Convoy." The name stuck, but their laughter sounded hollow.

One morning they were called into HQ in Lateral No. 3. MacArthur wanted a firsthand report of the morale and general condition of the troops on Bataan. He also wanted his personal encouragement and commendations carried to the trenches. The orders were passed on to Dick and Cole. They were to leave that night by torpedo boat for Bataan, accompanied by General Carlos Romulo, Philippine President Quezon's personal representative.

No matter how bad The Rock was, it was still more of a refuge than besieged Bataan, just two miles across the water from Corregidor. Cole and Dick knew that it was a dangerous trip, one that would expose them to the worst of battles several times over as they sought out the individual battalions and pockets of troops. Still, they accepted the assignment with surprising stoicism. Cole figured it was because they had lost so much and were resigned to eventual capture anyway.

The PT boat was a shadowed presence grumbling noisily beside the bomb-damaged dock. They hurried down and were informed that they would be met at the Bataan dock by an army vehicle for the general and an air corps vehicle for Dick and Cole because the two branches had their headquarters in different areas. If the dock was not clear of enemy activity, the commander of the boat had orders to take what evasive action he deemed necessary. While they were on the boat they were under his orders. Hopefully, his information on the mine fields was current. They were to report back to the Bataan dock at 2000 hours three days hence. If the dock was free of enemy activity, the boat would be waiting for them. If not, they must wait under cover until the area was cleared.

They acknowledged the instructions, saluted the general, and followed him on board.

The boat eased away from the dock and inched its way through the mine fields. Cole leaned on the rail and looked across the shimmering water toward the black bulk of Bataan. Flashes of gunfire and mortars lit the night like irritable fireflies. The noise gradually grew louder and could be heard over the sound of the PT's engines, like a whispered threat.

Presently, the mine fields cleared, the captain opened the throttle and the engines roared, the hull of the boat slapping on the waves with bone-jarring regularity.

It was absurd, Cole thought. He was barreling toward what was probably the most dangerous plot of real estate in the world, yet he was feeling no fear. Maybe he was numb, a kind of prolonged shock. He surely didn't count it as courage. He knew he would do anything to avoid death, to live to see Iris again.

That thought brought a searing pang of loneliness. Iris was so far away, so inaccessible, so vulnerable. He forced the tears so near the surface back into that hidden well deep inside him, that well he dared not drink from lest he lose all reason. *For you, Iris,* he thought, *I will go on.*

He pushed Iris from his mind, only to have Jake's face appear. *Another one lost, probably dead.* He also pushed Jake's memory deep inside him. How many others would be there before it was over?

The engine suddenly slowed. The bow scraped against the makeshift dock as they pulled alongside.

Cole and Dick were met by an air corps sergeant wearing a shabby uniform. In the pale moonlight his hair and beard looked gray, matching the weary creases around his eyes. His salute was more rude than military.

"Where we headed?" Dick asked as they climbed into the waiting jeep.

"Little Baguio," the sergeant said over his shoulder. "That's what we call air corps HQ—if you wanna call us an air corps."

The headlights wore blackout shields and Cole could barely make out the road three feet ahead, but the sergeant floorboarded the jeep. He not only seemed to know where he was going, he seemed to be taking a perverse joy in snapping their vertebrae like castanets on the rugged track he called a road. Obviously, men from Corregidor were not held in high esteem by the men on Bataan. Cole resolved to find out why.

The jeep traveled through a corridor of jungle. The thick overgrowth blacked out the sky, giving a nightmarish sense to their journey. It was in keeping with this illusion that a gruff voice called them to a halt from a black void at the side of the road and a soldier suddenly appeared from the shadows, his rifle at the ready. "Oh, it's you, Lefty. What's the cargo?"

"Messengers from The Rock."

"Oh." He paused, as if there was much he wanted to say but didn't dare. "There've been flares tonight. Take it easy."

"Yeah." The sergeant seemed more curt and angry than before. He ground the gears as they started on their way once more.

"Tell us about the flares, Lefty," Dick said. "We've had

them going off on The Rock recently. Do you think they're signals or just something to make us jumpy?"

Lefty spat over his shoulder carelessly. Cole leaned forward, both to hear better and to avoid being hit with the spittle. "They mean something, all right. You can bet your sweet ass on that. I was coming through right about here two nights ago." He gestured at the shadowed hill on their left and the pale opening in the foliage to the right. "A goddamn yellow flare sailed up right behind me, bright as day. Damned if the artillery group in that grove of trees over there wasn't right then put under a barrage that sure as hell wasn't no accident. I hightailed it out, fast."

As they drove through the indicated grove, a shiver ran up Cole's spine, making his hair prickle on the back of his neck. Even the shadows seemed to take on life, creeping up behind them as they rode on, watching, aiming.

"Sakdalistas?" Dick asked, referring to the Nippon-sympathetic Filipinos and resident Japanese reputed to have infiltrated the area to cause insurrection to fester among the troops.

"Can't trust anyone," Lefty said sharply. "I just know those flares ain't no accident and they sure as hell ain't helping the morale of the troops. You just tell old 'Dugout Doug' about that!"

Lefty was silent from then on, as if he felt he'd said too much. The tension caused by his words pulled tight in their throats, as they anxiously watched each passing shadow, straining their eyes to pierce each dark hollow, gripping their sidearms, instinctively tensing their bodies to jump at any flash of light, any sudden sound.

The shadows seemed to still stalk them as they got out of the jeep and walked to General George's headquarters (he'd just been promoted), a small bamboo shack with a lean-to on one side, nestled into the shoulder of the dark jungle. Similar lean-tos and tents were scattered around, completing the settlement. The windows were blacked out with a heavy curtain making the interior stuffy.

The general was carving a small wooden sculpture with a discarded scalpel as they were shown into the room. He greeted them enthusiastically. Of all the people they'd met on Bataan so far, he was the only one who did not seem to resent their being representatives from Corregidor.

"Sit down, sit down," he proclaimed. "You've been busy over there," he said to Cole. "I recognize some of your handiwork in the analysis reports."

"We do our best, sir," Cole said. "I just wish we could get some planes so we could really do something."

The general shook his head. "You can't believe what some of these youngsters can do. They tell me you taught them some tricks. Some of our men are alive now because of those techniques you passed on, son. Now, why are you boys here?"

"We're here mainly to get a first-hand observation of everything," Dick said. "We're supposed to carry General MacArthur's commendations and encouragement to as many men as we can, and to report back on the conditions and everything we see."

"Well, he was here a month ago. Can't think you'll be taking reports back of any improvements since then. However, the boys could do well to hear your words of encouragement from the general. But if you're going to find all the men, you're going to have to hit the dirt. A good percent of the flyboys are now eating mud with the infantry and marines."

"We're to go to them, too," Cole said. "General Romulo came over with us and the army is taking him around for the same purpose. We're supposed to split up so we can cover as much ground as possible."

"We're on pretty skimpy rations here," the general said. "A little less than half of what you get on The Rock. Out on the lines, sometimes they don't have anything because the cooks have left or they don't have anything to fix or what they do fix can't make it through the fire. Sometimes rice is all, sometimes not even that. It's affecting their night vision. Malaria, malnutrition, beriberi, scurvy . . . it's hard on the morale and the efficiency." He shook his head.

"Nothing's as bad on the morale as those flares," Major Ind, General George's aide, commented glumly.

The general nodded. "They're devastating. And we can't fight back. A plane is wheeled out of cover, and instantly a flare goes up. Just seems that no one can trust anyone. Even the shadows seem to send secret signals to the enemy. A flare goes up, the sentry fires several rounds into the place where it came from, and there's nothing there. Gives you the creeps."

"There's got to be a way to beat them at their own game," Major Ind said, shaking his head. Suddenly he looked up.

Cole had instantly caught the same idea, as had Dick and the general. They all started to talk simultaneously. It seemed so simple, so appropriate.

They would shoot flares too! The air corps had an ample number of flares. They also had an abundance of volunteers to shoot them, although it was immensely dangerous because the sentries and everyone else fired at anything in the night that looked like an enemy signal.

Later that night, they gleefully watched the first decoy flare sail through the night sky. It went off in a swamp some four hundred yards behind HQ. Enemy artillery fire immediately "killed" a swamp. The camp cheered ecstatically. The ominous flares would soon be a harmless joke. In the meantime, they would get enemy artillery to do some troublesome excavation work for them.

It was with a certain satisfaction that Cole and Dick went to their tent. In the morning they would separate and head toward the front lines.

Morning mess consisted of two pieces of sour bread with strawberry jam and a slab of Spam. Major Ind advised them to keep one piece of bread for later because they would not have lunch on their shortened rations. They took his advice and each stashed one piece of bread. With carefully studied nonchalance, they shook hands and promised to meet in three days.

Cole was to go north along the eastern coastline. He hitched a ride with a young corporal radio technician to a trapped squadron on the coast. A single volunteer had slipped through the lines with the message that if they could fix their radio and direct the artillery, the squadron would be able to fight their way out of the trap. Later, Cole couldn't remember the name of the young corporal, but he could remember waiting behind their jeep, squinting through the sun-heated air to see if their grenade had taken out a sniper who had them pinned down. He couldn't remember the face of the grateful sergeant when they managed to reach the trapped squadron, but he could clearly picture the rotting bodies on the beach, swollen and covered with flies. Their sickeningly sweet smell still clung to his clothes as he caught a ride the following afternoon, headed for the front line and a group of grounded air corps personnel doing quite well with their rifles.

As he rode along the bumpy road toward the front, he pulled a flier from his pocket. It was a Japanese propaganda sheet one of the men had given him. On it were roughly sketched pictures of chickens, fruit, roasts, vegetables—everything starving soldiers would dream of. In the center was a caricature of a fat soldier, perched on Corregidor, devouring a drumstick and a piece of cake. Hand lettered across the top was: "Don't fight MacArthur's War."

Cole held the dirty crumpled paper out to the corporal driving the jeep. "Have you seen these things floating around?"

The corporal glanced at the paper and shrugged. "Sure. They're all over."

"How many do you think believe this crap?"

"What does it matter how many? Everyone can see which group's getting pounded. Sure, the guys know Corregidor is bombed all the time. But here we have to crawl in the mud, not hide in reinforced tunnels. We hear the Japs every minute, not just when the planes go over. We can hear him cackling and laughing at night. Hell, we can smell him fart. We get pinned down like those guys you went in to see, and we don't eat for days. Those guys you just saw hadn't had a meal in two days. After the artillery fire got them out, they practically ran over one another getting to the food. Even half rations, when they're regular, are better than that."

"I see," Cole murmured. And he did. A black chill crept over him as he realized that the hopeless holdout of the men on Bataan was only postponing a useless holdout on Corregidor. They all faced the same grim fate. He shivered in the heavy warmth of the afternoon sun.

The jungle was thick and forbidding most of the way to the front. Pockets of men were dug in on hills and behind fallen trees, grouped under thick underbrush—whatever offered protection from detection by the enemy. Cole made his way by foot the last five miles.

He took messages, made notes, and encouraged, to the best of his ability. He was hungry, grimy, hot, and exhausted by evening. He'd been told that the farthest outpost of Americans on the north Bataan line was just at the top of the next rise. He set out alone, keeping to the lengthening shadows, his gun at the ready.

It was dark by the time he worked his way up the steep terrain through the thickly growing trees and clinging tangle of vines. The shadows were purple; the late evening scent of tropical flowers mingled with the acrid smoke of spent ammunition.

From the sound of the voices, he was close to the American troops when Japanese shelling began. He dove behind a tree, ducking splinters of shrapnel and broken rocks. There was a flash of light as an American gun began answering the shelling just ahead of him. It was almost as if the Japanese had spotted him. He ran in a crouch to a protective rock, closer to the Americans. Maybe he could make it to a foxhole behind the protection of the Yank firing. Suddenly the ground around him erupted in a sudden flash, spraying him with dirt and debris. He hit the ground, covering his head and rolling back behind the rock. The American was shooting at him, too!

"Hey!" he called between rounds. "The Yankees played the Dodgers in the World Series last year."

Silence. Then a skeptical voice called, "Yeah? Who's the Dodgers' manager?"

Cole froze, trying to remember what was so long ago, so far away. Then it came to him. "Leo Durocher!" he called triumphantly.

"Make a run for it and I'll cover you!"

Cole sprinted toward the spot where the flash of a machine gun rattled the evening air, spraying the Japanese lines. In the dark, he misjudged the distance, tripped, and fell head first into the foxhole of his protector. There was just one man there, and he quickly ducked back down as soon as Cole fell in.

"What the hell you trying to do . . ." grumbled a hoarse whisper.

"Sorry. Want a cigarette?" he said, offering the rare commodity. A shell whistled overhead and Cole ducked. The explosion shook the ground but was obviously a miss. To Cole's chagrin, his companion was lighting his cigarette, not even flinching. He looked up at the dirty bearded face, shadowed by the light of the match, and his breath caught in his throat.

"Wanna light?" the lieutenant said, holding the match out to Cole. Then he saw Cole's dumbstruck face. "My God . . ."

146

"Jake," Cole whispered, "is it you?"

"My God," Jake echoed. "You made it."

"You made it," Cole said simultaneously.

They fell into each other's arms.

"Who was the Dodgers' manager, you son of a bitch . . . since when did you become such a baseball fan?"

"I figured if it sounded familiar, I'd buy it."

Cole laughed, then suddenly grew serious. "I thought you were dead or prisoner. How did you manage this?"

Jake settled back and puffed on his cigarette, ignoring another shell blast that sent Cole cringing. "Well, you were right. I got caught behind the lines. Not that I didn't have time to get out. I just couldn't leave Rodrigues and his family moving themselves to the mountains all alone. They were burying the family jewels and silver, trying to pack enough things to last them through the war. They just needed another man around. There are five daughters and one son, and the boy is only seven years old. Anyway, I got them to the mountains, and we received word that Calumpit Bridge was gone and the Japs were in Manila. Rodrigues decked me out in some Filipino clothes and we set out with a cart. Went down the far side of the peninsula. Japs hadn't gotten to that side yet. Rodrigues left me with a packet of food where we figured was behind the lines. He drew me a rough map so I could make it over the Mariveles Mountains. Let me tell you, those babies are steep and unpredictable. Took me two weeks. I finally made it to an army engineers' camp. Found it by smelling the food. I hadn't had anything to eat for three days. They looked at me like I was a ghost or something. They fed me and got me a ride to Little Baguio. I told the staff sergeant my name and he told me to hook up with this outfit, which was heading out that afternoon. Before I left, I asked him if you were around. He checked all his rolls, said he didn't see your name. Where the hell were you? I figured you dead."

"They took me and Dick along with HQ to Corregidor."

"I'll be damned," Jake murmured. "How's old Dick doing?"

"First, what about Maria?"

Jake was silent for a moment. Then, his voice softer, he said, "She'll be fine if she stays out of sight. She's too beautiful for those animals to leave alone if she doesn't. I told her to cut her hair and wear boy's clothes. She refused—said she'd be ugly to me. I made her promise to keep out of sight. Told her I'd come back and marry her."

"I guess we both have something to live through this war for," Cole said softly.

"Yeah."

They were quiet for a moment, communicating more between them in their shared silence than they ever had with words. It was Jake who broke the spell. "How's The Rock?"

Just then a ghastly laugh shrieked through the night, followed by sudden, sharp popping sounds. "What the hell is that?" Cole asked.

"Japs. They don't want us to sleep. They think if they make noises like that all night with loudspeakers, maybe they'll wear us out. I've gotten sort of used to it. They throw a lot of firecrackers too, trying to make us think there's more of them out there than there really are."

"I have a can of salmon in my pack. Conned a cook out of it just north of Little Baguio. Want to split it?"

Jake grinned and pulled out a thin packet of dry ship biscuits.

They spread Cole's salmon on Jake's biscuits and enjoyed the first meal either one of them had had since the night before. They talked and laughed, trying to ignore the persistent shelling and noise from the Japanese. Late into the night, Jake leaned back against the rough dirt of the foxhole and said seriously, "We're liable to be captured, the way things are going."

"Yeah. Or worse."

"Well, the Filipinos will fight to the last man. I'll join them in a minute if I get a chance. You're with the brass. If anyone gets out, you might go along. We should have some way to send messages to each other. You never know what might happen."

"How do you mean?"

"I've read all sorts of things from World War I. You know—buddies in adjoining cell blocks . . . or even with some kind of radio connection between resistance groups, radio messages to headquarters from behind enemy lines, that kind of stuff. I can tell you this much. I'm going to risk everything I can to avoid capture. Rodrigues is part of a guerrilla band that's organizing up there. I left all the parts I would need for building a radio buried under his hut in the mountains. If I can, I'm going back there."

"So what are you leading up to?"

"Let's just say I can get to a radio. If I could get information to you, it would have to be in code."

Jake had thought about it all the time he had carried the heavy radio equipment up that mountain. He had thought about it all the time he had hiked through the jungles alone. Part of his code idea was to use the first letter of each word in a sentence to spell out the words of the message. For example, "Monthly Orders Vary Exceedingly. Some Others Use The House," would be translated as Move South. With the use of abbreviations and words having special meaning just to them, they could make the code more difficult to break. And they could change the pattern of the key letters at a given signal, making the message form from the third letter of each word instead, so it would be more difficult to break the code. He also thought they should concentrate on using words and events they'd shared in common. Places would be given by latitude as ball scores, with longitude degrees given as errors. The name of the winning team would designate who should be landing at various points: Dodgers for Japanese, Yankees for Americans. For a final backup code, they picked four books they could refer to in numerical count for words and messages. By the time they'd worked out the details, taking care to scrawl the important points on the inside of an empty cigarette pack, it was two-thirty, time for Cole to go.

"Cole?"

"Yeah?"

"If you get back here without me, will you look after Maria?"

"You know I will. Do the same for me. If I don't make it, find Iris?"

"Goes without saying." He stood up and looked over the edge of the foxhole. "Now get out of here," he said, slapping Cole on the rear as he clambered over the edge.

"See you in Tokyo. I'll be waving an American flag," Cole said over his shoulder. Stooped over, he ran for a banana patch, his rifle in his hand. A shell burst to his left, filling the black night with white and orange light. He fell to the ground and covered his head. Pieces of rock and dirt fell around him. Behind him, he heard Jake open fire, once more distracting the enemy. He got up and ran to the scorched trees, silently blessing his friend, hoping for the chance to return the favor someday.

By midmorning Cole was walking back to Little Baguio in the festering sun. The night before seemed a dream. He reached into his pocket and pulled out the cigarette wrapper. Scrawled on the back of it in Jake's looping handwriting was the essence of their code. It had been an amusing way to pass the night.

A jeep pulled up behind him. "Need a ride, Captain?" It was the same corporal he'd ridden with the day before.

Cole climbed in beside him. He would soon be riding back through the mine fields to Corregidor. From one nightmare to another.

Dick was thrilled to hear about Jake. Unlike Cole, he didn't think of the code as a whim; he thought it had great potential for what they both considered the inevitable. If on the outside chance any of them were able to escape the POW camp or death, they would somehow be able to reach across the miles to one another . . . possibly. "Possibly" was better than "impossibly." He insisted on including the idea in their final report.

Two weeks later, when Dick came out of conference in Lateral No. 3., his face was ashen. He invited Cole out for a smoke in the trees. They walked silently to their regular spot. Only two scarred and twisted trees remained of the grove.

"What's up?" Cole asked as they sat down on the hood of a burned-out jeep.

"Can you put everything you'll ever need in your shaving kit?"

Cole's heart was suddenly thudding in his ears. "Sure. Why?"

"Don't even let your face show what I'm telling you. Others might see. It can't go any further."

Cole looked down at his feet, fearful of what he was going to hear, fearful that he couldn't control his expression.

"MacArthur's been ordered out to Australia. He's taking a handful of men with him. You and I are included. We leave tonight. The chances of getting through the Japanese blockade are fifty-fifty. Better than here."

Cole's breath caught in his throat. He watched an ant crawl over his dirty boot. Cold sweat broke out on his forehead. The unthinkable was happening.

CHAPTER XI

To survive, one must adapt. Iris was learning the lesson well. She was no longer vivacious and confident. She was quiet, alert, and cautious. As Kiyoko had taught her, she was like the reed, supple and bending in the wind while keeping her roots firmly planted in the soil of her beliefs.

Since she worked only in the afternoons, she was able to continue her neighborhood obligation of standing in the morning ration lines until she heard the call, *Haikyu ga mairimashita!* telling her the rations had arrived. Eva's hours were subject to change, but she usually had a six-hour listening shift from late morning to late afternoon, allowing her to pick up rations that came into the market later in the day. It was a convenient arrangement not only for them but for their neighbors. In return for Iris and Eva's help shopping, three of the women took turns doing their laundry. With each passing week they felt more accepted into the community.

However, Kiyoko's persistent reminders prevented them from relaxing and letting down their guard. "Remember," she would say, "the Kampetei have spies in every neighborhood. No one knows who they are. Every citizen is obliged to report anything unusual to the Kampetei, and many do, thinking they are saving their family from future danger by getting on the good side of the Kampetei. Your every move and every word must be circumspect."

By the beginning of February, Iris was weary. She was tired of it all, tired of being cautious, tried of being "Japanese," of trusting no one. *When will it ever end?* she thought, as she returned from her morning chores. Her thoughts were interrupted by Kiyoko knocking at her back door.

"You honor me, my friend," Iris said, automatically going

through the obligatory formalities. "Please come in and I will make you some tea."

"The honor is mine," Kiyoko replied, returning Iris's bow and taking off her *geta* at the door.

"I have just delivered some rice and *nori* to the Big House."

"I know. That was why I came over."

"Oh no, I did something wrong again." Iris groaned as she began to make tea.

"No," Kiyoko laughed, "it just meant that you were home early and we would have time to talk before you went to work."

Iris smiled as she lit the charcoal, relieved that she hadn't added to her long list of ignorant mistakes.

"Your work goes well?"

"Yes. I spend most of my time typing and filing; they are just starting to ask me to correct the English in some of their broadcast scripts."

"Is it difficult?"

"A little," she admitted. "It's hard to correct so many mistakes without writing the whole thing yourself. I'm not a writer and I don't have any experience at broadcasting, so I feel as if I'm floundering."

"I see. Yet, they seem to think your work is all right?"

"Yes, I believe so. Why?" she asked, beginning to suspect something.

"I'm just concerned that you are not in any danger. You know if you note anything unusual, you should tell me so I can help you to interpret the meaning. If your superior calls you in, you must remember every word to tell me so we can try to see the true meaning."

"Oh, I'm careful, Kiyoko, don't worry so much," she said handing her a cup of tea.

Kiyoko accepted the handleless blue and white cup and bowed her thanks. As she sipped it, she glanced around the room. Then she suddenly stiffened.

Iris followed Kiyoko's gaze but saw nothing wrong. Four *tatami* mats covered the uncluttered wooden floor, three cushions, two green and one pale blue, lay beside a low wooden table at the side of the room; her book of poetry from Cole lay beside a pottery vase in which she had placed a single curved branch of pussy willow. The entire effect was quite

Japanese and one that Iris and Eva had worked consciously to achieve.

"What's the matter?" she asked finally.

"That," Kiyoko said, pointing to Cole's book. "It is written in English?"

"Yes." Iris smiled. "It is one that means a great deal to me. My fiancé gave it to me when he asked me to marry him."

Kiyoko picked it up gingerly, as if it might burn her fingers. "It is a lovely book, but you must get rid of it. It is forbidden to have English-language books in your possession. The Kampetei have ordered that ordinary citizens may not have them."

"Well," Iris said lightly, "I'm not an ordinary citizen. I'm an American, and it's only natural for me to have English books in my possession. Besides, I have none that are political in nature."

"The one which had the map. The one you showed me the first time I came here?"

"Oh, that's just an American history . . . oh, I see . . ." Her voice trailed off as she realized. "But the others are just fiction and poetry. Certainly nothing subversive."

"All in English and all written by Westerners. These are forbidden."

"But I can't part with them!" she protested.

"Easier to part with a book than with your life. Perhaps you can bury them in your backyard," Kiyoko suggested softly.

"Can't I at least keep out my book of poetry? Surely they won't find anything wrong with love poems."

"Read to me from the book," she commanded. "Read me your most favorite love poem."

Iris began reading the page where her ring had been attached:

> How do I love thee? Let me count the ways.
> I love thee to the depth and breadth and height
> My soul can reach, when feeling out of sight
> For the ends of Being and ideal Grace . . .

With each lovely word, Iris renewed her touch with Cole and realized anew the love they shared, which could never die. Long before she reached the end, her face was bathed in tears; she could go no further. She dropped the book and covered her eyes with her hands.

Kiyoko waited until Iris's sobs quieted, then said softly, "You see, that is reason enough for you to hide the book. You destroy your personal harmony with memories that are painful. When reading the book you lose your ability to remain truly Japanese. You are vulnerable. The Kampetei could imprison you merely for possessing an English book; should they ask you to translate it, you would lose any defense you might have left in your behalf. It must be buried."

Iris nodded. "How can I hide it without doing it damage?"

"Bury all your books in a corner of your bomb shelter. I will bring you some oilcloth in which to wrap them. Many old manuscripts have been preserved in that manner. Believe me, you are not alone when you hide your books. Many Japanese scholars have done the same rather than destroy what they cherish. I will bring the oilcloth tonight. You will not leave the house tomorrow until you have done this. Promise me?"

"*Hai, Kiyoko-san*. Eva will help me take care of it tonight."

After Kiyoko left, Iris sat quietly beside the warm ashes in the *konro*, stroking the cover of the book, Cole's engagement gift to her. It was all so long ago, yet her love had not diminished with the agony of time and separation. It seemed to have grown and strenghtened. Trapped behind enemy lines, her every day began with a renewed determination to prove her love, to make her way back to Cole.

When Iris had first realized that her job was to help the Japanese send propaganda to demoralize the American troops, she was horrified. She decided to quit her job; starvation was preferable to treachery. Then Kiyoko had pointed out that Iris would eventually be forced to work in a munitions factory, where the torturous, deadly work would involve making guns and bullets that would actually kill Americans. Better to help aim words at them than guns and bullets, Kiyoko had said.

But Iris knew that words could do more damage than bullets unless they were disarmed. It was that knowledge that made her decide to remain on her job. She began to sabotage the broadcasts whenever possible.

The scripts were very poorly written. She corrected all the grammatical mistakes and made the English passable, as she'd been hired to do. She sabotaged them by keeping in the phrases that sounded preposterous to American ears—phrases like "the sacred soldiers of Japan" and the "holy war of the Emperor." It gave her a glimmer of pride to do even that much.

However, those moments of imagined triumph were quickly overshadowed by the gloomy foreboding and increasing uneasiness that filled her days. When she left work the day Kiyoko had told her to bury her English-language books, the back of her neck crawled; she felt as if she were being followed.

"The Imperial Son of Heaven, descended from Emperor Jimmu, grandson of the Sun Goddess Amaterasu," was a ridiculous phrase that she had deliberately left in that day's script. Had that decision brought her under suspicion? Had they been testing her and she had failed?

Forcing her fears to the back of her mind, she examined the circumstances. She hadn't told Kiyoko what she was doing, for fear of a severe reprimand. She was on her own in this. Each time she had given her okay on a script filled with such ridiculous phrases, she had imagined suspicious eyes watching her every move. But today was the first time she felt she was being followed outside the NHK Building.

She kept stopping at newsstands, pretending to scan headlines she couldn't read as she glanced over her shoulder. Sure enough, she saw a uniformed Kampetei officer. He, too, seemed to be taking the slow way home, dawdling and looking in shop windows. Was her intuition right? Was she under suspicion? She forced herself to continue her routine, controlling her urge to run and hide.

It was her custom to stop at one of the marketplaces along the way home in case new rations had come in. She also checked with three bakeries each day on her way home, and the bakers and their wives had become friendly with her. Now, she turned a corner and quickly entered a *pan-ya*.

"*Konnichi wa*, Miss Hashimoto." The plump woman behind the counter bowed. "I was hoping you'd come today. We are just taking fresh bread from the oven."

"*Konnichi wa, Oka-a-san*." Iris kept her voice strong, hiding her breathless fear. "I could smell your always perfect bread from outside and knew I should stop."

"I will go get you a loaf. Please wait." The baker's wife bowed, then went into the back room.

Iris looked out the window, keeping her motions and expression casual. The street was empty. Then a movement caught her eye from the darkened corner of the shop. Someone had come in unnoticed while she had talked to the baker's wife. As she turned, he stepped forward. Iris's breath caught in her throat, yet she was able to hide it in a proper bow of greeting.

"*Konnichi wa,* Sergeant Ito. I didn't know you liked the taste of bread," she said, deliberately pretending that she didn't suspect that he had followed her, while also implying slight surprise at his not being completely Japanese in his tastes.

"Miss Hashimoto, what a surprise," he said, continuing the charade. He bowed only slightly, his thick lips barely parting, revealing his yellowed teeth. "I prefer our native rice, but am naturally willing to learn new tastes. It has been a long time since I have seen you. It is a fortuitous meeting. May I compliment you on your Japanese? Your accent is barely noticeable."

"*Arigato gozaimasu.*" She bowed once more, forcing him to bow again. "I value your compliment."

"Since the war goes so well for Japan and your language is so improved, I would assume that you soon will be registering your Japanese citizenship."

"The war news is most interesting," Iris replied vaguely. "Your frequent recommendations and visits of the past have not been forgotten." She turned and saw the baker's wife standing behind the counter, her face a mask of indifference.

"That will be three yen, please," she said, shoving the bread across the counter, obviously trying to protect herself in the Kampetei's eyes by overcharging Iris.

Iris pretended the price was her usual charge, paid, and went out the door, bowing to Sergeant Ito respectfully as she did so. Only after she was on the *densha* did she admit how frightened she was. But she had learned something about herself. She could be calm and calculating under stress. She could maintain a Japanese face. It was comforting to know.

Eva agreed that Sergeant Ito must be trying to intimidate Iris. However, since he had not called at their home, nor had he done anything other than follow her from work, he probably was not acting on official Kampetei business. They didn't believe he could possibly know of Iris's sabotage of the scripts.

156

"Besides," Eva reasoned over their evening tea, "you could always say that you didn't think you should edit out phrases that were so obviously pertinent to the political philosophy of the text."

Iris agreed. "That would probably cause me more trouble than leaving them in."

"Well, I think you handled it very well," Eva concluded. "I don't know if I could ever be so calm while facing such a horrid man." She suddenly jumped up and went to the back door. When she returned, she held a bundle of oilcloth. "I almost forgot. When I came home, I found this beside the door. Do you know anything about it?"

Iris explained Kiyoko's instructions to bury their English books. "Frankly, I didn't take her too seriously and just promised to keep her happy. Now, after my meeting with Ito, I think we'd better do it right away."

The air-raid shelter was hardly their favorite place. Over half the shelter was below ground; the other half was supported by rough beams they'd obtained by cutting down a tall thin pine on their property's edge. The beams were covered with dirt and rocks they'd excavated to make the hole. It reminded Iris of pictures she'd seen of pioneers' potato cellars, except that her shelter was only six feet square.

They were frequently sent to its dark confines at all hours of the day and night. Air-raid sirens would howl, and only after they had hurried out of their house would they find out that it was just another drill. Since an air-raid warden checked each house for compliance during such drills, they had no choice but to comply.

When the air-raid siren began that night, it worked to their advantage. They were just going out the door with their precious books carefully wrapped in oilcloth. Now if any prying eyes should see them, they had a reason to be hiding in that dreadful place with just the light of a candle between them. It didn't take long to dig the hole and hide the books. They covered the disturbed dirt with their regulation supplies kept in the shelter. No one would suspect contraband poetry was hidden under the ground. When the all-clear siren sounded, Iris and Eva hurried across the crust of snow into their house with a feeling of one more precaution taken.

One other time in February Iris spotted Sergeant Ito

following her after work. This time she conveyed a careless attitude, going so far as to wave at him as she emerged from a shop. Such brazen action apparently discouraged him from following her for several weeks.

The air-raid drills forcing them into the cold night air had caused their frequent colds all winter. Eva had to spend the last weeks of February in bed with a bad cough. Medicine was not readily available because it was all shipped to the military.

As bad as the air-raid drills were, the fire-brigade practices proved just as irritating. The worst drill usually came at night, when it was cold and the women were bone tired from a long day's work. The fire marshal would light a smudge pot and place it in a tree. They would then have to run up the hill with a full bucket of water and splash the smudge pot in an attempt to "put out" the fire. It seemed a silly way to prepare for a bombing.

Another irritation was the ridiculous supplies they had to keep in plain view outside their door. They'd been required to make sandbags and stack them outside the house. They were never told the purpose of the bags, but Eva thought they were supposed to pour sand on a fire if one broke out. Iris argued that the stacked bags were supposed to protect the windows from flying debris. Either way, they seemed as silly as the water bucket and the big fly swatter they were required to have outside the door as well. These were for putting out any fires that might envelop their house. Tokyo was a crowded city, built almost entirely of paper and wood buildings. It would be like using a pop gun to ward off stampeding elephants.

All these preparations and drills took their precious time and strength. Everyone worked long hours and no one had enough food. Iris and Eva both felt the toll and their health declined noticeably.

In the middle of March, as Iris was returning from a morning fire drill, she saw her aunt Toshiko coming down the street. Iris hastened into the house to tidy up. She had never had a visit from her family and feared bad news had precipitated this surprise. Iris peeked from the window as the gate bell rang. Her aunt seemed to be trying to avoid detection in coming in. She moved quickly to shut the gate behind her, keeping her head down and her face concealed in shadow.

"*Ohayo gozaimasu, Oba-san.*" Iris bowed. "I am honored by your visit."

"*Ohayo gozaimasu, Iris-san.* It is an honor I have postponed too long," Aunt Toshiko replied softly. She left her shoes on the stone *genkan* and followed Iris into the main room of the house.

"May I prepare you some tea?" Iris asked as her aunt sat down on a pillow.

"We must not waste our time with formalities. Please, let's talk," Aunt Toshiko said, with an uncharacteristic break in custom. "Your grandmother asked me to come to you. We have all missed you and have been most worried about your welfare."

"Thank you." Iris smiled. "I'm sorry I haven't come in several weeks, but I have been very busy with work and all these air-raid drills. But then I imagine it is much the same with you."

"Perhaps it is easier with three women to do the work. Your uncles were drafted into the army. We miss them very much." She lowered her eyes to cover her tears. "We have gotten one letter from each, but that was many weeks ago. We can only think thoughts of strength and make offerings at the shrines that they may be protected." She pulled a handkerchief from her sleeve and quietly wiped her nose. Iris noticed that her aunt's kimono hung loosely on her once rounded shape. "But the reason I came here," she continued, "is that we feel you belong with your family. Perhaps now that the war is here, you will register as a Japanese citizen. We want you to come back to your family. We will live through these difficult times together."

Iris was touched by their concern, something she had never felt was there, but now realized probably had been hidden by her inability to understand the customs and the language. Now that they could talk freely in Japanese, she felt closer to her aunt. "I'm sorry," Iris said quietly. "It is still the same as when I was living with you before. I cannot give up my American citizenship, nor can I endanger you with my presence."

"I see," Aunt Toshiko murmured. Then she reached into the bag she was carrying and brought out a wide belt covered with many stitches. "I have brought you Uncle Anami's thousand-stitch belt. Each person adds a stitch, and each stitch represents a prayer for your uncle's safety. When I have it covered with a thousand stitches I will send it to him for luck. He would be honored if you would add your stitch for him."

Deeply touched, Iris made a stitch, then handed the belt back to her aunt. "May Uncle Anami return to us safely," she said, bowing.

Aunt Toshiko began nervously twisting her handkerchief in her hand. "Tell me," she said finally. "It is whispered that America is larger and more wealthy than Japan. Is this so?"

Iris saw fear in her aunt's eyes—fear of defeat, surely, but even more, the fear that only women can feel at the prospect of conquering soldiers invading their homes. "Yes," Iris said gently. "America is very strong. Although it doesn't sound likely right now, I firmly believe Japan will lose the war. It is just a matter of time."

Aunt Toshiko looked at her lap for a long time, nodding slowly, as if she had suspected this all along. Finally she whispered, "I believe you loved your nieces and nephews very much when you lived with us. If Japan should . . . I don't care what happens to myself. I am ashamed to say that my worry is not for my husband's mother or for my sister-in-law. We will die or we will suffer, but we are adults. I can only think of what might come . . . of what might be done to the children." Her face was washed with tears. "The American soldiers . . . they tell such horrid tales about them. . . ." She broke down and sobbed, burying her face in her hands.

Iris was stunned by the depth of her aunt's emotion. "Aunt Toshiko, Americans are very kind. Please, don't believe all the lies the military is spreading just to keep people fighting."

"But if I am killed . . . or something . . ." She paused, collecting her composure. "Will you be responsible for the children? Because you are an American, perhaps they would be safe with you. If Japan really falls, perhaps you would even take the children back to your country to live with you and your parents. They would have food." Hope that her children might survive her, hope that this strange niece from across the sea could actually be the salvation of her children, flushed Aunt Toshiko's cheeks, giving her some of the beauty Iris remembered from when she first arrived in their home so long ago.

"Aunt Toshiko, I will do anything in my power to keep them safe. I would be honored to take them to America."

"*Arigato gozaimasu, Iris-san, arigato gozaimasu.*" Aunt Toshiko bowed low, touching her head to the floor. "You have brought peace of mind to an old woman and two worried mothers. In return, you may rest assured that should the war not go as you say, you will always have a safe harbor with your family. You will always be welcomed and we will help you to register on a moment's notice. And your friend is also welcome."

"I thank you, *Oba-san*, and I thank you for Eva, but should that time come, I would choose death over giving up my American citizenship."

Iris was greatly warmed by her aunt's visit. She actually smiled as she went to work. When she walked home, there was no shadowy figure following her, no prickly feelings of fear.

As she walked in the door, Eva greeted her with wonderful news.

"MacArthur made it through the blockade to Australia!" she exclaimed. "It came over the news today. He's probably been there a couple of days already."

Iris alternated between celebrating and mourning. "Was he alone?" she asked finally.

"I'm not sure. They always refer just to 'MacArthur,' whether telling about whole battles or his breakfast. It's clear that he didn't make any full-scale retreat of men, though. He's talking about going back and getting them out. He said, 'I shall return' at the end of his speech. 'I came through and I shall return.' The newscasts say it's the beginning of the turning of the tide, as they call it."

"He said 'I,'" Iris repeated numbly, not catching Eva's hopeful tone. "That means he left them all behind—abandoned them all in that Japanese trap. Why couldn't he die with them like a real soldier? If he could make it, why couldn't he get them all out?" She began to cry. "He left Cole there to die. . . ." She sat on the cushion, sobbing.

Eva put her arm around Iris's shoulders. "I can't imagine a general not taking out some of his staff. Maybe Cole got out with him."

"Oh, Eva, how would Cole have any contact with MacArthur when Cole's all airplanes and MacArthur's strictly army," she cried angrily. "I can't keep hoping hopeless things. I've got to face the truth sometime. Cole is probably going to . . ." She broke down again.

"MacArthur said he would go back to the Philippines and defeat the Japanese," Eva insisted. "Cole always said MacArthur was a man of his word, and he has the armies to command now. He'll probably be right back up there within a couple of weeks, rescuing our guys."

Eva had found it—a thread they could call hope, a slender, delicate thread to hold them together just a little bit longer . . . just until they were rescued.

Three weeks later, on April 9, the news sent them both reeling. Bataan had fallen. The Philippines were completely in Japanese hands. Iris's terrifying fears seemed certain: Cole was captured. How could she live with the thought? Eva also broke down. She reasoned that Sparky must have followed Cole to the Philippines, an idea she'd been keeping to herself for months.

Neither one could go to work the next day. On Saturday, Eva forced herself to report back to her job. They had to have further information, but there seemed to be none. Then, on the way home from work, the newspapers caught her eye. There were pictures of Japanese soldiers pointing guns at American troops who were holding their hands in the air. Silently, she bought a paper.

That night Iris and Eva grimly studied the picture with a magnifying glass, intent on deciphering each feature from the sea of tiny faces. They recognized no one. However, they determinedly bought every Japanese newspaper that had a picture of the Bataan surrender. For the next three days they scrutinized the pictures until their eyes burned. They alternated between seeing only the blur of a crowd and, at one point, seeing Cole's and Sparky's faces several times over in one picture. Once they even thought they saw a soldier, thin and worn, who had a hint of Jake's cocky stance. They finally realized that they were torturing themselves. They must return to their daily lives. They could do nothing but wait and see.

On April 18, ten days after Bataan fell, Iris sat with Kiyoko, having a cup of tea. Kiyoko had finally convinced her that she must feign normalcy lest her actions be reported as strange. Reluctantly, Iris had returned to work and her long waits in the ration lines, but she wasn't eating. Kiyoko was worried, and that morning had brought over a small roll and a piece of fish that she'd slipped out of the Swiss undersecretary's kitchen. Iris had to eat it after such a risk on Kiyoko's part.

"Thank you, my friend," she said as she washed the last bite down with her tea. "I see you are determined to fatten me up."

"You have very far to go before you reach fat. I jus. want you to not be all bones." She paused. "Are you going to work today?"

"Yes. I know you're right. I haven't missed a day all week."

"Good, then I will walk to the *densha* with you. I have to go downtown to the Ginza."

Iris put the cups away and got her coat. "It's a terrific day for a walk. We can take our time," she said with a smile.

The sky was a porcelain blue and the cool spring air was filled with the scent of cherry blossoms. Kiyoko pointed out a particularly lovely tree weighted down with blossoms, and explained, "Because the blooms do not wither but fall down from the tree in full flowers, we Japanese revere the cherry tree. To us, it symbolizes youth and courage and the fleeting beauty of life."

Musing on the poignancy of the cherry blossoms' message, Iris watched three young girls playing a game similar to jacks, using round stones. Sparrows were busy in the eaves of a house, noisily building a nest and squabbling over their territorial rights. It was a perfect spring day.

Suddenly an air-raid siren started to howl.

"Oh, why do they have to ruin it all with a drill right now?" Iris complained. "I'll be late for work if I go back."

Kiyoko looked around the street. Only a few people were lining up to observe the drill. "Why don't you just ignore it?" she suggested. "You are on your way to work. They couldn't mind. Most people ignore the drills these days anyway. You have a perfect reason to, now. I hear there's a demonstration of the fire squad downtown. We could stop and watch it; it would be most interesting to see."

Iris grinned.

They took a circuitous route to the downtown area so they would pass the park where the firefighting demonstration was being held. As they approached the crowd watching the maneuvers of the firemen, Iris heard the faint buzz of a plane, and glanced over her shoulder.

Kiyoko followed Iris's gaze. A lone two-engine bomber was flying toward the city. The sun reflected from its wings, and as it flew overhead, the crowd cheered. But Iris stood frozen to her spot. She recognized the red, white, and blue circles on the wings. They were American insignia, not Japanese. It was an American plane! An American plane over Tokyo!

The cheering of the crowd faded as the plane dropped three bombs. The ground shook with the not-too-distant explosion and black smoke filled the air. People screamed and began running. It was an American plane and it was bombing Tokyo! But it was also bombing her. Iris stood watching the sight, unable to run, unable to cheer, unable to move.

"Come," Kiyoko said, gently taking Iris's arm. "We must go to the railway station and hide."

"They say the leader of the bomber was named Doolittle," Eva said that night. "Roosevelt said the bombers were launched from an airfield in 'Shangri La.' Do you think it's the beginning of the end?"

"I don't know. I hope so. It was awful having to stand there and know that I was being attacked by the people I'd counted on rescuing me." She smiled at the irony of it. "I guess we'd better start figuring out a way to let the bullets know we're Americans!"

Eva laughed. They were both feeling lighthearted. The Japanese had been shocked; their homeland had never before been attacked. Iris and Eva saw it as the beginning of the breakdown of morale, which would make the American conquest come even more quickly. Perhaps within the week.

However, the week lengthened into two weeks, then three. On May 6 the word came. Corregidor surrendered. Once more Iris and Eva scanned the news photos to see if Cole and Sparky were among the vague and fuzzy faces surrendering on Corregidor.

CHAPTER XII

When Bataan fell, Major General Yoshikata Kawane was prepared to alternately march and transport twenty-five thousand healthy American prisoners from Mariveles, on the southern tip of Bataan, eighty miles north to Camp O'Donnell, where they would be interned. Instead, there were seventy-six thousand malaria-ridden, starved men who surrendered to the Japanese on April 8, 1942. Thus began the Bataan Death March.

The Fil-American Army was defeated as much by disease and starvation as by the Japanese. They had fought long beyond endurance without food, medical supplies, reinforcements, or hope. In the end, when the only thing left was futile defiance, entire companies of gaunt, dazed men came straggling out of the jungles, leaning on one another or their guns for support, dressed in rags, mere skeletons of men. They were then systematically searched by the Japanese, stripped of any valuables, and herded into groups of three hundred. Then came the eighty-mile march. Numbly, they set out in the scorching sun, one foot, then the other dragging in the dust. Very few could even comprehend what was happening. Jake Devon could.

As Jake started out from Mariveles, he told himself that he must survive, that he had hope of escape, and a place to go, if only he kept his head about him. He wouldn't be like the dazed, weeping men shuffling along beside him. He wouldn't let his mind dwell on the hopelessness of the situation. He wouldn't give in.

On his left was towering Mount Bataan, its peak shrouded in mist as usual. On his right were the blue green waters of Manila Bay. What had been a lush tropical jungle was now a smoldering, blackened desert of charred tree stumps, a grim testament to their defeat. The chalk white dust from the road clung to his sweaty skin, drying his throat and stinging his eyes as the relentless sun beat on his bare head. Men were staggering beside him; he couldn't let his mind dwell on their faltering, their suffering. Quietly, a silly ditty from the Bataan battlefields began reeling through his brain:

> *We're the battling bastards of Bataan:*
> *No mama, no papa, no Uncle Sam,*
> *No aunts, no uncles, no cousins, no nieces,*
> *No pills, no planes or artillery pieces,*
> *And nobody gives a damn.*

His mind played with the jogging rhythm of the words until a young man fell in front of him. Without thinking, he reached down to help him up.

The guard shouted behind them and suddenly Jake's head exploded with dizzying lights. He reeled under three quick blows of the guard's rifle butt. As he raised his hands to ward off further blows, his knees started to give out.

"For God's sake, don't fall," someone said hoarsely from behind as Jake struggled to remain upright. Just as quickly as it began, the attack was over. Catching his balance, Jake shook his head trying to clear it, then wiped the blood from his eye.

The guard had turned from Jake and was standing over the fallen soldier, who held his hand up in mute supplication. Screaming in guttural Japanese, the guard plunged his bayonet into the man's throat. Horrified, Jake watched the American's body jerk grotesquely and heard the cry gurgle in his severed throat as the guard twisted the bayonet and pulled it out. The Japanese guard turned and shouted a command at the staring prisoners, gesturing with his rifle.

The message was clear. Jake and the man next to him grabbed the dead man by the feet and pulled him off the road. Jake saw the throat still oozing dark red blood as he stepped over the corpse. The features on the twisted face were so young. Silently, Jake fell back in line under the prodding of the guard's bayonet point. And nobody gives a damn.

As they passed through the deserted remains of Cabcaben,

they began turning north. They weren't allowed to drink from the town well, and Jake's throat was burning with thirst.

They headed up the peninsula and Jake had one last glimpse of Corregidor, where the last free Americans in the Philippines were holding out. Was Cole still there, he wondered, or had he made it out with MacArthur?

The mind clings to monotonous, childish rhythms just to avoid insane reality. Now, seeing The Rock once more, Jake remembered another bitter battlefield ditty, a parody on General Douglas MacArthur, sung to the tune of the "Battle Hymn of the Republic." His brain grabbed the tune and silently rode the words around and around, finding solace in it:

> *Dugout Doug's not timid, he's just cautious, not afraid,*
> *He's protecting carefully the stars that Franklin made.*
> *Four-star generals are as rare as good food on Bataan,*
> *And his troops go starving on.*

Jake let his feet march to the internal rhythm of the song. He must survive. He had somewhere to go, a way to fight. He would escape. Somehow. *And his troops go starving on.*

They marched for five grueling days with no relief. There had been three stops for water in the past two days. Once, in Balanga, the Japanese had made an attempt to feed the prisoners. It was disorganized and woefully inadequate. Jake was lucky. He received a tiny parcel of rice and salt and a cup of water.

He had stopped counting the swelling, bloated bodies along the road after he'd reached thirty-five on the second day. Whenever he saw crows landing, he turned his head, refusing to watch them eating the carrion, fearful it might be someone he would recognize, their staring eye held in the beak of a black bird. The green bottle flies chewed mercilessly at the wound on his head from the guard's gun. He knew from the throbbing that it was badly infected.

By the sixth day, they moved at a snail's pace, the prisoners incapable of going any faster. Jake estimated they were leaving the peninsula and heading north, possibly toward Lubao.

Would it never end? Even at night there was no respite. The sixth night they were herded into some abandoned wooden storage sheds, maybe once used for sugar. Each shed was about forty feet by a hundred and filled with about 150 men, who were crammed in so tightly that they lay touching one another on all sides. The mosquitoes buzzed incessantly in Jake's ears as he lay on the hard, moldy ground. The oppressive, sultry air was filled with the sour scent of vomit and diarrhea.

Even when he dozed off, Jake couldn't stop the images of the past few days: the fetid rice paddy out of Orani where they were shoved in to sleep among feces crawling with maggots; the pit latrines that had bloated bodies floating among the excrement the next morning; the enforced "rest" where they sat squatting in the blistering noon sun; the turgid green headless bodies in the ditch. He couldn't escape the horrors even in fitful sleep.

He turned restlessly, the usual stench stronger than ever. His face was resting on moist rags. Suddenly awake, Jake sat up, wiping his face and looking at the rags in the bright moonlight filtering through the broken roof. The rags were the trousers of the man behind him, dripping with feces and blood. Jake gagged and swallowed hard to keep from vomiting. He kicked the man with his toe. He was motionless, dead from dysentery and God knows what else, having literally shit himself to death. Jake caught the movement of a guard out of the corner of his eye. He quickly took the man's feet and began dragging him down the aisle toward the door, gesturing to the guard to help him. It was a useless request, but it gave authenticity to his actions.

The guard stopped him and kicked the body; then, convinced it was actually dead, he allowed Jake to deposit it outside the door. There was a single spigot not far from the door. Jake gestured to the guard, asking to wash himself. The guard looked at his filth-covered body and grunted his approval. Jake turned on the water and scrubbed himself until he was raw, trying to wash off the smell of death. Then, sensing that the guard was tolerant, he drank from the faucet, then washed some more, trying to clean his wound, then drank some more. It was probably this indulgence that got him through the following day.

By this point most of the men were so severely dehydrated that they couldn't even urinate, despite the incessant urge to try. Compounding the situation was the fact that although there were few shade trees along the way, they were never allowed to rest under them. Some risked their lives to veer into a sugar cane field and break off a stem to chew. Jake didn't. It would only intensify his thirst.

By afternoon, Jake too was swollen and dehydrated. Painfully, he held out against the urge to urinate until he could no longer. A hoarse moan escaped his lips as he finally managed a tiny trickle. It felt like burning needles were shoved up his penis, but the relief was tremendous. As long as he could do that, he would not die. He had to survive. Lubao was near.

They had gone about forty miles in seven horror-filled days, seven days that blurred one into the other, seven days that Jake had recorded by scratching a mark into his belt each night, tenaciously holding on to sanity. However, by the time they reached Lubao, even Jake's mind was dazed, his vision blurred. He had to concentrate to put one foot in front of the other.

Weeping Filipinos lined the streets. Some tried to slip water or packets of food to the prisoners. Some were beaten for their kindness. Still, they tried. They were a blur, a colored haze in Jake's vision. He couldn't recognize a face, yet they all looked familiar. They all looked like Rodrigues. They all were Maria, crying. The cobbled streets tripped his lagging steps. Where could he fall? If only he could lie down . . .

He barely focused on the old woman swathed from head to foot in bulky clothes as she suddenly reached out. Instinctively, he braced himself for the blow. To his surprise, he was pulled abruptly to the ground, then dragged from the street. All light was gone, and a heavy, musty smell surrounded him. Dazed, he lay still. The old woman was covering him with her skirts. He couldn't move. Then Jake could remember no more. A peaceful darkness filled his mind.

If Cole had ever had any doubts as to why he had joined the air corps instead of the navy, he dismissed them forever on the escape from Corregidor aboard four navy PT boats. Headed by PT Commander John Bulkeley, the boats were to keep to a diamond formation, running full speed in the dark with their lights out over rough waters. As a Midwestern boy, Cole never had been at ease on the water. That interminable night, he learned exactly how much he preferred flying. The hull of the boat slapped the waves with a force calculated to grind their bones as they dodged in and out of the many scattered islands almost eight hundred miles south to the large island of Mindanao, where the Del Monte airfield was located.

The ebony night cloaked the other boats from view and by morning they were alone, struggling with a fouled engine to reach a hidden cove. Despite being stranded, they managed to reach Mindanao a week later, helped by sympathetic fishermen and a burgeoning guerrilla network.

Cole and Dick settled down in the little airbase, waiting for a plane to airlift them to Australia before it was too late. On April 8, word came that Bataan had fallen. Dick and Cole realized that most likely Jake was lost.

On April 18, too late to be of help to Bataan, bombers limped in from Australia. They were few in number and battered, but they had orders for a quick bombing of the Japanese in a last gesture of defiance. They would then refuel at Del Monte and take off for Australia, over Japanese-controlled waters, fully loaded with personnel. Cole and Dick were to be on the last plane out, if it made it through the bombing runs.

They were waiting as the planes were readied for the bombing, when a corporal ran out of the radio shack and into the officers' mess.

"Hey, everybody," he shouted, "we've bombed Japan! They say a bombing raid was carried out against Tokyo and Yokohama this morning under the leadership of General James Doolittle. The Japanese are complaining that we attacked civilian targets. . . ."

He was interrupted by howls of derision and screams of "What about Pearl Harbor" and "So was Manila."

He held up his hand and quieted his volatile audience. "President Roosevelt says that this first blow against the enemy was struck from an airbase in—get this—an airbase in Shangri La."

Cole sat at his table, buffeted by yells, whistles, cheers, and slaps on the back. He was torn by conflicting emotions. *Finally,* he thought, *we've struck back at the Japs, bombed them on their own soil.* But Iris was in Tokyo.

Dick put his hand on Cole's shoulder and stood up. "Where do you think they really took off from?" he asked the excited group.

This began a hot discussion, designed by Dick to give Cole time to recover. The arguments were leaning toward the United States using a secret base in China, but some maintained that the bombers had taken off from a carrier, although it would have been the first time such a takeoff had been attempted.

When their "escape" B-17 was due to return from its bombing run, Dick and Cole were waiting on the runway, scanning the darkening skies, "sweating in the pilot." Half an hour late, it landed and was refueled to capacity for the long haul to Australia.

When the men finally boarded, straddling flight bags and pineapples impulsively picked from fields on the way to the plane, they could hardly believe they were leaving the Philippines . . . alive.

Some hours later they made a brief refueling stop at a secret field in northern Australia. Several hours after that, they reached Melbourne, their final destination, and the men emerged from the Fortress, stiff, slightly dazed, and vastly relieved.

Melbourne was a city like many they might have seen back in the States. It had suburbs of red-tiled bungalows, a skyline that never aspired beyond thirteen stories, and a lazy river, the Yarra, meandering through the countryside.

Cole and Dick received more than a few strange looks as they walked into their assigned hotel wearing their wrinkled, dirty uniforms, which hung loosely on their thin frames.

A doctor examined them and declared them to be malnourished, battle weary, and in need of at least thirty days' leave, but otherwise well. They began following his orders immediately, enjoying the forgotten luxury of a hot bath and the exquisite joy of real food. They were like children at Christmas, turning on electric lights and bouncing on soft beds. They settled back to enjoy recuperating in their own Shangri La.

The next day, Corregidor was taken.

Once their bodies began to heal, and once they'd heard of the fall of the brave friends they'd left behind on Corregidor, Cole and Dick could no longer sit quietly waiting for their thirty day leave to pass.

Dick got an assignment in Brisbane with the intelligence

division to the north, and Cole begged a desk assignment there. He figured that from that vantage point, he might be able to finagle a plane. At least he'd be closer to the front.

Still, it was frustrating. MacArthur was commander of the Southwest Pacific Theater (SWPA), yet he received only a trickle of supplies; almost all the American war effort was being sent to the European Theater.

On a late-June evening, when Cole was feeling especially frustrated with all the meaningless paperwork on his desk, Dick came into his office and said, "Come on down to the radio room with me. There's something I just saw that they've been tossing around all afternoon. Didn't think it was worth much, I guess. When I found it a minute ago, I thought you might see what I did."

Cole followed him down the hall and into the radio room. Dick handed him the message. "It doesn't make any sense on the surface. The guys in the decoding say it's coming from an unidentified source in the Philippines and they figure it's probably some Jap trying to foul us up. They don't want to fool with it. It's worded like the Japs would probably word something. What do you think?"

Cole read the cryptic message:

Anxious in response but actually steady entry. Three more lend accurate knowledge again. Destroyed battleships sighted. Blue seals added to dead. All occupy real land once more. Actual light never observed west but ultimate intent leads drive in northern group.

"Did anyone even try to decode it?"

"They said why should they bother when they don't know the source."

"I do," Cole said, grabbing a pencil. "I'm afraid that if the Japanese pick it up, they'll figure it out as well. How many times has this been transmitted?"

"Twice that we've picked up. Seems to have been moved in between transmissions."

"Did they acknowledge it?"

"Yeah, just the standard sign-off."

Cole spent several minutes scribbling on a piece of paper, then held it up to Dick. "It's Jake all right," he crowed. "Look at this. Good clean information. You just take the first letter of each word until he says 'three more,' which means to begin taking the third letter of the words, then back again to the first letter when he says 'once more.' It's really too simple not to have the Japanese decode within minutes . . . if they pick it up and take it seriously. We'll have to hope he throws in the complications next time around."

Dick took the paper from Cole and read it: *Air Base NCoast Guadalcanal Now Building*. Then he walked over to the map and pointed to the Solomon Islands. "It's accurate information. We've been told the same thing by the coast watchers. Not the kind of information the Japs would throw away as bait. There's a little over a month to go before we land there." He walked back to Cole, his eyes dancing with excitement. "It's Jake," he said quietly. "He's alive."

The radio crackled with static. "Roger, Bataan HQ". Then the airwaves were clear, the volume of the static indicating that the receiving station had turned to another channel. Jake took off the earphones and wiped the sweat from his forehead. He didn't know if the message would be passed on. He'd deliberately used the simplest code possible, not knowing if Cole was alive to receive it. He'd call in again at the same frequency and time tomorrow. If Cole was there, he'd let him know, and they would switch to a safer, more complicated code. He massaged his temple where it was scarred from the Death March wound.

"Are you done?" Maria asked. He turned and looked at her; she was sitting on a bale of rice straw. Every time he saw her lovely face, framed by her thick dark hair, his heart turned over in newfound joy. To Jake, she embodied all that was beautiful and good in the world.

It was her quick-thinking grandmother who had spotted him in the Death March and had risked her life by pulling him to the ground and throwing her skirts over him. It was Maria's father who had concealed him in a wagon and taken him to safety. It was Maria herself who had nursed him these past six weeks. It was her loving care that had brought him from the edge of death. It was his desire for her that made him determined to live, his respect for all she stood for and believed in that made him a better man.

He went over to her. "Yes, my darling, I'm done." He held her oval face between his hands and softly kissed her lips, the fragrance of the plumeria in her hair filling his head. "Let's take our time getting the radio back to the house," he whispered.

"We can't," she said. "We have catechism with Father Domingo. Come on, don't make such a face. It's our last lesson before the wedding."

"Okay, darling," Jake said, putting his radio back in the case, "but I hope you realize how very much I love you. Just going through that old priest's instructions should be proof enough to assure both you and your father of the devotion your future husband brings to the altar." He grinned. "That has a nice ring to it, doesn't it?"

Maria ran to his arms, laughing. "Mrs. Jake Devon has an even better sound," she said, kissing him firmly.

"Mmm, almost as good as your lips taste," he said, reluctantly taking her arms away. "But we've got to hurry now. If the Japs got a fix on the radio, we've only got about ten minutes before they'll come busting through that barn door. Here, put the wire under the fruit in your basket while I get back in my white rags and hide the radio box under the sugar cane in the cart." Jake pulled the ragged white pants over his shorts. He'd taken them off to prevent getting them greasy, something a peasant wouldn't likely do to his clothes. Do you think your cousin Antonio will keep working at the Cavite docks? He's bringing some awfully good information."

Maria carefully tucked the wire under the pineapple and bananas in her basket. "He said he'll stay there as long as it's useful. Now hurry."

Within five minutes the barn doors opened and a Filipino laborer tugged at the yoke of a lumbering carabao pulling a two-wheeled cart. He whipped it lightly with a switch and swore something in Tagalog. His wife sat stoically on the cart with the sugar cane towering behind her, her dark shawl pulled tightly around her head and shoulders, a basket of fruit on her lap. If anyone was watching, they saw nothing unusual.

The wide-brimmed hat that shaded Jake's face was woven from pandanus, the same worn by many of the peasants in the fields. The deep blisters from the Bataan March sunburn had peeled away, and the merciless sun had baked his skin until it was as dark as any Filipino's. Only a close look at his face, his bone structure and Caucasian-shaped eyes, would reveal that he was not Filipino. Most villagers seeing Maria perched atop the family cart assumed that the shaded face belonged to her cousin Antonio, who lived not far from the family's country home. That was who the family had an identification card for, and who obviously helped Rodrigues plow the fields. Jake's existence was known only to a few trusted friends and relatives.

One of the villagers who did know of Jake was Father Domingo, a weathered, rotund, and very practical village priest. He had a violent hatred of the Japanese for their unjust and brutal treatment of his parishioners, but he was sure God understood and forgave his hatred. He had been the first of the village men to join Rodrigues's guerrilla group. Behind the soft facade of an aging priest was the steely will of a born fighter.

He knew his presence in the group was welcomed partly because they could use his church for meetings and clandestine communications. He also knew they relied on his judgment and ingenious ideas of subterfuge. He relished being able to use deceit to such a good end; it was like being given the freedom to be just a little sinful and not be chastised for it.

Father Domingo had quickly sized Jake up and had taken a strong liking to him. He had designed Jake's catechism to be as short and practical as possible within the letter of canon law. Part of his pleasure came from being able to catch another soul for the Mother Church. However, he had to admit that he was happy mostly because he was an incurable romantic. It was Father Domingo himself who had named and christened Maria for the Virgin Mary nineteen years ago. He openly admitted that she had remained his favorite ever since she'd opened her luminous brown eyes and smiled as he'd sprinkled the holy water over her. Now that she'd grown into the most beautiful, gentle, intelligent creature he'd ever known God to create, he wanted only her happiness and safety.

When the handsome, strong American had risked his life to bring Maria and her family to the mountain retreat, Father Domingo had fervently blessed him and offered prayers for his safety. When he was saved from sure death at the hands of the Japanese, Father Domingo knew his prayers had been answered. He knew that the Divine Plan meant for Maria to be cared for by Jake.

He watched them leave on their cart after the catechism and smiled with fatherly pride. They were such lovely children. Jake was so resourceful and so devoted to Maria. It was happiness such as this that made life endurable during the horrors of war.

Humming, Father Domingo turned back into his church. He would offer another series of prayers for the young couple and then begin making plans for the marriage ceremony. It would be simple, attended only by the family and a few friends in the guerrilla band. But it would be most blessed. Father Domingo knew, as Maria's confessor, that Jake had treated Maria with the proper respect, never threatening her virginity, even now, just days before the wedding.

He walked back to the altar and said his prayers in the flickering candlelight. Then, glancing to make sure no straggling worshipper had slipped in unnoticed, he leaned down and pretended to adjust the cloth. Yes, the radio was perfectly concealed beneath, safe until the next transmission, which would emanate from a deserted shack a mile down the road. To avoid Japanese detection, they must move the radio between each transmission.

"Are you sure you're not cold?" Jake asked, as he urged the horse to pull the cart a little faster along the darkening road.

"No," Maria laughed lightly, "I'm next to you and that warms me clear through. It's only a little ways now to Aunt Magdalena's house. I think you will like it. It's one of the old family places. Some even say it's haunted."

"It must be pretty old," Jake commented.

"Not as much as some—probably only three hundred years or so. Our grandfather back then came from Spain and married a Filipino. They began the family farms and businesses there."

"Does this farm we're going to have more than one house on it?" he asked suddenly.

"Well, there's the main house, and all the small houses for the laborers. But you don't have to worry about them. They're all very loyal to the family. They would die for me. Besides, they will not see you. Aunt Magdalena has instructed that we are to be served only by herself and my cousin for the two days of our honeymoon. And we will have the new wing all to ourselves. It was built in the 1800s and is much nicer than the old part; it has larger windows and higher ceilings. I used to go there to stay during my school vacations."

Jake shook his head. "You know, I don't think I knew what I was getting into when I married you."

Maria nestled her head on his shoulder and giggled. "You married my family, I'm afraid. But most of all, you married the one woman who loves you with all her heart. You know," she confided, "my mother was concerned that I would be afraid on my wedding night. I shocked her, I think, when I told her I couldn't wait. There," she said, sitting up, "take the right fork in the road."

They had passed through a street where the laborers' houses stood in neat rows. It was virtually a village. Jake was barely prepared by Maria's description of the house. It was an ancient, sprawling mansion, built in the European manner, high on a hill overlooking the valleys the family farmed. The main house had thick rock walls and dark beamed ceilings designed to withstand a siege of many weeks.

Aunt Magdalena greeted them warmly and escorted them to the new wing, a place of nineteenth-century elegance. After giving them a bottle of rich, nutty sherry with which to toast their marriage, she directed them to their bedroom.

As the door closed behind them, Maria turned to Jake. Raising her arms, she reached around his neck, holding her mouth up to his. She was so delicate, Jake was almost afraid of hurting her. He kissed her gently, longingly.

Maria leaned her head against his chest. "All these months I've dreamed of being alone with you and free to do everything we wanted to do with one another . . . but now I feel rather silly."

"Why?" he asked, kissing the top of her head.

"Well, before I go to bed with you, the one thing I want is a warm bath," she said, laughing. "I don't want you to hold me when I'm so grimy after the trip."

Jake tilted her chin up so that she was looking him straight in the eye. "Listen, darling, I would understand if you were afraid. I won't do anything that you don't want me to. You can tell me how you feel and I'll be very gentle when . . ." He stopped as she laughed, putting her hand over his mouth.

"Don't be silly. I'm not avoiding you. In fact, I was going

to suggest that you join me in the bath. It's a huge old tub and I'll scrub your back for you." When Jake hesitated, she said, "Who do you think bathed you all those days you were delirious? I know, and love, every part of your body."

As Maria pinned her long hair up on her head, Jake couldn't take his eyes from her. He undressed and slipped into the warm water. Maria's long, slender neck curved right at the hairline and he yearned to kiss her there, to kiss her everywhere.

Her almond-shaped eyes were wide and luminescent as she slipped into the other end of the tub. Her legs and firm breasts were like carved marble in the water. He was speechless at the delicate beauty of the woman who had vowed just two hours earlier to be his wife.

She scrubbed his back, then gently washed his body, touching him in a familiar way. "Here," she said, handing him the washrag, "now you scrub my back."

"I can't figure out why you aren't hiding from me," he said in amazement.

"Why should I? I have been taught all my life that my duty as a wife is to please my husband. Now I find that it's not only my duty but something that I've been yearning to do." As she dipped a cup in the water and rinsed off, a strand of hair slipped down from the twisted knot on top of her head and snaked its dark way over her creamy breast. "Ever since you held me so close to you back in Manila, before it all began, I began feeling . . . well, feeling things. I'd dream of you holding me like that. Then later, I would deliberately slide up close to you when you kissed me so I could feel you growing with desire. It made me feel as if I couldn't bear not to have you touch me all over. I've spent quite a few restless nights thinking about you." She smiled coyly. "Now I will have my night with you . . . tonight and every night from now on." She dried herself, then watched him get out of the tub as she unpinned her hair and let it fall about her shoulders in a shining, ebony cascade. She turned and picked up a filmy white gown from the chair by the vanity table. "Mother made me this gown for my wedding night. Please say I won't need it."

Jake picked her up in his arms, holding her warm body close to his. "You won't need it," he whispered, carrying her into the bedroom. He set her gently on the bed, and she pulled him to her, her moist mouth eagerly seeking his.

Jake trembled as he forced himself to go gently and slowly. He ran his hand over her body and she moaned with pleasure, raising her hips to meet him. Rolling over on her, he covered her with his body, holding her in his arms. As he penetrated her she cried out with pleasure, receiving him, pulling him more deeply into her. As their bodies joined together, Jake knew the beauty of all the earth. He possessed the most delicate fragrant flowers, gave himself to the rich musty land, exulted in a union so complete that the universe spun before his eyes as he cried out in joy.

She was crying softly as he held her to him, spent and warm with release. "Are you all right?" he whispered, suddenly concerned that he might have hurt her.

"Yes, my darling," she murmured. "I'm just very, very happy."

Jake spent the night and the following day knowing a happiness so complete he was dazed. How could he, the cynical one, know such joy, such consuming love, when all around them the world was writhing in despair? Maria was more than he'd ever imagined a woman could be—loving, laughing, playful, and sensual. They were alone in an enchanted world, protected from the insanity outside by their love. They awoke the last morning as the sun filtered through the lace curtains and a rooster crowed in the distance. From their pillows they could see the amber dawn outlining the hills and fields as the workers set out to till the land. It would have been hard to leave had Maria not been going back with him. From now on, he could take his paradise with him wherever he went.

The following two months, July and August 1942, were spent together in their own room in Rodrigues's mountain hideaway. Jake worked more feverishly gathering information, organizing the guerrilla activities, and teaching Rodrigues and Antonio how to use the intricate radio he had built.

The church reverberated with his whoop of joy the night that Australia acknowledged his message. "Leo Durocher, Bataan HQ. Message received." Cole was alive! Cole was receiving the code! Jake grabbed Maria, laughing and singing. Father Domingo rushed into the steeple, singing a loud, toneless chant, desperately trying to cover up Jake's indiscreet celebration.

Life was good, Jake thought as they drove away from the church that night. He loved his wife more than he'd thought humanly possible, and now he was able to work together with his best friend, whom he'd thought dead. It was because of these happy thoughts that he didn't hear what Maria was saying, but her last word, *baby*, caught his attention immediately.

"Whose baby?" he asked, staring at her in the starlight.

"Ours, silly. That happens between a man and wife, you know. We ought to have our baby in April."

"Our baby," he murmured, "in the spring . . ." He dropped the reins, leaned over, and kissed her laughing lips. "We're going to have a baby! Does your mother know? In the spring . . . I'll be damned!"

"I was hoping you'd be happy," she said, laughing and picking up the reins. "Now, we'd better keep on going before someone thinks I have a crazy man in the cart with me."

Jake took back the reins and looked at her with concern. "Are you all right? I mean, you don't hurt or anything? I couldn't . . ."

"Don't be silly. I'm fine. Women are made to have babies, you know."

"You're not going on any more trips with me," he declared. "I won't stand for you taking any chances. I hadn't thought about it much before, but now there are two to protect. And you won't go into the marketplace, either. The Japs are moving their troops into the area. It's not safe for a beautiful woman like you to be seen."

"Don't worry," she said lightly. "I will take care."

Father Domingo was as overjoyed as the rest of the family at the news. The union was as it should be—fruitful and full of love. He felt as if he were responsible for one of God's miracles. He knew of Jake's concerns and helped him pass the instructions on to the other guerrillas: Maria was to be kept hidden from the incoming Japanese soldiers. Maria was not to know of the horrid tortures and atrocities they were perpetrating on the people. She and her unborn child must be protected.

For that reason, Father Domingo was particularly surprised to see Maria come into town on market day the last week in September. Jake was out on the trails with the other men, watching the troop movements. Maria moved through the streets, dresed in white, her basket on her arm, chatting with her neighbors. Her body was still slim, only slightly rounded under her cotton dress. Father Domingo started down the church steps to chastise her.

A troop truck careened around the corner and stopped in the town square. As Father Domingo started forward, trying to catch Maria's attention, to tell her to seek safety in the church, one of the soldiers spotted her. He pointed and shouted something to the others. Leering, they jumped from the back of the truck and grabbed Maria by the arm. She pulled away, only to fall into the grasp of another soldier. She was dragged screaming into the back of the truck. Father Domingo ran after them, following long after they had disappeared from view.

Panting, he arrived at the Japanese camp. Maria was no longer able to scream. Hiding behind a large hibiscus bush, Father Domingo watched in horror as the soldiers took out their animal lust on her bloodied body one after another. There was no need for the leering, shouting men to hold her arms any longer. She was dead long before they sported further by shoving the bayonet repeatedly between her legs.

Back at the church, Father Domingo lifted his tear-filled eyes to the stained-glass window above the altar. "Please, Lord, take this cup from me," he prayed. He prostrated himself before the altar and begged what had become a cold God. He knew what he must do. He would comfort the family. It was his last duty as a priest. Then, he would throw away his worthless collar and join the men in the mountains, fighting to kill every Japanese animal on the islands.

Slowly he made his way to the Rodrigues hideaway, walking the dark road by memory, seeing only the horrors that filled his mind.

Jake was sitting at the table, berating everyone in the house for allowing Maria to go into town. Father Domingo cringed at Jake's horrified expression when he saw the priest enter. He knew even before Father Domingo could say the words, "Maria's dead."

Her mother cried out and fell to the floor in a faint. The four sisters screamed and sobbed. Rodrigues crossed himself and sat down, weeping. Only Jake was silent. He got up slowly and walked to the priest, seizing his shirt and nearly choking him.

"You lying bastard priest!"

Father Domingo clawed at Jake's powerful hands, trying to get his breath. "The Japanese killed her," he gasped.

"How do you know?" Jake demanded, loosening his grip.

"I watched the end. They grabbed her, pulled her on a troop truck. I ran, followed. I got there and she was already dead. They had killed her."

"How?" Jake demanded, torturing himself.

"They . . . they raped her. . . ." Father Domingo began to sob.

Jake let the priest go and slowly sank to the floor. His howl was the agonized scream of a dying creature. Then, much worse, was his silence as he lay there, staring out the open door.

Finally, he got up, his silence more terrifying than his one tortured scream, and started out the door.

"No!" Rodrigues commanded, grabbing Jake's arm. "You can't go out there and attack them single-handed. It will bring torture to the whole village. Children and women will die because of your empty vengeance. We can't let them know you are here. We can't let them think the village is responsible for your hiding here. You know what they've done elsewhere."

Jake hesitated, and his father-in-law rushed on. "Remember what happened to the Chinaman they found in the village to the south. He was roasted alive. They heard his screams for two hours. Don't bring that upon the innocent children."

Jake stood still, swaying slightly, his white-knuckled grip on his submachine gun frozen. They he said slowly, "Other children will not die because of me . . . just Japanese. I will not do anything foolish." His voice was barely audible, frightening in its control and quiet. He turned and walked into the night.

When Jake returned to the house a week later, he was cold and withdrawn, obsessed with plans for a relentless vendetta. Rodrigues and Father Domingo joined him and together they ranged far across the island, through the mountains, over rivers, in strange cities and towns. They manufactured explosive devices and traps of death. Troop transports overturned or were blown up in accidents on isolated mountain roads. Planes, ships, and ammunition dumps were sabotaged and destroyed.

Soon, the deadly three were hunted like animals, their identities concealed and elusive. Still, the Japanese officials offered rewards that were tempting to starving Filipinos. It was inevitable that as Jake became more bold, more reckless with his life in order to slake his thirst for revenge upon all Japanese, he would one day be captured.

It was without surprise that Father Domingo heard of Jake's capture in a faraway marketplace. Despite the brutal beatings, Jake was still grim and stolid as they took him away to Fort Santiago, where the wretched prisoners from Corregidor were held and tortured. "May God have mercy on his soul," Father Domingo whispered to himself.

CHAPTER XIII

The air was warm and heavy, swollen by the soft gray rain in the summer dusk. Iris slid open the back door of their main room, then sat down on the *tatami* floor and gazed quietly across the narrow porch that encircled their tiny house. The long rain of June had arrived.

A twisted pine bent over the curve of the garden path as if to hold the clean gingerscent of the air in its gnarled branches. The dark soil covering the roof of the air-raid shelter was striped with neat rows of bright green spears that held the promise of summer vegetables. Beyond them, almost obscured by the whispering rain, was the hedge of bamboo and pine. The tightly woven bamboo fence enclosed three sides of the yard, leaving the end bordered with the hedge, allowing access to the mansion next door.

Only on a clear day could Iris see the hidden opening in the hedge where Kiyoko frequently slipped through for her visits. It had been three days since Kiyoko had come to visit, and Iris was thinking how she missed her helpful advice and friendly chiding.

Kiyoko had transformed Iris from a careless, naïve young girl to a careful, serious woman. The only thing left from that other world, that other life, was her love for Cole—and that she kept carefully concealed even from herself, except in quiet moments when she brought it out. She was still an American, but now she was also different. With Kiyoko's guidance she'd slowly been able to assume the facade of a Japanese, and in so doing she had become molded by the mask she wore.

It was not that she liked Japan any better or would choose to live there if she were not trapped by the war. It was just that now she could see the strange kind of logic to the way things were done.

She still didn't like the food, nor understand their strange way of talking in circles instead of coming right out with what was on their minds, or a thousand other things, but she was learning to cover up her dismay.

Iris was brought back to the present by the faint swish of water in the bathhouse at the edge of the garden. Eva must be finishing her bath and it would soon be Iris's turn. She wearily got up and went to the *oshiire*, the heavy wooden chest in their sleeping room. Shedding her drab work clothes, she slipped into a pale green *yukata*, the loose fitting kimonolike dress the Japanese wore for bathrobes.

Iris looked forward to her bath. It had taken some effort, but once she and Eva had gotten the hang of it, the Japanese method of bathing not only made sense, it was the one luxury they allowed themselves at the end of each week. They had to make do with cold sponge baths the rest of the time because they couldn't afford the charcoal to heat the water more often.

Iris smiled, remembering her first bath in Japan. Aunt Toshiko had scolded, explained, demonstrated, and pantomimed, trying to tell Iris that Japanese don't sit in their own dirty bathwater. A Japanese scrubs and rinses himself first; then, all clean, he immerses himself in the hot steamy tub. It was an idea that Iris had grasped slowly, much to her aunt's dismay. It was several weeks before Aunt Toshiko had trusted her niece's newly learned manners enough to allow her any privacy in the bath. Iris had eventually caught on and had learned to splash buckets of water over her soapy body with cheerful abandon. Since the whole floor of a Japanese bath is drained, it gave her a feeling of childish carelessness to see just how much water she could splash around.

"It's all yours," Eva said, coming through the door, her face rosy and moist from the steamy water. "I'll start getting dinner ready."

"Don't hurry. I've got a lot to soak off," Iris said, taking her towel from a peg on the porch.

The rain was soft and cool on the back of her neck when she stepped off the narrow porch and slipped her feet into her *geta*.

As she walked into the tiny bathhouse nestled at the edge of the garden, the hollow clop of her wooden soles on the worn stepping stones echoed the sound of the raindrops in the cool gray dusk. The door creaked on its hinges and the pungent smell of moist wood tumbled out to greet her. She paused to leave her *geta* on the wood block that served as a stoop.

Although hardly bigger than a closet, the bathhouse seemed spacious inside. In the wall above the round wooden tub, which dominated the room, was a windowless opening framing the view of an old pine tree and a portion of the sky, hinting at a larger scene limited only by the imagination. A breeze drifted in the opening, cooling Iris's bare back as she hung her *yukata* on a peg.

Iris soaped herself from head to foot, then took the two buckets of water and poured them liberally over herself. The sound of the water running through the slatted floor to the pebbles beneath the raised bathhouse whispered of woodland streams.

The tub, made of wooden staves bound with copper hoops, was deep and set up on blocks over a charcoal heater. Eva had placed the flat wooden cover over the tub to hold the heat in for Iris. As usual, it was filled to the brim. The trick was to slip in as quickly as possible, letting the excess water spill over the side. With her knees up, Iris just fit into the tub. The steamy water was up to her chin as she leaned her head back against the side.

There had been a big sea battle over an American island called Midway. The reports concerning Midway were confusing. The Japanese claimed they'd won a great victory. Yet, when

185

Eva listened to the American broadcasts, she said they claimed the same victory, even to naming the Japanese ships and carriers they'd sunk. Iris didn't know what to believe.

Should they believe what everyone was saying about food shortages? The longer ration lines and the growing black market indicated that they should. In the beginning, they'd thought a garden would simply allow them to grow some of their favorite vegetables. Now they knew their garden could mean the difference between starving and surviving this winter . . . if they dried and pickled their crops.

They'd gotten some potato eyes from the Swiss undersecretary's kitchen, thanks to Kiyoko. Two long rows of white potatoes were now growing. They'd also gotten some tomato seeds in the same way. The spindly plants were growing beside the house. The rest of the garden was destined to be much more Japanese in character, boasting sweet potatoes, long Japanese cucumbers, onions, a kind of cabbage, some pumpkinlike squash, and daikon, the long hot Japanese radish. Now all they had to do was figure out how to squirrel those things away. They must be prepared in case the war waged longer, in case they couldn't somehow escape . . . in case Cole wasn't able to rescue her.

She shuddered. Looking at the sky, she saw the pearl gray of the clouds washed with the faintest hint of pink. It was almost dark now, yet it seemed she'd just gotten into the tub.

Climbing out, Iris reached for her towel of thin smooth cotton, not like the thick terry cloth of home. The first time she'd bathed, she'd stopped drying and had wrung out her towel under Aunt Toshiko's nose, indicating that she needed another. Her aunt had simply looked at the soaking towel, smiled, and nodded. The Japanese thought that wet towels dry better.

As she stepped out in the silken rain a chorus of frogs filled the air and each stepping stone puddle reflected the lantern's light. Back in the house Eva was sitting on a cushion, reading an English edition of the *Nippon Times* she'd gotten from one of her coworkers at the station.

"How about dinner?" Iris asked mischievously. "I'll take my steak medium rare, my baked potato with lots of butter, and some fresh sliced tomatoes on the side. And pumpkin pie and ice cream for dessert!"

Eva shook her head. "You're just making it harder. We

186

don't even have seasoning for that skinny pink fish in the kitchen."

Iris groaned. "What I wouldn't give for a bacon-and-egg breakfast. I'd even settle for a plain boiled egg. They're so hard to find now."

"*Gomen kudasai,*" Kiyoko said from the doorway.

"*Konban wa, Kiyoko-san,*" Iris called, jumping up and going to the door. "You do us great honor." She bowed as Kiyoko came in. "I was just wondering earlier when I would see you."

"It is an honor to be with you again," Kiyoko replied, bowing, with her arms held tightly in her black quilted jacket. "I hope I am not intruding."

Eva offered tea, but Kiyoko declined, saying, "I can only stay for a few minutes. I am expected back at the Big House."

Suddenly a sharp peep penetrated the room. Iris, thinking that a frog was in the house, looked around the room. It sounded again, this time sounding nothing like the chirp of a frog. She looked at Eva, who was staring at Kiyoko. Another peep pierced the air. Kiyoko returned their stares with a bland expression. Two more peeps came in rapid succession. They seemed to be coming from Kiyoko's sleeve.

"It sounds as if your arm needs oiling," Iris said, controlling her laughter as she sensed a great joke coming.

Kiyoko covered her mouth, but it was no good. Her peals of laughter filled the room. She pulled a wriggling rag from her big sleeve and asked, "Do you think my sleeve is too noisy?"

"What is it?" Iris asked, staring at the cloth, which seemed to have a life of its own.

"Here, open the *furoshiki.*" She shoved the wriggling cloth bag toward Iris. It peeped in protest.

Laughing, Iris untied the cloth and two chicks tumbled out like yellow marbles. They stood unsteadily on their spindly legs, blinking in the light.

"Where did you find them?" Eva cried.

"The gardener raises them for the Swiss undersecretary. So many hatched out from one hen this morning that he said it would be better to give some away than have the hen take care of so many. I took four, and you can have two of them."

"Thank you, Kiyoko-san!" Iris cried, with obvious pleasure.

"But how do we take care of them?" Eva asked.

187

"Ah, they are not for pets. They will grow and make eggs for you. If they are male, at least you will have a dinner from them. You can feed them *awa* seed. I left a small sack beside your door. I think you call it millet in English. It's still available in the stores because people don't eat it. You will also find that when they are bigger, they will keep your garden free from bugs and will eat what you throw to them."

Eva stroked the chicks with an appreciative gleam in her eyes. "We were just talking about how we would like to have an egg now and then."

"It's good you will have them. I must go now," Kiyoko said, bowing. "I will come back tomorrow for a longer visit."

Iris and Eva saw Kiyoko to the door, then brought in the sack of millet and scattered a handful on the newspaper for the chicks. After some confusion, the chicks scratched and pecked at it, then ate it.

However, as Iris and Eva began preparing their own meal, they found themselves constantly doing a little jig to avoid stepping on the fuzzy yellow chicks who dogged their every step as if they were the mother hen.

Iris laughed as she tripped for the third time to avoid squashing a chick. "We've got to pen them up." With that she scooped them up and plopped them into a wooden box.

"I don't know if this is worth it," Eva said, wiping a spot of manure from the mat.

"Sure it is. Just keep thinking of eggs. I'll make a pen for them tomorrow."

"I wonder why Kiyoko is so nice to us," Eva remarked. "Most Japanese don't do things like that, for fear of making you feel guilty with obligation to pay them back. The guys I work with call such an obligation *on*."

Iris was still thinking about what Eva had said long after they'd turned out the lantern and she'd curled up to sleep on her *futon*. Eva's explanation of *on* made a lot of sense. The Japanese felt they should keep their accounts clear, so to speak. That was why people didn't help someone who fell from his bike in the street. How would the victim ever pay back a stranger? He would have that unpaid obligation for the rest of his life. No one would wish that guilt onto another, even a stranger.

That all fit in with what Kiyoko had told her about fulfilling one's duties to others and repaying kindnesses. But then, why was Kiyoko helping them? She had no obligation, no ties to them, and they owed her much. When would their account come due?

What if Kiyoko had an obligation to someone else, like the Kampetei? No, that couldn't be, Iris quickly reassured herself. Still, the doubt remained, gnawing deep within her. She lay staring at the darkened ceiling for a long time. Only when she resolved to talk to Kiyoko about it the next day was she finally able to fall asleep.

The chicks awakened them with their shrill peeping, at the first pale light of morning. Eva glared furiously in the direction of the box and covered her head with her quilt. "I knew it was a mistake," she complained, her voice muffled.

"Just keep thinking of eggs." Iris groaned as she got up to feed them. It wasn't until she'd made the tea and sliced some bread that Eva reluctantly got up and joined her.

The talk of eggs so inspired Eva that she volunteered to go to the market. Sometimes at the end of the week, farmers eager to go home with full packs of supplies would have a few tidbits they sold on the black market rather than through the usual sources. With food scarce and ration lines long, the black market not only flourished, it was a necessity to keep from starving.

Iris was still trying to figure out how to pen the chickens when Kiyoko came.

"Ah, just in time, Kiyoko-san," Iris called. "Come have a cup of tea and help me decide how to keep the chicks."

Kiyoko sat down and sipped her tea. "It's too bad the fence is only on three sides," she said.

Iris stared at the pine and bamboo hedge at the end of the garden. It was quite thick and certainly sufficient as a privacy screen, but an enterprising chicken would take only a minute to get through it. Wire fencing material was unavailable because all metal went into the war effort. It was too bad the bamboo wasn't . . . "That's it!" she shouted, pointing to the hedge. "Isn't that the same stuff the rest of the fence is woven from?"

Kiyoko looked at the dark, tightly woven fence. "Yes," she said, grasping the idea. "But I don't know how to make a fence such as that."

The fence was a work of art, the intricately woven pieces forming a geometric design that subtly entertained the eye.

"I know I can't do that," Iris agreed, "but I could tie pieces of bamboo together like I've seen in other places, just not so pretty."

Kiyoko looked at the end of the garden. "Yes, I think you could. Make sure you place it very tightly against the ground. Otherwise, the chickens will escape. I will have to find you a post, so you can make a gate for me to come through."

Iris smiled. "We couldn't do anything to cut off our visits."

"No, we shouldn't," Kiyoko agreed.

"Kiyoko," Iris began, remembering her concerns of the night before, "what brought you to me and made you such a good friend? Most of the Japanese I know are very careful whom they reach out to for friendship."

"That is true," Kiyoko agreed. "Most Japanese feel a heavy obligation to the Emperor, their parents, and the rest of their family in that order, and then to their acquaintances who have done them favors or brought them pleasure. These obligations are very heavy and they do not wish to take on any more through casual friendship. Their actions are governed by these responsibilities, their *on*.

"But I was not raised in the old Japanese way," she explained. "My father, a great scholar and Catholic from the Meiji Reign, engaged German, French, and English tutors for me. I attended both traditional Japanese schools and a convent. You see, my education was broader than most, which is not always desirable in a wife.

"But I was lucky. Before I was too old the matchmaker approached my father on behalf of a man who wanted his scholar son to have a wife who was more than the simple flowers most Japanese women are trained to be.

"We married, and Kenichi and I knew the love of the poets. Our joy was unbounded when we were blessed with first a daughter and then a son. But such happiness tempted the fates.

"When the military rule took over, people with foreign interests and books were suspect. The Kampetei took my father to the station for questioning. Three days later he returned a changed man. Then the Kampetei came and forced Father to watch them burn all his library. I was afraid they were going to throw him on the fire, but now I think Father would have preferred that. Within a week he died of a broken heart. Before the year was out Mother followed him.

"Along with other intellectuals Kenichi and I buried our books in the countryside. When the Kampetei came to our house they found nothing, but still they harassed my husband. That was too much. Kenichi proved his love by divorcing me lest he endanger the lives of our children and me. The day after the children and I moved into my parents' house the Kampetei arrested Kenichi for thoughts disloyal to the Emperor. I've not seen him since.

"Angered by his father's fate, our son, Koichi, refused to comply with the increasing military rule in his school. Then he, too, was taken from me. He was sent into military training. I last saw my son when he left on his fourteenth birthday. Five months ago I received a letter from him saying he was going to war as a pilot.

"The same time Koichi was sent away, Hanako, our daughter, inexplicably lost her job as a teaching assistant and was ordered to work in a munitions factory with many foreigners doing enforced labor.

"Alone, I had to look for a job. I found this position working for the Swiss undersecretary caring for European guests and his household. For once my education helped me.

"Then last October there was an explosion in Hanako's factory. She was killed."

Iris reached over and took Kiyoko's hand. "I'm so sorry," she murmured, hot tears streaming down her face. "I wish I could help."

"You have already helped me in my sorrow," Kiyoko said simply. "I was walking in the garden of the Big House when I heard you moving in with Eva. Your voice is very much like Hanako's, so youthful and quick, like a sparrow. Your laughter helped heal my heart. It was as if you were sent to fill the void in my life. I'm sorry I made you cry with my story."

"Oh, no, *Kiyoko-san*," Iris said, wiping her nose with a handkerchief. "I think it's important that I know this. Now I understand and appreciate you even more. I can see why you want to take care of me, just like my own mother would want to take care of a Japanese girl caught in America away from her family by the war."

"Your mother is still alive?"

"Yes. Why do you ask?"

"I have a paper from the Swiss Red Cross. They have a message about your father. They don't mention your mother."

She reached into her baggy *monpe* and pulled out a folded envelope.

Iris tore it open and read anxiously:

To: *Iris Hashimoto, c/o Swiss Red Cross, Tokyo*
Re: *Chosu Hashimoto, previous address 1101 Pearl Avenue, San Francisco, California, U.S.A.*

Chosu Hashimoto, Japanese Issei, has been sent to the Manzanar alien relocation camp near Owens Valley, northern California. Correspondence can be directed to this person through the American Red Cross by writing c/o Camp Administrator, Alien Relocation, Newell, California.

Chosu Hashimoto is inmate #2341567. No word received to health problems so it is assumed that he is in good health.

Iris put down the letter. Confusion, fear, and rage churned within her. In her distress, she reverted to English. "Alien relocation camp? It sounds like a concentration camp! What's going on over there?" she cried. "And where's Mama?" She looked at the paper again, as if she might find something that she'd missed before. "This doesn't sound like the United States of America! They wouldn't take loyal citizens and put them in a concentration camp. That's what they do in Germany . . . and here!"

"Shhh," Kiyoko cautioned. "Speak quietly and in Japanese."

Iris looked around, suddenly feeling as if she were surrounded by dark forces. "This must be a false report," she said quietly in Japanese. "My father wasn't an American citizen on paper. But he was more loyal to the United States than most native-born Americans. This must be a false report," she repeated, "sent to make me lose faith and give up my citizenship. Well it's not going to work. I know they're lying!"

"I hope you're right," Kiyoko said gently. "Nevertheless, I asked them to confirm the authenticity of the cable, to make sure it was from the Swiss Red Cross. They said it was." She looked almost as sad as Iris felt. After a moment she reached into her *monpe* and brought out another letter. "There is another one for Eva," she said, handing it to Iris.

Iris looked at the envelope as if she were trying to see

through it. "I wish Eva would get back. If she doesn't hurry, I'll open it myself."

"Hi! Where are you?" Eva called just then as she came in the front door.

"We're out on the porch," Iris called. "Come on out—you've got a letter."

They waited in silence while Eva anxiously read. From her expression, Iris knew immediately that Eva's news was as puzzling as the note about Chosu. However, there was no outburst from Eva. She simply put the letter on her lap and reached for a cup of tea. Then she looked up at Iris and said, "Remember that evening I came home and said that there was something strange on the news about Japanese relocation camps?"

"Yes . . ." Iris said slowly. "We decided they must be talking about people who'd been bombed out in Hawaii or Japanese who were trapped in America like we're trapped in Japan."

"I've heard three other reports about these camps. I really didn't understand why they kept referring to issei, the Japanese emigrants, and the nisei, the second-generation Japanese—and about potentially dangerous aliens and protecting innocent Japanese from the wrath of Americans. I was so involved in trying to figure out who might be winning the war, and what might be happening to Sparky and Cole, that I just didn't think about it."

"You mean you think it's true?"

"Yes."

"They don't have these concentration camps for German aliens and German descendants. There were a lot of those around. What about Marta? People like her aren't locked up 'for their safety and to protect America' from potential German saboteurs," Iris said bitterly. "It's the same thing as the 'whites only' sign at the officers' club at Pearl. We're good enough to get bombed and shot at, but not good enough to trust. Yet someone like Marta, with a revolving door to her bedroom and the moral code of a cobra, can be trusted just because her skin is the right color and her eyes are the right shape."

"That is why there is war," Kiyoko interjected. "Japanese think that people who look Japanese are above all others; Americans think that only those who are Caucasian can be trusted. Maybe we'd be better off if we didn't see one another, just talked over the telephone."

Eva nodded wryly at Kiyoko's weak joke, then turned to Iris. "My father's in an internment camp in Owens Valley, California. Where's yours?"

"Same. I hope they can get together. I told the Red Cross to tell Papa that I was all right and wanted to come home but couldn't."

"Too bad he doesn't know you both have a lady who is your mama in Japan."

Iris looked at Kiyoko. Her face, always more animated and expressive than other Japanese, now seemed to be radiating warmth and affection. Iris paused, then knelt solemnly in front of her and bowed, her head touching the floor. "I am honored Mama-Kiyoko-san."

Eva bowed equally low beside her. "I am likewise honored, Mama-Kiyoko-san."

"May I live to hear your children call me *Oba-a-san*," Kiyoko whispered.

CHAPTER XIV

The third floor of the NHK Building always had the same stale smell of cigarette smoke mixed with a musty scent reminiscent of sandalwood. Iris was used to it. She noticed it only when she first came in and as she was leaving.

She paused at the coat rack to put on her *monpe* over her skirt and blouse and to slip into her raincoat. It was a funny-looking outfit, but the *monpe* made her less conspicuous in a crowd and kept her legs warm, and the American-made raincoat was simple enough to resemble those worn by the more modern Japanese women.

The trees were just beginning to turn color in the park across the way. She crossed the street so that she could walk under the branches on her way to catch the *densha* home. It was a brief pleasure that wouldn't take any extra time. That was something there wasn't enough of anymore: time.

The autumnal tapestry of topaz and bronze brought a wave of nostalgia sweeping over her. In San Francisco, she'd loved autumn best, that time of year gilded with afternoon sun and September leaves. But now it only made her remember that she had little time to store food from the garden and to provide for the bitter cold of December and January.

Ahead, workmen were repairing a spot in the street. It was nothing too unusual, but she slowed her pace and felt a hesitancy as she approached them. For the past five days she'd felt that one worker had been watching her intently as she passed. Since her experience with Sergeant Ito, she'd become extremely cautious and very much aware of anything that could be construed as surveillance. Now she saw the same man watching her again today. When she was almost there, he put down his shovel and walked slowly to a water can near the work site, a place she would have to pass in order to get to the streetcar stop.

She tried to pretend that she didn't notice his stare. She kept her pace calm and steady rather than running past him, as she felt like doing. It was even more disconcerting to notice, now that she was closer to him, that he was a handsome young man, about her age, with a bold bearing uncharacteristic of Japanese workmen.

As she passed, she glanced up to see if he was still staring. Their eyes met. He gave a slight bow and said quietly, *"Konnichi wa, Iris-san."*

Startled, Iris bowed ever so slightly, never slowing her pace. How did he know her name? Who was he? Why was he watching her? She turned and looked back as she started to board the streetcar. He was back at work, shoveling broken pavement with the rest of the workers. Strangely, it seemed more of an intriguing mystery to her than a threat. His eyes, although bold and daring, appeared friendly, not cold and cruel like Sergeant Ito's. Still, it was strange, and it made her uneasy.

Then as she settled down in a seat on the *densha* she decided he was probably harmless, and she dismissed the thought. She glanced at the clouds anxiously, wondering if there would be rain tonight. She'd have to bring in the drying vegetables before it did. While doing that, she would entertain Eva with her story of the mystery man.

Under Kiyoko's careful direction, they'd harvested their garden, cutting up the daikon, onions, and various vegetables and spreading them out to dry in the late summer sun. A few were still drying now at the end of September, but most were in boxes stacked neatly in the corner of the cooking room. Kiyoko assured them that such vegetables, boiled in water, would make the difference between a meal and hunger this winter.

She had also insisted that they purchase whatever was available in the marketplace with what money and ration coupons they had, including bags of rice and *nori*, black paper-thin strips of dried seaweed. Iris felt like a squirrel as she looked at their kitchen hoard when she came in the door.

"Eva!" she called, putting her coat away. "Are you home?"

"Out here," Eva answered from the garden. "I thought I'd better start digging the potatoes. Kiyoko said they'd begin to rot if I left them in the ground after the rains began. What do you think of using the air-raid shelter as a root cellar?"

"Makes sense," she said, stepping out on the porch. "Just leave room for us. I'd hate having to explain to the air-raid warden why we weren't in the shelter and all our potatoes were."

Eva laughed.

"I had a strange thing happen this afternoon," Iris said, as Eva put down her spade and came over to the porch.

Iris proceeded to tell her about the man who had been watching her and who had greeted her by name today. "The strange thing about it is that I wasn't really afraid after I'd looked him square in the eye. He just didn't seem to be threatening, for some reason."

"Well, maybe it's just some strange Japanese way of meeting a girl," Eva said. "But if you see any more of him, maybe you'd better ask Kiyoko's advice."

"I think I'll wait and see if anything else happens. I'd hate to have her start worrying over nothing," Iris said, walking toward the drying racks.

As she began taking the thin pieces of daikon off the racks and placing them in a wooden box, the two chickens fluttered over to her, clucking expectantly. Gertrude was a rusty red color, already showing signs of becoming a chesty biddy with a rather officious manner. Charlotte was a little gray-speckled hen and much more timid, given to following Gertrude at a respectful distance. They were growing awfully fast, and Iris and Eva were hoping to get an egg for Thanksgiving.

Even though they had scant knowledge about poultry raising, they had made the two birds into healthy, spoiled pets in the past three months, giving them full run of the yard as soon as the fence was completed. The garden had been virtually bug-free for the whole summer, which had helped their harvest.

"Hey, get away, you two!" Iris said, laughing at the pecking demands of the adolescent hens. "You couldn't possibly like this dried daikon."

"Say, would you look at that cabbage stuff?" Eva asked. "I had to move the pot away from the house. The smell is awful."

"Yeah, I noticed it this morning. Maybe Kiyoko was wrong about that. Just slicing it up and covering it with salt doesn't seem right. Smelled to me like it was really spoiling. I'd throw it out and stop turning it if Kiyoko didn't keep asking about it."

Iris walked to the crock resting on a rock beside the fence. "Whew!" she said, putting the lid back on quickly. "Well, maybe the hens will eat it."

"Let's give it to them before they start laying eggs. I'd hate to have to eat their eggs after they'd eaten this stuff."

Even though Iris had treated the subject lightly with Eva, she was plagued by the mystery of the strange workman. The next evening, she left the NHK Building reluctantly. If she dawdled, perhaps he'd go away, she reasoned with childish optimism. When she reached the park, the workmen were gone, the street was repaired, and her mystery man was nowhere in sight. She was amused to note that she felt a slight disappointment that she wouldn't see him again.

She was one block from the *densha* stop when the air was torn by the shrieking of the air-raid siren. Half in disgust and half in fear, Iris looked skyward. There were no planes in sight, nor had there been since the Doolittle raid. Like everyone else in Japan, she'd been frightened by that first and only bombing. They now knew that the islands were not immune to attack. Someday the bombers would return, and

197

when they did, they would not go without leaving a trail of fire and blood in their wake.

The instructions were that people caught in the streets during a raid were to go to the railway terminals or certain designated buildings. This made no sense to Iris, because it seemed that railway stations would be the first places the Americans would attack.

Today the nearest shelter was the terminal. The crowd surged toward it and Iris was swept along in the flow. She glanced at the sky again to assure herself that it was just another drill. If it really was an air attack, she decided, she would bolt for the open park. For that reason, she stayed near the terminal's entrance, her back pressed against the wall as she sat on the floor with the others.

The Japanese around her were packed in tightly, sitting on their heels in what she considered a decidedly uncomfortable position. Somehow, they managed through some peculiar manipulations of their fingers to plug their ears while covering their eyes. Iris never ceased to find it an amazing scene. She turned to look again at the patch of sky visible from her viewpoint near the entrance.

"It's just a practice. Don't worry."

Iris turned, startled to hear English whispered near her ear. She was even more shocked to find herself looking into the eyes of the mystery man. She looked around at all the packed bodies; she was hemmed in and couldn't escape. "Who are you?" she asked, almost in anger.

"My name's Bill," he whispered, with a perfect American accent. "I've got to talk to you. I went to your grandmother's and she wouldn't give me your address, just where you worked. Tell me where I can find you."

"Why should I?" she whispered suspiciously.

"No talking!" shouted the air-raid warden. Iris shifted uncomfortably on her heels and looked away from him. How was she to know he wasn't a Kampetei spy, or a criminal who preyed on unsuspecting young girls. He could have found out her name by questioning some of her fellow workers as they came out of the NHK Building. She tried to inch farther away from him. The all-clear sounded and she resolved to get away as quickly as possible. Jumping up, she headed toward the terminal entrance.

"I'll be selling baskets on the street outside your office

tomorrow afternoon. Buy one from me and leave your address on a piece of paper." Iris turned and glowered as she heard the English words whispered once more near her ear. He was looking in the other direction, apparently muttering to himself. Only Iris could understand him in the crowd. She started to move away from him, trying to ignore his insistent whispering. His next words stopped her cold. "It's important. I have a message from Cole."

Iris stopped. A Japanese woman bumped into her, then passed by, glaring. Bill was gone. Iris caught a glimpse of him going toward the train platform. Had she imagined what she'd heard him say? She turned and walked out into the street. Only through habit was she able to find her way home. The hoarse whisper, *"I have a message from Cole,"* kept echoing in her mind. Fear and doubt battled with the hope she'd been denying.

Her tension mounted as she walked into the house.

"Hi," Eva said. "Kiyoko was just here. She walked right up to the crock of rotting cabbage, lifted the lid, and stirred it. Then she told me it's just perfect and we should keep it under the house. I couldn't believe it. And then she packs it off and puts it there herself." Noticing Iris's expression she asked, "What's wrong? Did you see your mystery man again and he swept you away with his passionate stare?"

"You don't know how close you are." She quickly told of her experience in the train station during the air-raid drill.

When Iris finished, Eva let out a soft whistle. "Did anyone else hear what he was saying?"

"I don't think so. He spoke quietly and kept looking in the other direction so it seemed like he was muttering to himself, not to me. Why?"

"Well, assuming he's for real, we have to make sure no Kampetei informer was listening. But what if he isn't legitimate?"

"That's what scares me. I don't know what to do and I've got to decide by tomorrow."

"How would he know about Cole?" Eva asked logically.

"It would have been quite easy for the Kampetei to have opened all my mail before the war, and kept records."

"But how would he have such a good American accent if he wasn't authentic?" Eva persisted.

"There were over ten thousand Japanese-Americans caught in Tokyo by this war. They all are fighting to survive, and they will all choose different ways to do it. I know of several who've already changed their citizenship. Some of them are probably even working for the military and the Kampetei."

"All things considered, stay away from him," Eva said finally.

Iris's heart sank. "But what if he is for real?" she asked, close to tears. "What if he actually has a message from Cole?"

They argued both sides of the question long into the night. The next morning, Iris boarded the *densha* still in a quandary.

She leaned her cheek against the cold window and her warm breath clouded the glass. There were workmen on the road ahead and Iris watched them with curiosity. The mysterious Bill had worked in just such a crew, but these workmen seemed unusual for some reason. As they drew closer she could see that they were taller and more gaunt than most Japanese. As the *densha* passed the work crew, Iris's heart stopped. They were blondes, and light-complected, the kinds of faces she'd not seen in almost two years. They swung their spades and picks with the lethargy of the hopeless. Prisoners of war! Americans!

One of her fellow passengers was an elderly man dressed in a business suit. He caught her eye and made a derogatory gesture toward the prisoners. Iris looked down at her lap, trying to hide her tears.

That settled it, she thought as she got off the streetcar and walked to the NHK Building. She would take the chance that this Bill was legitimate. Perhaps Cole was being held prisoner here in Japan and was using Bill to get word to her for help. She would have to take the chance. If Bill proved to be a Kampetei trap, she would say that she had thought he was a spy and had merely been trying to get information from him as proof before reporting him . . . a transparent lie, but she'd try it anyway.

The day dragged on. Just before she left, she scrawled her name and simply "Gardener's house, Swiss undersecretary's residence" on a piece of paper, stuffed it into her coat pocket, then hurried down the stairs from her third-floor office.

The only man in sight was a basket seller, carrying his baskets tied to a long pole over his shoulders. Bent with age, he could not be the same man. She hesitated, then walked slowly toward him. She pretended to examine the baskets while she tried to make up her mind. Should she assume he was a messenger? But what if he wasn't, and she thrust her name and address into his hand? He'd report her. She fingered the slip of paper in her pocket.

"Do you wish to buy a basket?" The old man's voice was raspy and he spoke provincial Japanese.

"Oh, I don't think . . ." Her voice trailed off as she looked at him. The face was not as old as the posture indicated, and the eyes above the gray beard were clearly those of the man called Bill.

"My baskets are made of the finest reeds, dried in the sun." His eyes twinkled boyishly.

"I . . . I see," Iris stammered. "In that case, I will buy this one here." She pointed to the one on the end, which had a lid.

"That will be ten yen," he said, tipping the pole and cleverly catching the basket as it slipped off.

"Ten yen," Iris said, reaching into her bag, then stopping. "That's a little high, isn't it?"

The now familiar eyes were laughing. "For you I'll make the price two yen. But you must promise that you will never use my basket to cook *hamburgers*."

"What?" Iris was startled by his use of the English word. Then she realized that he was teasing her and enjoying it immensely. She bit her lip to keep from laughing. "Oh, of course," she said finally, handing him the paper money. She'd slipped her address note in between the bills.

The mystery man quickly looked through the money, treating the slip of paper as if it were a normal piece of currency and putting it quickly into the bag tied around his waist. "Thank you so much, *Ojo-san*," he said, bowing deeply. "May I have the privilege of your business a thousand times more."

Iris nodded, took her basket and walked across the street toward the small park. She was committed now, she thought as she kicked her feet through the autumn leaves. She didn't like the idea of not knowing when this person might show up on their doorstep. How would Eva react to her decision?

Iris needn't have worried. When she told Eva that evening about having seen the prisoners of war, Eva simply said, "I would have done the same thing." She was quiet for a while, then asked almost in a whisper, "Do you think he will know anything about Sparky?"

The evening was darkening and the frogs were beginning to croak in the garden. "I don't know. It depends on where and when he got the message from Cole."

They talked so long in the growing darkness that their dinner was late. Iris was hungry and the few Japanese *Choka Suba* noodles floating in thin vegetable broth looked especially good tonight. Just as she put the first spoonful into her mouth, the air-raid siren screamed.

"Oh damn, not again! Let's not go this time. It's just another stupid drill. There are no planes coming. We'd hear them."

Eva reluctantly put down her bowl. "You know the warden didn't check on us last drill so he's bound to start with us this time. We'd better go out. They can fine us, or worse, if we don't."

Iris followed Eva out to their shelter, grumbling all the way. "At least we should have brought our dinner along with . . ."

She was interrupted by Eva's muffled shriek from inside the shelter. As she stumbled out backward, Iris caught her.

"There's a man in there!" Eva cried, pointing to the black hole that was the shelter door.

Still holding on to Eva's arm, more for support than to keep Eva from running, Iris picked up the garden hoe and called in Japanese, "Come out of there."

"For chrissake, keep it quiet and get in here," came the man's voice in clear American English.

Eva gasped, and Iris dropped the hoe and took a step forward. "Bill, is that you?" she asked in a hesitant whisper.

"Well, who the hell else do you know who talks like this? Get in before the warden gets here and finds you talking to your air-raid shelter."

Bill struck a match and lit a candle when the door was closed behind them; then with the same match he lit a cigarette, squinting against the smoke in a roguish manner. "I thought you'd never come out tonight. I didn't know if you'd told your friend about me or not and didn't want to take the chance of scaring her to death. Guess I sort of failed in that respect," he said, by way of apology to Eva. "I didn't know the air-raid siren was going to go off tonight, or I wouldn't have hidden in here."

Eva seemed to be relaxing under his easy chatter. "That's all right. Next time I'll just bring a light with me and check the place out first. No telling what kind of creatures might be hiding here."

"And we don't know what kind of creature we've got this time, either," Iris said sharply. She'd been frightened half out of her wits after a long tense day and she wasn't in the mood to put up with any more. "The air-raid warden will be along any minute now and I want to know whether I should report you or hide you."

Bill eyed her steadily for a moment, then nodded. "You have no reason to trust me," he agreed. "See if this information is enough credentials for you. If it isn't, let me know so I can make my escape before this air-raid warden makes his appearance. I met Cole Tennyson in the Philippines. He was a lieutenant when he arrived in Manila, but he became a captain right after I met him. He's about six feet tall, maybe a little less, has blue green eyes, light brown hair that was sunstreaked almost to blond, a dimple that forms a crease on the right side when he smiles, a habit of running his hand through his hair when he's undecided or nervous about something, and a fiancée named Iris Hashimoto, whom he met while she was a secretary at the air force base in Pearl Harbor." He paused. Footsteps were coming down the path to the shelter. "Your warden is coming. Either scream and report me, or hide me."

Iris was shocked by Bill's description of Cole. His mention of Cole's habit of running his hand through his hair brought back the moment when Cole was proposing to her, uncertain if she would accept. She just stood there staring at Bill with tears in her eyes. Then she too heard the approaching footsteps and was filled with the fear that this single link to Cole might soon be snatched away from her. "Oh, dear God," she whispered. "How can we hide you in here?"

Bill threw his cigarette to the ground and looked around, taking off his coat in the same movement. "Throw this over me and pull those potato sacks up by my head and sit on my back," he commanded as he kneeled on his hands and knees.

Iris did as he said and they both sat on him as if he were a pile of supplies. Eva blew out the candle just before the warden opened the door and shone his torch inside. A quick sweep of the light, a grunt of approval, and he was gone. Iris and Eva sat trembling on Bill's back, listening to the receding footsteps.

"For chrissake," Bill complained in a hoarse whisper. "You can get off now."

They jumped up with a nervous giggle and heard Bill rummaging around in the dark. He struck a match and lit the candle again. "There," he said, settling down in the corner and lighting another cigarette. "You came through like troopers. Now, shall I tell you how I met Cole?"

"Please," Iris said eagerly.

Bill began his recitation of how they'd first met. Iris found it amusing that the letters addressed in Japanese had been done by Bill. However, she was dismayed to find out that he'd addressed many more than she'd received. He explained how he'd obtained information for Cole and Dick before the war, how they'd said good-bye, and his plans for becoming a behind-the-lines "freelance spy," as he called it.

They listened spellbound, delighted to hear another American accent, devouring his every word concerning Cole and the conditions in the Philippines. Finally, Eva broke into his narrative.

"I must ask," she said quickly. "Did you ever know or hear of a man named Irwin Sparks? Cole would have called him Sparky."

"Sparky," Bill said, rubbing his chin. "Let's see . . . I know I never met anyone by that name, because I only talked to Cole and Dick and once a guy named Jake." He paused again. "I do remember Cole once complaining about getting things fixed or something and he said if Sparky wasn't still in Hawaii . . . yeah, I'm sure the name he used was Sparky. Said he was great for coming up with something out of thin air, a kind of wheeler-dealer."

"When was that?" Eva asked eagerly. "Do you think he was in Hawaii when the war broke out?"

"Far as I know, he was. Only time I heard about him was that once. Must have been in October or later, because Cole was pretty desperate to get some things ready for the attack we were expecting by then."

Iris grabbed Eva's hand. "That's great!" she said. "At least Sparky wasn't captured on Bataan."

"If he made it through Pearl Harbor," Eva said, torn between tears and a smile.

Just then the all-clear sounded. "I don't want to chance being seen in your house," Bill said. "Go inside and make like you're getting ready for bed and turn out the lights. When it's dark, I'll come to the back door."

"We haven't eaten," Eva said hesitantly. "We don't have much, just a thin soup, but . . ."

"Put some extra water in it," Bill said with a grin. "I've got some flavoring powder and some tofu in my pocket. It was going to be my dinner. Heat it up, and when it's ready, turn out the lights."

They went into the house and began following his directions. Iris even laid out the *futons* in the sleeping room. Then she slid the door closed and turned off the light.

The faint glow from the coals gave the room a pale rosy hue and Iris could see only the shadow of Eva's motions as she quietly put the bowls and the soup pot on their low table, then put the teapot over the coals.

There was a soft movement on the path outside their door, then a light tapping on the edge of the porch. Iris opened the door.

Bill entered and Iris smelled a mixture of tobacco and soap that reminded her of Cole. Warm memories washed over her, leaving an echo of sorrow deep inside.

"Where's that soup pot?" Bill asked quietly. Eva took him to the table. He sat down, pulled an envelope from his pocket, and sprinkled its contents in the soup. Then he took a square packet from his other pocket and unwrapped it. Iris could see a cube of something white in the moonlight filtering through the window. Bill opened a pocketknife and cut it into smaller squares. It was obviously soft, like a stiff pudding. "It's tofu," he explained as he threw the pieces into the pot. "If you haven't had any, you'd better start getting used to it. It's bean-curd paste and a pretty good source of protein. It takes on the flavor of whatever you mix it with and it may be one of the few things we'll be able to get to eat before this war is over."

Eva dished up the soup and they sat down in the darkness. "This tastes pretty good," Eva said as she tasted the soup.

"Yeah, a little like meat, just sort of soft," Iris added. "You'll have to tell us what was in your magic envelope."

"Just some soup seasoning. Spices and some ground-up dried seaweed and things like that."

"How did you learn how to cook?" Iris asked.

"My mother. She's Japanese and so is my father. They

moved to the States just after they were married. My father was the youngest of nine sons and didn't have much of a future here in Japan," he explained. "They took what little money my mother's dowry contained and some gifts from their wedding, and moved to a place in Oregon called Hood River, where I was born.

"I worked in the orchards through high school, saving for college. But after one year of college, I'd had a stomachful of prejudice. I quit in a huff, hitchhiked to Portland, and jumped the first freighter out. Got my seaman's papers the same week I got the news my folks were killed in a car wreck, so I just kept on going. When I got to the Philippines I liked it so much I stayed. I got a job in a Japanese hotel in Manila and saw the war coming.

"That was when I realized I was an American. It was *my* country they were plotting against," he said. "I realized that if the Japanese really did start a war against the United States, I would never be welcomed back there unless I'd done something to stop it. You see, we're locked inside a skin that looks like we're Japanese. But inside, we're as American as apple pie. The only way we're going to convince the rest of America that our 'wrappings' don't count is if we work like the devil to help win this war."

"I think that's the best way I've ever heard it put," Iris said, pouring the tea. "That's really why I left Hawaii. I was afraid that my 'wrapping' was going to cause Cole a lot of problems."

"That's what I figured when Cole told me how you'd bolted like that," he said softly. "The message he wanted me to give you was that he loves you and is working in every way to get you out or to get to you as soon as possible. That was before the war broke out, but I'm sure he's still trying and still feels the same way."

Iris was quiet for a moment. It was a voice calling to her from the past, throbbing with hope she'd buried long ago. "You don't know if he's a prisoner of war, if he was captured on Bataan?"

Bill shook his head. "I'm sorry. I hit the hills on December eighth. It took me a while to work my way from Manila to Tokyo. I had to figure out a way to avoid getting shot by both the Americans and the Japanese. While I was hiding out, I heard that Cole's friend Jake was a guerrilla in the hills north of Manila. He was trying to send messages to someone in Australia. Since Cole had been working with the brass, I assumed it was Cole that Jake was trying to reach. I don't think they would have let him stay behind when he'd been so . . ." He stopped and patted Iris's hand. "I didn't mean to make you cry."

"It's just that," Iris sniffed, "just that I've thought all this time that there was no hope, that he was a prisoner of war or worse. We've been looking at all the pictures in the papers with a magnifying glass, trying to see if we could see Cole and Sparky. We were hoping they weren't dead. . . ."

"Those horror pictures?" Bill moaned. "No wonder you two are . . . oh, hell. Listen, I'm fairly sure that Cole isn't a prisoner. Maybe he is, but all indications are that he had a chance of making it out of there. As for your friend Sparky," he said, turning to Eva, who was also crying quietly, "I honestly don't know, but there's reason to believe he never left Hawaii. From everything I heard, the ones who took the worst beating were the navy. The Army Air Corps was pretty well smashed, but not as bad. Since he was an airman, he has a better chance of being alive today. I don't want to raise false hopes but . . ." He paused awkwardly. "Anyhow, I'm counting on that being the case."

"Thanks, Bill," Iris said finally. "We appreciate you taking the time coming here to give us the message."

"But why all the secrecy?" Eva said, suddenly cautious.

"Well, you're known to be Americans and therefore suspect. You see, even the Kampetei think I'm Japanese; in fact, everyone here does, except you. Granted, they don't all think I'm the same Japanese—some think I'm an old basket seller, others think I'm a young worker who just hasn't been drafted yet. You've already seen two of my identities, Iris. It gives me the ability to float in the society here, and that's useful."

"But how do you get your identity cards?" Iris pursued.

Bill looked uncomfortable. "I have my ways. Somebody dies, someone can be bought."

"About a week ago I heard at the Domei, where I work, that the Japanese are landing in Australia now," Eva cut in. "Do you know if it's true?"

"They're claiming to be on some islands north of Darwin," Bill said in a suddenly professional tone. "But you shouldn't believe everything you hear. Both sides tend to cover up the worst and glorify the best. But the Japanese lie, deny, and ignore when they aren't doing so well. Keep that in mind when you hear conflicting news reports."

He put his hands on his knees and leaned forward. "You see, your jobs can be pretty useful, too. But we'll talk about that another time." He got up and went to the back porch. "I'd better let you working girls get some shut-eye." He paused. "If you don't mind, I'll drop in on you from time to time. I don't know if I can manage to give you warning every time so that I won't scare you like I did tonight, but I'll try."

"Don't make it too long between surprises," Iris said with a smile.

They stood watching him from the doorway. When he looked back with a final wave Iris blurted out, "Bill, wait. . . ." He stopped and half-turned, the moonlight shadowing his strong-boned face, his dark eyebrows lifting in question. "I just wanted to say thank you," she said awkwardly. "I mean, it really meant a lot to hear what you had to tell us. I'm sorry if I was rude before."

Smiling, he nodded and turned to leave.

"Be careful," Iris said softly before he was out of hearing.

He looked at her over his shoulder and said quietly, "Thanks."

CHAPTER XV

Cole threw his weight back, pulling on the stick to bring his plane out of a loop. The P-40 was a heavy plane and making a dive was hard work. A few more maneuvers like that and the kids following him would have a lot more confidence against the Zeros. He turned and looked behind him. There were four planes left of the eight he'd started with. One had blown a tire on takeoff, two had turned back with engine trouble, and one had gotten lost in the "rat race," the training exercise of follow-the-leader that Cole was taking them through. In Hawaii, before the war, such a poor performance would have appalled him, but they had had more planes and supplies then, and there had been no enemy flying over every day shooting holes in their equipment.

He waggled his wings, signaling that they should get into the finger formation, so called because it formed the shape of the four fingers of an outstretched hand. They were learning, he thought with approval. Hunt in packs. That's what he kept drilling into them. It wasn't that they weren't good; it was that they hadn't had the right kind of training before they were shipped out. On top of that, they were working with planes and equipment that weren't serviced or repaired properly. Broken or worn parts couldn't be replaced because there were no replacement parts.

He flipped the switch on the throttle for his throat mike. "Red Fox to cubs. Let's head for the den." They tried not to use the radio more than was absolutely necessary because the Allied warning systems weren't very good and there was no telling when the Japanese might be listening in. He'd used it now so that the lost plane might pick it up. They banked and set their course for Seven Mile Strip, Port Moresby, New Guinea, the last Allied outpost between the Japanese and Australia. It wasn't much, but it was their home base.

The outline of New Guinea soon loomed ahead like a sleeping dinosaur. Just a few miles behind the coastline, the dark mass of the Owen Stanley Range soared sharply to cloud-wrapped heights of more than thirteen thousand feet. It wasn't a place to get shot down. The steep, jagged slopes were covered with a rain forest so dense that sunlight seldom penetrated through the vine-tangled canopy to the black, moldy floor. It formed a forbidding jungled backbone the length of the country, a formidable barricade the Allies had naïvely thought would keep out invaders, until the Japanese began slashing their way through it. At this moment they were clawing their way to Imita Ridge, just thirty miles from Port Moresby.

Cole picked up the familiar reef with its opalescent blue and green coral encircling the two-mile-wide lagoon. Port Moresby was a small town with wharves lining the shimmering blue harbor on one side and picturesque native huts rising on spindly stilts above the water on the other side.

Seven Mile Strip was just north of Port Moresby. Cole led the pack in to buzz the field, then roared his engine to gain altitude, did a quick split "S" turn, cut his throttle, and coasted in for a flashy landing. Each one of his formation followed suit at five-second intervals. It created an aura of bravado and daring that he liked to encourage in his pilots. When anyone on the ground saw one of Cole's pilots landing with a straight-on approach, they knew something was wrong and stood by.

As he was climbing out of the cockpit, Cole heard another plane engine. It was the one he'd lost in the "rat race." The pilot was coming in straight and the engine was coughing. No wonder he hadn't kept up with the rest of the pack.

"Damn!" Cole slapped the side of his plane.

"What's the matter, Captain?" Lefty, his crew chief, was watching him with troubled eyes.

"Same old thing. How the hell can we fight a war when we can't keep our planes in the air? We need a miracle worker out here to keep things going with the meager supplies they dribble down to us."

"What about that friend of yours in Hawaii you keep talking about?"

"Sparky? Boy, he'd be great." Cole grinned. "I asked the colonel to see if he could steal him away from Hickam. Haven't heard yet."

"Maybe that's why the colonel wants to see you. He sent word out for you to report to him as soon as you get in."

"He probably wants to know why I haven't released this green crew for combat duty yet," he said, watching the rough landing of the stray plane. "By the way, you might check the elevator cable. Seemed a bit stiff in the dive."

"Roger."

Colonel Blackwell looked up as Cole came though the door, casually returned his salute, and pointed to a chair beside the desk. He had been tall and thin to begin with, but New Guinea had made him gaunt. There was a look to his cool blue eyes that made Cole think of the men on Corregidor—a haunted, shadowed look.

"How are the new pilots shaping up, Tennyson?" he asked as Cole sat down.

"They ought to be ready for combat in a couple of weeks . . . if we have planes for them to fly."

"I don't know if we'll have them or not. Right now there are ten off the line and I don't have the parts to fix them."

"Another one just barely landed, sir."

The colonel grimaced. "Four have been shot down in the past week and six have been shot up in raids on the strip here and will have to be patched up somehow. Then there's the five that are scattered in bits and pieces around the mountains. Don't know how much longer we can keep this up without replacements.

"And look at this," he continued furiously. "Those lily-hearted asses in Australia won't send us what supplies we have there if we miss crossing a *t* in the requisitions." He threw a handful of returned requisition forms on the desk.

Cole shifted uneasily in his chair.

The colonel suddenly leaned forward. "What do you know about that man Sparks you told me to get from Hawaii? Is he the kind to go AWOL?"

"Sparky? Well, he's a bit unorthodox, sir, but he'd never . . why do you ask?"

"I took your word that he was the kind of mover and doer we need out here and sent for him. There was a shipment of B-24 Liberators coming out from Hawaii and they said they'd put him on with those. Just got a radio from Brisbane. Not only do the Liberators have cracked antishimmy collars on their nosewheels, but they don't have your friend with them either. They do have the papers for him there, though. Just wondered if you could give me an idea of where to start looking for him."

"He's no shirker, sir. Did you check back with Hickam Field? Maybe he didn't make it on board. Knowing the army, they forgot to tell him to go, just sent his papers on."

"If you're sure he didn't go AWOL, I'll stir up some questions. But I don't want to take a chance of losing him just because of a momentary misjudgment on his part," the colonel said, standing up.

Cole got up, saluted, and turned to go, then stopped in the doorway. "I hear a big engine coming in, sir. Are we expecting anything?"

"There's a C-47 coming in from New Caledonia, carrying a cargo of supplies. Let's go see if the navy has robbed us again."

They walked out to the strip and watched as the twin-engine cargo plane came in. As it taxied to a stop at the end of the field, Cole said, "That ought to serve us pretty well, sir. Too bad it doesn't have a couple of fighter planes stuck in its belly."

"Hell, I'd be happy to see a couple of B-25 wheel bearings come out of it."

"You're right about . . ." Cole stopped and stared at the man jumping down from the C-47 hatch. "You can forget that missing sergeant we were talking about, Colonel. I'd recognize that swagger anywhere."

"Hey, Tennyson!" Sparky called, coming up and pounding Cole on the back. "What kind of orders did you write up for me? They were going to take me clear to Australia."

"Well, that's how you get to New Guinea, you stupid son of a bitch. What are you doing on that C-47?"

"Hell, that's a pretty roundabout way to go. I thought you said you needed help right away, not through the back door with a vacation in the middle. When we landed in New Caledonia, I saw this ship coming here, so I just jumped aboard. They needed another for poker anyway. I figured you'd be able to fix it up with the brass and get the paperwork done up right. In the meantime, we could get going on your engines here."

"Uh, speaking of brass, Sparky, this is your commanding officer, Colonel Blackwell."

Sparky's face registered surprise as he saw the colonel, but he was quick to regain his composure. "Reporting for duty, sir," he said with a snappy salute. "Hope you don't mind if I sort of rushed past my orders in my eagerness to get to you."

The colonel returned his salute and laughed. "It's not recommended, Sergeant. However, General Kenney, our new air boss, says the one thing we need out here are operators. Tennyson, see to Sparks's quarters, get him settled in. I'll have to wait until his orders come from Australia before I can officially put him on the roster, but you might be able to figure out something constructive for him to do in the meantime."

Sparky put his arm on Cole's shoulder. "I could use a cup of coffee."

Cole took him to the mess tent, nodding and laughing at Sparky's steady stream of chatter. On the way, he saw his crew chief. "Hey, Lefty," he called. "Come on over here. I've got someone I want you to meet."

Sparky and Lefty began talking like long-lost brothers, barely noticing when Cole left to arrange Sparky's quarters. When he returned, Lefty got up and shook Sparky's hand saying, "I'll see you out on the line in a couple of hours. Hate to see you getting bored early on."

Cole sat down and said, "With Lefty on your side, you ought to be able to get this outfit back on its feet in no time. Of course, we don't have anything for you to do it with, but I told the colonel that that wouldn't stop you. That's why he didn't throw you in the brig back there. He thinks you'll help keep us in the air."

"Yeah, you son of a bitch." Sparky laughed. "Sounds like I'm supposed to walk on water while fitting a cowling blindfolded. I don't need that kind of prepublicity. 'Sides, I told Lefty there I wasn't such a hot-shot mechanic. I'm at my best when I comes to procuring."

Cole roared with laughter. "*Procurement!* You old thief, you'd break out in a rash if you even saw a procurement form."

"Well, I didn't say I was conventional about it. Besides," he added, "that's what you need the most. Went with Lefty and looked over the supplies. This place looks like Old Mother Hubbard's cupboard . . . after the dog died."

Cole agreed, and said, "It's taken this long for the factories back home just to get their steam up. The European front gets first dibs on everything that comes off the line. 'Get Hitler first' is the plan. The Pacific theater is the poor cousin that has to take what's left over. Then the navy pirates what goes through their hands. Out here in New Guinea, we get the very dregs, if we get anything."

"I suppose those guys back in Washington think they don't use real bullets out here." He looked seriously at Cole. "You think we can win in spite of Washington?"

"Well, if we can cut them off from their supplies, wear 'em down, we'll win . . . if we last that long. But we don't know how much stuff they have or how long they can hold out. For all we know, they've filled up all the Japanese islands with years' worth of supplies they've stolen from Southeast Asia, China, and the Philippines. No telling what life is like in Tokyo. They could be living really well."

Cole paused, then added quietly, "I can't help hoping on one hand that that's the case. I'm worried about Iris. Have you heard anything?"

"Not since that letter I got last January. Eva wrote it the September before Pearl Harbor. Said she was living with Iris now and had a job. Nothing else. Hell," he said angrily, "she's so damned helpless and little. I don't know how she'll survive."

"Well, at least they're together. They can look out for each other. You and I just have a bigger reason than most to get this war won fast."

"You're damned right," Sparky murmured.

Cole sighed, then began again in a more businesslike tone, "Well, it'd help a lot if we knew we were wearing them down. As it is now, they shoot down one of our planes and we're out of a plane. We shoot down one of theirs and in a week they've got another one to take its place."

"I see my job's cut out for me," Sparky said, standing up. "I think Lefty said he'd meet me somewhere on the line. If you'll show me a tent to throw my gear in, I'll get out there."

Sparky had his sleeves rolled up, his cap on the back of his head, and his knees covered with grease before the hour was up. Cole couldn't help feeling that things were getting better. It was reassuring that some people just couldn't be changed, even by a war. Sparky was one of them.

Cole hadn't realized all that he'd gotten them in for until a week later, when he saw a major grabbing a tin can from a garbage pail and scolding the cook for throwing it away. Sparky had everyone in the camp saving their tin cans so the flight crew could hammer them out and use them for patching the smaller bullet holes in the planes. It was soon apparent that no piece of metal was safe around Sparky. Rumor had it that the colonel was hiding his jeep just in case Sparky got any ideas. But no one was complaining. Planes were getting repaired.

Two weeks later, as Cole was talking to the colonel at the edge of the flight line, Sparky joined them. "Colonel Blackwell, sir," he said, giving a smart salute. Cole knew he had something up his sleeve; it was not like Sparky to approach an officer and to act so regulation army.

The colonel returned Sparky's salute with a surprised look.

"Sir, I was wondering if we could try a new idea here."

"What do you call all those things you've been doing?"

"This is about those B-25s sitting around here. We can't get them up in the air because we don't have any wheel bearings, and one of these days those Japs are going to blow them up on the ground. They won't ever be used if we don't get the parts."

"Sergeant, how well I know. But there just aren't any wheel bearings to be found here or in Australia."

"But, Colonel, I know how to get some," Sparky persisted. "I heard of a B-25 that was shot down over Bena Bena. There's a Lieutenant Hanson who says he can land his C-47 on that field up there. If you'll give me about three men, some guns, rations, a kit of tools, and Hanson, I could go in there and bring out the wheel bearings we need. The plane didn't burn when it went down, and I could salvage lots of usable stuff."

"Sergeant Sparks, Bena Bena is up on a plateau in the middle of New Guinea. It's inhabited by only partially reformed cannibals. We don't even know whose side they're on. We don't know if the Japs patrol that area regularly. Sure, Hanson's a good pilot and could set that transport down up there, but the C-47 is unarmed and you'd be flying it in easy range of enemy fighters at Lae and Salamaua. You don't know what you're asking."

"Yes, sir, I do. I'd heard all that. We were talking about it over at the shop, and if you'd be willing to give us permission to try, there's more than enough volunteers."

The colonel sighed and said, "We need those wheel bearings. I'll talk to the general."

"Yes, sir." Sparky beamed. "Just tell him that they can land us there, take off, and come back in about four days and pick us up. That's how long it will take us to strip the plane."

Two days later, Sparky had his scavenging mission okayed to leave immediately.

The next days were difficult for Cole. He had gotten permission to be among the pickup crew for Sparky—but three days was a long wait. He went out on two missions, strafing the trail where the infantry said the Japanese were dug in, in a frantic drive to attack Port Moresby by their overland route.

The morning of the fourth day, Cole was out before breakfast, checking the guns and ammunition, asking Lefty to go over the plane "just in case," and insisting that the ground crew take the doors off because they were going to have to make quick loading of the salvage and men when they touched down.

After circling the area to let Sparky and his crew know they were there, they landed at Bena Bena at 2:55 P.M., praying that they hadn't been spotted by the Japanese.

They sat steaming in the plane's interior, engines running, guns bristling from the window and door, waiting. There was no Sparky, no corporals, no natives—nothing. An hour went by. Cole watched the edge of the jungle, seeing every undulation of the sun-baked air, every flutter of a breeze, jumping at every bird call.

It had been a bad idea from the beginning. He should have fought it. Maybe the Japs had found them. Maybe the natives had a meat shortage. . . . He shuddered and wiped the sweat from his face. Sparky was lost. They couldn't wait much longer. The gas was running low. It would get dark.

"We can't wait much longer," Lieutenant Hanson said, as if reading Cole's mind.

"We'll wait until the last minute," Cole snapped.

"The way I have it figured, Captain, that last minute comes about twenty-five minutes from now."

Another three minutes passed, then five.

"Maybe I should go down and turn around," Hanson suggested. "You know, get downwind for a quick takeoff."

"Yeah, go ahead," Cole said reluctantly.

They had just swung around into position when Cole saw movement in the trees. A man was coming out, waving his arms furiously and yelling. Cole jumped from the plane and ran to him. It was Corporal Johns, all but unrecognizable because of his torn, dirty clothes and four-day growth of beard.

"Where're the others?" Cole called, his gun at the ready.

"The gang will be here in a minute. It took us longer than we thought. Don't go away." He ran back into the jungle.

"The gang?" Cole repeated as he turned and gave the okay signal to Hanson.

Within three minutes Sparky came into the meadow with "the gang." He was followed by two corporals and about a hundred naked natives. Every last one of them was loaded to the hilt with airplane parts. Wheels, landing-gear parts, rudders, aluminum sheeting for future repair work, radios, ailerons, fins, and the precious wheel bearings. Sparky had just enough energy for a slight swagger. "Ya got the bag?" he asked, referring to a duffel bag he had stowed in the tail of the plane before setting out on the mission. He'd asked Cole to keep an eye on it.

Cole pointed to the plane and nodded. "What's all this?" he asked in astonishment.

"Found a downed P-40, too. Think we stripped both planes of everything they had. These New Guinea guys are great. Just a minute, I have to pay them off." He ran to the plane and came back with his special bag.

He held the bag open to one of the older natives, a large, sinewy, grizzled man with a mop of curly hair, blackened teeth, and tattoos the length of his body. The man looked into the bag and nodded to the rest. A murmur of anticipation ran through the troops. Cole shifted his weight, gripping his gun nervously.

The head man turned to the rest of his men and motioned that they should put their gear in the plane. There was a momentary hesitation as they looked doubtfully at the rumbling C-47, then longingly at the bag in Sparky's hand. Then the first of them moved toward the plane and the rest followed, quickly deposited their load in the belly of the plane, and darted back to the edge of the meadow.

When all was loaded, Sparky took the bag and somberly handed it to the head man. He reached inside and held up a seashell. The rest of the natives cheered. Sparky waved and turned to the plane. "Come on. Let's get this stuff back before the Japs find out we've been here," he called back to Cole.

"I don't understand what you were doing with those shells," Cole shouted when they were airborne.

"I talked to some of the Aussies around the base. Wanted to know what the New Guinea natives valued—what they used for money. Seems they're just crazy for cowrie shells. So, the day before we took off to come here, old Johns and I did some shell collecting. Figured I'd have to have something that would make me look like a real friend . . . also something I didn't keep with me while we were traipsing around waiting for you guys to get back and pick us up. I just sort of used the plane like a bank. I took along a few free samples and got us some pretty good labor. Those buggers are strong."

Cole laughed. "I can't believe you, Sparky! You always land on your feet."

"Sure." Sparky grinned. "Anything else you want to know?"

"Yeah—how much longer can the Japs hold out?"

Sparky glanced over his shoulder and saw that the two corporals were sound asleep. No one was within hearing distance. "I don't know," he said seriously, "but I hope that Eva and Iris can hold out longer."

Cole looked around at the piles of metal and parts that they'd gotten. "It's going to take more than salvaging two planes to get to Tokyo. But it's a damned good start. Before you know it, we'll be walking down the streets of Tokyo with our girls on our arms."

CHAPTER XVI

"Bonzai Tojo! Bonzai Tojo!" A group of young boys chanted as they ran beside Iris's streetcar. Their faces were alight with the glory of victory. She shuddered and tried to look away, but her eyes were drawn back to their faces—faces that should have been laughing in childish play, but instead were aged by the grimace of carefully nurtured hate. "Death to Americans! Bonzai Tojo!" The *densha* pulled away from the stop and the chanting boys faded into the distance.

It was easy to guess the reason for their celebration. The script for the propaganda broadcast that she'd just gone over at work carried enough gloating words of triumph to last her a lifetime. Then, on her way from work to the streetcar stop, she had heard much the same news blaring on the Japanese national radio station.

They were claiming victory after victory for the Japanese

forces: the Nippon Army had virtually vanquished the Americans from an island called Guadalcanal; the American soldiers were cowardly and hiding in the jungle; the American planes were dropping like flies. The wild wind of victory fired frenzied demonstrations celebrating Nipponese supremacy and their leader, Tojo, throughout the city.

Still, Iris had her doubts. She had reason to hope that the Japanese victories were not what they claimed. The script she'd edited that afternoon had included a final jab at the Americans, claiming General Kenney was a "gangster" and the air force he commanded was nothing more than an unethical "gang of gangsters." Iris doubted that the Japanese would complain like that if the Americans weren't doing some kind of harm.

If Cole was still alive, maybe he was part of this "gang of gangsters." She smiled at the thought of her gentle Cole being called a gangster; then her smile faded in fear. If he was one of the "gang," was he also flying the planes the Japanese said were dropping like autumn flies? She quickly shoved that thought to the back of her mind. She needed what little energy she had.

Maybe the cold weather was taking its toll, or maybe poor food was affecting her. Maybe she was just tired—tired of war, of worry, of hunger. The only time she wasn't exhausted was when she was frightened, but when the fear dissipated, her exhaustion was worse.

The *densha* was approaching her stop. Tonight she would talk to Eva. Maybe between them they could glean some new hope; maybe they could get an idea of how the war was really going. But for now, the most pressing issue was what they would eat for dinner.

They were luckier than many Japanese. Kiyoko's insistence that they raise their own food and store it had already proved its worth. They had been able to trade some of their vegetable ration cards and purchase twenty-five pounds of flour, because there weren't many Japanese who used it. They might be able to get through the winter by eating thin soups with tofu and tough flour noodles and dried vegetables. They were better off than the pale, emaciated people they saw standing in the ration lines.

"Bonzai Tojo!" an old woman in a black *monpe* suddenly cried as she got up to get off at Iris's stop. Catching sight of a poster tacked on the fence, Iris knew what had inspired the outburst. She probably had a son in the army. "Bonzai Tojo!" the other passengers responded. Iris hurried for the exit, fearful of being caught in a mob demonstration and detected as an American.

She jumped from the *densha* steps and found herself looking directly at the poster, a grisly representation of an American soldier holding a dead baby in his grip and writhing under the bayonet of a noble-looking Japanese soldier. "Bonzai Tojo!" the debarked passengers shouted behind her. "Death to all Americans!"

Iris shuddered and quickly walked down the street toward the protective wall surrounding their little house and yard. She could let the mask fall away there. She would be safe at home.

As she opened the gate a blast of cold wind whipped around her legs. Maple leaves the color of dried blood swirled across the crust of December ice on the stepping stones. Eva would be home in an hour. In the meantime, Iris would start the *konro* and heat water for tea and soup.

Fatigued and fearful, Iris didn't notice the loose latch on the door. Her ears were still ringing with the violent cheers and chants, so she didn't hear the movement inside as she slipped off her shoes.

The blow was sudden and violent. She was sprawled on the floor before she was even inside the main room. Stunned, she turned over, trying to focus her blurred vision. Her assailant stood spread-legged over her, sneering down a black gun barrel. The detested Kampetei uniform frightened her more than the gun.

A crash came from the cooking room and she turned to see Sergeant Ito pull down their stacked boxes of dried vegetables and break them methodically with the butt of his gun. A small sack of rice under the table was slashed open; the white grains spilled across the mat. Against the wall, their hardgained flour sack was likewise split open, its precious contents wasted on the floor. Muddy boots had trampled through it all.

Horrified, Iris could see the gaunt face of starvation in the damaged food. "Stop!" she yelled, and before the officer knew what she was doing, she pushed the gun barrel away and jumped up. "Stop it this instant!" she demanded, running to Sergeant Ito. He turned and looked at her, his gun held in midair.

"Just what do you think you're doing?" she demanded.

Sergeant Ito was taken aback by her outburst. Clearly, he was not used to being called to account for his actions. He arranged his face into a mask of authority and said stiffly, "We are searching for English-language books. They are forbidden. You cannot have them."

"I know that," Iris said indignantly. Her anger overwhelmed her fear. "I also know that if you'd waited politely, we would have allowed you to search our house without having to destroy irreplaceable food. Surely your orders do not include instructions to waste valuable food and ransack personal property of honest people."

Sergeant Ito straightened to his full height and looked Iris in the eye. "You are not a citizen. We have orders to search thoroughly every suspicious house, every suspicious person who might be harboring disloyal thoughts. Unfortunately," he said with a sneer, "you have refused to register as a Japanese citizen, much to the pain of your family and myself. You must therefore be subject to such searches."

"If my family is in pain, you caused it."

"Nothing has hurt them except the excruciating embarrassment of your continued stubbornness."

"In that case, they are no more pained by my actions than they must be to know that the Japanese government allows its officers to harass innocent people and destroy their household goods with no cause."

The puzzled look on Sergeant Ito's face gave Iris courage. At that moment Iris knew only that she couldn't go on cringing at every noise, fearful of oppression from an irrational authority. The thought of this slimy character rummaging through her personal possessions made her furious. "If I am such a threat to the state, I demand that you arrest me now. Put me in the prisoner-of-war camp and treat me like the traitor you say I am."

There was a sound behind her as the other officer stepped forward for the first time. Her heart sank. Maybe she'd gone too far. Yet, she didn't regret her challenge. She'd rather know the worst than live in fear and starvation, groveling and whimpering at the sight of every uniform for the rest of the war.

Sergeant Ito held up his hand, stopping the other officer. "That is impossible," he said. "We would never be able to feed all the American-born Japanese in Japan if we put them behind fences. Instead, it is our policy to warn you that your actions are being watched. You may yet come to see our side when you realize the Americans are losing."

"You can watch me all you want," Iris said defiantly, "as long as you refrain from destroying my property, and obey the law."

Ito looked at her calmly, almost smiling. "But I am the law."

That cold truth chilled her, but she kept her mask in place. "No wonder there's a war. If you have any questions, I am willing to answer them. Until then," she concluded, stepping to the door and sliding it open, "I regret having taken your time. I trust that if I see you again, it will be more pleasant."

The young officer was obviously awed by her speech and bearing. He was almost deferential as he followed Ito out the door. He even bowed slightly in Iris's direction. Iris nodded almost imperceptibly in return. She looked at the muddy footprints across their clean *tatami* floor, and could not resist adding, "I have learned during my stay in your country that all decent Japanese take their shoes off as they enter a home."

Sergeant Ito stopped in the entryway and turned to her, his thick lips drawn in a triumphant smirk. "*If* the home is Japanese," he said. Then as he looked down at Iris's shoes on the pad, he added, "I'm glad to see that you are more Japanese with each meeting."

Hiding her chagrin at his comment, she said with forced dignity, "Good day, Sergeant Ito," and slid the door closed.

As soon as they were gone, she opened the door again and slipped out to the entryway to close the heavy wooden night door. Then she went back into the cooking room and surveyed the mess.

Her anger churned anew as she considered the violence. Their precious food had been maliciously, wantonly scattered across the floor. Rice and flour was intentionally wasted, and the dried vegetables were thrown across the mess. Mud from their boots had fouled the food.

Iris went into the sleeping room and saw that the *oshiire* had been thrown on its side, their clothes scattered and trampled on the floor. Their underwear lay in a separate pile, obviously the object of curious examination. The *futons* had been slashed open with bayonets.

Trembling with rage, Iris stared helplessly at the chaos. The Kampetei had violated the last vestige of privacy they had.

"Bastards!" she exclaimed, as she returned to the cooking room. Falling to her knees, she scraped the rice into a pile. She wanted to get rid of every sign of their presence. Her hands froze in revulsion as she touched the damp mud. Suddenly she was crying, gasping her anger, frustration, and fear in deep racking sobs. "Damn, damn, damn," she cried, pounding the floor with her fist.

Her sobs filled the room. She was so caught up in her anger that she heard only her own crying. Then a firm hand touched her shoulder. Screaming in fear, she jumped back.

"Hey, it can't be all that bad," Bill said sympathetically, pulling her into his arms.

"Bill!" she cried, leaning gratefully on his shoulder. "Don't scare me like that. I can't stand any more." She hastily wiped away her tears and stepped back, gesturing at the house. "Will you look at this? Sergeant Ito, the Kampetei officer I told you about, was here. He said—"

"I know. I was outside, waiting for you to come home. I heard them come in and ducked under the porch. I heard everything."

"Why didn't you stop them?" she demanded.

"Sure," Bill laughed, "and get a bullet through the skull. And then the Kampetei would find out I wasn't a Japanese citizen. And since I was discovered in your house, you'd soon be wishing that the bullet had been in your head instead."

"I guess you're right. I'm sorry," she said sheepishly.

"For a minute there, I thought I was going to have to spend the rest of this war trying to spring you from some rat-infested POW camp instead of what I'm supposed to be doing here."

"I sort of lost my temper," she admitted.

"Well, it worked. You were pretty brave," he added admiringly. "Don't know that I would have stood up to a couple of guns with nothing but my indignation for a shield. You probably won their respect in the process."

"I don't think Ito knows what respect means."

"Well, you don't have to worry about that now. Let's see if we can salvage some of this food and get the mess cleaned up before Eva gets home," he said, stooping down beside her and sorting out the dried vegetables. He looked at her and winked reassuringly. "You'll feel better as soon as we get things back into order. Why don't you wash that bump on your head . . . it's still bleeding a bit. Then see if you can salvage some of those boxes over there."

Iris dabbed at her head with a wet cloth, then quickly began sorting out the broken boxes, straightening and trying to repair the wooden slats that Ito's rifle hadn't shattered completely. As she handed him two boxes, she said, "We haven't seen much of you lately."

"Keeping busy. Went fishing a couple of times. Saw some interesting scenery." He put the dried sweet potatoes into one of the boxes. "What about you? Still transcribing radio scripts?"

"More and more. They seem to be relying on me quite a bit these days for several programs."

"Do you ever write any of it?"

"Me? Never. They have it all written up and translated. I just go over the English and clean it up."

She paused, remembering how she'd deliberately left in the stilted, ridiculous language. She was about to tell Bill about that, then decided not to. He already knew too much about her and Eva. It would be foolish to make herself more vulnerable by revealing something even more damning.

"Well, let me know if you can ever slip anything in. We might need it." He tied a knot in the rice sack where the bayonet had sliced it and began dumping handfuls of dirty rice back into it. Then he stopped, and looked at Iris intently, as if he were trying to decide how much to reveal.

"I think maybe I should tell you something," he said finally. "When I left Cole that last night in the Philippines, I told him I would try to get any information I could and send it to him. I told him I'd send things under the code name 'Flower of the Pacific.' I guess I was sort of thinking about your name because he'd talked about you so much. Anyway," he continued, turning back to the rice on the floor, "if anything happens so that I can't send messages out and you have something to say and some way to do it, you're welcome to use my sobriquet."

"Oh," Iris said, feeling inexplicably embarrassed. "I doubt . . ."

"My God! What happened?" Eva cried from the doorway.

"Welcome home, Eva," Iris said bitterly. "Sergeant Ito and friend searched for English language books."

Eva slowly slumped to the floor, tears streaming down her cheeks, her hands covering her ears, shaking her head slowly as she looked around in shock.

"It could have been a lot worse," Bill said comfortingly as he went to her. "You're both all right. And we can save most of the food."

Eva looked at him as if she didn't recognize him.

"Pull yourself together," he said firmly, taking her by the shoulders and standing her up. "You can't let them get to you like this. That's what they want." Iris started to reach out and put her arms around Eva, but a sharp look from Bill stopped her. "Here." He pulled a match from his pocket. "You go light the *konro* so we can warm the place up and make some tea. Iris and I will work on the food cleanup. You find a needle and sew up those *futons* so you have someplace to sleep tonight."

Eva looked at him solemnly for a moment, then took the match and began arranging the charcoal in the brazier. Bill nudged Iris into the kitchen area to continue picking up the food, but they kept an eye on Eva as she mechanically and silently went about the chores Bill had outlined for her.

"Do you think she'll be all right?" Iris whispered as Eva went into the sleeping room and began rummaging through the mess, looking for their sewing box.

"I think if we can keep her going in sort of a routine, she'll snap out of it."

By the time daylight faded and Iris lit the lantern, they had pretty much put the kitchen back in order. "Would you like to eat with us?" Iris asked. "I think we can make some kind of a soup."

Bill shook his head congenially. "Nah, I've got to go. Thanks, though." He looked at Eva, who was mending one of the *futons*.

"Hey there," he said lightly, "tell me what the radio was saying today. Any news from the States?"

Eva shrugged. "It's a lot different from what we hear in Japanese." Then she listed the main points of the news she'd translated today. "They're still holding out in Stalingrad. The Nazis are even being pushed back in a couple of places. The Allies are bombing occupied France. They're fighting in someplace called Tunis in North Africa. There are some strikes threatened by labor unions back home. And they say that the Americans have the upper hand in Guadalcanal."

"That sounds a lot brighter," Iris said.

Bill had listened intently, nodding at each piece of news. Now he turned at Iris's words and said, "That's the spirit." He winked. "Now I've got to get going. It looks like you have everything under control." He paused on the porch as he put his shoes on. "I'll drop in on you in a few days and see how things are going." His words were cut short by a strange squawk from one of the hens under the porch.

"What was that?" Eva asked, getting up and running to the door. "Did you step on one of them?"

Bill laughed. "No, but I think one of 'em just laid an egg. You'd better bring the lantern and find it. See you later." With a cheery wave, he went down the path and through the hedge.

"Our first egg?" Iris whispered excitedly. Then the air was pierced with another clarion call, from the other side of the porch. "Two eggs?" She looked at Eva. "Come on, gal! I have a feeling this is just what we need."

Both hens were clucking proudly over the eggs in the nesting boxes Iris had built under the porch. Caught in the glow of the lantern, the smooth, warm eggs looked like pearls to Iris's eyes.

That night, they finished putting the house back in order while the soup simmered and two eggs boiled merrily in the pot. Eva extravagantly added an extra lump of charcoal and the room almost seemed warm. The hens got an extra ration of millet and both Iris and Eva lingered over their dinner, savoring the first egg they'd tasted in months. That night as they fell asleep, they felt that somehow they had won a very private victory over the Kampetei.

The wind was rattling the thin walls of their house, blowing skiffs of snow under the doors and around the window frames. They had just finished an early dinner of scrambled eggs and broth when the back door opened, letting in a howl of cold air and Kiyoko. Her hair glistened with frozen crystals around the edge of her scarf.

"Kiyoko," Iris said as she closed the door, "you're early for the *tonarigumi*. Would you like a cup of tea?"

Kiyoko sat down, warming her icy fingers on the bowl of tea Eva gave her. "The Kampetei have been visiting the neighborhood," she said bluntly. "They've been asking everyone about you. I think it would be best if you visited your grandmother tonight instead of going to the meeting. They will want to discuss you and it will be easier for them to do so if you are not there. I will tell them I saw you both going to catch the *densha*. It is good for them to hear that you are devoted to your grandmother. I brought three extra eggs I had in the house which you can take to her for a gift."

Suddenly the air seemed colder, the night darker. The campaign was spreading against them. Iris shivered as Kiyoko explained further.

Ito had come to her that afternoon and asked about Iris and Eva. Kiyoko had pretended that she knew them only from the *tonarigumi* and casual meetings in the street. When she'd told Ito that they were helpful to their neighbors and seemed to be obedient citizens, he'd grunted and left. Then she had asked the other neighbors and heard much the same story. She felt that the neighbors might not turn against them, but they were frightened by the questions.

Before she left, it was agreed that Kiyoko would convey an invitation from Iris and Eva to hold the meeting next week in their home. It was their turn.

They took their last egg, added it to Kiyoko's gift, and bundled up against the storm. As they walked to the *densha* stop hidden eyes seemed to be watching. They met Kiyoko on the street as arranged, bowed, and pretended to convey their message. It was a cold charade, acted out on an icy black stage.

The darkened *densha* was filled with blank faces of weary workers and exhausted housewives. Iris and Eva kept silent, feeling even more threatened and vulnerable in the crowd. What was happening at the *tonarigumi*?

The latch on Grandmother's garden gate was frozen shut. Iris had to hit it with her gloved hand before it released. Even the clapper on the gate bell was frozen fast. "It doesn't look like anyone's been out all day," Eva whispered as they went down the path.

A faint glow of light could be seen through the walls as

227

they reached the house. Iris rang the bell beside the door. She felt a rising expectation. It'd been a month since she'd come to visit and she had been anxious about them for some time.

Aunt Toshiko opened the heavy *amado* and held her *bonbori*, a small lantern, high above her head. Iris stood still, staring at her aunt's thin, lined face. Her hair, which had always been twisted into a gleaming, intricate bun, was now dull and carelessly knotted, with loose ends straggling down. Eva and Iris bowed deeply in greeting.

"*Konbawa, Oba-san,*" Iris said. "My friend and I come with great respect and affection to see *Oba-a-san* and, of course, you and Aunt Teiso and the children."

Aunt Toshiko's face beamed as she bowed. "My niece and Eva-san, you are most welcome to our home. Please come in and lighten your grandmother's heart."

They left their shoes on the *genkan* and followed Aunt Toshiko to the main room. Pale lantern light mellowed the stark white of the paper walls, and it was nearly as cold as it was outside.

Iris couldn't help smiling as she entered the room and bowed deeply to her grandmother, going through the prescribed formalities with a heart much lighter than usual. As she sat up, she noted that the entire family was in the room, obviously trying to use the little heat available from the *kotatsu* in the middle of the room. Grandmother sat wrapped in a quilt, her feet extended down the warm sides of the sunken fire pit, her nose red with cold. Perhaps it was just the bulky wrapping, but she looked smaller and more wizened than Iris had ever noticed before. Aunt Teiso sat next to her, baby Kibo wrapped in a blanket, sleeping in her arms. The other four children were huddled in blankets around the fire. The eldest girl, Mieko, was awake; the others dozed fitfully. Aunt Toshiko took her quilt and pulled it around Iris's and Eva's shoulders, then got a thin blanket to wrap herself in.

Iris politely answered her grandmother's probing questions in a way that would not cause the old woman undue worry. She thought she was doing well, until Grandmother asked, "And Sergeant Ito . . . has he questioned you or visited you?"

"Actually, he did stop by our house the other day," Iris

said slowly. "He wanted us to know that there is a law against having English-language books."

"You must abide by his warnings," Grandmother said softly.

"Oh, we didn't have any," Eva said quickly.

"Yes, we'd known of that law for some time," Iris put in.

Grandmother seemed to relax. "And do you have enough food?"

"Yes, *Oba-a-san*." Iris smiled. "In fact, we've brought you four eggs." She reached into her pocket and brought out the carefully wrapped packet.

Grandmother smiled her approval as Iris handed them to Aunt Toshiko, who said, "The children will thank you as well."

When Iris and Eva finally took their leave, Aunt Toshiko walked with them to the door. "My niece," she said softly in Iris's ear, "I fear that Sergeant Ito did not have a pleasant visit."

Iris decided to tell her the truth. "No, it wasn't, but I didn't want to worry Grandmother or frighten the children." She went on to explain how Ito had ransacked their house, and how she had stood up to him.

Aunt Toshiko listened in silence, then said, "He's fulfilling his *on* in a very strange way."

"What do you mean?" Iris asked.

"I thought you knew. Your grandfather was his father's teacher many years ago. Grandfather helped his father many times, even teaching him when he could no longer afford the tuition. Your grandfather got him his job with the police. When Sergeant Ito grew up, Grandfather helped him also get a job, this one with the Kampetei. We did not know what they were like in those days," she added apologetically. "So, you see, Ito's family has a great responsibility, a great debt, to our family. It is his duty to repay your grandfather's family for both himself and his father. For that reason, I cannot imagine that he would hurt you. But perhaps he feels he is repaying Grandfather by trying to force you to become a Japanese citizen."

"You've helped me to understand more about what's happening," Iris said. "Thank you very much, *Oba-san*."

Aunt Toshiko bowed. "I thought you knew of your grandfather's great kindnesses to his students. Many families in

Tokyo today owe a great *on* to our family. That is one reason why we have not starved this winter."

"Thank you again for telling me, Aunt Toshiko. It gives me a feeling of pride to be his granddaughter, even though I never knew him."

"Your words will make your grandmother happy. I will tell her."

Iris and Eva bid her aunt good night and walked quickly down the icy walk while her aunt held the lantern high to light their way.

They rode the *densha* home in silence, watching the shuttered city with its blacked-out shadows of buildings. Tokyo was anticipating a blow, hiding in a shroud of darkness and blackout curtains.

Once safely home, Iris and Eva talked over the information Aunt Toshiko had revealed. Knowing how strongly the Japanese adhered to their customs, Iris took some comfort in her aunt's words. Eva was less confident. She feared that the burden of such an *on* might create a resentment and backfire on Iris.

Christmas was fast approaching, and Iris and Eva began to plan their private celebration. It came on a Friday and they would have to work, but they wanted somehow to take note of the day, to capture the memory and warmth of their childhood.

Then one evening Kiyoko appeared on their doorstep and unwittingly planned their second Japanese Christmas.

"Kiyoko," Iris exclaimed, "we were beginning to wonder what had happened. It's been four days since the *tonarigumi*. Have we been rejected by the whole neighborhood?"

"No," Kiyoko smiled, "but some were very worried. Old Mrs. Okimoto stuck up for you—she's the one who does your laundry when you stand in the ration lines for her. The others felt better because she trusts you. Then I told them about your visiting your grandmother and that you had asked the honor of having the *tonarigumi* at your house next time to make up for your absence this time. They seemed to think that was just fine."

"Thank you so very much, Kiyoko," Eva said gratefully. "When do we have to be ready for the *tonarigumi* in our house?"

"It will be in five days, next Friday evening at seven-thirty."

"But that's Christmas," Iris objected. "We were going to have a little celebration."

"Ah," Kiyoko nodded, "now you will have the whole neighborhood to join you. Remember, you should have a special treat prepared."

Iris and Eva spent hours after work searching the shops for a special treat. Wanting to assuage any lingering doubt about their loyalties, they felt it was important to serve something special to these people who hadn't turned against them.

Sugar had not been available for years because of the military requirements for it. Iris and Eva couldn't think of any substitute that might allow them to make a dessert, yet they knew everyone craved sweets.

The day before the meeting, Iris walked twelve blocks from her *densha* stop to a foreign grocery she'd heard about. As she walked into the shop, she was disappointed by the many empty shelves. Then she spotted a tin of butter on the bottom shelf. She grabbed it, hoping that her ration cards would be accepted. Then she noticed some glass jars filled with a crystal-clear liquid.

"What's that?" she asked the proprietor, pointing to the jars.

He bowed and smiled proudly. *"Hachimitsu."*

"Honey? But it's clear. Where did it come from?"

"From China, *Ojo-san,*" he said, taking down a jar and handing it to her.

"It's so clear," she said suspiciously. "Are you sure it's honey?"

"Oh, yes, *Ojo-san,*" he assured her. "See, there's the bee."

She looked at the jar more closely. Floating in the bottom was a bee, captured in the clear sticky liquid.

It had taken most of her week's ration cards and she wasn't sure what they could make with butter and honey, but she hurried home with her prizes, hoping Eva would be able to think of something. She was making the tea as Iris came in the door and set down her package.

When Iris showed her what she'd bought, Eva laughed. Just then one of the hens cackled triumphantly. "I've got it," Eva declared. "Pancakes! We'll use that egg Gertrude just laid, along with the butter and some flour. Then we'll top them with honey and roll them up and serve them with tea."

The following evening, Iris and Eva had cleared both the main room and the sleeping room and opened the *shoji* screen that separated the rooms. Then they nervously awaited their first visitor. It was exactly seven-thirty when they heard, "*Gomen kudasai,*" at their door. It was the *kumicho-san,* the head of the neighborhood group. "Merry Christmas," Iris whispered to Eva as they went to the door to welcome him in. The others were coming down the path.

Each neighbor came in the door, bowing properly and curiously looking around the room out of the corners of their eyes. Eva had made their small place look as Japanese as possible, going so far as to set up a tiny alcove to look like a *kamidana,* a kind of household shrine. They could see by the approving look in Kiyoko's eye that they had done well. Everyone squeezed in against the walls and the meeting began.

There was much discussion about finding food and fuel and the new government regulations regarding fire-fighting practice and a mandatory thirty minutes of calisthenics daily. The weary people accepted these additional duties without a murmur of protest.

When the business was finished, Eva and Iris brought out the pancakes and tea they'd prepared. The neighbors were thrilled with the honey-filled pancakes, and Eva and Iris were greatly relieved. The meeting was an unqualified success. They had taken one more step toward becoming an accepted part of their neighborhood. Granted, they were still different, but at least they were no longer feared as foreigners.

January was bitter cold. By the first of February, Iris's lips were chapped and her fingers and toes ached constantly from the cold. Their dried vegetables were nearly gone. Eva developed a chest cold that persisted for three weeks; a wracking cough kept her awake each night and left her exhausted each day. More and more she was forced to miss work. Each day, Iris's face grew more sallow. Something was wrong. They ached all over.

It wasn't until Kiyoko came in the second week of February and found Iris holding a handkerchief to her bleeding nose that something was done. "Do you bleed also inside your mouth?" she demanded.

"Yes," Iris admitted. "But I don't have the awful cough

that Eva has. I'm *nantu u no*—how do you say 'achy' in Japanese?"

"Ah!" Kiyoko said, "you have the sailor's disease. Have you been eating the cabbage?"

"Cabbage? What cabbage?"

"The cabbage you salted and put in the crock."

"Oh, that. Kiyoko, I'm afraid it's no good. It smells awful. We left it under the porch and forgot it," Iris explained, rinsing out her handkerchief and hanging it on a peg beside the door. "And why are you talking about a sailor's disease? You know Eva and I haven't been seeing any men, much less sailors."

Kiyoko laughed as she went out the door. "Silly child, it's what sailors get when they don't eat fruit and vegetables while at sea. Go bring Eva out of the bed."

By the time Iris had Eva sitting up on a cushion with a quilt around her shoulders, Kiyoko had dipped two huge helpings of the fermented cabbage onto plates and handed it to them with chopsticks, commanding, "Here, eat. You will get well."

Eva shook her head in refusal and Iris took her plate reluctantly. Kiyoko shoved the plate into Eva's lap and said fiercely, "Eat."

Iris hesitantly tasted the strands of tan cabbage. It was sour. She tasted it again and her face lit up. "Eva, it's sauerkraut. It's Japanese sauerkraut. Eat it. It's pretty good." She took another bite. The tart, salty taste was surprisingly good. She ate until she could hold no more and Eva followed her example eagerly.

Gradually, the scurvy symptoms dissipated. By the end of February, Eva was back at work. Iris's legs and arms no longer ached. They obediently ate their Japanese sauerkraut each day, embarrassed that they hadn't followed Kiyoko's advice from the very beginning.

In the first week of March 1943, Yakumo, Iris's boss, called Iris to his office. "Sit down," he ordered brusquely. Adjusting his glasses, he asked with studied nonchalance, "Tell me about the American radio programs you heard when you lived there."

Iris was puzzled. "If you would tell me why you're asking, I would know how to answer you."

"I want to know what Americans like to listen to on the radio."

"Oh. Well, most everything, I guess. Drama, news, music, that sort of thing."

"Be specific. What was most popular?"

"I don't know. Different people like different things."

"Why don't they like the news we broadcast?" he blurted out.

So that was it, Iris thought. They must have heard that the propaganda broadcasts were a flop. "I only know what you broadcast by the scripts I edit," she said evasively.

"We give them news. What does your American news sound like?"

"There's an announcer who comes on and tells what's happening around the world, in the United States, and around the hometown. Sometimes there's gossip about movie stars. Things like that. It's pretty fast-paced. There's not much we can do to imitate that. We don't have an American announcer." Then an idea struck her. The less news, the better. More real entertainment would keep the propaganda down. "Music!" she exclaimed. "If we played music, they would like it."

Yakumo pressed his fingers together and leaned back in his chair. "Ah, yes, the jazz-mad Americans . . . And how do you introduce the musical numbers? Are there bands playing music at the stations?"

Iris thought for a moment. "Sometimes they broadcast live bands, like Guy Lombardo and the Royal Canadians or Jimmy Dorsey and his Orchestra, playing from a ballroom in a fancy hotel, but most often it's records."

"Do you have any musical records?" he asked.

"Me? Oh no, that's against the law," she said quickly.

"It wouldn't be if you gave them to me. Do you have any?" he persisted.

"No. I'm sorry. I didn't bring anything like that with me."

Yakumo was silent, rubbing his chin slowly with his fingertips and gazing at the ceiling. Finally he said, "We will be developing some new programs in the near future. I will depend on your help. See to it that you are not as ill as you were earlier this month."

Iris's head was spinning. "Yes, Yakumo-san," she said, bowing deferentially. "Is that all for now?"

234

Yakumo nodded distractedly and continued rubbing his chin, deep in thought.

So that's it, Iris thought as she went back to her desk. *They've found that propaganda, Japanese-style, isn't working.* She needed to talk to Bill so that she would have a plan when they asked her for guidance.

CHAPTER XVII

As winter lingered into March, chill winds pierced the thickest coat and ice-crusted mud mottled the streets and sidewalks. Eva's cough returned, causing her to wheeze constantly. In bleak misery they waited for spring to bring warmth and hope.

It had been two weeks since Iris had been asked about American radio programs and almost three weeks since she'd seen Bill. Two more consultations with Yakumo had made her increasingly anxious to talk to Bill. Now that there was a chance for her to be of some real use to the Allied cause, she needed his guidance. She searched the face of each worker on the street, hoping to see Bill. Each night she went to bed filled with impatience.

When the same empty house greeted her again one afternoon, she finally gave vent to her frustration. She threw her coat on the floor and stomped into the cooking room, railing at the silent walls. They hadn't even seen Kiyoko for several days.

Iris lit the coals in the *kotatsu.* Maybe by the time the tea was ready and Eva came home she would feel better.

The teakettle was whispering in lonely harmony with the wind outside. Iris had wrapped herself in a quilt, with her feet tucked beside the glowing *kotatsu* and her red hands wrapped around a steaming bowl of tea, when Eva came in.

Putting away her coat, she said, "Boy, I sure could use

some of that hot tea." She wrapped the quilt around her shoulders, shivering from the cold. As she sat down, she was seized by a fit of coughing and Iris looked on helplessly as her friend's body was wracked with spasms.

Iris put her hand on Eva's heaving shoulders and murmured, "There's got to be something to help that. I wish Kiyoko would come; I bet she has some home remedies for coughs."

Eva closed her eyes against the pain. "Me too," she said hoarsely. "How long has it been since she's been here?"

Iris thought for a moment. "It must be at least ten days. You know, she's never stayed away for longer than a week," she added with concern. "I wonder if something's wrong."

"What if the Kampetei took her away because she's been so helpful to us?" Eva asked with frightened eyes. "Or maybe she's sick and can't help herself."

Iris put down her cup decisively. "We'd better go check on her." Then she stopped, feeling rather silly. "We don't even know where she lives."

It was curious that despite their deep friendship with Kiyoko, they had no idea where she lived. Iris remembered her story about moving into her father's house when her husband divorced her but she couldn't recall ever hearing where that house was. It must be nearby, since Kiyoko attended their neighborhood meetings.

"Maybe they'd tell us at the Swiss residence?" Eva suggested. "We could tell them we were concerned . . . no, any Japanese would wonder what kind of *on* we had, and we couldn't explain that satisfactorily."

"How about if we tell them that she showed us how to preserve our vegetables last summer, and now we want to share some with her?"

"That sounds good. They would tell us so we could rid ourselves of the debt we owe her. Let's try it."

It was the gardener who answered their question. After hearing their story, he pointed the way to Kiyoko's house. They couldn't miss it because of the venerable long-needled pine beside the red gate. They thanked him and left, following his directions down the street.

Behind the decorative fence lining the street, the large peaked roof surprised them with its size and dignity. The gnarled long-needled pine spread its branches to repeat the curve of the massive carved gate. The impression of noble splendor was incongruous with the simple Kiyoko they knew. However, the grandeur dimmed as they opened the gate and saw the ruins of a once-beautiful garden. Weeds crowded the curving walk; the skeletons of dead shrubs clawed at the trunks of tangled trees gone wild. A cold wind blew dried leaves from a deserted fish pond to rattle across their path. No one answered the ringing of the gate bell, so they hesitantly entered the yard, uninvited.

The old gate was stiff on its hinges and creaked loudly. Brittle chips of red paint crumbled from the wood and clung to Iris's worn gloves.

As they walked down the broad curving path to the front entrance, Iris's eyes strayed from the sagging front steps and the wide spacious porch to the second story. Shuttered windows were set in white plastered walls beneath the soaring, curved red-tiled roof. Echoes of lost prosperity answered the clack of their wooden *geta*.

"Cozy little bungalow," Iris murmured sardonically. "Do you really think this is Kiyoko's house?"

"If it isn't, I want to get out of here fast. I'd bet there's a samurai ghost lurking up there." As if in response, the wind whispered in the pine and piped a minor chord through the rounded roof tiles.

"Well, we've come this far," Iris said, reaching out for Eva's hand and walking up the creaking steps. She rang the entry bell. A scurry of dead leaves blew across the wooden porch and they jumped at the sound. She rang the bell again. "I'm getting worried," she finally admitted.

"Me too. Do you think we should go on in and look? What if she's ill or hurt and can't come to the door?"

Iris lifted the latch and opened the door. It was heavy and the hinges groaned. Inside, pale light filtered through the interior walls, casting a gray tone onto the worn *tatami* floor. They left their shoes in the *genkan* and stepped cautiously into the corridor.

"*Gomen kudasai*," Iris called tentatively. "Kiyoko-san . . ."

There was no answer. The air was stale, filled with the moldering smell of neglect. "Kiyoko," Iris repeated into the silence.

They slid open a door and saw a darkened room of generous size, filled with massive pieces of furniture shrouded in dustcovers. Quietly, they closed the door and went down the corridor. Two more rooms held the same scene, each one more eerie in its silence than the last, inhabited only by the dust of the past. The fourth room was at the end of the corridor. She slid open the screen.

This room looked out over the back garden and had obviously been lived in recently. Pillows were on the mat by the window; a cooking brazier with cold ashes sat beside a low table; a faded quilt lay near the empty *kotatsu* in the center of the room.

Whether she was shivering from the chill or from nerves, Iris didn't know. Eva jumped when the wind blew a branch against a window.

"This is silly," Iris said, trying to find courage in her own voice. "There doesn't seem. . . . Wait, look over there by the window," she said, pointing to a bundle of blankets.

"Kiyoko?" Eva whispered, following Iris.

Iris gasped as she pulled back the covers. "Kiyoko-san! Oh, Eva . . . Mama-Kiyoko-san, are you all right?" she cried, reaching out and touching her still, cold face. She was gray, her skin clammy to the touch. "Kiyoko-san," Iris called, gently shaking her shoulders. Kiyoko's thin arm fell limply on the mat.

"Is she . . .?" Eva began crying softly.

Pulling back the covers, Iris put her ear to Kiyoko's bony chest and was relieved to hear a faint rasping sound from deep within. "She's alive," she said tentatively. "Mama Kiyoko-san," she called softly in Kiyoko's ear, "wake up. Are you all right? Mama Kiyoko?"

Kiyoko stirred slightly, murmuring.

"What did she say?" Eva whispered anxiously.

Iris shook her head and leaned over Kiyoko once more. "Mama-san."

Kiyoko turned her head restlessly. "Hanako, stay . . . don't go. . . ."

Iris felt Kiyoko's forehead and said, "She's burning with fever. And her chest is all gurgly sounding, like when you have pneumonia. We've got to get help."

"How can we find a doctor? I don't even know where there's a hospital."

Iris shook her head. "Me neither. Tell you what," she said, "I'll stay here and try to clean her up and cool her off. You go back to the Swiss residence and tell the head housekeeper what's happened. If she's Japanese, give her the same story we told the gardener. Find out how to get Kiyoko to a hospital."

Eva ran down the corridor. Iris heard her stop at the doorway, seized by another fit of coughing, and then go out the door and down the path.

"Oh, Kiyoko-san," Iris whispered, touching Kiyoko's fevered brow. She looked around and found a cloth by the table. She dampened the cloth with water from the teapot and gently began bathing Kiyoko's body, starting with her sallow face. There was the musty, sour smell of old illness about her. She must have been ill for many days. Her flesh hung pathetically on her frail bones.

Iris gently combed out Kiyoko's graying hair, silently crying, whispering with each stroke of the comb, "*Mama Kiyoko-san, shinanai de kudasai.*" Please don't die, Mama-san.

By the time she heard Eva's footsteps on the path, Iris had bathed Kiyoko as best she could. She was still unconscious.

Eva ran breathlessly in the door, then stopped and held on to the wall, overcome by a coughing spell. "How is she?" she managed to ask between coughs.

"The same. What did you find out?"

"They're sending an embassy car around to take her to a hospital," she said hoarsely. "The chauffeur will help us carry her to the car. We'll need to take her sheets and blankets."

By the time the Swiss chauffeur had arrived, they'd found all the supplies they needed for Kiyoko's hospital stay. The ride was a blur. Iris didn't take her eyes from Kiyoko's unconscious face resting on her lap. Occasionally Kiyoko would murmur something about her dead daughter and Iris would gently reply, "*Hai, Mama-san, hai.*" By the time they arrived, the dark chill night had enveloped the city.

The doctor was overworked and tired. He quickly examined Kiyoko, then pronounced that she had acute pneumonia and would have to be hospitalized. Assuming that they were her daughters, he turned to Iris and Eva and told them they must provide their mother with clean linens and food every day. He stopped his instructions when Eva began coughing. Without a word, he took out his stethoscope, listened to her chest, and began a perfunctory examination. "You will stay as well," he said with finality.

"Stay?" Eva gasped, then began coughing again.

"You have pneumonitis. If we don't catch it now, you'll be just like your mother in a week. It's best to keep you here for a couple of days. Your sister will take care of things."

Without waiting for a response, the doctor motioned for a nurse to check Eva in. She started to protest, but began coughing.

"Go, Eva," Iris said with false confidence. "It's for the best. I'll be back tomorrow right after work." The doctor was already walking away, but Iris stopped him. "I'm sorry," she said quietly, "but I don't even know which hospital this is. Could you tell me how to get back to the Azabu-ku perfect? Where do I catch the *densha*?"

He looked exasperated. "You're in St. Luke's Hospital. It's in Tsukiji-ku. You can't take a streetcar at this hour of the night. I'll have the attendant arrange for a taxi." He left before she could thank him or protest that a taxi was too expensive.

Within a few minutes, a driver approached her. When she explained that she had only two yen in her purse, he assured her that he would take her to her house for that amount.

She rode home in misery, knowing that she was spending the last yen she had until her next paycheck, knowing that she was going to an empty house, knowing that they couldn't afford the hospital and medicines, yet thankful that they'd gotten help for Kiyoko and Eva in time. She felt desperately alone as she paid the driver and stood in the street before her gate, dreading going into the empty house.

Once inside, she fumbled in the dark to find the small lantern and their precious matches. The darkness pressed on her back as she kneeled on the mat beside the lantern and struggled to strike the match. It broke in her hand. She struck the head once more and it flared, nearly burning her fingers before she lit the lantern.

Too cold and tired to fix a meal, Iris pulled out the *futon* and bedding. Then, remembering to check on the chickens, she went out the back door and shone the lantern light on the sleeping hens. Shivering in the cold wind, she went back into the house.

As she closed the door behind her, she spotted something white on the *konro*. Holding the lantern high, she stooped and picked it up. It was a piece of paper, a note. Iris looked quickly around the house, shivering at the thought that someone else might be there with her. Seeing no one, she opened it and read: *Meiji Jingu. 10 A.M. B.*

Iris stared at the cryptic message for a moment. Then suddenly it struck her. Bill—it must have been Bill. He came while they were with Kiyoko. Meiji Jingu was the huge shrine built in 1920 in memory of the great restoration Emperor, Meiji. But it was a huge place in the center of Tokyo. It would be difficult to find Bill there. Meeting him at ten o'clock would give her two hours to wander around the grounds before she would have to leave for work. If she didn't find him by then, she'd go back at ten the next morning, and the next, until she did. She looked at the message once more to make sure she hadn't missed anything, then held it over the flame of the candle. As the paper caught fire, she placed it on the *konro*. No incriminating evidence. With that, she blew out the light and went to bed.

Iris awoke at dawn to the muffled bong of a distant temple. It had been a restless night, fraught with disturbing sounds, real and imagined. She turned and watched a patch of blue sky through the window.

The south-facing Japanese houses were designed to catch every ray of sunshine. It was only after Kiyoko had explained this that she and Eva had learned to take the screens from the roof of their porch in the cool months to allow any sunshine to reach the inner house and warm it. Now, with the screens properly removed, the pale morning sunshine crept in across the *tatami* mat, until its faint warmth reached Iris's face, promising a hint of spring. A wave of deep loneliness rolled over her as she remembered that Kiyoko and Eva were in the hospital, that she was miserably alone and without any money. Then she remembered the note from Bill.

She got up quickly, lit the *konro*, and began making her tea. While the water was coming to a boil she went outside to feed the chickens and pump another pail of water for a sponge bath.

By nine o'clock she had finished her breakfast, having thanked the two fat hens for their three eggs, cleaned the house, packed some food and linens for Kiyoko and Eva in the hospital, and was ready to walk to the Meiji Jingu for her meeting with Bill.

Since she could not afford the bus fare to the shrine, she left an hour early and walked through the streets, using the

241

time to try to think of a solution to their financial problems. The early morning household smells of charcoal, boiling rice, and sewage blended with the smells of the neighborhood shops she passed: the dark musty smell of the tea shop, the delicate sea smell of the fish shop and the pungent incense of the fresh-cut cypress coming from the shop of the old cabinet maker.

It was the sight of the cabinet-maker's shop that brought to mind the tiny hidden compartment she'd discovered in the *tansu* after Ito had ransacked the house. She'd been so pleased that Ito hadn't found the secret compartment that she'd taken one of her last five-dollar bills and slipped it in the compartment, telling Eva that it was good luck, that they'd use it to buy hot dogs and Cokes when they got back to Hawaii. Now, that last forgotten American money held a promise of medicine and food, a promise of life. Perhaps the Swiss Embassy would help her convert it into Japanese yen.

She'd passed the Meiji Shrine many times in the *densha* and knew it was large and protected from the bustle of the city by thick woods. However, she hadn't realized how immense it was until she approached it on foot. It was exactly ten o'clock.

She passed under the large *torii*, the soaring gate post of the shrine, and found an air of serenity. The shrine itself was a magnificent edifice, in pure traditional Japanese architecture, made of natural wood with the typical sweeping eaves of Japanese temples. The white-pebbled courtyard shone like ivory in the clear morning sunlight. She copied the other visitors' actions because she didn't know the proper manners in a shrine.

No one was going into the shrine itself, so she wandered around the outer grounds, walking pebbled paths laced with the shade of lush, budding trees, searching each care-worn face. Each person was a stranger, obscure and wrapped in private thoughts.

She'd given up hope of finding Bill by the time she'd reached the lovely pond surrounded by thick woods and carpeted with fat lily pads, so she paused by the water's edge to watch the wild ducks. Only one other person was within view, a Shinto priest walking slowly along the shoreline. His black kimono fluttered in the morning breeze, and he seemed pensive.

She felt terribly alone, and turned to look once more at the water before leaving. Despite the cold that nipped her nose and penetrated her scarf, there was something promising in the sight.

"*Ohayo gozaimasu, Ojo-san.*" The priest had silently approached her from behind and was bowing politely.

"*Ohayo gozaimasu,*" Iris said, returning his bow. Then something about the line of his cheek, and a certain arrogant stance even as he bowed, made Iris stop.

"You'd better bow lower than that," the familiar voice said, "or someone watching may think you're disrespectful of the clergy."

Iris giggled while bowing still lower. "You don't know how good it is . . ."

"Don't talk now," he said quickly. "Just go straight down that path into the wooded area behind the pond." He bowed again and continued walking.

Iris bowed, then slowly walked down the path into the shaded woods. She'd not gone far before Bill appeared.

"This way," he said, "where we won't be seen or heard." He turned abruptly and set a fast pace down the path.

She followed, hurrying to keep up with him. They ducked under some branches, then picked up a faint trail into the heart of the woods. He stopped in a tiny glen, warmed by a column of sunshine. Evergreen trees towered above them and shrubs concealed the spot from view.

"Where've you been?" Iris began breathlessly as she sat down on a large rock. "I've been frantic."

"Shhh, we'll have to whisper," Bill cautioned, sitting beside her. "I've had quite a bit going. The Kampetei have still been hanging around your neighborhood and I don't want to use up all my disguises." He reached inside his kimono and took out a cigarette.

"I've been working with a young Japanese-American student from Seattle. With his help, I was going to set up a radio to try to get messages out of the country. We'd just gotten most of the equipment last week, when Ted was suddenly drafted. They came to his school and got him just like that. Now I'm back where I began. Maybe I'll go south and try my hand at being a fisherman—one with a radio hidden in the hold of his boat."

"Does that mean we wouldn't be seeing you anymore?"

Bill grinned mischievously. "If I thought you'd miss me, I'd do it just to prove a point."

"We both would miss you, silly."

"You've come a long way from threatening me with a hoe in your air-raid shelter." He chuckled, then added more seriously, "No, I'll keep in contact with you whatever I'm doing. If I'm going to be gone for more than two weeks, I'll let you know ahead of time. Now, what was it you were so frantic to talk to me about?"

Iris quickly told him that Eva and Kiyoko were hospitalized. Then she told him about her conversations with Yakumo at work, explaining that the NHK propaganda broadcasts were going to change in character and that perhaps she could keep them from being effective.

Bill listened intently, his clear seal-brown eyes urging each detail from her. When she finished, he whistled under his breath. "Wow," he whispered, "it's just dropped into our laps. How much influence do you think you can have?"

"I don't know. There are other Japanese-Americans around the station, but from the way they act, they're mostly loyal either to the Emperor or their own skins. I've had some words with a couple of the women because they turned in their American citizenship." She smiled and admitted, "I'm not the most popular one there. I've also heard that down on the second floor there are even some POWs they've brought in for that purpose, but I think that's just another one of those rumors because I haven't seen them. There's no telling what kind of help I could be. I'd like to try, though."

Bill was quiet, his dark eyebrows knitted in a frown of concentration. With his face thrown into relief against the dark traditional robe, he was very Japanese, very handsome. He turned to her and shook his head. "Let me think about it. We'd better work out a master plan for every possibility we can think of, so you'll know what to do. I'll come to your house tonight, probably pretty late."

Iris nodded. She didn't feel so alone anymore. "Thanks. I'll wait up. Since I've got to cook for Kiyoko and Eva at the hospital, I probably won't make it back home until late myself. Ten o'clock?"

"Fine." He got up abruptly. "You'll have to worry about finding food enough for Kiyoko and Eva, so leave dinner to me. I'll find something to tide us over. Incidentally, don't spend your precious yen on a taxi again—you're perfectly safe on the bus." As they began walking toward the main path, he said, "You go on ahead. Don't be late getting back tonight. I have to leave in time to get to Yokohama by dawn."

"I won't," she promised. "Don't you forget."

He grinned and waved her on her way, saying, "Small chance of that."

A small yellow butterfly flitted across the path in front of her as she hurried out of the woods. She felt almost lighthearted.

Exchanging the five-dollar bill at the Swiss Embassy took much longer than Iris had anticipated. She was two hours late by the time she got to work. As she hurried up the stairs of the NHK Building, she was stopped abruptly on the second-floor landing by a sight that made her heart stop. An office door was just closing, but not soon enough to prevent her from seeing three men, sitting with their backs to the door. From their weary posture, pale shaved heads, and thin frayed American uniforms, she knew. POWs. So, the rumor was true. That was how they were going to make a real "American" program.

With leaden feet and thudding heart, Iris went on up to her third-floor office. Yakumo immediately approached her and told her in very firm terms that his superiors frowned upon such tardy appearances, especially the powerful Major Tsunieshi, the army officer who had set up an office in NHK just for the purpose of controlling the radio broadcasts. After sitting numbly through the lecture, Iris forced her attention on Yakumo's fat face and shiny round glasses and said, "Please accept my apologies. Even in the face of wartime hardship I will try to faithfully do my job."

Yakumo hesitated, obviously startled by Iris's acquiescence. Then, once more taking his authoritative stance, he said, "We might be asking you to work longer hours soon. Please arrange your schedule to accommodate such a change." With that he turned and left.

Eva looked better than she had the night before. Kiyoko was sleeping, but Eva assured Iris that she'd been conscious and had even talked for a few minutes that afternoon. Iris set up the brazier between their beds and began preparing the bit of rice and dried vegetables she'd brought with her. At the suggestion of one of the nurses, Iris used her seasoning powder to make a soup for Kiyoko. Once it was boiling, she cracked the two eggs she'd brought and dropped them into the boiling broth.

Eva ate with enthusiasm while Iris gently awakened Kiyoko and spoon-fed her. It was after Eva had put down her bowl and Iris was still feeding Kiyoko that she caught sight of an orderly who was working nearby. He seemed to be edging his cart of supplies closer to them, deliberately trying to get within hearing distance.

"It looks as if even the beds have ears," Iris whispered to Eva. "We'd better speak only Japanese and choose our subjects wisely."

Eva glanced in the direction of the orderly and said out loud, "Hai, one-e-san." Yes, sister.

Kiyoko until that time had saved her strength for eating. However, when she heard Eva call Iris her sister, her eyes brightened and she whispered, "Ichihatsu no hana, kemmeina watashi no musume."

Iris understood that Kiyoko had called her a wise daughter, but she didn't know what else she'd been called. "Wakarimasen, 'Ichihatsu no hana,'" she told Kiyoko softly.

Kiyoko smiled wanly. "It is the name of the Japanese iris." With that she leaned back against her hard pillow and whispered, "Thank you, my daughter." From her even breathing, Iris could tell that she'd drifted into sleep again.

It was nine-twenty before she was ready to go. Not once in the time she'd been there had Iris felt free to talk to Eva about the POWs at NHK or her coming visit with Bill. The other patients were too close and the attendants had a disconcerting way of appearing when least expected.

By the time she got home, it was after ten o'clock. She eagerly opened the gate and stepped into the garden, then felt a twinge of disappointment when she saw no light coming from the house. Leaving her shoes on the pad in their entry, she slipped on her soft house slippers and slid open the door to the main room. A soft glow of coals came from the kotatsu.

"How's Eva?"

"What are you doing here in the dark?"

"Don't you think it'd be rather suspicious to have your

lantern light itself? Or have you forgotten the eyes and ears in this neighborhood?"

"I guess I just wasn't thinking. When I saw it was dark, I thought you weren't here. You surprised me." She took off her scarf and put her coat away. "Are you hungry? I'll start dinner."

"It's all made. Just pull up a pillow and I'll go get it."

"How'd you do that in the dark?"

"I have a black-out flashlight. Sit down."

Iris was famished after her long day. Bill must have anticipated that, because he brought out three large pots. As he lifted the lid of each, Iris exclaimed excitedly. "Potatoes! Where did you . . . oh, Bill, is that really fried chicken? And fresh carrots! I can't believe it. Is this gravy in the bottom?" She eagerly filled her plate from each pot. "I should feel guilty because of the meal I just served Eva and Kiyoko, but all I can do is cheer. You're magic! How'd you do this?"

Bill grinned and went back into the kitchen; he returned with a loaf of bread and a small tin of butter. "Now, maybe we can start getting some meat back on those bones of yours. Do you know how thin you're getting?"

"I only know I'm in heaven," she said, with her mouth full. "You're a miracle worker. I don't know how to thank you."

Bill was laughing at Iris's enthusiastic attack on the meal. "I think it's enough just to see your performance at finishing this off. Now, slow down and tell me how Eva and Kiyoko are."

Iris forced herself to put down a drumstick and briefly tell about their progress in the hospital. She also mentioned the orderly who was trying to overhear their conversation.

Iris went back to her dinner, then suddenly her expression sobered and she pushed away her plate. "I was wrong about there not being POWs working at NHK. I saw three of them today. I asked Ruth Takata, one of the nisei workers at the station, about them. She says that the POWs have been there for a couple of months. I asked her if there was any way to see them; she asked me what on earth for. I told her I was just curious and felt sorry for them. She said that I'd better watch out because there are too many Kampetei agents working in the office."

"She's right, but you should try to figure out some safe excuse to at least catch a glimpse of them. If they're American or Australian, you might be able to work it that they'll help us."

"Oh, I'm sure they are. Ruth said they were captured in Southeast Asia, so they'd probably be Australian. What do you have in mind?"

"You said they're going to change their programming and ask for your guidance in doing it. So, let's see what we can do to sabotage it."

It was Bill's contention that for now, the best they could hope to do would be to diminish the demoralizing effect of the propaganda. Eventually they might figure out some way to convey real information, but that idea was pretty farfetched, in Bill's estimation.

However, he felt that if Iris could write some of the scripts, they would have more control. Comedy shows with subtle satire might be effective, he felt; but Iris insisted that she had no talents in creating scripts or any other kind of writing. She was hesitant to try her hand at writing even brief lead-in announcements.

"Well," Bill said, "if you have editorial control over the news announcements, you might be able to do something."

"Hopefully. But remember, there are other nisei in the American division who appear to be quite supportive of the Japanese cause. If they pick up on something, it could be bad."

"Maybe until we see how it's going, we'd better concentrate on the kind of programming. What do you think is the least depressing?"

"I guess I'd stick by what I was telling Yakumo that first day—music programs. If the station has access to any American records, that'd be the way to go."

Bill nodded. "If you can swing it, that seems to be our best bet. If you get a chance, you might tell Yakumo that you'd be glad to help him work on the programs. You might get in on the ground floor and be really helpful in a crunch." He watched Iris thoughtfully, then added, "But don't take any chances. Keep your head about you like you did today with your humble apology for being late for work."

Iris smiled faintly. "If I pour it on too thick, they might get suspicious. After all, I've been outspoken all along."

"Well, have a slow conversion . . . one that makes them think they're actually winning you over to their side."

Iris shook her head. "It's hard to keep plugging when you don't even have an idea about how things are going. With Eva in the hospital, I miss my nightly briefings on the world news."

"You know about the Battle of the Bismarck Sea about a week and a half ago?"

Iris frowned. "Not really. Eva mentions so many places. That one doesn't stand out in my mind."

"Well, it should. Just like the Battle of Midway should stick in your mind. The Japanese lost again. American planes bombed the stuffing out of a Japanese convoy that was trying to reinforce some Japanese troops on New Guinea. MacArthur claimed it was a major victory and made sea power obsolete. He says Allied ground-based airplanes will win the war."

"How do you know all that?"

"I have other sources for news besides Eva," he replied. "The interesting thing is that there are indications that now, since the Battle of the Bismarck Sea, the Japanese command is going on the defensive."

When the candle in the lantern sputtered out, they were left in the rosy glow of the charcoal. So, they sat, warming their feet near the ceramic brazier, talking about home and dreams and what they could possibly find to eat that would ever taste as good as Bill's fried-chicken dinner.

At last Bill looked at his watch and moaned softly. "Do you realize we've been sitting here for three and a half hours? I've got to get going if I expect to catch that train to Yokohama," he said, standing up. "I'll be back day after tomorrow, and we'll do the same thing. I'll have dinner waiting when you get back from the hospital. Maybe you'll have something to tell me about the decisions on the propaganda programming."

Iris beamed. "I can't wait," she said, following him to the back porch. "Yakumo will probably have a meeting tomorrow or the next day, so there should be something."

Bill paused before the sliding door, the light from a chilly full moon silhouetting him against the window. "We should avoid meeting in public. I realized today at the Meiji Jingu that we're both considerably taller than the average Japanese. When we're together, we stand out too much." He reached out and touched Iris's cheek. "Don't take any chances with Yakumo," he said, tilting her chin up with his fingers. "I'd hate to see anything happen to you." He leaned down and kissed her gently on the lips, lingering tenderly for a breathless moment. Then he walked out the door.

Iris stood watching his shadowy departure, holding her fingers to her warm, tingling lips.

CHAPTER XVIII

Iris tossed and turned for two hours after Bill left. When she finally drifted off to sleep, an air-raid siren sounded, causing her to retreat alone to the dark, damp shelter in their garden. It seemed she'd just crawled, shivering, back under her quilt when the cry, *"Haikyu ga mairimashita!"* announcing that the rations were in, forced her out into the chill morning to stand in the long line. By the time she arrived at work she could barely hold her eyes open, much less concentrate on her editing job.

When she was summoned to her boss's office, she was surprised to find several of the NHK management sitting there. She was even more shocked to see Major Tsuneishi, who was the power behind the NHK American division. Fearful, Iris hesitated at the door.

"Please come in, Miss Hashimoto," the major said in an ominously pleasant tone. As Iris slipped into the chair he had indicated, he added, "We were just discussing you. I have been told you spent most of your life in the United States."

"Hai," Iris said nervously.

"Then you can be of great help to us. We are going to design some new programs for the American troops. Tell me what you think they would like to hear. Perhaps news, uplifting lectures, stirring military music?"

She knew that if she was going to have any credibility, she must speak knowledgeably in putting forth the ideas she and Bill had discussed.

She bowed politely. "I can only offer you my own opinion, which is simply based upon what I have observed. What you decide with your complete wisdom will obviously be the best. I believe that you would achieve a great audience of Americans if you were to play popular music." There was a long pause, as if they were waiting for her to go on. "Americans will turn to any station that offers them good music—jazz, classical, or semiclassical. Americans crave music." There was another waiting silence, so she slipped in a subtle challenge. "Of course, I know it would be most difficult even for you to find popular American recordings. . . ."

"It would be no problem, Miss Hashimoto," Major Tsuneishi assured her. "What kind of American music program are you talking about? Please explain how it proceeds."

Iris paused, choosing her words carefully so her Japanese would not be heavy-tongued, so as not to say anything that might discredit her. "In my limited opinion, a good American music program would be like many I have heard in California. It would have an announcer, what Americans call a disc jockey. This announcer keeps up a lively kind of chatter, telling what each record is and maybe something about the artist who performed it—that sort of thing. Then the record is played. Then the announcer comes back on and does much the same thing for another record. The program is mostly music, you see. The announcer just identifies the music and tries to make it sound exciting."

There was a brief silence when Iris stopped. She knew that when she'd come in there was more than one opinion; now she'd taken sides. She held her breath.

An army captain sitting next to Major Tsuneishi seemed the most displeased. He spoke up first. "We can only influence the wrong thinking of the Americans by explaining the righteousness of the Imperial Way. We do not exist to entertain them. We must prepare them to accept their inevitable defeat and to become loyal subjects of the Emperor and members of the Greater East Asia Co-Prosperity Sphere."

"Ah, but we also know that the reason the Americans are so decadent is because they are jazz-mad. We must talk to them in their language, so to speak," put in a nicely dressed man whom Iris had seen around the studio many times. The army captain glowered at him.

Major Tsuneishi inclined his head. "The sound of a falling tree

251

is not heard if a man's ears are stopped. We cannot explain a thing if they won't turn the radio dials to our station." He turned to Iris and added, "I think Miss Hashimoto is correct. We must give them what they want to hear in order to say what we want to say. We thank you for your help, Miss Hashimoto. You may return to your work now."

Iris got up and bowed, then stopped. "I am most grateful I could be of help. If it would please you, I will offer my services in setting up this musical program."

"Why would you do that?" Yakumo asked suspiciously; this was the first time he had spoken.

Iris had anticipated his suspicions and had her answer ready. "When I lived in America I wanted to work for a radio station. This would be a very good opportunity for me. I think it would be fun."

"Your answer is honest and reasonable for one so young," Major Tsuneishi said. "You may be of use to the Emperor while gaining valuable experience as well. It is the kind of situation which would create a good worker. Yakumo, you will see to it that Miss Hashimoto is allowed to help and advise in the production of this program if we decide to do it. Good day, Miss Hashimoto."

Iris bowed very low and said her thanks before going out. As she went back to her desk, she made a point of walking with a light step, which seemed to disappoint some of her co-workers, who'd expected that she'd been called to the boss's office for a reprimand.

As she walked past Ruth's desk, Ruth whispered, "What did they want?" She held up a piece of paper as if she were asking Iris a question about it.

Iris stopped and leaned over, looking at the decoy paper. Ruth was one of the few who'd been pleasant to her and was the only one Iris considered a potential friend. "They just wanted to ask some questions about what American radio programs are like." She took the paper from Ruth's hand and added, "They're finding out that lectures aren't too popular with the troops." Ruth had done some radio announcing for the American division herself, and several times as she had come back from the studio, she had put the script down on her desk and made a grimace at Iris.

"What did you say?"

"Told the truth. Americans like music."

252

Right before Iris's quitting time, Ruth called her over again and handed her a three-page script, imperiously saying, "I don't have time to finish what I have here. Take this on your way out and deliver it to the office on the second floor."

Iris took the script, astounded that Ruth should use such a haughty, commanding voice with her. Then Ruth whispered, "It's your chance to see the POWs." With that she turned back to her work, dismissing Iris abruptly for the benefit of the rest of the office workers.

Iris bowed slightly, carrying out the charade. At last she would see the POWs—maybe even talk to them. It would mean a lot for them to know that there was another American working there, an American who was still rooting for their side. *Maybe they'll even know Cole,* she fantasized as she went down the stairs.

She walked briskly into the office, smiling encouragingly. Two men were leaning over their desks, reading and marking scripts. They looked tired, beaten, and emaciated. Iris's heart went out to them.

"I brought a script for you," she said, handing it to the man closest to her. He looked up, his thin face sallow, the dark circles under his eyes deep and hollow. His light brown hair was beginning to grow out from the shaving he must have been given upon capture. Iris was startled by his blue eyes; she hadn't seen blue eyes since she'd left Hawaii, two years ago.

"Just set it down," he said listlessly. "Another turncoat Yank, huh?"

"A Yank, yes. But I'm no turncoat. I've gone through a lot to keep my American citizenship." She looked proudly toward the other prisoner. He was staring at her as if hypnotized.

Then she saw his eyes and the cynical twist of his mouth. Despite the gaunt face, skeletal build, and thinning hair, she knew the eyes, the mouth, the tilt of his head. She barely had breath to speak. "Jake . . . ?"

He eyed her coldly, his mouth curling in distaste. Then, without a word, he turned back to his work, his silence more eloquent than words.

"Oh, Jake, it isn't . . ." she whispered.

"Better leave, lady. We can't have visitors," the other POW said bitterly. Then he too turned back to his desk.

Slowly, Iris went out the door, shocked beyond words. An

office worker stopped and looked at her strangely, bringing her back to her senses. With an almost superhuman effort, she composed her face back into an indifferent mask and went down the stairs and out the door. Behind the blank facade, her mind was whirling, echoing, spinning.

The first days after Jake's capture were nothing more than a blur of pain, exceeded only by the burning inner torment and agony of his loss of Maria and their unborn child. The tortures his captors conceived for his body could never exceed the wounds they'd inflicted on his soul. Finally, just when he'd given up, just when he'd given in to the pain, they quit. He was left alone in a dank cell under Fort Santiago, keeping company with rats and the distant screams of other prisoners. Jake assumed they'd abandoned hope of getting information from him and would soon execute him. It was only a matter of time.

When they removed him from Fort Santiago, he was prepared for the firing squad. When they put him, instead, in Bilibad Prison, where some prisoners from Corregidor were held, he assumed they were merely waiting until they got enough for a mass execution and grave.

Gradually, days slipped into weeks, weeks into months. With each day more men died in Bilibad Prison. Some crawled off to curl like dried worms beside the fence that kept them cut off from freedom. Some simply died in their sleep. Others bartered away their meager rations for green Japanese cigarettes and deliberately starved themselves to death, crawling under the buildings and dying in the maggot-infested mud. More than three-quarters of the prison population died in the eight months that Jake was there. Disease was rampant, starvation universal. The thin gruel they were served each day was nothing more than a few grains of rice boiled in water and seasoned with a bit of soy sauce.

Then came the day in December—ironically, December 8, by Jake's reckoning. Without explanation, they singled Jake out from the other prisoners, shoved him into the back of a truck, and took him to the docks. Seeing the troop ship waiting there, Jake balked, thinking they must be taking him to Tokyo for further interrogation. He was hustled onto the ship and locked in the dark, damp, miserably crowded hold with what must have been four hundred other prisoners, and countless hungry gnawing rats and cockroaches. Most of the prisoners were Chinese, Malaysian, and Filipino, whom Jake figured were being enlisted for slave labor in Japanese factories. He knew that he was a political prisoner to be pumped of information and then summarily executed.

At sea he watched those around him die from the malicious neglect of their captors, and wondered why he was still alive. Once again his nostrils were filled with the scent of death. Once again he awaited the time when he too would weaken and fall. Once again, he survived.

They docked in Tokyo in late December. Jake was herded off the boat. While the prisoners stood barefoot in six inches of snow, the officers came and once more separated Jake from the rest. He was taken to the Sanno Hotel in the center of Tokyo.

Still under guard, Jake was allowed his first bath and shave since leaving the Philippines. There was a blanket for him to wrap up in, and a meal that exceeded all he'd had the whole time on the boat.

The following day, still weak from dysentery and wearing his shabby, peasant trousers and loose shirt, Jake was taken to a building in downtown Tokyo that housed offices and radio equipment. A small Japanese major greeted him.

He came right to the point in accented English. Jake was known to have been a radio commentator before the war. Now he was to use his special talents for the Japanese. Weak and tired, Jake reminded the major of the provisions of the Geneva Convention. The major reminded him the Japanese had never ratified the Geneva Convention, and said he could not guarantee the safety of any POW who refused to cooperate with the Japanese army.

Jake said he could only broadcast POW messages home. Then, as his old sarcasm surfaced, he added that he could mop floors, because he'd also done that in civilian life. The major's face got red and he stood in stony silence, glaring at Jake. It wasn't hard to see where it would go from here. Long ago prepared for such an end, Jake added, "Or you could save us both a lot of time. Just give me a loaded pistol and I'll put a bullet in my brain."

The major barked an order in Japanese and Jake was taken back to his hotel. The next day he was taken to a prisoners' compound somewhere in the city. Most of the men there were Allied prisoners who were doing enforced labor in factories, defense sites, and other strategic work areas. Nothing was said as Jake was placed in his cold cell.

The following morning as he walked out into the courtyard, he felt a palpable air of terror. None of the men had been taken to their various job sites. Instead, they sat around the walls, crouching on their heels, staring at the center of the yard like cornered rabbits.

A thin, naked man lay splayed on his stomach in the center of the yard, his hands and feet tethered to stakes, his pale flesh blue from lying on the icy ground. Two armed guards stood back to back at his head.

As Jake came out, one of the guards stepped forward and shoved him to a post near the man's head. Jake's arms were twisted roughly behind him and his hands were tied tightly behind the pole. The guard pushed Jake's face and pointed to the man on the ground, grunting something in Japanese. Jake could clearly see the naked prisoner's shivering body, wracked by each terrified breath he took.

The commander of the prison came out, hitting his polished boots with a swagger stick as he strutted up to Jake. Another prisoner was called over. "Say who this prisoner on the ground is," the commander ordered in heavily accented English.

The man's eyes rolled from the staked prisoner to Jake and then to the commander. "He . . . he's Avram Rosenburg, from New Jersey."

"Before army, what profession?"

"He was a . . . an accountant for his father's firm and," he blurted out, "and he's never done no one no harm, not even a Jap."

The informant prisoner was shoved back to the wall. The commander looked up at Jake. "You watch."

One of the guards took a pail and began smearing a liquid over Rosenburg's bare back. The pungent smell of benzene reached Jake's nose and he could see the man's thin buttocks quivering as the caustic liquid was poured over his genitals. Avram Rosenburg, from New Jersey, began to whimper as the guard stepped back.

Suddenly the commander stepped forward, struck a match, and threw it on Rosenburg.

Instantly Rosenburg's back was a sheet of orange flame.

Screaming, he twisted in agony, tearing the skin from his ankles and wrists as he pulled at the ropes pillorying him to the ground.

"No!" Jake's long scream mingled with the shrieks of the burning man.

Repelled by the sight, Jake turned his head, unable to look at Rosenburg's burning flesh as it began to curl in blackened ripples on his back. Still, the smell of burned hair and scorched flesh filled Jake's nose. His screams ricocheted off the prison walls and reverberated through Jake's very bones. Jake's stomach rose to his throat and he began to gag, tearing the sinews of his shoulders as his body was convulsed with dry heaves.

The commander reached up and grabbed a handful of Jake's hair, forcing him to look once more at the burning man. Then he barked an order and left. The guards threw sand on Rosenburg's back, killing the flames, exposing the white bones protruding from the burned flesh. Now mercifully unconscious, Roseburg was untied and dragged from the courtyard.

To his surprise, Jake was then untied and taken to the commander's office. "You see what your stubbornness creates," the commander said as he casually lit a cigarette and leaned back in his chair. "That man is an example. How many more will suffer before you're convinced to aid in the Imperial Way?"

". . . Convinced?"

"Major Tsuneishi of the NHK has asked me to convince you to help him with his radio broadcasting. Will it take much longer?"

"Rosenburg was . . . because of me?" Jake said, swaying on his feet.

"Of course. You will have today to think about it." Just then one of the guards came in, said something in Japanese, saluted, and left.

"Rosenburg is dead," the commander said to Jake, almost with pleasure. "You think about it. We will talk later today. Perhaps you will talk to Major Tsuneishi."

That afternoon, Major Tsuneishi handed him a radio script to read on the air. Jake was still shaken by the horrible death his captors had staged to force him to do their propaganda. Weak and light-headed, Jake sat in front of the microphone and gave a slipshod delivery of the virulent attack on Roosevelt that the Japanese had written for him.

Back at the hotel, Jake had time alone to ruminate on what had happened. He couldn't get the smell of Rosenburg's roasted flesh from his nose. His head echoed with Rosenburg's screams. The strange familiarity of the radio mike haunted him. Then, suddenly, he saw some hope. He would cooperate. He had no choice, lest other men be martyred. Maybe he could do some good by reading POW messages as well. When doing the Japanese-prepared scripts, he would deliberately slide over the most offensive parts, using his tone of voice to minimize the effect. If he saw mistakes in the phraseology or grammar, he would deliberately emphasize them. If possible, he would slip in his own words, words with double meanings, sarcasm, puns, and humor. Thus, he could maintain his honor while weakening Japanese propaganda and preventing the torture of other innocent POWs. He fell asleep that night, knowing that it would be all right . . . if he was careful.

Jake had little contact with the other POWs working at NHK, primarily because they had different assignments and schedules. Noting that some were complacently writing their own propaganda programs and broadcasting them, Jake was leery of their loyalty, fearing that they might turn informer to save their lives. Yet, Jake couldn't really blame them for whatever they did.

The Japanese paid them in yen for their work, according to the Geneva Convention, although Jake had been told they didn't adhere to it. They even issued him a few ration cards, allowing him to buy, through his guards, some bits of shoddy clothing and strange food. After about a month, Tsuneishi brought Jake a winter uniform he'd had made for him, which warmed Jake's body, if not his heart.

Jake couldn't tell how many Allied POWs worked at NHK, but he didn't think there were many. There was at least one Filipino, an Australian, Major Charles Cousens, whom as far as Jake could tell was not a willing conspirator, and Sammy Delaney, the young corporal who'd just arrived from the Solomons. He was more of a journalistic clerk, having had very little broadcasting experience. He was also pretty outspoken in his dislike of the Japanese, American "turncoats" as he called the nisei working in the office, and anything that wasn't American. At the first opportunity, Jake cautioned him about Kampetei spies. When he balked, Jake told him about

Avram Rosenburg. After that, Sammy limited his bitter sarcasm to the nisei women who worked in the office and frequently found excuses to come down to the second floor and see them.

Jake thought he was prepared for anything, until that afternoon in March. He'd heard the door open and a bright female voice talking in straight American English. It was a new voice and he couldn't resist just a glance at this new traitor. His eyes were held by the face.

She was thinner, and now wore long, thick braids, and the deep hollows under her eyes were strange—but, yes, it was definitely Iris. He could not mistake the fine bone structure and the delicate mouth.

Jake's mind swam with images: Cole laughing, sharing the news of his engagement; Cole brooding, hurt and confused when Iris had left; Iris's American smile lost in her Japanese face. It had been Japanese faces raping and killing Maria, Japanese faces torturing him in Fort Santiago, Japanese faces setting fire to Rosenburg's back, Japanese faces each day trying to make him betray his country and himself. Then Iris looked at him and whispered his name, her Japanese face revealing shock at being discovered in her betrayal.

It was well after ten before Iris got on the *densha*. The doctor had stopped her on the way out of the hospital, telling her she could take Eva home the day after tomorrow if her temperature stayed down and if Iris could care for her at home. Kiyoko would take at least another month. Iris had trouble understanding him because she was so distracted. Finally, she'd taken out a piece of paper and asked him to write down the instructions. He'd obliged, and returned the slip of paper covered with Japanese characters. Iris had bowed her thanks, hoping Kiyoko could read it to her the following night.

Now as she hurried down the darkened street toward their gate, she wasn't sure that Bill would still be waiting for her.

Kicking off her shoes in the entryway, she hurried inside. "Bill? Are you here?" she called as she felt for the lantern and struck a match.

In the fluttering of the match she could see him sprawled out on two *zabuton*, the sitting cushions beside the low eating table. He sat up slowly, smiling. "Hey, calm down. I thought the place was being raided or something. Can't a guy get some shut-eye without . . ."

"Oh, Bill, if you weren't here I would have just died," she said, moving the lantern into the main room. She saw Bill's smile fade to a look of concern. "But I think everything's all right," she added quickly.

"Well, take off your coat and let me bring out your dinner before you start telling me your story. But I'm sort of disappointed. I thought all your eagerness was just to see me again . . . or at least my terrific cooking."

He brought out two plates heaped with steaming fish, deliciously seasoned rice, and fresh vegetables. As they started eating, Iris quickly told him about her meeting with Major Tsuneishi.

"You handled it just right," Bill assured her. "Now, if you can only get to writing one of those programs . . ."

"But that's not all," Iris said, waving her hand. Then she told him about her encounter with Jake. "And I'm sure he recognized me," she concluded. "His look has been haunting me all day. It was so . . . so accusing." Her voice trailed off as she remembered Jake's cold stare.

Bill stared at the coals in the *konro*. Finally, he said, "You're sure it was Jake? People change, and when you're away from home, every strange face looks like it should be someone you once knew."

"It was Jake," she said firmly.

Bill continued looking at the coals. "And you felt he was hostile?"

Iris nodded. "I always thought Jake sort of liked me," she said softly. "I know he didn't really approve of a mixed marriage between Cole and me. Maybe he thought it was going to hold Cole back, like Marta said, but I don't think he disliked me personally. We always joked around and got along fine."

"There are two possible reasons, then," Bill said. "One— he's embarrassed that you caught him collaborating with the enemy. Or, two—he thinks *you're* collaborating with the enemy."

"That's ridiculous. Surely he wouldn't think I'd conspire with the Japanese."

"Don't jump to conclusions. There's no way he could know what you're doing. Remember, Jake's been through a lot.

There's no way he could still be the same Jake you knew in Hawaii. Anything that looks like you might be part of the Japanese machinery, is bound to be resented. Being his best friend's fiancée would make you even more of a traitor in his eyes."

Iris was silent for a few moments. "Then what do I do now?" she asked softly.

"Win his confidence."

"How?"

"Every way we can think of. You said he was thin?"

"Emaciated. I wanted to cry."

Bill got up and went to the back porch. He came back carrying four oranges. "I was going to save these as a surprise for you. Now I think we can use them to win Jake's favor. They're almost impossible to get."

Iris stared at the oranges as if they were diamonds and rubies.

"Don't ask. I have my sources. Now," he said, taking out a knife, "let's share one; you can save one each for Kiyoko and Eva, and take the other one to Jake." Iris's mouth watered as the sharp citrus smell filled her nose. Bill handed her half the orange with the peel still on, saying, "Eat the peel. As starved as we are for fruit and vitamins, we can't afford to waste any. Besides, it'll taste good."

He was right. Iris savored each tangy bite, sucking the juice from her fingers, holding each golden section up to the light to admire its translucent beauty. She was sure she'd never seen a more beautiful creation. Even the bitter sweetness of the rind was a treasure. "Oh, Bill, it's just heavenly," she said, licking her fingers. "You've topped the chicken dinner, I do believe."

Bill polished off his last bite. "When you give the orange to Jake, be careful you're not seen. I don't think even the black market around here has them. That would really put you under suspicion. And tell Jake when you give it to him that it's a gift from Bill. If he remembers me, that ought to help him start trusting you. There's no way you could know about me unless I'd actually contacted you," he explained. "Now, I've got to be going," he said, heading for the door.

Iris was suddenly very self-conscious, remembering how Bill had kissed her before leaving last time, remembering how she'd enjoyed it. But this time there was no lingering good-bye.

"I'll check in with you in a week or so. In the meantime, keep working on getting Jake's trust. It's important." He touched her cheek lightly and said, "Be seeing you, kid." Then he was gone.

Iris wondered why she felt so disappointed. Probably just tired, she told herself. She put out the lantern, got ready for bed in the dark, and slipped under the quilt on her *futon*. She was instantly and peacefully asleep.

When Iris went to work the next day, she stopped first at the second-floor office. Two strange POWs were working there; she simply bowed and excused herself. All day she tried to go back down there, but every time she was about to, either Yakumo or one of the other office workers prevented it. Finally, as she was leaving the building she tried once more.

She carried a blank piece of paper, so she looked as if she were delivering something again. Quickly opening the door of the office, she slipped in. Jake was there alone. He turned at the sound of the closing door; seeing Iris, he turned his back to her.

"Things are not what you think, Jake," she said quickly. She put the orange down in front of him and he stared incredulously. "It's a gift from Bill." He turned and looked at her, hatred mingled with curiosity, then his eyes strayed back to the orange. "Eat the peel, too," she instructed, "but don't let anyone catch you with it. They're rarer than hen's teeth." She heard footsteps pass by the door and knew she'd better leave quickly. "I'll check in with you whenever I get a chance. Just remember what I said. I'm still American. I haven't changed my colors."

She left him still staring. He'd not said a word.

When Eva finally came home from the hospital, they worked together devising ways to win Jake's confidence. Iris ate only half her lunch, slipping the other half to Jake. She gathered from his terse comments that on those days, he gave his rations at night to the other POWs to divide among them.

Within two weeks Eva was back at her job at the Domei News Agency, translating American broadcasts. Once more she had access to news of the war. They both felt that if Iris could somehow pass on news of Allied advances in New Guinea, Jake would be heartened and perhaps more trusting.

In the meantime, Yakumo had asked Iris to begin working on the development of a music program. It was at that time that she took a bold chance and said, "If you will allow me to make a suggestion, I have an idea that will make this a very popular radio show."

Yakumo gestured for her to continue.

"I was asked to deliver a script downstairs to the office on the second floor the other day. One of the POWs I saw in there was an American whose face I recognized. He was a famous radio announcer from Seattle; I listened to his program when I was a schoolgirl. If you will allow me to work with him, I think we can create the program you have dreamed of." Yakumo was silent, his skepticism thinly veiled. "Perhaps," she continued, "if you will allow us a short segment of time, maybe fifteen minutes, I can convince you. If I fail in the effort, you will be able to stop me without much loss."

Yakumo leaned forward, one eyebrow raised over the top of his rimless glasses. "You will have a very steep road to climb with that prisoner. He has not given us much cooperation. He has been uncooperative even with his fellow prisoners, making them uncomfortable in his presence. We have gone to great expense to use his talents and have not been as successful as Major Tsuneishi and I had hoped. Perhaps you can see the difficulties involved."

"But if he will work with me on the type of program we've discussed, it will be a great credit to you."

Yakumo was silent for a moment, then he nodded. "*Hai*, Miss Hashimoto. You might be able to do it. Ingratiate yourself with him. When he begins to appreciate your pretty face, convince him he must cooperate in order to save you great pain. It is something he will understand. Try to make it your best program ever. If you are successful, there might even be a slight raise in your paycheck in appreciation of your work for the Emperor."

It was the first of May when Iris met with Jake and showed him the rough draft of her first script. She knew it didn't sound quite like a radio announcer should sound, but she hoped Jake would help make it right . . . once he understood she was no traitor.

"What's this crap?" he asked, looking up from the script.

"A new idea for a radio program for the Allied troops."

"It's a mess. What do you have to do with this?"

"I've convinced them this is the kind of program that will get a listening audience in the American sector."

"And you say you're not a traitor?"

Iris looked around, to make sure there was no one to overhear them. "Don't be a fool, Jake. This is the most innocuous thing to come out of here. Just try to cooperate for once, instead of being so mean."

Jake eyed her coldly. "You can't expect me to work with the same people who raped and murdered my pregnant wife, can you?"

Iris gasped.

"Or to help people who set innocent victims on fire just to get their own way?"

"I don't understand. . . ."

"I'll bet you don't," he said, handing the script back to her.

"Jake, please. We've all been through a lot. You've obviously suffered more than most. But you've got to at least think this over. Maybe we can do more good, more help than harm. Bill says to tell you that we're all counting on you."

"Bill who? You mentioned that name when you gave me the orange. We didn't know a Bill in Hawaii."

"Not Hawaii, the Philippines. Bill Ando."

Jake looked at her, startled. "Now I know you're part of them. Take your goddamn script and get out of here. I'll stick to the crap they shovel out to me. At least I know no one will listen to it. Some poor soldier might want to turn your program on."

"Don't be a fool. If one of our boys turns this on, he's not listening to the depressing drivel you spout." Just then a Filipino POW came in the room and began typing. "At least think about it," Iris whispered. "I'll come back tomorrow."

She took her script back to the third floor and pretended to revise it for the rest of the afternoon. How could she convince Jake that she wasn't part of an elaborate conspiracy? Every time she thought about what he'd said, she shivered and understood why he was so suspicious.

The following night, Bill came to their house, bearing a

264

whole fish, an onion, and two carrots. While he began cooking, Iris sipped a bowl of tea and told him about her latest frustration in trying to win Jake's confidence and get her radio show started. "I have the whole program pretty well worked out. Yakumo came in today with a whole box of old records. I couldn't believe it. There was Bing Crosby, Tommy Dorsey, Frank Sinatra and the Pied Pipers, Carmen Miranda, the Ink Spots, and Dinah Shore. I was all excited, and then Jake drops this bomb on me. He doesn't believe anything I've been telling him."

"Well, how did he think you knew about me, then?"

"He said that was all part of the conspiracy. Apparently, he thinks the Japanese know about your supplying information to the Americans before the war and are using it to trick him into complying with Japanese plans."

Bill was quiet for a moment. "Then maybe we'll have to try harder to convince him," he said, putting the food on the *shokutaku*, their low dinner table. "Eva, what news do you have from Domei today? Maybe some good news would cheer him up."

"Well, the Americans are fighting for Dobodura in New Guinea. They're making progress slowly, but it's still progress. Maybe the American announcement that they shot down Yamamoto's plane two weeks ago would cheer him up. Admiral Yamamoto was the one who was behind the Pearl Harbor attack."

Eva tasted the fish and smiled. "Iris was right, Bill. You're a magician. You'll have us actually enjoying Japanese food at this rate." She took another bite. "Do you think that was an accurate report and not just a bit of propaganda on the part of the Americans? About Yamamoto, I mean. The Japanese haven't breathed a word of it."

Bill nodded. "You bet it's true. Do you think they'd admit to such a loss? Wait a while. They'll come up with something saying he died happily in his sleep." He helped himself to another bowl of rice and dipped his *hashi* into a small side dish, pulling out a small pickled plum. "Actually, I think the Yamamoto news might intrigue him. It's the biggest thing we know of recently, and certainly it's not available to the Japanese. Tell him about it, Iris. And I'll try to arrange something tomorrow that might make him more receptive."

"What's that?"

"Wait and see. I don't want to promise something I'm not certain of."

As Yakumo had indicated, Iris was now working longer hours, starting before noon and often not leaving the studio until after seven o'clock. Besides working on her own program, she had to correct the English for the scripts of several others. The day after Bill had come to their house, she was hurrying along the street more carelessly than usual because she was late for work again. When she bumped into a farmer, his back loaded with merchandise for the market, she stopped briefly and bowed her apology. Then she saw Bill's laughing eyes under the farmer's hat, his broad shoulders stooped under the weight of the pack on his back. Wisely, she kept her surprise to herself and hurried on her way without letting on that she knew him.

When she reached her office, she was greeted by Yakumo, who bluntly told her that she had today only to convince Jake to cooperate. Otherwise, the program would be abandoned and Jake would be considered a waste of time. Iris had no doubt that that meant his death.

Her heavy heart was not lightened when she opened the door to the second-floor office. Jake was not alone.

"I've brought another revision of the script," Iris said, handing it to him. "Will you please consider how it can be improved and how you could work with me on producing this program?"

Jake took the paper silently, looking furtively toward the other POW, who was working at the typewriter. He scanned the words, then began crossing out words and inserting new ones. Iris held her breath. Was he finally giving in?

Just then the other POW began a fit of coughing, and Iris took advantage of it to whisper quickly to Jake, "Admiral Yamamoto was shot down by the Allies two weeks ago over the Solomons."

Jake stared at her for a moment; then, in the silence following the man's coughing, he said simply, "I got an idea as we were brought into the office this morning. A farmer was on his way to the market. It was such a good sight, I thought maybe we could include some comments about familiar sights back home when we talk about the records."

Iris smiled. They would make a good team.

266

CHAPTER XIX

Once more Iris turned the soil, carefully planting with each seed her hopes for peace, her dreams of home. Once more she watched the tender green sproutings with wonder, finding in their fragile leaves a promise of order and constancy in a world of violent instability.

But this year was different. They could only grow Japanese vegetables, all other vegetables having been declared frivolous by the government and therefore forbidden. Where last year she saw the garden as an opportunity to eat more familiar and better food, this year she knew it was the single thing that stood between them and winter starvation. Last spring, at Kiyoko's suggestion, they had planted a small plot. Now, with Kiyoko slowly recuperating in their home, they spent March and April digging up the whole yard and planting it. Kiyoko supervised from her convalescent pillow, which they had brought out on the porch. Then they had left Kiyoko to sleep as they spent their afternoon planting another garden behind Kiyoko's house so she too would have vegetables this winter.

Kiyoko was strong enough to return to her own home in the first part of May. Once more on her own, she quickly returned to her old self. She remained thin and pale, as everyone was, but she was as well as could be expected and Iris and Eva were grateful.

Now, two weeks later, as Iris washed her hands under the pump after a long, back-breaking weeding session, she looked at their garden and saw how far they had come. In the straight rows of tender green leaves she could see the beginnings of what they would harvest that fall.

Her thoughts were interrupted by Kiyoko's robust voice. "Iris-san, is Eva home yet? I have something for you," she called as she shut the gate behind her. She was carrying a large parcel wrapped in pale green cloth.

Iris laughed, rejoicing in the return of such visits after Kiyoko's long illness. "Yes, Mama Kiyoko. She's in the house getting ready to prepare supper."

Just then Eva came out on the porch, holding a tray of teacups and a teapot. "Mama Kiyoko, what on earth are you doing carrying heavy packages like that?" she scolded as she set down the tray and helped Kiyoko up the step.

"Oh, not so heavy," Kiyoko said mysteriously. "Shall we drink our tea before you see what I have brought?"

"Oh, please, Mama-san," Eva pleaded, "you know I can't stand to wait."

Kiyoko giggled as she slowly unwrapped the cloth. "I wanted to bring these to you before it was too late. It is right that as my children you have them. Besides, they will help you to understand the part of yourselves which you are discovering, your Japanese part." She reached in and lifted out a small curved sword of about two and a half feet in length, sheathed in an intricate gold-and-black-enameled scabbard. A cord of crimson silk wound around the top of the scabbard like a graceful scarf around the neck of a beautiful woman. The curved handle was of ebony, its simplicity a stark contrast to the elaborate filigree of the scabbard.

"This was the sword of one of my grandmothers," Kiyoko explained, drawing out the gleaming, etched silver blade. "She was samurai. You see the small spot of orange on the blade? They told me it is the blood of a lord who presumed upon her affections. She was much admired for her courage, faithfulness, and honor."

"She killed him just for saying he loved her?" Eva asked in astonishment.

"No. He did not love her or wish to marry her. He forced her to . . . to pillow with him because he was such a powerful and arrogant lord and she was very beautiful, very noble, and most of all was married to a man he wanted to shame. Had she not been married and had he been more polite, things might have been different. As it was, he forced himself upon her, and when he was done he turned his back to leave and she cut off his head with this sword."

"Was it the grandmother with the sword who told you the

story?" Iris asked in awe as she ran her fingertips over the scabbard.

"Oh no." Kiyoko laughed. "The grandmother who used the sword lived many years ago. Long before I was born. I think it was around 1680 in your way of counting years."

"What happened to her?" Iris asked.

"She had no choice. She committed *seppuku*."

"She killed herself? Why?"

"She had been an instrument of hurt and caused her husband to lose face. It was all very brave and honorable."

Eva's eyes widened. "Do you think that's really his blood on the blade?"

"No, I think his blood rusted the blade. Only truly evil blood could rust such a fine blade. It is a story of courage and faithfulness, and the sword has been in my family for many years. Because it is a woman's sword and a woman's story, the women of the family are the ones who keep it. Now, you are to keep it and learn its wisdom. Even the most peaceful have occasion for use of a sword. Now," she said, turning back to the package, "this is for you as well." She pulled out a creamy silk scroll wound lightly around an ebony dowel. "This *kakejiku* is for you to hang in your *otoko*, your honor alcove."

She unwound the long scroll, separating the yellowed tissue from the silk, revealing beautiful hand-brushed letters soaring up the creamy column like the song of a bird. Even though Iris couldn't read the characters, she felt the beauty of the writing. There was the slightest hint of blush washed through the letters and down the blank side of the scroll, creating an impression of flower petals in the sunset.

"It's lovely," Iris whispered.

"The message is important too," Kiyoko explained. "The writing of our language is as much an art as the drawing of objects. Not only is there beauty in the shape of the characters, there is beauty in the thoughts they bring forth. Such a scroll in the *otoko* is a Japanese custom. You can sit and meditate while looking at the beauty. It says, 'That orchids might blossom in profusion . . . .' That is the beginning of a poem by a famous T'ang emperor from China."

She paused, then said, "I understand that in Chinese the word is not quite *orchids*, but it translates most nicely that way. This is the rest of the poem:

269

That orchids might blossom in profusion—such was my hope,
But the Autumn winds destroyed them all.
That imperial deeds might shine before the world—such was my
wish,
But scheming ministers wrought havoc in the land.

"It is most appropriate for us now." She sighed. Then, more brusquely, she continued, "I thought that you should have this scroll, because it too will help you understand your Japanese face, your Japanese soul. The influence of China is strong in Japan, but we have adapted their customs and art to fit our needs. It seems that much of what happens in Japan is like the poem—a desire for beauty even when crushed under the heel of evil. My scholarly great-great-great-uncle chose to write only the beautiful wish. The rest is implied."

"How sad," Eva murmured.

"Yes," Kiyoko agreed. "But a lovely thought is sufficient and the sad ending is of no importance. Very Japanese. Like today."

Kiyoko fondly gazed at the scroll, then smiled as she handed it to Iris. "When we are finished with our tea, we will place these in your home. You must understand both the sword and the scroll if you are to understand what you are."

Iris and Eva bowed deeply as they took the gifts. "*Arigato gozaimasu, Mama-san*. They will be in a place of great honor," Iris said.

Deeply touched, they found the proper place on the wall for the sword and carefully arranged the scroll in the *otoko* with a graceful twig of cherry blossoms in a leaf-brown vase. Kiyoko looked on approvingly, clucking her directions and explanations from her pillow in the middle of the *tatami* floor.

Before she went home, Kiyoko told them that she was keeping the family house ready for the return of her husband, should he be released from prison. With that, Iris and Eva were relieved of their concern that Kiyoko might insist that they come to live with her. They had talked a great deal about it. They didn't want to hurt her feelings, but they felt that not only would they be a burden and a possible danger to her, but that their plans and clandestine meetings with Bill would be severely curtailed. That was a part of their lives they had carefully kept hidden from Kiyoko, because they knew she would not only worry but possibly become involved and therefore endangered.

Kiyoko had been right. More and more Iris found herself thinking on the meaning of the two objects, the sword and the scroll. So often she condemned the war, the use of the sword. Yet, now she knew that she was hoping for that very thing—hoping that the Americans would use every sword at their disposal. It seemed that the flowers of peace could bloom again only through the effective use of the sword. And the words she used daily, like the words on a scroll, were written to move the minds of men, sword-wielding men. It was all so intertwined. Perhaps she had a Japanese soul after all.

"Here, take a look at this," Jake said as Iris came in. He was waiting for her at the desk they had set up for her in a corner of the large office. She'd just leaned her umbrella against the wall. She paused to wipe the perspiration from her upper lip before she took the script from Jake. The soft, warm rains of June had arrived.

She took his script and read it, her eyes widening. "What're you doing?" she whispered. "You've written here that the Japanese shot down twice as many planes over New Guinea as even the Japanese are claiming they shot down. We can't say that."

"Why not? They want us to say things that will deflate the morale of our troops. Now, what do you think about this record to follow it?" he asked, putting on a scratchy copy of a Tommy Dorsey arrangement. Then, using the music to cover his conversation, he quickly added, "That's more planes than I think we have in the whole Pacific theater. The guys will hear that and laugh their heads off. I'm just out-lying the liars. What do you think?"

Iris suppressed the laughter that bubbled up inside her. "For a minute there, I thought you'd lost your senses. But you're right. They'll see right through it. But what if we're called on changing the numbers?"

"Simple. We're just trying to help out," he said with wide-eyed innocence. "If they don't approve of our enthusiastic efforts, we'll promise to try to control ourselves in the future."

"I doubt that they'll listen. Seems the program is considered adequate, though not stupendously successful."

"That's another thing I wanted to talk to you about," Jake said, taking the needle off the record. "So you think it's too scratchy, eh?" he said loudly, for effect. "I'll see what else I can come up with. In the meantime, I think we ought to jazz up the program a little, give them something more to listen to. Like a female announcer that I can banter around with, someone for a little repartee."

"I think you're crazy, Jake," Iris said, looking around to see if anyone was paying attention to their conversation. "We've only had you on the air for a month. Let's stick with what we have until we get it right." She picked a record out of the box beside her desk. "Let's use this one instead of the scratchy Tommy Dorsey," she said, putting it on the turntable. As the Ink Spots began crooning, she whispered, "You could foul everything up by bringing someone else in."

Jake laughed. "Not if that someone else is you."

"That's even more ridiculous. I don't have the faintest idea about radio announcing."

"You're right. I'd have to train you from scratch. But what we need is a flippant female voice. Someone who could read all these disaster reports in such a way as to make our boys understand that it's all a joke. With some intensive training, I think you could do it. Your voice is light and you have a natural inflection that can come off real smart-ass, if you'll excuse the expression."

"I doubt they would approve the change."

"Well, leave that to me. When the time seems ripe, I'll put it to them. But you've got to promise me you'll cooperate."

"Haven't I always?"

"Good." He smiled. "Now go over the rest of the script. We have just an hour before air time."

Iris went right to work. She was always able to find words that Jake had put in that would sound too good to an American ear. With a deft mark of the pencil, she'd substitute words that had a delicate Japanese sound, words that were sure to please the NHK listeners while amusing the American troops. Today she was more daring than ever. The gem she chose to alter was the sentence, "Victorious Japanese troops, after winning the slugging match for New Guinea airfields, are now resting, eating plentiful meals, and enjoying the commendations of their comrades." She changed it to read, "Victorious Japanese troops, after winning the slogging match for New Guinea airfields, are now resting, eating meals of rice, and annoying the recommendations of their comrades."

Jake glanced through the script and smiled. "We haven't tried malapropisms before. I'm sorry I didn't think of it first. Come on down to the studio and listen in, why don't you?" It was his standard invitation and Iris always accepted.

In the glass recording booth, Jake began his introduction, read a brief news report, then played a record. While the music was playing, Iris slipped him her box lunch of rice, vegetables, and a hard-boiled egg. While the records played, he ate voraciously and she whispered to him the latest news Eva had heard monitoring the shortwave broadcasts from the States. It was a good time for them both. Iris was glad to forgo eating lunch in order to keep Jake from starving, and the news she brought him seemed to forge their relationship even more strongly. Their shared hope sustained their lives.

That night on the *densha* Iris began counting the days since she'd seen Bill. He had promised to tell her if he was going to be gone for more than two weeks. It had been ten days. She no longer pretended that the only reason she wanted to talk to him was because she needed advice on the radio show. Life had become more bearable since his arrival.

The rain pattered on her umbrella as she walked to the garden gate. She was tired after waiting in the long ration lines, and there had been both a fire-brigade practice and an air-raid drill last night. It seemed as if she hadn't slept for weeks.

As she took off her shoes in the *genkan*, Eva came out, saying, "You got a letter today, addressed in Japanese. Kiyoko's here and she'll translate it for you. Hurry in and see what it is."

Iris smiled at Eva's curiosity. Kiyoko translated the letter: Iris's grandmother asked her to come visit on the following Thursday at five o'clock. There was no explanation.

"In the meantime, we'd better save some eggs. I can't go empty-handed," Iris said.

So it was, with a packet of the first tender beans from their garden and six fresh eggs, that Iris set out the following Thursday for her grandmother's house.

She felt rather guilty. It had been several weeks since she'd even thought about her relatives, and at least two months since she'd seen them. It wasn't that she didn't care about them, it was just that there seemed to be no time. Her mind had been filled with the plans for the radio program, with Jake, with caring for Kiyoko and Eva, who were still not as strong as before, and with talking to Bill and, when he wasn't around, wondering where he was.

It was raining when she reached her grandmother's house. Aunt Toshiko responded quickly to the bell, as if she had been waiting by the door for her. She welcomed her into the home and led the way to the main room, chattering all the way. Grandmother was seated on her usual cushion in the center of the room. The outside walls were open, admitting a soft breeze and revealing the spacious view of the garden.

"*Konnichi wa, Oba-a-san,*" Iris said, bowing deeply. "*Gokigen ikaga desu ka?*"

"Well enough, my granddaughter," Grandmother answered warmly. "*Mah, hisashiburi desune.*" It's been a long time.

Iris bowed again at the gentle reprimand. "Because our time is spent finding food and serving the Emperor, we are not allowed the pleasures we would prefer. Would you accept the first harvest of some of that hard work?" Iris asked, offering Grandmother the packet of beans and carefully wrapped eggs. "Please take them with our respect."

Grandmother thanked her, and Aunt Teiso quickly took the package to the cooking room.

They sat quietly visiting, Aunt Toshiko and Grandmother asking about Iris's work, her garden, and her home, in a general and polite way. The children were called in from their weeding in the garden to greet her and Iris was amazed at their growth and pained by the hollow, joyless look in their eyes and their thin little bodies. When they left, the conversation once more turned to unimportant topics. There was no tea brought in.

After about fifteen minutes of idle chatter, the gate bell rang. Aunt Teiso quickly got up and left the room. When she returned, she was accompanied by an elderly woman whose hawklike eyes shone with intelligence. Grandmother greeted her cordially and introduced her to Iris as Murasaki Sadako.

At once, tea and rare sweet-bean cakes were brought out. Iris had no idea what occasion they were celebrating, but she politely took part in the seemingly innocent conversation.

It wasn't until Murasaki Sadako turned her bright eyes on

Iris and began asking some rather direct questions for a Japanese that Iris began to feel she was under scrutiny.

"Your grandmother says you grew up in America," she stated pleasantly. "But you returned to Japan for your education?"

"Not really," Iris said honestly; then, sensing that this wasn't quite the right response, she added, "But it was here that I learned to speak Japanese, so I guess you could say that my education continued in Japan."

She glanced at Aunt Toshiko in hopes of getting a clue to what was going on. Her aunt's face was a mask of politeness, but when she caught Iris's eye, she reached up and fidgeted with the pendant she wore, which held Uncle Anami's picture. Iris was baffled.

"You have had occasion to meet Sergeant Gosei Ito, the very important Kampetei officer, I understand," Murasaki Sadako said casually. "I know him and his family well. He treats his mother very well even though he is busy with his work."

Iris's heart stopped at the mention of Sergeant Ito, but she carefully averted her eyes and kept her expression neutral. "Yes, Sergeant Ito has talked to me on official business," she said carefully.

Then the idea came to her in a horrifying flash. Murasaki Sadako was a matchmaker. For some unknown, ridiculous reason, it was being proposed that Iris be married to Sergeant Ito. She took a long sip from her bowl of tea to allow herself time to gather her wits.

"Since Gosei Ito has no wife, his family is much concerned that a man of his position and rank obtain a wife worthy of him," Murasaki Sadako was saying.

She was right. Iris took a bite of her bean cake and chewed it slowly, stalling for time. The image of the fat-faced sergeant with his thick lips and flat nose almost made her gag. Still, she kept her face immobile. If she were to refuse the sergeant outright, she might bring real danger to her family or herself. But why would he want to marry her in the first place? If she could understand that, she might know how to reply. It was both terrifying and absurd.

Iris suddenly had an inspiration. She said casually, "I can imagine his family's concern. It is a great responsibility. I know my father, too, is very concerned that I should have a proper marriage. That is why he made me promise, out of respect to his judgment, that I would not marry without his permission while away from home." It was a blatant lie, but perhaps it would work.

There was a long silence. Aunt Toshiko exchanged glances with Aunt Teiso. Iris glanced at her grandmother; she was looking down at her hands, but from the tiny smile wrinkle around her eyes, Iris sensed that she might have just pulled off a coup.

Murasaki Sadako, a professional matchmaker, was obviously facing one of the most tangled problems of her long career. "But surely your father wouldn't want you to lose your youthful bloom waiting for his permission when his mother is here to act in his stead," she persisted.

"I cannot presume to guess my father's mind. I only respect his wisdom above all things. I would not shame him by presuming on his judgment," Iris said piously. "It is my fate to wait upon my father's wishes, despite any desires I may feel."

Then, warming to her role, she couldn't resist adding, "I can imagine the pains Sergeant Ito's family must be taking to find him an appropriate wife, one who would know all the proper Japanese customs from birth, and who could help him to raise even higher in rank and respect. Yes, they must be facing a very delicate job."

Murasaki Sadako fidgeted with her teacup, her bright eyes almost piercing Iris's mask. "Yes," she murmured, "they have a most delicate task before them." Then she asked hopefully, "Your Japanese parents, even though you weren't born in the land of the gods, must have taught you Japanese customs and language from birth."

Iris shook her head sadly. "*Iie*, it is unfortunate, but I not only did not learn the language until I arrived here two years ago, I also did not understand the proper Japanese way of doing things. I put my aunts and grandmother to great shame when I first arrived. They were most patient with such an unworthy pupil and the very best of teachers. I owe much to them for their understanding and help."

"Yes, as it should be," Murasaki Sadako murmured, as she gathered her crimson kimono around her more tightly. She turned her attention to Grandmother, asking seemingly innocuous questions but obviously trying to gather whether Grandmother confirmed all that Iris had said.

"Sergeant Ito and his family have known of my son's departure to the United States for many years. Sergeant Ito was most kind to visit Iris upon her arrival here and pay his respects," Grandmother said. Iris wished it was within Japanese custom to kiss her. Eventually, Murasaki sighed with disappointment, ate the last bean cake, and bade her formal farewell.

Aunt Toshiko saw her to the door and returned with another pot of tea.

"Was she really a marriage broker?" Iris asked.

"Yes," Aunt Toshiko said, "and we had much discussion as to how to handle her proposal. It was Aunt Teiso who suggested we let you make the decision."

Iris thought for a moment. "Did I answer in a way which will do you no harm?"

"You answered very wisely, my granddaughter," Grandmother said affectionately. "You have learned quickly since you arrived. I don't know why we didn't think of saying what you did when we were approached."

"It was because Sergeant Ito is so powerful," Aunt Teiso said softly.

"Yes, and he seems to have it in his mind that it is his duty to make you a Japanese citizen," Grandmother said.

"I think he believes he will have fulfilled all his obligations to our family if he accomplishes that one thing," Aunt Toshiko said bluntly. "He is a man weighed down by many obligations. His father before him recklessly became obliged to many for his education and his profession. Then Sergeant Ito took on more obligations when he became a powerful Kampetei, just adding to the accumulated *on*. Such a burden would make a man unreasonable at times. I think Iris's refusal to become a Japanese citizen has become a symbol to him of all the impossible repayments hanging over his head. He is not of the noble nature to take his life to end such obligations. He is the kind to force the rest of the world into his teapot."

Grandmother nodded sadly. "I'm afraid you're right. He cannot force marriage on her and thereby make her a citizen, and he has no other way to repay Grandfather's many kindnesses to his family. Perhaps he will turn his attentions to one of the other debts he faces."

"Sometimes the caged bird will fight the cage for so long it will not even notice the open door," Aunt Teiso commented.

"Do you mean he might harass me in other ways?" Iris asked directly.

Aunt Teiso looked startled by Iris's bluntness. "I would hope not," she murmured.

Iris bowed politely to her aunts and grandmother, thanking them for their guidance and assistance and promising to visit more often. Then she bowed once more and backed from the room.

Aunt Toshiko escorted her to the door. "I'm sorry you had to go through this ordeal, my niece," she whispered as Iris gathered up her umbrella and put on her shoes. "We felt we had no choice but to accept the startling offer from the marriage broker to meet with us. Under normal circumstances, it would have been just Grandmother and the marriage broker. However, we insisted that you were unique and should be present."

"Please convey my appreciation for the special waiver of custom on my behalf," Iris said, smiling. "I suspect that you had a lot to do with it."

Aunt Toshiko blushed. "I think Sergeant Ito is acting very strange. Perhaps he is losing face with his superiors concerning your citizenship. Perhaps he is just overburdened with *on*. Desperate men do strange things."

Iris paused at the door and looked at her aunt. Once again, she had lifted the mask and revealed a caring woman beneath. Iris didn't know if she were more grateful for that glimpse of love or for the warning she gave. "I am greatly indebted to you, favored aunt," she said finally, bowing deeply. "Please don't worry, because I'm sure there is nothing he can do to me."

"Yes," Aunt Toshiko said, returning her bow. "Murasaki Sadako is sure to report back to Gosei Ito's family that you are a most unsuitable wife for him because of your strange background. No one would ever force a daughter to disobey her father. Besides, your ignorance of Japanese customs is unsuitable for someone of his position."

Iris again wished that the Japanese customs did not forbid spontaneous hugs and demonstrations of affection. She wanted them to know how much she had come to love them all.

It was a strange country which would allow such evil aggression against the world and prevent any open expression between a grandmother and granddaughter. Just when she began to think she understood Japan and the Japanese, it revealed another face more strange than all the others before it.

CHAPTER XX

Cole leaned back as the C-47 gained altitude, enjoying relief from the summer heat in the cooling cabin. The general had been right: he had needed this leave. He'd been given sixty days and military transport home, and it had been some homecoming.

After one year and seven months of war, he'd returned home as Major Cole Tennyson, air force ace, and his hometown had a real wing-ding. It was great to ride at the head of the Fourth of July parade with his father. They'd put a banner around the Packard convertible saying ACES FOR VICTORY, WITH A TENNYSON FROM STEATOR WE'LL DO IT AGAIN. He'd thought his father was going to pop his buttons. He'd told his story to the local newspaper and the wire service had picked it up; people from all over Illinois were writing letters to his parents, telling them how wonderful their son was, even strangers.

Then there were his mother's apple pies, slabs of roast beef dripping with gravy, real eggs, and real mashed potatoes. Living on a farm, they were not too greatly affected by rationing. As a result, his uniform was tight where before it had hung loosely.

What he hadn't been prepared for were all the girls: he could have had them all, if he'd wanted. They were just crazy for anyone in uniform, and if they thought a man was a bona fide hero, he could just about write his own ticket. The guys back at the base were going to think he was out of his head for passing up the offers he'd received. But he knew Iris would have been proud of him.

That was where all the confusion had started. He'd heard so much hatred of the Japanese, so many violent, cruel racial slurs, that he was beginning to worry about what it would be like after the war. He couldn't imagine taking Iris back to Illinois. Hawaii seemed the only solution to that problem, or maybe somewhere on the West Coast.

Then there was that strange feeling he got when talking to people back home. They had no idea what war meant. They complained about food and gasoline rationing. They threatened strikes when they felt they weren't making enough money working at the defense factories; they actually felt they were suffering, while staying home making profit from the war.

As he listened to their complaints, he pictured the faces of the men who'd died fighting; he could smell the muck they'd died in; he could see the starvation in the eyes of the men he'd left behind on Corregidor. Then he would get so angry that he would have to get up and leave the room.

These people had no idea what hardship, sacrifice, war, or courage was, and Cole doubted they ever would.

Still, it hadn't been a bad time. He'd slept like a baby in his childhood room, only twice waking up with war-torn dreams. Most of the time, he sat perched on the kitchen stool, gorging himself on his mom's cooking, and visiting with people who dropped by.

He'd quietly told his family about Iris again. It had started when his mother tried to get him to go out with the daughter of her best friend. His insistence that he was still engaged almost led to an argument. His parents had thought "that" was all over with when the war began. They brought up all the questions Cole knew he was going to have to deal with after the war: How did he know she wasn't right now helping the enemy? After all, she was one of "them." How could she possibly have gone to Japan and stayed there even after the war had started? Orientals were, well, different. . . .

They didn't understand his love for Iris. That was what bothered him most. It was a wall he could never tear down. While the whole world was falling apart, everyone at home had stayed the same. But he hadn't. He knew that he could never go back. War had changed him irrevocably.

Now, he was taking the last week of his leave to help Iris in the only way he could think of. He was going to San Francisco and try to find her family. Perhaps he could make them feel better, letting them know that someone else loved her too. But he was doing it also for selfish reasons. He desperately wanted to talk to someone who was as worried about her as he was. He wanted to hear stories about her childhood, see pictures from her school days, immerse himself in her memory so that he might be sustained through the rest of the war.

Cole had heard of the relocation centers but had not thought much about them, thinking it a necessity in time of war to remove potential spies and enemy sympathizers from the vulnerable population centers. However, when he found a fat, greasy man behind the counter of Iris's father's grocery, he began to have second thoughts. No, he was told abruptly, this was no longer Hashimoto's Grocery. It was Gus's Continental Deli. The Jap had been taken away with the rest of his kind. Someplace called Owens Valley Reception Center, where they wouldn't be able to do any of their dirty yellow tricks.

Cole controlled his urge to snap Gus's fat neck. Instead, he went to a phone booth. After several calls, he found one person who knew. The Japanese camp Manzanar was outside Owens Valley. There was a bus leaving that afternoon; he could make connections to arrive the following morning.

His uniform was wrinkled and his disposition grim as he sat eight hours later in a bus stop café, drinking bitter coffee and counting fly specks on the wall. He was sitting next to a middle-aged man dressed in a brown suit and wearing dark-rimmed glasses.

"Do you have friends at Manzanar?" Cole asked, trying to make conversation.

The man pursed his lips and drew himself up stiffly. "It is my job to go there once a week and confirm that they are getting the same food rations as the rest of the country. Can't allow aliens to operate in the black market, can we?"

"I see," Cole said, although he didn't really. "If you're with the government on this business, could you explain why these people are in these camps? I thought the relocation centers were just for the spies and those who were Japanese sympathizers. Have all the people in these camps committed some kind of treason?"

"The fact that they had done nothing up to the time of their relocation is obvious proof that they were merely waiting for the time when our guard was down. You can be sure it's a good thing they're locked away."

"You actually believe that kind of crap?"

"Real patriots, real Americans, are concerned with the welfare of all the people in their country. Soft bleeding hearts would turn the other cheek and lose the war to the Japs for us."

Cole's temper flared. To keep from punching the man's face, he clenched his fists and walked to the bus.

A little gray-haired lady, who had overheard the exchange in the café, leaned across the aisle and said, "I agree with you, young man, but it won't help to get angry. There's too many of them to waste your time and energy on. We need you elsewhere. In fact," she said confidentially, as she inched closer to the edge of her seat, "some say that this is the safest thing we can do for the Japanese-Americans because of the real anger people feel after Pearl Harbor. There're some crazy people who might take it upon themselves to lynch anyone whose eyes are shaped wrong." She warmed to Cole like a lost nephew. "I'm going to visit Mrs. Tanaka. She was my neighbor for years. I miss her. Are you going to see a friend?"

Cole's anger faded under her pleasant chatter and he smiled. "Yes, I am."

"How nice. Where are you stationed?"

"New Guinea."

"Is it really as awful there as they say?" she asked.

Cole looked past her through the window to the rolling straw-colored hills of California. New Guinea and war were so far removed, so far away. Like another world. Another life.

He politely described the thick, steaming jungles and cloud-shrouded mountains, the ebony natives, and what the soldiers ate and how they lived. By the time he'd finished, the bus was slowing down.

As Cole descended the metal steps, a hot, dry wind blew dust around his legs, pushing the desert heat through his summer uniform.

The compound consisted of wooden barracks-type buildings perched on stone pile foundations and lined up institutional-style behind a barbed-wire fence. "It's a goddamn concentration camp," Cole muttered in fury. "They might as well be POWs." He checked in at the gatehouse and found out where the Hashimoto family was located.

Cole made his way through the maze of unpainted rectangular buildings. The sun beat down mercilessly. Children were playing baseball in the dirt behind one of the wooden buildings he passed. Another building caused his heart to turn with its carefully arranged rocks and raked dirt. The lovingly created dry garden, in its simple beauty, shamed its sterile surroundings. A group of old men sat listlessly on the front stoop, their hands idle, their talents lying fallow. Three young women were behind another barracks, washing clothes on washboards in soap-filled tubs, chatting over their mundane chores.

He found the building he was looking for. The door was open to the heated wind and white curtains blew out the windows. An old man sat, in his suspenders, his white shirtsleeves rolled up, drowsing in the throbbing afternoon heat. He was leaning back in a chair fashioned from boards and hand-sewn pillows. No one else was around as Cole knocked on the door frame. "Are you Mr. Hashimoto? Chosu Hashimoto?"

The old man started from his sleep. "Yes, yes. Come in. Who is it?"

"Sir," Cole said hesitantly, walking across the bare wood floor. "I'm Cole Tennyson. I'm a friend of Iris's. Did she ever tell you about me?"

"Cole Tennyson," he said carefully; he had the typical Japanese problem with the *l* in Cole's name. "Yes. I know of Iris's friend Cole. She writes and says Cole is one of her friends. Come in. Come in, please." He got up gingerly and welcomed Cole with outstretched hand, offering him a seat in a homemade chair next to the one he had been in. Behind a curtain at the back of the room, Cole could see an iron bedstead and handmade shelves holding clothes, books, and pitifully few personal items.

"Please, let me make tea. My daughter and son are at a meeting somewhere in camp. You must meet them. Iris would want that. Tell me, please," he continued as he bustled to the hot plate and put on a pot of water, "you hear from Iris? She tell us she likes you."

It was as Cole had suspected. Iris had not told her parents about their engagement. "No, sir, I'm sorry. I haven't heard from her since the war. I was hoping you might have had word."

"No letter. But," he added more brightly, "Red Cross come one day with message that she is well and wants to come home . . . but nothing since. I can do nothing to help," he added sadly. "Before Pearl Harbor we had letter asking for birth certificate. She said I am not to come to Japan and that she needed help to leave. She was right," he said with a sad shake of his head. "I sent papers, but then war and nothing from my daughter."

Cole wondered why she needed her birth certificate when she had her passport with her. "I had written to her several times telling her to leave Japan. I'm glad to hear she was really trying. That may mean she got some of my letters."

"Yes, yes, she tried. I should not have told her to go to Japan," he said forlornly.

"You had no way of knowing," Cole said gently, stifling the urge to agree. He hadn't the heart to accuse the old man of such misjudgment. "Tell me," he asked, "how are Mrs. Hashimoto and Iris's brother and sister?"

"My wife died."

Cole felt as if he'd been slapped as he looked at the old man's passive face. "Dead? When? I mean, I'm so sorry to hear . . ." he stammered.

"She died four months after we come to this place," he said simply. "Her heart could not take sadness to lose everything and so afraid for Iris. I say her heart break. It carried too heavy load. They say heart attack. I say heart break."

"You lost everything?"

"Yes. We told we must sell everything or get nothing. We put more than thirteen thousand dollars in the store. The Italian man, Gus, pay me only one thousand. He says fair price for Jap place. I must take what offered. Then, our other possessions, we give most away. People pay," he waved his fingers in an empty gesture, "for lovely lacquered chest, beautiful silk, all gone. All old family things."

Cole's eyes burned with tears of anger. "I'm sorry," he

murmured. "It's not right. Have you told Iris about her mother?"

"No. I not try. She has sorrow enough. When she's home is soon enough to know. It not help her mother now. And my letters to Red Cross have no answer. I think she not get them." He poured Cole a cup of tea. "I'm sorry I have nothing to offer with tea except cracker. We not have many visitors."

"Thank you," Cole said self-consciously, "it's quite enough. You know," he went on, "Iris is very important to me. I care for her very much. I must admit to you that I tried to stop her from going to Japan. I wanted to—"

"Yes, yes, I know Iris happy in Hawaii. She talk about Cole in letters. My fault. I had fear she would have sad life married to a man who was not like her. Now, she may never marry. She may . . ." He looked quickly out the window to conceal his tears. "The land is harsh and dry here," he said softly. "Few things can grow."

"Mr. Hashimoto, I came here to let you know that I'm doing everything I can to get to her as fast as I can. When the first American goes into Tokyo, I promise you, if I'm alive, I'll be there. And I won't be shooting, I'll be running to find Iris. And when I find her, sir, I'm going to marry her. I'm going to take care of her. That's why I came to see you. I was hoping you'd understand, and maybe feel a little bit better about it."

Mr. Hashimoto turned slowly to look at him, his head slightly tilted, as if he were trying to absorb the full impact of Cole's words. Cole waited. He felt he'd bared his inner soul.

Finally, Mr. Hashimoto spoke. "A father finds comfort in knowing a good man cares for daughter, helps her when her father cannot. I tell you honest, like you tell me honest. Before I see you today, I hope Iris find man and stay in Japan, raise Japanese babies, even though I thinking Japan stinking place with bad leaders. Now you here, I not want daughter in stinking place." He bowed his head toward Cole. "Good people come from all kinds people. You show me you strong. You good. In your eyes I find hope for my daughter. I think you find her. Then you tell her Papa-san says marry with heart, American style, marry good strong man like you."

He paused a moment, then smiled wistfully. "Iris's mother was very, very good woman. Iris make you very good wife."

Cole's composure was shattered by the old man's speech. His simple statement of faith moved him deeply. He nodded in response, then looked down at his feet, not trusting his voice.

At the sound of feet on the wooden stoop, Cole looked up and his breath caught in his throat. With the white-hot afternoon sunlight behind her, he could have sworn it was Iris, standing in the doorway, the dry desert wind blowing her pink cotton dress around her knees. A slender teen-age boy came in with her. They stopped in the middle of their conversation when they saw Cole.

"Hello," the girl said, stepping into the room. Once she was closer, once the sunlight wasn't behind her, Cole could see it wasn't Iris. Her face was more square, where Iris's was fine-boned. Where Iris was slender and pliant as a willow, this younger woman had the stolid grace of a young elm, squared of shoulder with strong legs and firm steps. Still, the heart-turning moment when he thought it might be Iris had left him speechless.

"I said hello," she repeated. "I'm Ruby Hashimoto. Are you here on business with my father?"

"Oh, no," Cole said, getting up politely. "I'm sorry. I came here on leave to meet you and your family. I'm Cole Tennyson. Iris—"

"Yes, she wrote me about you," Ruby interrupted anxiously. "Do you have any word from Iris? Do you know anything?"

"No, I'm sorry. You've heard more than I have in the message from the Red Cross."

Her voice was lower than Iris's, but her quick, easy way of talking, was so much the same as Iris's that Cole just wanted her to keep on talking to him. She turned as the young man moved toward the window. "Oh, I almost forgot my manners. This is our younger brother, Joe. Joe, you remember how Iris wrote us about Cole?" she said with a warning look.

Joe was about fourteen, slender, with dark wind-tousled hair and a serious look in his eyes. He grinned shyly, a smile that echoed Iris's dimpled charm, and held out his hand. "I'm pleased to meet you, Cole."

Cole took his hand and smiled. "When Iris told me about her baby brother, I didn't expect to meet a young man."

Joe laughed easily, warming to Cole. "Ruby and I were hoping we'd have a chance to meet you before . . ." He stopped, caught by Ruby's sharp look. "Ah . . . ah, before Iris left Hawaii," he ended lamely.

Cole laughed. "That's all right, Joe. I was just talking to your father. I told him how I felt about Iris and that as soon as I got to Tokyo, I was going to find her and marry her."

Ruby shot her father a shocked look, braced for the worst. He smiled benignly and inclined his head. "I learn today," he said quietly, "that to find gold nugget on dusty road, one must not close eyes."

Ruby and Joe beamed. "Hey, Dad, that's just great," Joe said enthusiastically.

"You know about Iris and Cole?" Mr. Hashimoto asked.

The brother and sister exchanged uneasy glances. "Iris wrote and told us she was in love with Cole, Papa-san," Ruby admitted. "She was afraid . . . that you might not approve of him. We thought . . ."

He raised his hand. "She's a good sister," he said simply. "It's good she kept her heart open to part of her family."

Joe and Ruby gave a collective sigh of relief and Cole found himself joining them. He'd not only received his future father-in-law's blessing, he found he'd had two allies all along in Ruby and Joe. Not a bad start for a marriage.

Cole spent the remainder of the afternoon poring over old family albums, black-and-white pictures capturing the essence of Iris and her family. The shared laughter and stories made Iris once more a living part of himself. He felt accepted, as if he were already a part of this family.

When Cole had to leave, Iris's father was reluctant for him to go. He kept finding excuses, new things to tell Cole just to keep him a few seconds longer. He rummaged around through the back of one family album, finally saying, "Here, there is something for you." He pulled out a snapshot, more recent than the others, and looked at it lovingly before handing it to Cole. "It is right that you take this with you. Then Iris know you saw us. This is the last picture of her. She sent film from Japan right after she got there. My brother took this picture of her with my mother, her grandmother. See, she looks sad, but smiles anyway. You take it. When you marry, you come back."

Cole spent his journey on the bus to San Francisco and on the military planes to New Guinea staring at the picture. Iris's thin face smiled wanly, her eyes frightened and weary.

Had she lost weight because of unhappiness or because of a hard life and poor food? It was a strange new Iris that looked at him from this picture, yet it was the same young woman he loved so deeply. What was happening to her now in Japan? His heart was torn. In order to rescue her, he must plan to bomb and destroy the very place in which she was trapped.

The heat of New Guinea hit him with all the force of a Joe Louis right hook. From the moment he stepped from the plane, the heavy, moist air settled on his limbs, slowing his movements and soaking him with perspiration. It took a full week of the regular schedule before he even began to adjust.

The Allies had captured Buna in January and had set up the airfield at Dobodura before Cole had gone on leave. It had been the first real step on the road to Tokyo. Now, large Japanese bases in Rabaul, Wewak, and other points the Japanese had thought impervious to American air attack would be within range of American bombers and, more important, within range of the fighter planes that provided cover for the bombers.

Sparky greeted Cole, brimming with news and questions. They spent his first night back drinking warm beer in Cole's old tent.

"Come on, Sparky," Cole was saying, "you're not trying to tell me my P-40 was shot down?"

"Yep, the old *Iris* took a bath in the drink when Chervik was flying it. He was picked up later on, but the plane just sank out of sight," Sparky said, referring to the plane by the name Cole had painted on its fuselage. "Maybe it's for the best, though," he added. "They're bringing in the P-38 and it's a real honey. You'll probably find yourself in one of those."

Cole nodded. "That must be why the colonel told me to take up a P-38 in the morning and stay in it until I liked it as well as the P-40." He opened another bottle of beer. "Tell me what you've been up to. Last I remember, you were shipping out to work at Dobodura. What are you doing back down here?"

Sparky grinned and held up his arm, showing off a brand new watch. "The guy who owns the Bulova Company gave General Kenney a hundred watches to give to the hundred best crew chiefs."

"Congratulations," Cole said. "It's a pretty good idea. The pilots get all the medals, but they wouldn't get anything if they didn't have a good ground crew keeping them up there. If you can't show off a medal to the girls, at least you can show them your watch."

"Yeah." Sparky shrugged. "They weren't too impressed with the medal I got for that quick salvage work I did when the Japs hit Pearl."

Cole laughed. "You SOB, you never wore it. You told me yourself."

"Yeah, well, it seemed like bragging. When I get back home I'll pin it on so the folks can see it. But this watch is something. It's worth a pretty penny, I'll bet."

"Well, they couldn't have given it to someone more deserving."

Sparky grinned mischievously. "That wasn't all. They tried to promote me to lieutenant. I wouldn't have it. Told 'em they couldn't promote me in Hawaii when I was dating Eva, so I wouldn't take it now that she's gone. That set 'em to talking. Then I told 'em that some fool coming along behind them might get the wise idea that because I have rank I should be flying, and they'd lose the best damn mechanic and parts-procurement officer they have." He leaned back, drained his beer, and added, "They laughed and said they agreed. Got off my back for a while."

Cole leaned back on his pillow, laughing. Sparky never changed.

The next morning, Cole circled his new plane like a cat warily reconnoitering a new neighborhood. It had twin in-line engines mounted in bullet-shaped nacelles that extended rocketlike to the twin stabilizers on the broad tail. The cockpit was a third nacelle mounted between the engines. The end result was a plane that looked like a dragonfly with a tail extending back from each side of its head. The wing span was fifty-seven feet—twenty feet wider than his old P-40. However, it wasn't much longer. The propellers rotated in opposite directions, eliminating the need to compensate for torque, which had caused Jake's accident in Hawaii. Overall, it seemed aerodynamically sound. With those twin tail booms, it would be the easiest plane to identify in the whole Pacific theater. He climbed up and signaled his crew chief he was ready to go.

Within three hours he was back on the ground, proclaiming the virtues of "his" P-38. It was maneuverable, although it should never be expected to take on the Zero in an actual dogfight. It could reach altitudes of over thirty thousand feet and speeds of more than four hundred miles per hour. Like the P-40, it could probably outdo any Zero in a dive because of its heavy armor. The twin engines were a priceless safety measure out here where much of their flight time was over the ocean. It could make it back with one engine shot out, whereas the P-40 was done for if hit in the engine coolant or some other vital place. He christened his plane *King Cole*.

He reported his enthusiasm to the colonel. The colonel promptly told him to chalk up a few more hours in the P-38 and then prepare to take a squad up north to Marilinan, where he would take over the command of fighters stationed there. Cole spent almost every waking hour of the next week testing the plane in every maneuver and situation he could devise. By Sunday, he was ready to take it anywhere.

"Hey!" Sparky called as Cole walked toward his plane. "Are you going out again today? It's Sunday, remember?"

"I thought I'd put in a couple of hours. We're going out tomorrow morning. I want to be ready."

"Well, don't take too long. Word's out that they're using women to ferry planes out here to us now. The first batch is going to land here this afternoon. Imagine—real American women!"

"If they're anything like the ones I saw back home, they'll all have hot pants. Is that what you're looking for?"

Shrugging, Sparky kicked the dust with his toe. "I'd sure like some lovin', but I doubt it would help me forget Eva. What about you?"

"Same. Why do you think I'm so anxious to get to Tokyo?"

"Yeah," Sparky said, putting his arm on Cole's shoulder as they walked out to his plane. "That's why I got myself shipped up with you to Marilinan. I'll be in the C-47 you're covering."

"Hey, that's great," Cole said, slipping on his leather flight jacket and pulling on his five-hundred-hour cap, the regular officer's billed cap that had the stiff lining removed in order to fit under his headphones in the plane. It was one of the status symbols of the air force pilots. Since Cole had managed to bring his out of the Philippines, it was looked on with awe by the other pilots; he was one of the few that actually had in excess of five hundred hours' combat flight. "I'll be back around 0300. Have a beer cooling for me," Cole said as he climbed onto the wing.

When Cole landed, Sparky rushed up to him as he walked off the landing strip. "Hey, hurry it up! I've got a surprise you won't believe. Meet me at the rec room!"

Cole reported in, then went to the long, canvas-topped recreation hall. The place was buzzing with excitement. He'd noticed the C-47s sitting at the edge of the field and assumed that the women pilots were the reason for the mob scene.

He stood in the doorway, peering through the smoky interior, then spotted Sparky in the center of the room. He maneuvered his way through the crowd, and as he did he saw the women air-transport pilots in trim uniforms at the center.

One tall blonde turned as Cole approached, and he stopped in surprise. She was wearing her thick blond hair neatly pulled up and tucked under her cap in front, but the pageboy hanging down behind and the familiar, inviting tilt of the head, were still the same. Even the severe military cut of the uniform couldn't hide Marta's sensuality. As she saw him, she broke away from the others and ran to him with open arms and a genuinely delighted smile. "Cole!" she cried. "Thank God you're all right. It's so good to see you!" She threw her arms around his neck and planted a kiss on his surprised mouth.

Whistles and whoops rose from the crowd before she let go and stepped back to look at him. Cole's face felt hot; he knew he was blushing, for the first time since seventh grade. "Hey, Tennyson," one of his squadron called, "how'd you manage to get your fiancée out here?"

"She's not . . ."

"Don't take her away," another called. "It's been too long since we've seen a beautiful woman."

"Come on, Tennyson, sit down and just let us look at her. You can have all the kisses."

They were jostled and kidded as they made their way to the table in the center of the room. There was little conversation that could take place, with all the men clamoring to talk to the women seated at the table. Apparently they had arrived just half an hour before. The excitement began to subside in another half hour, when the women had spread around the room, several men to each table graced with a smiling female.

That allowed Cole a chance to try to put their conversation on the correct footing. Mercifully, Sparky stuck around to help.

"Well, you finally got your pilot's license," Cole observed.

"You bet," she said, beaming. "Actually, I was working in the Women's Auxiliary Ferrying Squadron as soon as they started it up in forty-two. I was working in the European theater for a while. Now they've sent me out here. They're reorganizing us into a bona fide women's branch of the service this month. We'll be called the Women's Airforces Service Pilots."

"WASPs." Cole chuckled. "That fits. Tell me, how was it in Europe?"

Marta shook her head. "Seeing what's going on over there, even at a distance, gave me some second thoughts about the things I believed before the war. Hitler's a real monster. There's no superman—at least not on a race basis. Now, on an individual basis . . ." she added, in her familiar seductive voice.

"Speaking of that," Cole said, refilling his glass, "have you heard anything of Jake?"

A shadow of sadness passed over Marta's face. "No, I haven't heard a thing. I thought you might know."

"We think he's being held prisoner in the Philippines. He was working with the guerrillas for a while. I received some radios from him. Then everything was quiet. We can only hope he wasn't killed." He looked glumly at the foam clinging to the side of his glass. "Then again, from what we've seen and heard, it might be worse if he wasn't killed."

Marta's face was pale, her blue eyes stricken. "Jake was a good friend, and a good man. I can only hope the best for him." She looked down and twisted her paper napkin into a spiraling cone. "This whole damn war is full of nothing but worries and fears about people you care about. I didn't even know that you'd made it out of the Philippines until I landed here and saw Sparky."

"Yeah," Cole said with embarrassment. "Well, it's hard for us all." Then he added confidentially, "Iris is caught in Tokyo, you know. She couldn't get out. You think we have it hard in the States, but you can imagine what it's like in Tokyo."

Marta looked at him strangely. "Haven't you been listening to Radio Tokyo lately?"

"Nah, we don't listen to that drivel," Sparky cut in. "All

they do is make us laugh at their silly attempts to depress us."

"Well, you should. What time is it?"

"Five-twenty. Why?" Cole asked.

"Turn on the radio!" she called to the bartender. "Tune in Radio Tokyo."

He shrugged and turned on the radio. There was static and interference, then the room was filled with the mellow, distant strains of Tommy Dorsey's band playing "I'll Never Smile Again," with what sounded like a vocal by the popular Frankie Sinatra. The bartender looked at Marta apologetically. "That's where it usually is, but it sounds like American music. Want me to keep looking for it?"

"No, that's it. They have a new program," Marta said confidently. Then, turning to Cole, she said, "I want to know if you think the same thing I do when you hear it."

Some of the men started dancing with the WASPs. The excited chatter died down and the talk was more subdued as the men tried to soak up the moment, a momentary haven from the war.

When the band finished, a woman's voice came on the air, speaking in a fresh American tone. "That was Tommy Dorsey playing for you folks," she said, "and you're listening to Radio Tokyo. Speaking as one orphan to another, I can tell you that that song brings back some nice memories for me." Her voice was light and lilting, a Lorelei calling to the men from the enemy's camp with the most enticing and deadly weapon of all, a female play on the universal homesickness of soldiers away from home. Before, the Japanese had broadcast propaganda programs that were the laughingstock of the American forces. But now they were playing familiar music, with this lovely, cheerful, American-sounding woman to enchant them between records. . . . Now they had an effective propaganda weapon, Cole thought with a chill.

He looked up. Marta was watching him intently. "What do you think?" she asked with a curious smile.

"It's going to be hard keeping the men from wanting to hear what she has to say," Cole admitted.

"Listen more carefully."

Cole looked sharply at her unwavering gaze, then turned his attention back to the voice of the woman announcer.

"I'm sorry, fellas," she said, smiling over the airwaves,

"that old clock on the wall says I'm going to have to go. But I'll tell you what, I'll sign off with an old favorite of mine which I know must be one of yours too. Songs have special meanings for us all and this one means a lot to me. So your Flower of the Pacific will say good-bye by playing for you 'Pennies From Heaven.'" She continued, cheerfully explaining the artists on the record label, but Cole didn't hear another word. His mind was frozen. He felt as if his world had suddenly stopped. Sparky's face was pale as he watched Cole. Marta was glowing.

"You think so too," she said. "I can tell by your face."

Cole nodded stiffly. Then, looking at Sparky's pained expression, he whispered hoarsely, "It's Iris."

Just then, as the song ended, a man's voice came on the air. "Well, our Flower of the Pacific has folded for this week, folks, but be sure to tune in next Sunday when we bring you . . ."

Marta's smile faded, first to puzzlement and then to shock as she listened to the pure baritone voice rolling through the air. Cole was still reeling from hearing Iris's voice, but as he saw Marta's startled look he listened more carefully. Sparky was looking up, his hands stopped in the motion of rubbing his temples. He knew, too.

"No," Marta whispered.

"It can't be . . ." Sparky cried.

Cole's head was turned toward the radio, his fist tightly wrapped around his beer glass. "Not Jake too . . ." he howled. The glass shattered in his hand and he sat looking numbly at the crimson thread of blood running down his fingers.

"Cole!" Marta exclaimed, as she took out a handkerchief and quickly wrapped his hand. "Bartender," she called. "Bring a rag and another round. There's been a little accident here."

"No," Cole said suddenly. "I don't want any more beer. Come on, Sparks," he said, getting up. "I have a bottle of good stuff back in my tent."

"That does sound better," Marta said, following them. It wasn't Cole's intention that Marta should hang around. He needed time to think and to talk to Sparky while emptying that bottle of Scotch. But his mind was too dazed to tell her to go back to the club.

Back at the tent, Sparky found some bandages and Marta

bathed and doctored Cole's hand, while Cole downed a glass of straight Scotch. Sparky joined in disconsolately.

Finally, Marta broke the silence. "We know why Iris is in Tokyo, but Jake? Why did he turn traitor?"

"We don't know that he did. Don't judge others," Cole said sharply. "We all have enough to do trying to take care of ourselves."

"If we weren't being judgmental about this, we wouldn't be so depressed," she snapped back.

"I'm sort of finding it a good omen that Jake's still alive," Sparky put in.

Cole looked at Sparky's hopeful face and shook his head. "I know what you're thinking. If Iris is alive, then maybe Eva is too. But don't get your hopes up. No telling whose side she's on either."

Sparky looked at Cole and sighed. "I don't know, Cole," he said, getting up. "I don't have the time to argue with you. I just feel that we don't know the whole story. I've got to get back out on the line. There's a crew waiting on me to get those planes ready for tomorrow. We'll have to talk this out later. See you, Marta."

Cole poured himself another tumbler of Scotch. Marta leaned back against the cot. "It sure is a furnace down here. I thought when the sun started going down it'd cool off, but I'm still roasting. Besides that," she added, when Cole didn't answer, "I'm starving."

Cole remained silent, lost in his thoughts and barely aware of Marta.

"What say I go to the mess hall and get us something from the cook? Do you know of a place where we can go and have a picnic on the beach? Well, never mind," she said to Cole's continued silence, "I'll go see what I can find. Do you mind if I check out a jeep in your name?"

Cole grunted noncommittally and took a deep swig from his glass. Then he poured another glass and leaned back in his bunk. He couldn't sort it out. His first shock was slowly fading. The joyful echo of Iris's voice contradicted the horror of hearing her on the enemy's propaganda program.

Comments from his mother and father kept running through his head. *How do you know that she isn't right now giving aid to the enemy?* How could they have known? What would they say if they knew now? But how could she be a traitor?

Why? *Orientals are, well, they're different.* Was it true? Was it some quirk of the Oriental mind that made Iris so glibly transfer her allegiance? After all, she'd inexplicably deserted him, leaving him, her fiancé, on some wild goose chase for her family. Maybe there was more pulling her than even he could fathom. Maybe she had found that she was sympathetic to the Japanese because they were really her people. The hurt burned inside him, leaving a bitter taste in his mouth.

There was no way around it. Iris had turned her back on America; more important, she'd turned her back on him. He threw the half-filled tumbler against the side of the tent, splintering the glass on the wooden side.

"Hey," Marta said as she came in. "You have another accident or just a bit of temper?" She was carrying a pack and had taken off her uniform jacket and tie. The blouse was opened at the neck, lightly covering her rounded breasts while still hinting at their fullness.

Cole looked up, startled by his own outburst, the pain still raging inside him. "Oh. I guess I lost my temper. Sorry, I didn't know you were around."

"Hey, that's all right. I understand." She sat down beside him. "Here, look in this pack. I got Cookie to give me some sandwiches and some bananas. He said they grow right around here someplace. He also told me where we could find a great beach for a moonlight picnic. I got a jeep waiting right outside the door. Come on, let's go," she urged softly, whispering in his ear.

Cole turned and looked at her. He could feel her warmth, see her softness. It'd been so long since he'd touched a woman. "Sure, why not?" he said with a shrug. "But I get to take the bottle."

"I've got it," Marta said, putting it in the pack. "Want me to drive?"

"You think I'm too drunk?" Cole said evenly.

"Not at all," she said, leaning against his arm. "It's just that I was the one who got the directions to the beach. You can drive if you want to."

Cole was amazed at how clear his mind still was. The alcohol hadn't numbed his hurt and anger. Still, he didn't want to drive. He just wanted oblivion. He reached into the pack, brushing against Marta's breast as he did. "No, I don't want to drive," he said, taking out the bottle. "I've got some serious drinking to do on the way."

They were soon on a rough road going northwest. Cole noted the Southern Cross in the sky as he tipped his head to drink from the bottle. He still wasn't drunk enough to lose his bearings. He took another deep pull of Scotch. Marta was handling the jeep like a pro. He watched her as she concentrated on the road framed in their headlights. Then he leaned his head back and watched the stars above. He wasn't going to think about a thing tonight.

"Wow!" Marta exclaimed as she rounded the bend. "This is some deserted beach. I don't think anyone could find us if they spent their whole life on it. Come on, let's get out."

Cole raised his head, startled out of a drowsy contemplation of the sky. "Not so bad," he said laconically as he slid from the seat and walked to the sandy shore.

They sat on a sheet Marta had pulled from his bunk as they'd left the tent. Marta spread out the feast and voraciously dug in, exclaiming that she'd never tasted such good Spam sandwiches. All meat was rationed back home and was hard to come by even in the PX. Cole ate halfheartedly, commenting that as soon as this war was over, he'd never eat another bite of Spam or chipped beef for the rest of his life.

The oblivion he'd sought so desperately still eluded him. He watched the white scalloped pattern of the waves on the sand, feeling the heavy warmth of the evening settle over him. "I'm going to take a swim," he said suddenly. Before Marta could respond, he stripped to his shorts and headed for the water. The lukewarm waves washed over his legs and he threw himself into the lap of the ocean.

"Cole, wait!" Marta called from the beach. He stopped and looked back.

She was standing on the shore, kicking off her shoes and unbuttoning her blouse. Cole stood shoulder deep in the ocean, the gentle waves rocking him from behind. He watched, fascinated, as she shrugged out of her blouse and dropped her slacks. Her bra and panties were white in the moonlight as she reached up and took the pins from her hair, shaking her head to let her blond hair tumble over her white shoulders. Then she reached back and took off her bra, releasing her full breasts with their dark nipples to shine in the bright moonlight. Then she stepped out of her panties and walked to the water, naked. Cole felt a tightening in his loins and began walking slowly toward her, never taking his eyes from her.

As she waded into the water closer to him, her breasts moved invitingly as her long legs pushed against the water. Then she swam to him with long, bold strokes. His head was spinning as she came up splashing and laughing, her hair streaming behind her. Without a word, she reached up and put her arms around his neck and pressed her lips tightly against his, rubbing the length of her body against him. Before he knew it, he was holding her and she was wrapping her legs around him, tugging impatiently at his shorts.

His head was pounding, filled with turmoil and desire. Somehow he was naked on the wet sand, with the waves lapping against his legs as he rolled on top of her and savagely crushed her mouth with his. She gasped as he violently thrust himself into her, then raised her hips eagerly to meet his. He possessed her with a pounding, angry heat, pushing away all his hurt in one pulsing, hot release. Then he was suddenly aware of her beneath him as she shuddered and wrapped her legs around him, an anguished moan escaping from her parted lips.

Suddenly nauseated, he withdrew and dove into the water, swimming furiously through the cooling waves, washing everything from his mind. Finally, exhausted, he turned back to shore. Marta was lying on the blanket as he staggered, across the sand, oblivious of his nakedness, careless of where he was. He dropped face down on the coarse sheet and rested his head on his folded arms, panting from the exertion.

Marta's cool soft breast caressed his shoulder as she leaned over him. "It's all different now," she whispered. "We're finally together. I can't imagine anything coming between us now."

"Can't imagine . . ." Cole murmured; he was lost in a rolling black fog of sleep.

CHAPTER XXI

"Jake," Iris whispered while the record was playing, "Bill has some information he thinks we should try to get out. There's a lot of planes all bunched up like sitting ducks at a place called Wewak in New Guinea."

Jake glanced at the record to see how much playing time was left, then turned to Iris. "I don't know that we should try that kind of stuff," he argued softly. "I think you're still looking at this as some kind of a game. It's one thing when we can water down their propaganda and make jokes behind their backs, like when you said, 'Watch out, flyboys. You know what the Japanese are flying—Zero.' Maybe we can talk our way out of that kind of thing if we're called on it. It's a whole different ballgame to be passing military information over the airwaves."

Iris shrugged. "What good is it to live if the Japanese win the war? I'm willing to take the chance."

"Personally, I have nothing to live for. You might," he said, casting a wary eye at the record. "Besides, you don't know what you're bargaining for."

"I haven't forgotten the awful story you told me about them burning that man. I know the risk. I just think we should plan carefully and do what we can."

Jake held up his hand in warning and reached for the arm of the record player. As the record ended, he said, for the benefit of anyone who might be listening, "This one's good enough for Sunday. Do you have any others to try out?"

Iris smiled as she handed him a paper-jacketed record. "Dinah Shore singing 'Careless.' I used to dance to it a lot."

Jake put it on. "It looks like it's scratched," he said. The band came on with the introduction, skipping over one scratch for the first few bars. "How important is this one?" he asked.

"Cole and I had our first argument when the band was playing this. We used it ever since to signal that there's something wrong." Her eyes clouded in wistful remembrance. Then, more businesslike, she added, "it might be useful."

Jake nodded. "If Cole is out there to pick it up. I doubt that anyone else would understand your personal code."

Iris fought back sudden tears. "You don't want to take any chances. You try to make me think that Cole isn't even alive. What else do you have to say to make the day pleasant?"

"Iris, you've got to face reality. The odds are that a pilot with over five hundred combat hours will be shot down. Cole's already been shot down once and was lucky enough to survive."

Iris gasped. "How do you know?"

"I was there. It was on the first day of war. He tangled with a swarm of Zeros and came out second best after knocking one of them out himself. He parachuted out of the smoking plane and was picked up by a Filipino fisherman. He had a sprained ankle and a light concussion, but was back in the air within a month."

Iris leaned back, biting her lower lip. Jake's story made her face, for the first time, that Cole was actually flying in battle, being shot at. Through all her worries, her fears had been without mental images. Now her mind was filled with visions of Cole going down in flames while a Japanese fighter pilot calmly marked him up as another "kill." She shivered from the sudden cold sweat washing over her.

"We just can't count on you getting a personal code off to Cole. And I don't think we should try to get such detailed information out over the air. It's too dangerous to you, to Eva, your family, and that lady you call Mama-Kiyoko," Jake said matter-of-factly.

Iris sat silently while Jake put on a selection of Strauss waltzes by the Boston Pops Orchestra. As the light rhythms of the strings filled her ears, her mind slowly started circling around the one fact: Cole was risking his life to win the war. Finally, she said firmly, "The least I can do is take some chances too. I'm willing to try. Bill says you had a code you used in the Philippines. Surely others besides Cole picked that up and knew it. Can't we use that?"

Jake's face clouded at the mention of the Philippines. His dark eyes became black pools of sorrow; his eyebrows knotted in pain. He shook his head violently and turned away from Iris. Then he stopped, half-standing, his face drained of all color as he stared at the doorway. Iris followed his gaze. Major Tsuneishi was standing in the doorway, looking around the office. Then he marched over to their work area.

"Good afternoon, Miss Hashimoto." He bowed. "I trust is well with you, Captain Devon?" he said in English. Jake answered the major with silence. Iris quickly got up and bowed politely, saying in English, "Good afternoon, Major Tsuneishi. We are planning our program for this week by checking the records. I'm afraid that Captain Devon is feeling a bit ill. Please forgive him."

Major Tsuneishi nodded brusquely. "We'll have the doctor look at him this evening. I have a request for program. Is very good that program is popular with American soldiers. Now we have audience, we want you to include words to say they cannot win against the superior Japanese soldiers. Now, you tell them they must give up."

Iris looked to Jake for help, but he was still staring at Major Tsuneishi's uniform, his jaw clenched, his face pale. "We will do our best," Iris said, bowing. "However, I hope you will be patient with us. If we speak so openly to the Americans it might be laughed at. We will try to find a way that will be acceptable to you and to the Americans."

"So good," he said with a shallow bow. "I will be listening. Americans use puzzling language. You talk so they listen." He turned and left.

"Jake," Iris whispered, "are you all right? Why didn't you answer him?"

Jake dropped into his chair like a marionette whose wires had suddenly been clipped. He put his hand over his eyes. "Why did you tell that bastard I was sick?"

"I had to say something. You were looking so strange. What's the matter? You kept staring at his uniform."

"The uniform. They were wearing that uniform when they raped Maria. That was what she was looking at when she died. That goddamned, fucking uniform."

Iris gasped. "Oh, no . . ." she whispered, touching Jake's arm softly. "Oh, Jake . . ." He sat silently, never taking his hand from his eyes.

Finally Jake raised his head slowly. His tormented eyes were dry, rimmed in red, hollow with a consuming sorrow.

"You're right. We'll take those chances. It's the least we can do to beat the bastards. Here, tell me the message again."

Iris smiled in relief at seeing a glimpse of the old fighting Jake again. She quickly explained what Bill had told her at their last meeting. She and Jake then worked to reduce the information to the most basic elements. Finally, they came up with "Planes Wewak," surmising that if someone was decoding their message, they'd know that they were giving them critical information.

Jake spent the rest of the afternoon explaining the simple code he'd used in the Philippines, along with all the intricate variations he'd worked out for Cole in the foxhole that night on Bataan. By the end of the day, they had two stacks of records in two boxes, labeled "Usable" and "Defective: Don't Use" and a determination to figure out a way to work in their message on their next program. Bill had said it must be sent out within the week, and they promised to give it their best shot.

That evening, as they sat on the porch, Iris told Eva about what had transpired at the radio station that day.

Eva was frightened. "You're planning on sending military secrets on a Japanese-sponsored radio program that practically the whole world can hear. Surely someone out there will catch on."

"That's what we're hoping. Only our gamble is that the ones who catch on will be American. The whole beauty of the plan is that no one is going to be looking for secret messages in something sponsored by the Japanese, something that's intended to be a propaganda program that they're sending out themselves."

"But remember what Jake said about that man they burned . . . and about his wife, Maria?"

"All I know is that if Cole is alive today, he's putting his life on the line. The same goes for Sparky. If they're doing that, this is the least I can do."

There was a pause in the muggy summer night, a pause heavy with Eva's fear.

Finally, Eva said quietly, "You're right. It's the least we can do. But I've been pretty scared because of the warnings we've been getting at the listening station every day. They say it comes 'from the very top of the army' that we're not to repeat anything we've heard that might be construed as de-

302

moralizing to Japan. In other words, don't tell how the war is really going. And I've been telling you everything and we've both passed it on to Bill. I can't help wondering if they're not giving these warnings because Bill's been found out and they're trying to trace his source before taking care of us all."

"I wouldn't worry about that," Iris said brightly. "Bill said you're not his only source of foreign news. They're just being cautious now that the news isn't all in favor of the Japanese. Since Midway, really, they've got to pad it more and more with daydreams and lies." Iris put her hand on Eva's arm. "Just wait and see. We're going to help get the Yanks here before you know it."

The next day Iris found that Jake had written a dialogue for them to do that held a hidden, coded message. It was almost like a sassy little part in a play that Iris was supposed to read, except that each one of the words meant something other than what the Japanese would think. Jake began coaching her. She worked hard under his guidance, trusting his judgment and professional expertise. She had to slow down her delivery to make it perfectly clear. At the same time, she had to sound chatty. They practiced all afternoon on just a two-line exchange.

Finally, exhausted, Iris whispered, "Jake, I don't know how they're even going to know it's us. By the time some of the places pick it up, it's going to be filled with static. We can't count on our voices being recognized."

Jake wrote in three more lines. "I'll use some slang from Seattle. We'll give every clue we can. Now, see, you're going to be just coming in to see me. We'll keep calling you Flower of the Pacific, or Flower. That's sort of your identity already. You've got to keep it bouncy. Then, try to make your voice almost have that kind of pout that you girls have when you pretend you're feeling sorry for a guy but you're really teasing him. Do you know what I mean?"

Iris read the words he'd written. "Maybe I do. Let's try it a few times."

A few minutes later, Jake interrupted Iris's delivery for the fifth time, "No, no. You've got to sound much more lighthearted. Just like you did when you were all excited about going to a movie—you know the kind of bouncy sound."

"Ah, so good you rehearse." Major Tsuneishi's voice boomed from behind them, causing them both to stop in fear. "You keep on. I already hear. It's so good you have things to say. Good idea to feel sorry for Americans. You make me proud of program." He beamed and bowed slightly to them. "I not interrupt more. You keep practice. Make good show."

Iris and Jake silently watched as he walked away. "I think we just passed the test," Jake whispered, smiling. "He could have stopped us right then."

With relief they returned to the practice, encouraged that they sounded convincing to a Japanese ear. Now, if only they would be heard by an American ear. If only the turncoat niseis didn't catch on. If only they were able to send it out without getting pulled off the air and shot. If only . . .

It was the first week of August and Iris was once more affected by the stifling heat of Tokyo. She was exhausted by her day's work with Jake and could barely drag herself to the *densha* stop. The heavy humidity had settled over the city like a lid over a kettle, steaming those caught under it.

Kicking off her shoes in the *genkan*, she had nothing more on her mind than splashing her face with cool water from the pump. She stopped on her way through the main room as she caught sight of Eva sitting in the corner of the sleeping room. "Hey, are you all right?" she called. "I expected you to be out in the garden fighting the battle of the weeds and making me feel guilty for not helping."

"Yes," Eva said listlessly.

"It doesn't sound like it," Iris murmured as she went into the sleeping room and looked at her friend's pale face. "Do you think you're coming down with something?" Eva shook her head. "Well, has something happened?" Iris persisted. Then, seeing a tear trickling down Eva's pale cheek, she kneeled beside her. "Something's happened. Tell me, Eva."

Eva looked at Iris, her eyes filled with fearful tears. "I'm . . . I'm afraid," she whispered. "Sergeant Ito came here today."

"Did he hurt you?"

"Not really."

"Come on. What is it?"

"He said that we'd both better go down and register as Japanese citizens. He said it could be pretty bad for me especially, if we don't. Iris," she said more intensely, "it was almost as if he's . . . he's obsessed by this thing. He said something about how his superiors expect him to be able to pay his *on* to your grandfather, and something about you maneuvering to thwart him. I'm not sure what it was all about because he talked so fast. I think he was drunk. He smelled sour, like saki. And then he started in about me. He said you take good care of me and treat me like your sister, but I'm not as good as you. I'm not from a good family. He said I'm almost an orphan and I shouldn't expect any help from influential people. He said if he can't hurt you, if he can't make you do what he commands, he'll show you his power by making me submit to his will. Then he said some crazy things about the Kampetei and their control over everyone. He even said there were kinds of torture, including something called *shikijo no*. That means 'erotic.' He kept getting more and more worked up. It was so hot, and we were standing outside in the sun. I thought I was going to faint. He stood there waving his arms and dripping with sweat, talking faster and faster. He kept saying something about *ikujinashi ni suru*. It means to take away his manhood. To emasculate." Eva was holding on to Iris's arm, her frightened eyes telling Iris more than her words. "Iris," Eva said tentatively, "could he have been doing this because of what you and Jake are doing at the station?"

"I don't see how. We haven't even broadcast our first message yet."

Eva nodded and silently looked down at her folded hands.

"Are you okay now?" Iris asked softly.

"I'm still scared."

"Me too," Iris admitted. "But I don't think we have anything to fear from Ito. He's crazy, from the sound of it. Pretty soon his superiors will see it and he'll be taken away. In the meantime, we'd better take some precautions. Maybe we could ask Kiyoko to stop over during the day and maybe some of the other neighbors. You know, at times when we know one of us, especially you, will be home alone."

Eva's face brightened. "Do you think that would help? What will we tell Kiyoko?"

"The truth. I can't imagine him giving too much trouble when there's a witness hanging around. We'll work it so you're checked up on all the time. If he's watching the place, he'll soon find out that he'll find no privacy to carry out his dirty, drunken threats."

"I don't know where you get your courage. You always come through when things get rough."

"Not really. I just know that if we're going to survive, we can't give up and hide."

Cole wandered in a dazed confusion for days. The fact that Iris was a traitor gnawed at him, making his life a mockery. The fact that he had succumbed to Marta's seduction confused him. It didn't seem right that just as he was mourning the loss of Iris he could so thoroughly enjoy making love to Marta. But he had. He'd found an angry release in sex. She had told him when she'd left Port Moresby that she would be ferrying the next group of planes being sent to Amberly Field outside of Brisbane, Australia. Her hot, moist kiss before she left promised him a night of passionate forgetfulness if he could manage to visit when she arrived.

Then Dick came to Port Moresby the following day and Cole persuaded him to arrange the conference he'd been talking about for the weekend of August 7, the same time Marta's group was expected to arrive. To ease his conscience, Cole told Dick the whole story. Dick was his usual taciturn self, merely nodding and saying, "Those things happen."

"Not having your fiancée turn traitor," Cole protested. "That's not the kind of thing that most guys have to face up to."

"No," Dick agreed. "Are you sure it was her?"

"No doubt about it. I'd recognize her voice anywhere. And Jake too."

"Jake?" Dick said with more interest. "Are you sure?"

"There aren't many voices like his."

"Still, that's pretty hard to believe. How'd he make it to Tokyo? We'd thought he was dead."

"Well, he might as well be," Cole said bitterly.

Dick grunted and shook his head. They spent the rest of the night in a serious game of gin rummy. Nothing else was said about Iris and Jake. Dick left the next morning on an intelligence junket to Dobodura and then back to Australia and headquarters.

The week passed with difficulty for Cole. He threw himself into training a new group of pilots just in from the States during the day, but at night he was overwhelmed by the lust Marta had released in him. His mind spun with images of her making love to him, seducing him.

Sparky's attitude didn't help. He was remote and business-like and avoided Cole. Cole knew he was upset about hearing Iris on Radio Tokyo, but he suspected that Sparky was also disapproving of Cole's liaison with Marta.

Cole had been back in New Guinea only two weeks, but two weeks was more than enough to make him appreciate the civilization of Brisbane. He was greeted by a ruddy-faced corporal as he got off the transport. The young man saluted respectfully and handed Cole an envelope.

The note was written in Marta's sweeping handwriting. She urged him to waste no time getting to his hotel. Eagerly, he caught a ride there, where the clerk handed him a key and said that his wife had already registered.

The room was dusky gold as the sunlight filtered through the drawn blinds. He closed the door behind him and tried to focus his eyes. There was a rustle on the bed and Marta murmured, "It's about time. I didn't think I could wait.' Her naked body was burnished in the dusty sunlight, round and soft with the promise of pleasure. Cole forgot all nagging doubts, all guilt.

That evening, he pulled himself from her arms long enough to check in with Dick at headquarters. The meeting was scheduled for Sunday at noon. The night was his and he spent it with Marta.

Sunday morning he rolled over in bed, still partly asleep but gloriously aware of Marta's naked body next to his. Her long legs were entwined with his and her hands were caress-ing him, embracing his awakening desire. Her moist lips trailed warm kisses up his chest and she buried her face in his neck, eagerly reaching for his hardness. "Now, aren't you glad I got you out of that mess in Hawaii?" she murmured, her warm breath filling his ear.

Cole was suddenly alert; his hands stopped caressing her buttocks. "What did you do for me in Hawaii?"

"Why, when I got you off the hook, of course," she said, wide-eyed.

Cole was still, feeling as he had when he'd gone pheasant hunting as a boy. One wrong move and he might scare her away. "What do you mean?" he said with forced casualness.

"When I told that Jap that she was holding you back. I was right, too. As soon as she left, you started getting your promotions." She wriggled against him. "But let's not talk about that. No thanks expected. I've got my reward."

Cole slid out from under her and sat up on the edge of the bed. "You told Iris she was holding me back because she was Japanese?" he asked coldly.

"Hey," Marta complained, reaching out for him. "Let's not talk about that. We were . . ." He caught her arm and held it, feeling her bones with his tightening fingers. "You know I did," she said, pouting. "She told you. That had to be why you told her to go back to Japan, where she belongs. You're hurting my arm."

"I told her no such thing. I never knew why she ran away from me. Now I do. Some jealous slut wanted another cock to ride," he said, enraged. "Get out of here!" He threw her arm away from him and got up from the bed.

"You can't talk to me that way," she said, rubbing her arm. "Not now. You know you love me. You couldn't wait to have me last night!"

All desire was gone, replaced with disgust. He picked up his uniform and went into the shower, saying, "When I'm done, I expect you to be packed and ready to go."

As he showered, he realized that the disgust he felt was more for himself than for Marta. She wasn't the one who'd changed character; she wasn't the one who'd betrayed anyone; she'd merely been acting as she always had. He should have known. He was the one who was wrong.

He looked at himself as he shaved. His face was the same, but his eyes were different. They weren't confused as they had been this past week; they weren't in mourning anymore. They were clear. His mind was clear, too.

Marta was sitting at the vanity table brushing her hair. Her packed suitcase lay open on the bed. "Honestly, Cole," she said with tear-filled eyes, "I don't know what I did that was so wrong. It was true, you know."

Cole looked at her and said, "Actually, you probably did me a favor. Not in Hawaii . . . what you did there was despicable, but here in this room . . . and last week on the beach. You helped me learn a lot about myself . . . and now you've explained a two-and-a-half-year-old mystery. If I could return the favor, I'd help you learn to see yourself as clearly as I've learned to see myself. No, I'm not mad at you. But I don't love you. I never have." He shook his head. "I guess I was just horny and you came along when my defenses were down."

"But can't we . . ." Marta pleaded.

"No. A few minutes ago, when I realized what you'd done, when I realized that it was you who actually drove away the one woman I'll ever love, drove her to her possible death, I hated you. I could have killed you. Then I realized that you were only acting on your same old instincts. You were just surviving the only way you knew how. I just expected too much from you."

He walked to Dick's office and talked him into going down to a coffeeshop for breakfast. Over coffee, steak, and eggs, Cole told him the whole story, including his own degrading part. When he was through, Dick leaned back in his chair and said, "Well, does that change your mind about your Tokyo Rose?"

"I don't know. There's been something that's been bothering me since I first heard that broadcast, but I just can't put my finger on it. At first I thought maybe it was because it wasn't really Jake announcing. I'm still not sure it was Jake, but maybe my subconscious picked up on something that I didn't recognize right off. What do you think?"

Dick shrugged. "I don't know. I've had pretty much the same feeling. I think there might be something you missed in the first shock. Let's turn on the radio this afternoon in my room. Maybe in privacy we'll be able to concentrate and hear what it is that's bothering us."

They agreed that after the meeting they would go directly to Dick's quarters.

The purpose of the meeting was for Cole to talk to the colonel in charge of Dick's intelligence unit. Knowing that Cole had worked with Dick in intelligence in the Philippines and occasionally since then, the colonel wanted to put more ears where the action was. Since Cole was a group leader for the fighters, he was in a position to see things firsthand, maybe pick up on some clues as to what was happening that the G2 wouldn't get in ordinary debriefings. Cole agreed.

Once Cole's unofficial liaison position was established, he and Dick went to Dick's room. The program would not begin for half an hour. Cole paced the room, smoking and lost in his own thoughts. Dick put paper and pencils in front of the radio set. "Just in case we want to note anything down to talk about later," he explained.

At 4:25, Dick turned on the radio, filling the room with static, and then a stilted, amateurish Japanese voice gave some kind of lecture on morals and the American lack of courage. Then music filled the room: Glenn Miller's Orchestra playing "Imagination." As the music faded, Jake came on, announcing the Sunday afternoon program, "Call of the Pacific." The first few minutes were devoted to POW messages of twenty-five words each, which Jake read. Cole and Dick leaned forward, straining to hear every word and write it down. They all seemed to be authentic messages sent by prisoners of war in various Japanese POW camps throughout the Pacific. The last one read was, "Hi, Mom and Dad Roberts. I'm doing okay. I haven't seen Joey since Burma. Kiss Sis for me. You can send Red Cross packages. Love, Tommy."

The music began again, and then Jake came back on. Dick reached for his pad and pencil.

"Now, all you Yanks out there, how about some music, the kind that brings out the poet in you, the kind you used to dance to back home," Jake said in an informal, chatty manner. Then he seemed to interrupt himself, saying, "Hey there. Look who just walked in to join us. If it isn't the Flower of the Pacific—and is she looking good. Hi, Flower, how're you doing today?"

"Oh, everything's just Jake with me," Iris chirped back. Cole and Dick exchanged startled looks.

"Well, come on over here, Flower, and help me choose some records to play for the Yanks. They need some cheering up out there. They seem to think that their planes are holding up for them. What do you have to say to that?"

"Poor little airmen, nearly exhausted," Iris said, as if she were pouting. "Such wishes exhibit warped Allied knowledge."

"Well, that's some message," Jake joked. "Maybe we'd better pick out a good record for them to do a few turns with. What do you suggest?"

"How about something for you?" Iris asked. "I have Wayne King and his Orchestra with Buddy Clark doing the vocal. They tell how 'We Could Make Such Beautiful Music Together.' "

The strains of Wayne King came on and Cole turned to Dick, beaming. "That's it!" he crowed. "Did you hear her?

310

How could I ever doubt her? Did you get it all written down? I think I might have missed something. My hand was shaking too much."

Dick laughed. "I don't know, but I'm sure now that she's trying to communicate with us. 'Everything is Jake with me' is an old Pacific Northwest slang term, but obviously she was making it clear that is was Jake she was with. Then that part where Jake said the music would bring out the poet in you . . . your name . . . Tennyson. . . ."

"I know!" Cole said enthusiastically. "They used to tease me, calling me their poet in Hawaii."

"Then that part where Jake said 'some message' . . ." Dick added. "I hope to hell they aren't caught doing this."

"Oh, God . . ." Cole pushed away the unthinkable.

"Did you hear what he called her?" Dick asked.

"Flower of the Pacific. I could hardly believe my ears. Then he kept calling her Flower. I used to call her Posey. Her name's Iris, you know. That's a flower."

"Yes, I know." Dick grinned. "Flower of the Pacific was also a code phrase."

"Bill!" Cole shouted. "I'd forgotten. That was so long ago. Surely, you don't think . . . could he possibly . . . ?"

"It's what he said he'd try to do. Wouldn't you know he'd pick the most flagrantly dramatic way of doing it. I had thought a while back that he was trying to send a code via some shortwave at sea. We'd picked up some partial message a couple of times that had his sound. Then they stopped. But he just could have found her; you said you gave him her address. There always was the possibility—shhh, they're back on," he said, turning up the volume.

They listened intently to the rest of the half-hour program. There seemed to be nothing else of significance except for Jake's frequent reference to Iris as the Flower of the Pacific. She teased him some about his Seattle background. When they signed off, there was no doubt in Cole's and Dick's minds that they had heard Iris and Jake. They could hardly wait to put together the pieces of what had been said. There had to be a code in it.

They compared their notes, then sat in silence, each scribbling frantically on his pad. "I've got it," Dick said at the same time Cole cried out, "That's it."

Cole leaned over with his paper. "Is this what you got?"

311

He looked at Dick's paper. He'd written the same thing as Cole. They'd taken the second statement that Iris had made, "Poor little airmen, nearly exhausted. Such wishes exhibit warped Allied knowledge." Taking the first letter of each word, it spelled out *PLANES WEWAK.*

"Wewak," Cole said, sitting back and lighting a cigarette. "That's the place Sparky was telling about, that forward Jap base in New Guinea, isn't it?"

"Well, you'll know about it soon enough," Dick said wryly.

"Why?"

"There's an attack scheduled for next Tuesday."

"On Wewak?"

"Yeah. We've got plenty of other information that it's the end of the line for the Jap ferry system. Planes are all bottled up there with nowhere to go until they can prep them and send them on to their final destinations. Wing tip to wing tip. We're going to send a group of you up there on August seventeenth to see what we can do about helping them thin out the parking problem."

"Can't help but wonder why they're making the same mistake that we did at Clark and Pearl."

"They don't think we can reach them yet. That new field we've built at Marilinan can, though. We've just been holding back to catch them off guard." Dick leaned forward, his elbows on his knees. "You know, this will be a good chance for us to check out the reliability of this message. If it's like we think it will be, we just might have ourselves a direct line to Tokyo." Cole shook his head in wonder as Dick went on cautiously, "Just to make sure it stays a nice surprise, don't breathe a word of this to anyone, even Sparky."

"You can count on me, but don't you think we should take this information to the colonel?"

Dick tossed his pad on the table and leaned back. "I think we'd better confirm this first message before you go off half-cocked and tell anyone that your fiancée is a Japanese in Tokyo sending out secret coded messages as one of the Tokyo Rose announcers." He paused. "We don't know what either of them have been put through. We don't want to fall into a Japanese trap."

Cole nodded. "How do you think we should handle it?"

"Let's just check this one out. When it's proved, I'll tell the colonel that I received a message that was then verified by the reconnaissance and the raids. If it's actually verified. Then, when we get another one, I'll pass it on to him for analysis. When we've finally built up his confidence in the information we've been getting, you'll have to come forward and explain the whole thing, if you want to chance it."

It was arranged that Dick would be on a routine swing of New Guinea each Monday after the broadcasts. They would meet and compare notes on anything they had picked up from the radio program. From that point, the information was Dick's, to do with as he saw fit.

Cole left for New Guinea the following morning, barely able to control his exhilaration. Now he really had something to fight for. The overwhelming thought in his mind was that Iris had left Hawaii not because she didn't love him, but because she loved him so very much. And now she was reaching out, after two and a half years, her bright voice cheering him and telling him enemy secrets. She wasn't a traitor. She was brave and faithful. How could he have doubted her? He could hardly wait for August 17.

On August 16, one hour before midnight, a dozen B-17s and thirty-eight B-24s took off from Moresby in the biggest mission since the Battle of the Bismarck Sea. They returned at 3:00 A.M., reporting success. Within hours Cole was warming the engines of his plane in Dobodura.. They were about to fly the five hundred miles to Wewak for the deepest daytime bomber penetration into Japanese-held New Guinea, and Cole was in one of the P-38 Lightnings covering them along the way.

Approaching Wewak, they crisscrossed Japanese roads, seeing soldiers swimming, sitting around, and obviously not expecting to be strafed suddenly by a swarm of American planes darkening the sky. As they approached the field, Cole's heart turned in slow elation. It was more than they could ask after the bombing of the previous night, but they had caught the Japanese completely off guard. "This must have been what Clark looked like to the Japs," Cole murmured. Just as Dick had said, the planes were lined up wing tip to wing tip the whole length of the runway. Several fuel trucks were parked alongside airplanes. Crews were busy. In the revetment area, some planes were being loaded with bombs.

Not one plane got off the ground; not one puff of antiaircraft fire rose to stop them. The strafers went in slicing down the line. They dropped their parafrag bombs, General Kenney's ingenious invention, with a supersensitive nose fuse that sent out fragments that could cut off a man's legs or rip through a plane a hundred feet from the point of impact. They were dropped in clusters of three, making the field look like milk-weed blowing in the wind. Cole watched the whole show from above as the bombers and strafers did their business. It was an easy job. Then, as the big planes turned to go, their bombs gone and their fifty-caliber cannons blazing, the P-38s took a turn, swooping in for one last strafing run and a parafrag drop of their own.

As they turned and flew back behind the ridge, they lifted now and then to gloat over the results of their raid. Fires were blazing over twisted wreckage everywhere. The mission was an unqualified success. They hadn't lost a plane. Most important to Cole, Iris's information had been right on the button.

Over the next two weeks they continued their strikes against Wewak, reducing the Japanese stronghold to a skeletal operation, keeping them busy filling in bomb craters on their airstrip instead of causing trouble with Allied operations. Iris's next message was a cryptic: "Good job." The following Sunday's message took more work to understand.

Dick and Cole sat through the entire program, chewing their pencils as they listened for some indication of a message hidden in Iris's sweet chatter. Finally, in the last five minutes of the program, the tone of her voice changed and they leaned forward in anticipation.

"Well, fellas," Iris said slowly and confidentially, "I'll tell you this: We have three more records. You'll listen to a two-step, a beguine, exceptionally upbeat, and thirdly, the Decca hit, Great Daddy's number-one song, 'Adios.'

"Listen—all men ache usually about love and embraces. Under three years of fanatical opposition hurts them in a lopsided trampling of careers, dreams of ladies, and finally love. But don't worry, fellas, you'll get a change of scene soon enough. In the meantime, sit back and relax. Dream with Bob Chester and his orchestra, Judy Garland, and finally, Glenn Miller."

The strains of "Practice Makes Perfect" came on. Dick shook his head. "I hope she played that one just to encourage us."

Cole grinned and leaned over to compare notes with Dick's copy of her message. Then they were silent as they worked over the decoding. The only comment they made for the next fifteen minutes was Dick's terse, "She's changing the letters pretty fast, to make it harder to decipher. Use the 'three more records,' then change when she says 'two-step.'"

"Yeah," Cole said, "every time she says some kind of number. Can you tell where it ends?"

"Not yet." They worked a few minutes longer in tense silence.

"I think it ends when she says, 'finally,'" Cole said at last.

"Looks like you're right. Have you figured it out?"

Cole held up his paper and read slowly, "U.S. expected Salamaua Lae unprepared." What do you get?"

"Same." Then, seeing Cole's frown, he explained, "Salamaua is a Japanese base south of Lae on the Huon Gulf of New Guinea. American and Australian forces are within sight of Salamaua and both sides are gearing up for a major offensive there. However, HQ is hoping the Japanese are anticipating the Salamaua offensive first and don't have a thing waiting at Lae. With luck, we'll be able to make a brilliant leapfrog jump over the Japanese forces and take Lae, which is an excellent base. Iris has just confirmed what our sources are saying."

Cole nodded with obvious relief. Again, Iris was right on the button. "Too bad it isn't original info," he commented.

"Don't worry. She's like money in the bank. One of these days she's going to come up with something we don't know a thing about, and all these previous confirmations will have built up a pretty good reputation for your 'Flower of the Pacific.'"

Dick passed Iris's message on to the colonel that afternoon, saying he'd received it from one of his sources.

On September 1, Cole got final word. They were going to make a combined assault on Lae under cover of foggy weather. Cole was part of the group slated to provide cover for the landing of Australian troops. American bombers blasted Japanese bases all around the area in an effort to discourage any reinforcement.

About two o'clock in the afternoon, as the support ships were withdrawing, one of the ships picked up a Japanese formation approaching from the southwest, less than a hundred miles away. The report was flashed to Dobodura. Cole's group of P-38s was already on patrol over the area and intercepted the message. With Cole in the lead, sixteen Lightnings raced toward thirty Japanese planes intent on stopping the Allied landing.

Cole dragged the nose of his P-38 up a little as the Zeros saw the Lightnings and changed course to meet them. One tried to turn and get on Cole's tail. Cole hit the rudder and climbed left, turning the other way to get level and behind the Zero. He used the heavier weight of his P-38 to dive down on the enemy plane. As the Japanese pilot tried to dive away from Cole's maneuver, Cole squeezed the trigger and his fire chewed into the Zero's right wing, and smoke streamed back. Smoldering pieces of metal flaked from the enemy fighter until the whole thing tore off and tumbled past Cole's plane.

Another Lightning was boxed in by Japanese fighters, so Cole pulled out of his dive and zoomed in on them. Several Zeros spotted him and turned to meet him head-on. The nearest one opened fire but was too far away. Cole waited, then fired a short burst. The Zero broke to the left, and Cole fought the stick to keep to the right. The planes whipped past each other and Cole felt a shudder through his plane. The Zero's wings had nicked his.

He had little time to regain composure because another enemy fighter was now headed straight for him. Cole wrenched the Lightning into firing position and pressed the firing button. Cole saw sudden jagged holes as his bullets struck the Zero's fuselage, and black smoke poured from it.

Cole watched his second victim a moment too long because a pattern of holes suddenly opened up in his right wing. He instinctively pushed the stick forward, initiating a dive. The Zeke followed, blazing shells around Cole. The heavier Lightning outdistanced the Zero in the dive and Cole pulled back on the stick just above the water, hoping the shells hadn't weakened his wing. As the P-38 strained out of the dive, Cole was crushed into his seat. His vision blurred and sweat rolled down his face. He fought to keep from blacking out until the P-38 gradually leveled off.

Land was about fifty miles away, and he now had several fighters coming in his path head-on. He knew his ammunition was low and he was hearing the telltale ratchet discord that meant that one of his guns was jammed.

A Zeke flashed past, tracers streaking from his guns. Shells shook Cole's P-38 once more. He pressed his mike button. "King Cole calling Headhunters. Mayday!" No answer. Where were they?

He was now flying right on the deck with one engine running rough and only a few guns firing. Five Zekes were on his tail. His choices were few. He could try to dogfight, which he'd always taught his men not to try against the agile Japanese, or he could bail out and hope to survive. He tried a bluff. He pulled back on the stick and managed to reach six thousand feet, then peeled into a dive for more speed. Some ships of the U.S. invasion fleet were in the water off to his right. He headed within their range.

As he skimmed across the tops of the whitecaps, bursts of fire from the ships began exploding near him. His one last hope was in their recognition of him as a besieged American. He stood his P-38 on one wing to show the unique P-38 silhouette to the navy gunners, and prayed that they knew their identifications.

The American ships suddenly realized what was happening and adjusted their fire to form a barrier between Cole and the Japanese on his tail. The enemy fighters fell back and Cole was left alone to try to limp home. He decided to try for Dobodura. Forty minutes later, he pulled himself from the shattered cockpit. He fell into his bunk, too exhausted even to take off his flying suit. His last thought before dropping into a deep sleep was that once more Iris's information had been good. The battle for Lae was already set in the Allies' favor.

CHAPTER XXII

Corporal Conlan was getting on Sparky's nerves. He was on detail with three other men, and one of them, Conlan, just wouldn't shut up about his hatred of the "slant-eyed Jappos," "yellow dogs," and every other epithet he could think of. Sparky tried to ignore it by concentrating on the job at hand. They were installing an AA gun and its protective machine gun at the end of the airfield at Marilinan, the Allies' once secret base in the heart of Japanese territory in northern New Guinea. Once that was in, everyone would breathe easier. No telling when some crazy banzai squad might break into their backyard and try to stop the planes that were bombing the Japanese with such deadly regularity.

"Conlan, shut up and hand me that wrench!" Sparky snapped as he tightened one last bolt on the machine gun.

"Pipe down," crusty old Sergeant Malloroy added. "It takes some quiet to work sometimes." He winked at Sparky over the gun barrel. Malloroy had twenty-two years of service under his sagging web belt.

"There, that's about it," Sparky said, stepping back from the machine gun. "Now all we have to do is go back and tell them to man this son of a bitch. That—" He stopped, his eye caught by a furtive movement at the edge of the jungle. Instinctively he ducked behind the sandbags. The others followed suit.

"Do you think it's a . . . Jap sir?" Private Harlinger whispered, his face paling beneath his sparse mustache.

"Stay down!" Sparky ordered in a hoarse whisper. "Maybe we'll take him by surprise."

Corporal Conlan dove for the machine gun and turned the barrel to the spot where everyone was looking. Sparky rasped, "Don't be a goddamned fool, Conlan. Could be one of our own men coming in from patrol."

Conlan clutched the gun with sweaty hands. "I can smell a stinking Jap. I'm going to get me one of those bastards yet . . . and you're not going to stop me."

Just then Sparky saw a movement of white. It was a man. A lone Japanese soldier waving a white flag of surrender. Was it a trap? Sparky hesitated. The ammunition clicked against the metal brace as Conlan aimed the gun. Sparky spun around, grabbing Conlan's shoulder and throwing him back against the sandbags. "I gave you an order," he said fiercely, "and you damn well better obey it." He slid the bolt of his rifle and turned back to the approaching Japanese soldier. "We'll just wait and see what he's got on his mind."

"What are you, some kind of Nip lover?" Conlan protested. "We got one dead in our sights and you say lay off? We're supposed to be killing—"

"Shut up," Sparky hissed. "He's waving a white flag."

Conlan started to protest but was interrupted by Sergeant Malloroy's soft drawl. "When a master sergeant tells a corporal to shut up, that's what they're supposed to do, son. Sparks is in charge here. Just watch and see what's going to happen. They don't often give up."

"All I can see is that it's a goddamn stinking Jap monkey trick," Conlan whined. "And Sparks is going to get us all killed."

The man was within hearing distance now; Sparky stood up in full view. "What do you want?" he called.

"I surrender," came the distant answer. Sparky gestured for him to come forward and the man broke into a run, crouching low and looking furtively over his shoulder.

Sparky heard a movement behind him and a click. Corporal Conlan was back at the gun, squeezing the trigger. Sparky spun around, catching the corporal's jaw squarely with his fist. Conlan was lifted by the blow and fell back against the sandbags once more. "I said hold your fire," Sparky said evenly.

The corporal rubbed his jaw. "I would have had the bastard if it wasn't for forgetting to take off the goddamn safety."

"I'll have you for disobeying a superior," Sparky growled over his shoulder, still watching the approach of the soldier. "You're on report."

"Not after I report you for aiding and abetting the enemy," Conlan threatened. "Jap lover."

319

For a brief flash Sparky seriously considered the joy of seeing a bullet go through Conlan's empty head. Instead, he kept his eye on the soldier, who'd stumbled, gotten up, and was now about twenty feet away. "Hold it right there," Sparky called.

The Japanese stopped short and began waving the white flag once more. "I surrender!" he called. "Honest. I surrender."

"You speak pretty good English," Sparky said.

"I should. I was born in the States."

"A goddamn traitor on top of it!" Conlan shouted, struggling against Sergeant Malloroy's hold.

Sparky ignored the tirade behind him. "Where you from?"

"Seattle."

Sparky remembered Jake's descriptions of his hometown and called back, "What's the highest building there?"

"Smith Tower."

"Are you alone?"

"Yes."

"Throw down your guns and come on. Just remember you've got four guns on you."

The Japanese eagerly threw down his rifle and a pistol and then ran toward the gun emplacement. He threw himself down behind the sandbags, panting for breath, his eyes closed in relief. Private Harlinger held his sidearm unsteadily on him, anxiously watching Sparky for orders.

"Let's hear it," Sparky said.

"I'm Ted Watanabe from Seattle. I was in Japan, seeing my grandparents, when the war broke out. The Japanese wouldn't let me go home. They drafted me into the army," he said breathlessly, eyeing Private Harlinger's gun with obvious fear. "Honest," he pleaded, "I've spent the last year shooting over the heads of the Americans, praying for a chance to get away from the Japanese. I'd . . . I'd like to talk to an intelligence officer if I could."

Sparky looked at him, incredulous. He was hearing a story so similar to Eva's that it sent chills through him.

"Sure you were," Conlan jeered. "Don't believe him. They're all a bunch of sneaks. It's one of those yellow monkey traps you always hear about."

Sparky turned to Malloroy. "Take care of Conlan. See that insubordination charges are filed. Witness and I'll sign.

Harlinger and I'll take care of Ted Watanabe. That's what you said your name was, wasn't it?"

He looked at the Japanese cowering in the corner of the revetment. His eyes were filled with tears of relief as he nodded. His English was perfect, with no accent. Maybe it was because of Eva, but Sparky couldn't help believing his story. "Get up," he commanded gruffly. "I'll take you to intelligence myself." He turned to Sergeant Malloroy. "Take Conlan to the brig," he said with a jerk of his head.

"Yes, sir," Malloroy said, walking off with Conlan in tow.

"Why are you out here alone?" Sparky asked as he and Private Harlinger walked their prisoner back to camp.

"They sent me out on patrol and I just kept going. I'd heard there was an air base up here. You've sure been plastering the Japanese from it. I'll tell your intelligence officer where to find the squad I was patrolling for." He was talking with his hands up, glancing uncertainly at Sparky as he talked. "I have some pretty good information about some other things, too," he added in almost a pleading voice.

Sparky's intention was not to take Ted Watanabe to the regular intelligence officer first. They headed straight for the tent where Cole was resting before his mission that afternoon.

"Hey, Tennyson," Sparky said, sticking his head in the tent flap, "I got a surprise for you."

Cole got up off his cot, obviously shocked at the sight of a Japanese soldier holding a white flag in front of Private Harlinger's aimed rifle.

"Here, Watanabe," Sparky said, shoving him into the tent before he attracted any more attention. "Tell him your story."

"Are you an intelligence officer?" Ted Watanabe asked fearfully.

"I do some intelligence work. Tell me what you have to say and I'll make sure it gets to the right place," Cole said cautiously.

"Well, sir . . . does 'Flower of the Pacific' mean anything to you?"

"I don't know, Jake," Iris said, wearily leaning back in her chair. "New Guinea seems so far away. Besides, I don't see how any of these broadcasts could even be heard there, much less understood. I don't think they're ever going to get here. They've been in New Guinea for two years now."

321

The soft strains of Guy Lombardo's Royal Canadians played in the background. It was a terribly depressing statement, coming from Iris, but it had been a difficult week and the program they were broadcasting right now was even more difficult.

"Come on, Iris," Jake said. "You're just depressed because it's winter. We can't give up hope. If our message about the bigwigs on the Jap transport landing in Wewak gets through, February 28, 1944 will be a black day for the Japs. Ever since we sent that message, the Yanks have been bombarding it like crazy. It'll take a while for our boys to inch close enough to Japan for a strike, and then *bang*! Before you know it, it'll all be over."

Iris smiled ruefully. "Here we are, you a prisoner, and you're the one who has the courage to bolster my spirit. Look at you, you're nothing but skin and bones."

Jake shook his head. "You should talk. I think you'd blow away in the wind."

"Is that camp where they put you really bad, Jake?"

"Bunka camp?" He shrugged. "It's not like home. But there're worse camps. I've been in a couple of them, in fact. Here they have to keep us on our feet because most of us are working, either doing propaganda or in factories." He shrugged again under Iris's penetrating glance. "Yeah, it's hard to keep up your spirits when you're caged. There's a guy in the cell next to mine—they beat him pretty bad and took away his blanket. I'm afraid he's going to freeze to death. I'd give him mine, but it's too thin even for skinny me."

Iris had known that there was something on Jake's mind these past two days. She was glad he trusted her enough to tell her. "Let me see what I can do. With these baggy pants, I can smuggle a lot of things in, if only I can get them. Maybe Kiyoko will have an extra blanket. I'll stop by her house on the way home."

Jake smiled gratefully. "Nothing too big. Remember, I've got to fit it under my uniform." He turned to the record, lifted the needle, and read his script to introduce the new song. Iris's cue would come after the next record. As Bing Crosby crooned, Jake turned back to Iris. "How's your family?" he asked.

"I don't know. I haven't been across town for a couple of weeks now. It's pretty hard on them. My oldest niece is being taken out of school and forced to work in a paint factory. She's only eleven. I've got to go over there sometime this week." She pointed to the record, which was nearing the end, and picked up her script. If she was heard this time, a plane of Japanese generals and other high-ranking officers would not survive to conduct the war in New Guinea.

Sleet was coming down as she left the building that evening. She pulled her thin coat more tightly around her shoulders and dashed across the street to her *densha* stop. The other passengers in the car were cold and dripping; the smell of wet clothing filled the chilled air. She got off the streetcar a block early and hurried around the corner to Kiyoko's house.

"Oh, you're shivering," Kiyoko said as she opened the door to Iris. "That coat is no good for you. It's good that you stopped by. I was going to come to your house." She led Iris down the corridor to the single room she occupied. The screens were tightly closed and a ceramic charcoal burner glowed cheerily. Kiyoko then took Iris's wet coat and replaced it with a brown quilted *dotera*, an oversized kimono with wide sleeves to wear for warmth around the house. Iris gratefully pulled it around her and accepted a bowl of hot tea.

"Why were you going to come see us?" she asked.

Kiyoko went to the side of the room and brought back a package. "I was cleaning out some things. I found these *hanten*. They belonged to my daughter, but I think they will fit you and Eva. They will help you keep warm when you go to work. They are very strong and warm and the *sashiko* stitch holds together many layers of cotton batting."

Iris held up the top jacket. It was dark red, with a pale turquoise crane on the back. Kiyoko was right: it promised much warmth. The second jacket was black with a thin gray stripe running through the cloth. The lapel running the length of the front was embroidered two-thirds down on the right-hand side with a geometric design of bronze thread.

"That is my family crest," Kiyoko said, pointing to the bronze design. "You wear that one."

"They're lovely Kiyoko," Iris said. "Are you sure you want us to have them? I mean, if they were your daughter's . . ."

"You are my daughters now. You must be kept warm. You will be very Japanese wearing them over your *monpe*. That is good," she said wisely.

"Thank you, Mama-san," Iris said, bowing deeply. "You honor us. We will wear them and remember your love."

Just then the bell rang at the gate and Kiyoko got up to answer it.

There was the murmur of a man's voice at the door, then the muffled sound of footsteps. Iris stiffened as she saw the military uniform of the man Kiyoko bowed into the room. He stood at attention, while Kiyoko bowed and graciously offered him tea.

"No," he said with a nod. "I come on business. It is with great honor I tell you of the noble sacrifice your son made to the glory of the Emperor. His plane carried him down in flaming courage over New Guinea; his brave actions and faithful attendance to duty were of great honor to you and his father and will be long remembered by his fellow soldiers. He took two American planes with him in honorable death."

Iris gasped in shock. The soldier gave her a sharp look and she quickly looked down at her hands.

Kiyoko was silent; then, swallowing, she bowed and said, "You do me great honor by bringing this news. Thank you for filling his mother's heart with pride."

The soldier bowed quickly and turned to leave. Kiyoko followed him to the door. Silently, and properly, she bowed him out the door and waited as he went down the walk. Iris sat in the chill silence of the house, awaiting her return, hearing her own heartbeat, feeling her own sorrowful pain for Kiyoko's loss.

Then the muffled pad of Kiyoko's slippers returned down the corridor. Kiyoko came into the room, her face placid, her hands folded inside her kimono. "Mama-san, I'm so very sorry," Iris murmured.

Kiyoko bowed, her eyes brimming. "It is an honor a mother never wishes to have," she said quietly. "I'm sorry my sorrow disturbs your harmony. If you will please excuse me, I wish to watch the rain in the garden. If it is acceptable, I will have dinner tomorrow evening with my two daughters." She bowed deeply from her waist and Iris got up to leave. She ached to put her arms around Kiyoko and hold her, comfort her in her loss. But that was not the Japanese way. Kiyoko would find solace in her garden, in her own quiet meditative thoughts. Kiyoko followed Iris to the door. Iris bowed very deeply to her as she took her leave.

As Iris walked to her house, the sleet mingled with her tears. The clapper was frozen on their gate bell and the hinges squealed in the cold. Iris looked futilely around the garden as she walked up the path. If only there were some small flower blooming early that she could take to Kiyoko. Ice crystals hung from the drooping limbs of the plum tree.

"I'm glad you're home," Eva called as Iris slid the door closed behind her.

"Why?" she asked, putting down the package of coats from Kiyoko and hanging up her rain-soaked overcoat.

"I don't know." Eva shrugged. "It's silly, I guess. I was a long time going through the ration lines after work and I just got home a few minutes ago myself. But the whole time I was standing in line, and the time it took me to walk home, I felt as if I was being watched and followed. It really gave me the shivers."

"Did you see anyone?" Iris took the bowl of tea Eva offered her and and warmed her hands as she sipped the hot liquid.

"No; that's what's so silly." She paused and looked at Iris. "Is anything the matter?"

Iris put down her tea and slowly told Eva of Kiyoko's son's death.

"I wish there was something we could take to her," Eva murmured.

"I can't think of anything." They looked at the coals glowing in the *kotatsu*. Then Iris added, "But there is someone who needs something we do have. That wool blanket I use over the *futon*—you know, the one I brought with me? I want to give it to Jake. The padded quilt should be enough for me." She quickly explained the situation Jake had told her about.

"Then take mine too," Eva volunteered. "Jake could use one if all he's got is a thin blanket. No wonder he's sick half the time."

The following day Iris wrapped one of the blankets around her, donned her *monpe* and the black jacket Kiyoko had given her, and went to work. When she and Jake were alone in the recording booth, on the pretext of getting some records, she gave it to him and he wrapped it around his middle and pulled his prison shirt and pants over it. He attracted no notice from the rest of the office staff when he emerged.

Iris left work a bit early because she was more concerned

about Eva's feeling of being watched than she'd let on last night. The feeling of uneasiness increased as she walked from the *densha* stop to their house. She opened the gate and hurried in. As she left her shoes in the *genkan*, she heard a soft crying coming from inside the house. "Eva!" she called, sliding the door open. "Eva? Are you all right?"

Eva was sitting beside the *kotatsu*, the ashes cold and untended.

"What's the matter? Are you all right," Iris demanded, sitting down next to her.

Eva nodded. "I'm okay. It's just that I can't put up with any of this anymore." She started crying. "It's just too much, with the war and all. . . . And Ito . . ."

"Did he come again?" Iris prodded.

Eva nodded. "He came in just like last time, no knocking or anything. Only this time he acted . . . well, different. He kept reaching out and touching my neck, leaning very close to me and saying threatening things. He said he wanted our passports. I told him we didn't have them in the house. I . . . I lied. I told him that you carried them both with you. He said for you to leave them in the house and the next time he came around to get them I'd better give them to him. Then he reached out and grabbed me and pulled me against him and said he had ways to make me sorry if I didn't have them. Oh, Iris, his breath smelled all sour with saki and he made me feel all dirty all over." She shuddered. "I don't know what's going to happen next. He'll come in here like this and then disappear for a couple of months and then he'll come back with no warning just when we start to let our guard down."

"We'll arrange it so that you're simply not home alone anymore," Iris said firmly. "Maybe you can change your schedule at the station—or maybe we can arrange for you to go to Kiyoko's after work."

"We can't tell her about this. It'd drive her crazy after just losing her son and everything else she's gone through."

"Well, it wouldn't hurt to stop by her house each day anyway."

Eva nodded. They agreed not to tell Kiyoko the truth. They would have to deal with the problem on their own. If Bill showed up within the next week, perhaps he would have some solution to offer. In the meantime, neither one of them would be in the house alone for any length of time.

That night over dinner they put on a brave front for Kiyoko. Laying the groundwork for Eva's safety plan, they asked Kiyoko if she would mind if Eva came after work each night to bring by the rations she'd obtained in the morning. Thus, Kiyoko's sorrow was eased by their daily companionship and Eva's safety insured at the same time.

The following day, Iris smuggled the other blanket to Jake. He reported getting the first one to the suffering POW. With luck he might survive, although Jake suspected that the man now had pneumonia. The second blanket would go to Jake so he could give his thin prison-issue blanket to the sick POW as well.

The following two weeks were busy ones. Iris and Eva made the trip across town to visit Iris's family. Grandmother was coughing deeply, and the children were thin and sickly. The niece, Mieko, who was working in the paint factory with her classmates from school, was so exhausted that she could barely stay awake to eat the egg Iris had brought her. The war was wearing on everyone, making the cold, wet winter seem long and vicious.

By March, the tips of trees swelled with the sweet promise of buds. Iris and Eva had made it through another winter.

It had been a long day but Iris took the time to stop at four bakeries looking for bread. The air smelled of new grass as she walked through the park. Then, right before her *densha* stop, she found a tiny spring flower peeking through the muddy grass in the park. Gambling that such a thing was not illegal, she quickly stooped and picked it. On the way home, she got off a stop early and walked to Kiyoko's house. Eva would still be there and the flower would cheer them both.

But when she reached Kiyoko's she found that Eva had already gone home. "She left here twenty minutes ago," Kiyoko said. "She said you'd be home waiting for her because she was late. She invited me to come for dinner and wanted to hurry home to prepare it. She is such a dutiful daughter and so kind to her Mama-san."

A small stirring of concern began in Iris's heart. "That long ago?"

"Yes, maybe a bit more. Is something the matter, my daughter?" Kiyoko asked.

"I don't think so. I'll just hurry on home and see if I can help Eva with dinner. When will you be coming?"

"As soon as I put on my jacket and take care of the coals. But I can see you don't want to wait. You go ahead. I want to borrow Mr. Kawasake's handcart to bring some tools home so I can begin working the garden. You go ahead," she repeated pleasantly.

Iris smiled and bowed as she left the room. Then she ran all the way home. Something inside her was churning; this was the first time Eva had been alone since Ito's last visit. As she stopped to kick off her shoes outside the door, she heard a sound from inside, muffled and harsh. Suddenly her heart was racing. There was a grunting sound again, followed by a cry and the sound of flesh hitting flesh. Iris threw open the door as Eva cried, "No, no more . . . please no more . . ."

Eva was on the floor, her face battered and bloody, her clothes torn and scattered. Ito knelt above her naked body, his short bowed legs straddling Eva, his wet penis flaccid and loose above Eva's stomach. He was still wearing his brown Kampetei shirt with its insignia and leather strap. He was holding Eva's arms down on the floor and her face was turned from him as she cried out.

"No!" Iris screamed. "No! You bastard! Get out!" Then as she ran to the startled Ito, she cried, "Stop!" She began hitting him with her fists.

Battered and bloody, Eva still struggled under his grip. He turned and grabbed Iris's wrist and twisted it painfully. "You will pay for your American arrogance," he hissed, as she cried out and fell to her knees. Still holding Iris's wrist, he turned and struck Eva with the back of his hand. She lay there still and unmoving. He gave her a satisfied glance, then stood up and turned back to Iris.

Her arm was burning with pain as he continued twisting it, his tiny eyes gleaming with a strange joy at her cry. He loosened his grip and the pain subsided slightly.

"Now we talk," he said slowly. "We will talk on my terms." His breath was sour with rice wine and his face was reddened by drunkenness. "I have used a good torture on her," he said with a jerk of his head toward Eva's still body. "She will remember me and obey. Now you will learn."

Even through her pain and anger, Iris could not help thinking how ridiculous he looked in just his uniform shirt,

328

his small penis dangling between his legs, his toes splayed against the mat. She forced herself to look him in the eye, controlling the urge to gag at the sight of his fat lips. She swallowed hard and said evenly, "You have a strange way of repaying an *on* so deep. I'm sure the spirit of my grandfather is outraged and your father is deeply shamed."

It was as if she'd struck him with a hammer. Stunned, he released his grip on her wrist and shook his head, tottering slightly in front of her. Then his hand moved so rapidly that she had no warning. There was a crushing blow to the side of her head and the room blackened. She felt his sudden weight on her, his hands tearing at her clothes, but she could not fight back. Darkness filled her eyes.

Suddenly a scream filled the air from across the room. *"Yamete! Yamete! Kedamono!"* No, beast! The weight lifted from Iris and there was a scrambling on the mats near her. She shook her head, inhaling deeply to catch her breath. The fog cleared from her eyes and she saw Ito crouched on the floor with Mama Kiyoko clawing at his back and screaming. Iris struggled to her feet to help Mama-san.

Just then Ito rose with the roar of an angered bear, spinning around toward Kiyoko, catching her shoulder with his fist. Before Iris could do anything, he raised his hand again. As Mama-san staggered under his first blow, he struck her once more at the base of the skull. She fell face forward to the floor and didn't move.

Eva stirred in the corner and Ito turned toward her, not seeing Iris struggling up. Without thinking, with only screaming anger, Iris reached up to the wall above the *otoko* with Kiyoko's scroll and pulled the sword from the scabbard. In one raging movement, screaming all her fears, she threw her whole weight behind the sword and brought it down on the back of Ito's neck. She felt the sharp blade cut through bone and cartilage. She saw the blood spray around the room and his head fall forward, held to his neck only by the torn white flesh in the front. His knees crumpled and he fell down, dead.

Eva was covered with blood as she crawled out of the way of his falling body. The screens were splattered with dark spots. Iris's arms were suddenly heavy and she could no longer hold the sword; it fell to the *tatami* floor. The room spun around her and she was violently ill. She ran to the *benjo* and vomited into the toilet.

When she came back into the room, Eva's bruised, naked body was leaning over Kiyoko, shaking with deep sobs. "She's . . . she's dead!" she cried.

"No!" Iris leaned over the limp form. "No, Mama-san, you can't . . ." she cried softly. *"Shinanai de kudasai."* Please don't die. Kiyoko had a pale blue tinge around her nose and mouth. Her eyes were still open in a startled expression. Iris put her head to Kiyoko's chest and heard nothing. She felt for a pulse and found nothing. She moved Kiyoko and she was limp. "No, Mama-san!" she cried putting her face against Kiyoko's, washing it with her tears. *"Iiye, Mama-san . . . Shinanai de kudasai."* You shouldn't have done it. . . . Why?"

Eva sobbed. "She died for us."

"Oh, God, what will we do?" Iris cried, looking around the room, suddenly filled with the realization that they were going to have to explain two dead bodies in their house. They had to do something. If found out, they would be tortured and killed for what they'd done to a Kampetei officer. No matter what he'd done to them, she knew they would not be justified in the eyes of the authorities for killing him . . . even though he'd killed Mama Kiyoko-san, beaten and raped Eva, and tried to rape Iris. Such was the official Japanese attitude toward blind obedience and respect for any official.

"They'll kill us," Eva cried, looking around the room and shivering as much from fear as from the cold. "There's nothing we can do! Mama-san," she cried, looking at Kiyoko's body, "oh, Mama-san, we will die too."

"No!" Iris said harshly. "Snap out of it. There's plenty we can do and it starts with you cleaning yourself up and getting dressed. I'm going to look outside and make sure no one heard all the noise."

Eva looked at her, startled by Iris's sudden tone of authority. She dried her eyes and, still sobbing, painfully went to bathe and dress.

Iris looked out the door and saw no one looking around the garden, peering over the walls, or coming to their rescue. For once, she was grateful for the Japanese custom of minding one's own business and pretending not to hear anything. She turned to go back into the house when her eye was caught by the handcart. Kiyoko had brought it with her as she'd said she would. A plan slowly evolved in her mind. She cast an eye to the graying sky. It would be dark within an hour.

Once inside, she set Eva, still sobbing, to washing all the bloodstains from the mats and the walls. Iris pulled Ito's decapitated and half-naked body out the door and shoved it under the porch.

Then she and Eva gently closed Kiyoko's eyes and wrapped her body into one of their quilted blankets. "I'm going to take Kiyoko home," Iris announced. "Help me put her in the handcart."

"Why?" Eva asked. "What good will that do?"

"I think her neck's broken. If I can make it look as if she fell in her house and we can discover her tomorrow, that will clear us in her case."

Eva nodded, then looked over her shoulder toward the back porch. "What about . . . him?"

"I've got that figured out. But we'll have to wait until it's dark. I'll explain it when I get back. You can't help me while it's still light because your face is so swollen. We'll have to think of an explanation for that, too." She paused and really looked at Eva for the first time since she'd come home. "Are you all right?"

Tears flowed down Eva's face. "I hurt. I can move everything. It's just that . . . he . . ." She started crying brokenly, staring helplessly at Iris.

"Don't think about that now," Iris commanded. "We've got to take care of this mess first. There'll be time later. . . ." She started to reach out and put her arms around Eva, then stopped. "Later . . . now, we've got work to do."

It was almost dark when they put Kiyoko into the handcart and covered her body with tools, empty boxes, and a blanket. Afraid to leave Eva alone, Iris told her to cover her head with a scarf and come with her. They went out the gate and started down the street. Old Mr. Kawasaki was shuffling down the street and stopped when he saw them. With their hearts in their throats, they put down the cart with Kiyoko's body hidden in it and bowed to him. He bowed back and murmured that they were so good and dutiful to Kiyoko-san. They forced smiles and bowed once more before going on, their knees shaking so badly that they could hardly push the heavy load.

They tearfully arranged Kiyoko's body to make it look as if

331

she had tripped going out into her back garden. Her head would have struck a rock as she fell down the steps. Iris then went into one of the closed-off rooms and began rummaging through some trunks. Eva came in as she was opening a *tansu*.

"What're you doing?"

"Looking for her son's clothes. And I think I've just found them." She pulled out some trousers, a loose jacket, and a straw hat, the kind that workmen often wore when delivering goods in the streets. "These should do. See if they fit you," she said, tossing them to Eva.

Puzzled, Eva climbed into the clothes and stood there under Iris's scrutiny. "They're a little big, but they'll do just fine," she pronounced finally.

"Fine for what?" Eva asked timidly.

"Fine for making deliveries to the waterfront warehouse district of Tokyo." She pulled out another similar outfit, then picked up the lantern and said, "Now let's get out of here before we're seen."

Eva started weeping silently as they wheeled the cart to their own yard. Iris heard her sniffing beside her and felt a rising panic, a feeling of anger and fear at her helplessness. She needed Eva to complete what had to be done. If only Eva could pull through just a bit longer . . . if only she would wait before she thought about what had happened to her. . . .

Once inside the gate, Iris turned to Eva and grabbed her shoulders. Shaking her, she said firmly, "Snap out of it! I need you. You can't fall apart on me now."

Eva was limp in her grip, startled yet responding to Iris's sudden outburst. "I'll . . . try." She sniffed. "I'm just sort of dizzy." She staggered and Iris caught her arm.

"Come on inside. Maybe some hot tea will help. I'll see if I can find an egg."

Eva seemed to calm down once she drank the tea. Iris poached an egg and made her eat it, then dumped some noodles and dried vegetables in the water and made a quick soup for herself. She got up and brought in Kiyoko's son's clothing, handed Eva the outfit, and said, "Go put this on. Then braid your hair and pin it up really tight to your head. Don't let any stray ends hang down."

Seeing that Eva was silently obeying her, she turned and did the same thing. Then she checked herself in the mirror.

She looked like a thin, rather frightened young boy. She took some ashes from the *kotatsu* and smeared a line along her jaw. She now looked like a dirty, frightened young boy. It would have to do.

Eva was still trying to pin up her hair. Her hands were shaking too badly to be effective. Iris took over, pinning up Eva's hair and smearing ashes on her face. Eva winced under Iris's brusque movements, as Iris tried to make her swollen and cut features look merely dirty.

Iris stood back and looked at Eva, her heart aching for her friend. "You look a little tough, and if you walk right, you'll pass for a man. Now come on. We're going to have to load him into the cart and cover him with some kind of rubbish." Her plan was to take Ito's body through Shiba Park and down to the warehouse district on the bay. "We'll just dump the whole load into the ocean. With luck, he'll wash out to sea or wash up on some far shore. Even if he just floats in right there, they can't tie his death to us."

Eva had been strangely quiet since they'd returned from Kiyoko's. Now she merely turned and limped to the door. Iris followed her with increasing misgivings. In order for this to work, she had to have Eva's strength combined with hers. Otherwise they would never be able to make it the long distance to the waterfront. They must not look as if they were struggling with the load. Workmen were accustomed to the loads they carried, and they had to look like weary workmen.

Grabbing Ito's feet, Iris tugged and pulled him out from under the porch. Then she gestured for Eva to grab hold of one side and help her get him into the cart. Woodenly, Eva went to the other side of the body and reached down to pick it up. Iris pulled, and found that she was pulling the full weight. "Come on, Eva, lift. I can't do it without you."

Eva reached down once more and lifted up an arm. Then her knees buckled and she fell down, sobbing hysterically. "I can't . . . I just can't. . . ."

"Eva, you've got to," Iris said, trying to make her voice strong. "I can't do it without you. I'm not strong enough. Get up. Try," she pleaded, her voice starting to break.

The hat had fallen over Eva's eyes and she continued to cry. Iris went over and took her arm, trying to pull her up. She was limp and trembling uncontrollably as Iris tugged at her. "Eva, stop it!" Iris said desperately. "You can't do this."

It was no use. Eva was hysterical, her sobs coming faster and deeper with each breath. Iris lifted her up and guided her into the house. Pulling out the *futon*, she laid Eva down, carefully setting the hat aside and taking off the man's jacket.

"I'm sorry . . . I can't . . . we'll die. . . . He looks so . . . so . . . What will happen?"

"I don't know," Iris said soothingly. "I'll have to try to do it by myself. Here, drink what's left of this tea." Eva sipped from the cup, still sobbing. Iris handed her a handkerchief and said, "If I'm caught, you'll probably know in the morning and it'll be over for both of us. In the meantime, the only thing you can do is sleep." She took the cup from Eva and was amazed that she was instantly asleep. Iris wondered if she had fainted.

She got up and went back outside. Fighting back the urge to cry as hysterically as Eva had, she once more pulled and lifted the body. She was desperate; cold perspiration covered her body in the chill night air, yet she felt a frantic fever inside. After fifteen minutes she had managed to get the partially decapitated torso into the cart. Now she had to get the legs to fit in. She rested for a moment, then went back to pushing and bending the legs. She couldn't use up all her energy now. She still somehow had to find the strength to push it across the district and to the waterfront. She shoved once more, and one of the legs fell into the cart.

"Tomare!" A man's voice suddenly cried from the corner of the house. "What are you doing?" he demanded gruffly in Japanese.

Iris froze, her breath caught in her throat. Then she turned and ran. Perhaps she could get away. She stumbled through the garden, heading for the back gate. She could hear footsteps running behind her, getting closer. She reached the gate, and pulled it open, and slammed it behind her, hoping to slow him down. Then she was hit from behind. Bright white spots filled the darkness in front of her eyes.

She fought against her attacker, kicking, hitting, scratching, struggling to get free. Then her arms were pinned and the weight of his knee crushed her stomach against her backbone. She was immobile, helpless.

Then he jerked her to her feet, the hat dangling ridiculously to the side of her head and her braid falling over her ear. He shone a flashlight in her face. "What the hell . . ."

334

Caught by the three English words, Iris turned abruptly toward her captor. "Bill?" she whispered.

"My God, Iris. What are you doing?" he asked, putting his arms around her. "I could have killed you. What's going on?"

"Bill, get out of here," she said brokenly, half-clinging to him. "You can't be part of this. Just leave and don't ask any questions."

He held her more tightly. "You know that won't work," he said softly. "You'd better tell me."

Iris buried her head in his shoulder and fought back the burning tears, trying not to give in after all she'd done to keep strong. Finally, she looked up at him and said, "I'll tell you, but you've got to promise to leave and not get involved."

"I won't promise that. I've been involved since I first saw you threatening me with that hoe. Come on. Are you all right?" he asked as they walked back through the garden toward the porch. He kept his arm around her shoulder and she felt herself gathering strength from his calm. "What were you loading in this cart? I thought you were a burglar or something," he said shining his flashlight into the handcart. "Oh, my God . . ."

He shone the light back to Iris's face. Then he looked at his watch and said, "You'd better tell me what's happened, and fast. It looks like you had the right idea about getting rid of this."

They sat on the edge of the porch and Iris quickly told him what had happened. She heard his gasp as she told of the rape and murder. Then he wrapped his arms around her, murmuring, "Thank God you're all right. How's Eva?"

Iris told him about what they'd done with Kiyoko and how Eva had finally collapsed after that. "She's sleeping, I think, right now," she ended.

"Sounds like a bad case of shock. We'll have to check in the morning, though. You've done everything just right so far," he said, kissing her cheek softly. "It'll be all right now. I'll take the handcart and dump the body."

"I'll go with you."

"No, you won't."

"I can't allow you to do this without me," Iris insisted. "I'll be fine, and there's more sense in two of us pushing it across the city in the dark. We'll need one just to dump it and one to act as lookout."

Bill held her more tightly for a moment, then stood up. "You're right. Let's go. I've got a pack of wares beside the house there. It's not too heavy. See if you can carry it. It makes more sense to have both workmen delivering merchandise. Go pin up your hair. My tail-end tackle didn't do you much good."

Iris quickly followed his orders while he covered the body with rubbish. They were soon on the street, plodding slowly over the cobblestones toward the wharf. They walked in silence, Iris concentrating on shuffling her feet and bending her back in the same way that Bill did, imitating the walk of a weary deliveryman. The night was black and cold. Most of the time they had to feel their way because of the semiblackout conditions being enforced in the city.

After an hour of walking, Iris knew that she would never have been able to make it without Bill.

Bill knew the district well. They ducked between buildings, through hidden alleys, down forgotten streets and past musty storage sheds. Finally, Bill turned toward the waterfront. Stopping in the shadow of a stack of wooden boxes, he waited for a moment, listening.

Iris heard a scratching, scurrying sound and jumped. "Rats," Bill whispered. "Go walk in that direction, as if you know where you're going. Then stop and look around as if you've discovered you've missed the correct building, and go back the other way. If it's clear both ways, set your pack down and rest, keeping a sharp eye open. If you see someone coming, stomp your feet like you're cold. Got it?" Iris nodded and walked down the wooden wharf.

The iodine smell of seaweed and the pungent smell of creosote filled the air. She heard the water gently lapping against the underside of the dock. There was a tiny light at the end of the dock area, half-blocked by a blackout shade. Probably a night watchman. There was no other light, except the thin starlight of the clearing night. She stopped and listened; perhaps she would hear footsteps or breathing if someone was watching. Nothing. She turned, looking confused, and walked in the other direction. Then, looking around, she set down her pack and wearily put her hands on her back. Looking. Listening.

There was the sound of the cart wheels on the wooden dock. She listened more intensely. No one could come now.

Then there was a distant splash and the lighter sound of the empty cart returning.

"Let's get out of here," Bill whispered. "Here, put some of those pots into this cart. That will lighten your load."

Iris did so, and they headed home. Iris's hands were shaking and she felt nauseated as they left the warehouse area.

It was nearly 4:00 A.M. when they finally reached Iris's street. Her legs were heavy with exhaustion, and she felt lightheaded and she couldn't see clearly. They had made it, she thought incredulously as the gate closed behind them.

Eva was still sleeping soundly. "She'll be all right until morning," Bill said reassuringly. "Make me some tea and something to eat, will you? I'm going to make a quick trip to Kiyoko's and make sure you didn't forget anything." He turned and went out the door, adding, "I'll be right back. Why don't you unbraid your hair while I'm gone?"

Almost in a trance, Iris followed Bill's suggestions. She was brushing her hair when he returned. Silently, she brought out his soup and tea. He ate quickly, watching her from the corner of his eye. When he finished, she said wearily, "I suppose you'd better go."

He looked at her softly. "Got any more hot water?" Iris nodded. He went to the pack that Iris had set down on the mat and pulled out an oblong ceramic container. "Ever see one of these? It's a Japanese hot-water bottle. Go get your *futon* while I fill it." Iris did as he told her. He set the hot-water container at the foot of the *futon* and put the quilt over the top of it.

"There, you will keep warm and cozy. Get some sleep. I'm going to stay here and keep watch, just in case." He reached out and stroked her cheek.

The gesture was simple and genuine. Iris looked at him, and suddenly the horror, the fear, the grim truth of what had happened filled her and her sorrow poured out in uncontrollable shaking and sobbing. Bill pulled her to him, warming her against his chest, shutting out the world with his arms. "It's about time you did this," he murmured.

Then, sitting down on the *futon* and leaning against the wall, Bill pulled Iris down next to him and held her. Her sobs slowly subsided and a heavy peace settled around her. She was safe in his arms. She went to sleep smelling the smoke of his cigarette.

CHAPTER XXIII

Cole was unusually quiet as he walked with Dick to the colonel's tent. No matter what they told Colonel Whiteside, it was going to be tricky. Yesterday they had received Iris's code message about the planeload of Japanese generals. They had tried to arrange a mission through the lower echelons, to no avail. The Japanese had been working day and night repairing the damage to the Wewak airstrip. A planeload of generals was scheduled to land there at six o'clock tonight. Unless Cole and Dick could get a mission cleared, it would land safely, bringing in fresh Japanese top brass to lead further assaults against the Allies. Cole and Dick had to convince the colonel that this was a legitimate intelligence report.

Whatever happened, Cole wanted this mission to go—and he wanted to be on it. He would put his life on the line, trusting Iris.

The colonel listened to Dick's precise report of the information, then quietly read and reread the coded transmission and the decoded message it contained. Finally, he leaned back in his chair and said with a bemused look, "You really believe that this American POW is broadcasting information over a Radio Tokyo propaganda program? You believe that a POW has access to such vital military secrets and is blatantly using the Japanese's own propaganda to relay them?"

Dick handed him another file, explaining. "You may remember me telling you about Bill Ando, the Japanese-American working undercover for us in Manila right before the war broke out. On December seventh he told Tennyson that he was going to try to slip into Japan with the repatriated Japanese and send information to us from there. At that time he chose the code name 'Flower of the Pacific.' The fact that

338

he made it to Japan and has tried other methods of getting information out was confirmed by the Japanese soldier, Ted Watanabe, who surrendered a couple of weeks ago. He'd worked with Ando in Tokyo, trying to send messages out from a fishing boat before the Japanese forced him into the army. We'd received some partials on those transmissions. That's how Watanabe knew the code name. You will note that phrase was used several times in the broadcast yesterday. Ando is obviously getting the information and slipping it to Jake Devon, the POW." He handed Colonel Whiteside another worn file.

"Devon, the male announcer, worked with Philippine guerrillas after the fall of Bataan. He's a close personal friend of both of us. Before Bataan fell, he gave Cole a personal code for them to use just in the event he could escape and work with the Filipino friends he'd made in Manila before the war. We received several transmissions from him in the Philippines after we'd arrived in Australia and New Guinea. It was all reliable, clean information, as it says in the file there. Then, nothing. He'd obviously been captured and we'd given him up for dead. Then, a while back, we heard his voice on these Sunday programs. He was passing information again. It was also clean—corroborated by other sources. We think this particular message is too important to sit on. That's why we've come to you."

The colonel lit a cigarette and reread the transcript of the broadcast. "Most of this information was spoken by the female announcer. I cannot believe that Devon would have been able to enlist a Japanese woman to relay military secrets." He shoved the files back across his desk. "I'm sorry. It's too tenuous for such a dangerous mission."

Dick was silent. Cole could keep his secret or speak up now. He would be gambling his entire career in admitting that his fiancée was a Japanese propaganda broadcaster in Tokyo. He could lose all credibility, even be sent home for the rest of the war, considered a security risk. He was already a major, decorated with a handful of air medals, a Distinguished Flying Cross, and a Bronze Star. He was a respected leader, one of the top aces in the theater, with fifteen victories to his credit. He could keep silent and continue his exemplary career. Or he could speak the truth.

He looked the colonel square in the eye. "Sir, the female broadcaster is my fiancée."

The colonel stared at him dumbfounded, his cigarette halfway to his lips. A heavy silence filled the room as the midday sun pulsed down on the tent roof. Then the colonel leaned forward and said quietly, "Go on."

Cole explained how he and Iris had met in Hawaii, why she'd left him to go to Japan, their coded letters as she'd tried to return before the war began, and even his visit with her family during his leave.

When Cole finished, the colonel said, "She left so as not to hinder your career, yet you're putting that same career on the line right now. A career, I might add, that shows great promise. Why?"

"I believe in her, sir. She isn't a traitor. Her information is good. Past messages, as you now know, have proven that. Perhaps future messages will be vital. Besides, my career isn't worth a spit in the wind if we don't win this war. Shooting down a planeload of Japanese generals will help to accomplish that. If it costs me my career to accomplish it, it's worth it."

The colonel smiled tightly, his face lined with worry. "You must recognize that even though Watanabe has led us to a few ammo dumps and a couple of Japanese patrols, he still could be a red herring sent by the Japs. We must take that into consideration. You must also recognize that this could be a trap. No matter how much faith you personally have in the people transmitting this message, they could also have been fooled . . . or tortured into doing it." He paused to let his meaning sink in. "I will authorize this mission on three conditions: One, I will send you out, Tennyson, to fly cover for the two best aces we have in the theater, Bong and Lynch. Second, you will not go aloft until I get some kind of corroboration on this message. I'll check with the decoders right away and see if they have anything coming in over the Jap radios."

"But, sir," Cole cut in, "it's after noon now. If we have to wait around for corroboration, we'll be too late. The plane will land and the brass will be hidden away."

"Sir," Dick put in, "these are proven codes passed on by proven agents in the past, all of them personally recognizable to both of us, two of them by voice identification and one by code name previously known only to us."

The colonel started to reply with a shake of his head, but was interrupted by an aide coming into the tent. "We just decoded this radio between Tokyo and Wewak, sir. Thought you might want to see it right away." He saluted and walked out.

The colonel glanced at the paper. "Go warm up your planes, Tennyson. You've got a mission on your hands."

Cole let out a whoop of approval and started to get up, but Dick grabbed his arm and said, "Hold it." Then he looked at the colonel and said cautiously, "You said you had three conditions, sir. You only told us two."

"The third is that Tennyson's story is not to leave this room. You will both continue receiving and decoding these transmissions. Tennyson, according to your file here, you have enough combat hours under your belt for me to want to pull you back a bit anyway. You will continue with your training work and this intelligence work, but I'm cutting back on your combat missions. We can more profitably use you in intelligence and planning."

"But, sir . . ." Cole began.

The colonel raised his hand. "You are going today only as an observer and to offer top cover. You are to shoot only in self-defense. We may be on to something here and I want you around." He smiled quickly, then saluted and said, "Dismissed, and good luck."

Time was short, and they were almost too late. By flying wide open, the three P-38s were able to arrive at Wewak about two minutes before six o'clock. But the Japanese must have had a tailwind; the plane was already on the ground, rolling to a stop. There was a greeting party of about a hundred Japanese in full dress waiting at the end of the runway. Cole stayed aloft while Lynch dove to the attack. However, halfway down, Lynch found that in his hurry to get away, his gunsights hadn't been installed. He called to Bong to come down and take it. Bong roared in and fired one burst. The plane was enveloped in flames for a second; then a black explosion filled the air. No one was seen leaving the plane. However, just to make sure, they machine-gunned the waiting party. There was no interception and the P-38 trio returned to base unscathed.

Cole was elated. It would have been privilege enough to have flown with the two top aces of the theater, but to have been the one responsible, the one with the secret information, the one with the fiancée working to help from Tokyo, made him walk on air for the next week.

Subsequent radio communications intercepted between Tokyo and Wewak indicated that the victims were a major general, a brigadier, and a whole staff of other high-ranking officers, not to mention their strategies, expertise, and carefully planned orders.

Iris glanced worriedly at Eva, sitting in the corner knitting. She had not cried once since that horrible night. She'd remained in bed for over a week after the attack, mostly sleeping, sometimes staring at the ceiling. Then, in the middle of March, she'd gotten up from bed and, with the last of the woolen yarn they'd brought with them from Hawaii, had begun knitting socks, slowly, methodically and quietly. Sitting on a pillow, with the sliding doors closed to the outside, she spoke only when spoken to, answering in soft, short replies. At Iris's insistence she'd gone back to work, but she'd requested shorter hours and spent the rest of her time in her own silent world. Her jaw had been badly swollen, perhaps broken, and she'd been forced to eat only liquids for a month. Her tiny body had wasted away. Iris knew that Eva's lethargy was in part a sign of advancing starvation.

"I have to go to work now," Iris said softly. "Will you be all right? I'll hurry home right after the broadcast."

"Yes," Eva said, without raising her eyes.

Iris slipped out the door with a leaden heart. She didn't know what to do. A drizzling rain misted the late March sky as she hurried to the *densha* stop. It was time to start the garden again. Would Eva be able to help? Then there were the poor hens: they'd nearly starved and frozen during the bitter winter. The few eggs they'd laid had been soft-shelled.

Even before she hung up her coat, she heard that the cough Jake had been fighting for months was settling in his chest. It sounded almost like pneumonia. She was worried as she looked at his face with the dark purple circles under his fevered eyes, his sallow complexion and trembling hands, while his deceptively strong voice announced the Judy Garland record "Over the Rainbow." It was amazing how he could make his voice sound so good when he looked so terrible.

"I think you'd better see a doctor before you need a mortician," she said as the record began.

Jake's body was wracked with coughs before he could answer. He shook his head finally, whispering, "I don't think they make prison calls."

"If they want to keep an announcer, they'd better start."

Jake doubled over in a fit of coughing. With a shaking hand he sipped from the teacup Iris offered him. "We'd better get this program out. Then I'll sleep for a week," he whispered.

They sat in silence, waiting for the record to end. The words of the song rang painfully clear in Iris's ears. Then Jake's baritone voice came on:

"I imagine all you Yanks out there are wondering where our Flower of the Pacific is today. Well, she's just now coming in the door. Hi there, Flower. Gee, that's some hat you're wearing. I'll bet the fellas out there would like to see you tip it to them."

"Why, this little thing?" Iris came in on cue. "It's just something I picked up to make those poor Orphans of the Pacific feel better."

"Why, Flower, what makes you think those honorable boneheads need cheering up?"

"Well, I just know it's going to make them turn inside out to hear this, but they're fighting a losing battle down there in New Guinea. There's just no way they can take that big old base the Japanese have put in at Hollandia."

"Tell me more, Flower."

"Okay, now. There are just scads of Zeros and bombers and all sorts of fighting men all lined up ready to take off after the Americans. Like I said, this will just turn them inside out, but the Yanks can't do anything about it. There's no way they can stop all those planes. They're sitting there safe and sound out of the Yankees' range. That's why I thought this little hat might make the program more cheery for them. Okay?"

"Hollandia, huh? Maybe they do need that cheery little hat. Well, Flower, why don't you tell me what record you've picked out to play for them today?"

"Oh, I want to play my favorite, 'Pennies from Heaven.'"

Jake put the needle down on the record and gave in to

another fit of coughing. Iris handed him the tea and a small container. "Here. I was able to trade a skirt for these. They're probably the last aspirin in Tokyo. You look pretty fevered."

Jake took them gratefully.

It had been the result of a long search on Iris's part. She'd kept half the aspirin in case Eva needed them. The rest she'd wanted Jake to take. If it could keep his fever down, if it would help ease some of his pain, perhaps he would heal faster.

As soon as the program was over, Iris requested a few minutes with Major Tsuneishi. She explained to him that Jake was coming down with pneumonia and that NHK was in danger of losing him if they didn't find him quick medical attention. Tsuneishi agreed to have a doctor check Jake's condition, but he didn't seem to appreciate it when Iris added that hospitalization seemed the only sensible thing.

"How is your health, Miss Hashimoto?" he asked politely.

"I'm sure it's the same for many in Tokyo," she said. "I'm very run down. I have many colds and get very tired because of poor food." Such an open admission of the problems they were facing was not considered correct. However, Tsuneishi merely bowed his acknowledgment, and shoved a newspaper clipping across his desk, and told her to read it.

It was from Switzerland originally and had come to Japan through Lisbon. Written in English, it told of the propaganda programs Japan was broadcasting to the Allied troops in the Pacific and how the programs were enjoying a good deal of popularity. It made specific mention of a female announcer with a soothing voice on Sunday evenings. They called her Tokyo Rose.

"That's interesting," Iris said, putting the article back on his desk. "Who do you think Tokyo Rose is?"

"It could be either you or Ruth Hayakawa. She also has a Sunday program and her voice is quite melodious."

"I see," Iris said simply. She would have to think of the implications of this strange kind of stardom later, when she had time. Now she had to get home to Eva.

By the first of April, Iris had managed to get Eva out to the garden. However, it didn't have the effect she'd hoped for. Eva remained quiet and robotlike, methodically doing her chores, finding no joy in life. Iris talked constantly, hoping that her chatter would trigger something in Eva to snap her out of it. She mourned the loss of Kiyoko even more than before. She was the one person who probably could have brought a response from Eva.

Once, when Iris had bumped into the wall, Kiyoko's sword had fallen to the floor. As she'd stooped to pick it up, everything that had happened rushed into her memory. Bitter tears burned her eyes.

When she'd finally stopped sobbing, she'd looked up and seen Eva standing in the doorway, watching her as she stood holding the sword. Large, silent tears streamed down Eva's cheeks. She'd taken the sword from Iris's hand and quietly hung it back on the wall, then turned and gone back out to the garden. The ceaseless, gnawing grief was creating a void in their lives. Even together, they felt alone. The loss of their beloved Kiyoko-san was a wound that could never heal.

Although nothing had ever come of Ito's death, no indication that it had even occurred, Eva seemed still to expect another attack. She jumped at the slightest noise. Iris knew that the only reason she'd agreed to go back to work was so that she would have fewer hours alone in the house while Iris was at work. She obviously preferred to have Iris within earshot, even though she seldom spoke. Iris felt even more alone.

Bill had remained close at hand for the first week after the attack. However, when nothing more was heard, when Kiyoko's body was "discovered" and a respectful neighborhood funeral was arranged and her ashes placed in the family cemetery, he assured them that they were safe, and went back to his old pattern of unpredictable appearances. However, when he did appear, Iris felt a warmth and comfort with him that she felt with no one else. When they were alone, he openly reached out and held her in his arms. Iris had no idea if he was merely being affectionate as a brother or loving as a lover. Nor did she know why she was so happy when he was near. She knew only that he was the one remaining bright spot in her increasingly difficult life.

When she and Jake were told at NHK that the Americans were "silly enough to try night bombings at Hollandia and were merely splashing the water of Lake Sentani all over the place," they were confused. Why didn't the Allies stage an all-out attack? Perhaps the information Bill had given them to transmit was wrong. Perhaps it had not been understood.

After all, the "inside out" code only meant something to Iris and Cole. What if Cole wasn't around to receive it? Maybe the direct approach would be best. They should at least be told that they weren't hitting the target. The next time, they didn't stray from Tsuneishi's suggestions. Iris used her mocking voice and hoped that straight news would help.

"This next song is for all the pilots out there in New Guinea. It might help improve your disposition. All you've been doing lately is going out at night and dropping bombs blindly around Hollandia. And that just splashes the waters of Lake Sentani all over the place and messes up the pretty view. Maybe once you've cheered up, you'll reconsider the whole thing."

Tsuneishi clapped his hands in glee at her derisive tone. "Well done, well done," he crowed after the broadcast. "That will make them lose face."

To Iris, it all seemed so useless. Obviously, Cole wasn't around to receive her transmissions. Then there was Jake: he wasn't getting any better. If he had to be replaced on the broadcast, she couldn't continue as the counterpart of someone seriously intent on passing real propaganda. It was with heavy footsteps that she approached the gate to their house that evening.

She walked around to the back, expecting to see Eva working in the vegetable garden. She was nowhere in sight; just the hens scratching at the dirt, clucking in the warm April dusk.

She went in the back door. "Eva?" Increasingly concerned by the answering silence, Iris looked around the cooking room. Seeing nothing disturbed, she went to their sleeping room. The air had a closed, musty smell, as if the room hadn't been opened all day.

There was a slight rustle from the rumpled pile of Eva's bedding. She moved swiftly across the room and lifted the cover.

Eva was shivering, her face contorted in silent pain as she doubled up in a tiny ball. "Eva! What's the matter?" Iris said, kneeling beside her.

Her face was dripping with perspiration and she moved her mouth in a pained whisper. "I'm sick. . . . But don't worry."

"Don't worry? You've got to see a doctor!"

"No," Eva protested hoarsely, kneading her stomach in pain.

"You could have appendicitis," Iris said. "Of course you'll see a doctor. You can't walk. I'll go to the corner and get a taxi."

"We can't afford it. . . . I'll be okay," she protested tearfully.

Iris ran down the block to the main thoroughfare, looking frantically for a cab. She didn't know where they would get the money, but she had to get Eva to a doctor.

She had to run three more blocks before she was able to find one of the dilapidated coal-burning cabs. She urged the driver down their narrow street and told him to come in and help her carry Eva. They got her out to the car without much difficulty. She was only semiconscious by that time. Iris urged him to drive faster and faster to the hospital, as she held Eva's damp head in her lap. The fumes of the engine made her feel lightheaded. She would give him the money she had put aside for their food for the rest of the week. It would have to be enough.

They arrived at the hospital where Eva and Kiyoko had been treated for their pneumonia, and the kindly driver helped her carry Eva inside, accepting only half the coins she offered in payment.

Eva was wheeled into a room and Iris was left to wait in the green-painted foyer, wringing her hands with anxiety. There was nowhere to turn. Nowhere to go.

Finally, a doctor came out and asked, "Is she your sister?"

"She's . . . like my sister. How is she?"

He shook his head. "Are you American also?"

What had Eva said in her delirium? Iris had no choice but to trust the doctor. "Yes, why?"

"Let's go where we can talk in private," he said, leading her to a tiny alcove. "I will speak English," he said. "I went to the University of California in Los Angeles. You don't have to worry," he said reassuringly as Iris stiffened in fear. "No one else will know about this. Your friend is very sick. She apparently tried to terminate a pregnancy with a sharp instrument—a knitting needle, she said. She achieved that, but she also damaged herself and has a very bad infection."

"Pregnancy . . ." Iris whispered in shock. Tears filled her eyes as she suddenly realized the horror that Eva had silently been bearing. "Will she be all right?"

"She will probably die within a week," he said gently. "I have no medicine to combat the infection. I need sulfa drugs,

347

but they are all being sent to the front. There is nothing left for civilians. I'm sorry."

"What if I can find some?"

"Black market? I doubt there's any even there. But you're welcome to try. If you can find some, get as much as there is. If you manage to get them, I'll make that the payment for her hospitalization. But don't get your hopes up. I have the small son of a very important official in there right now who might die if I can't find any, and even his father hasn't been able to help."

"Can I see her?"

"I still have some morphine and I've sedated her because of the pain. She might be awake enough for you to say good night. Don't expect her to be too coherent. You can come back tomorrow. I'll be here." He smiled wanly. "Sometime when all this is over, you can tell me about life in the States." He got up and wearily set off on his rounds.

Iris quietly opened the door and went in. There were several beds lined up around the room and one at the end that was screened off. Iris tiptoed around the screen. Eva's face was pale against the sheets, her eyes closed. "Eva?" she whispered, lightly touching her arm.

Eva turned her head slowly and large tears began running down her cheeks at the sight of Iris. "I'm . . . I'm sorry," she murmured.

"It's going to be just fine. Don't worry. The doctor told me everything."

"It was like . . . I was . . . so ashamed. I had this monster growing inside me, not a baby. Babies come from love. This was hate and evil. . . . It was evil growing inside, eating away . . . I couldn't . . . I'm so ashamed." She started to cry piteously.

"You have nothing to be ashamed of. Don't worry . . . it's going to be all right. Just get some sleep. I'll come back in the morning."

Eva nodded weakly, then fell asleep quickly. The morphine was working. Iris left quietly, wiping the tears from her own cheeks before she stepped from behind the screen.

Where to go? What to do? How could she possibly find sulfa drugs to save Eva's life if the Japanese had sent them all to the troops? Iris pondered the problem all the way home on the bus.

The house was black and empty, as she wearily went up the walk. Crickets were beginning to chirrup in the evening. The peaceful sound only emphasized her loneliness, her sorrow.

"Where've you been?"

"Bill!" she cried, jumping back and dropping the lantern in surprise. He reached down and picked it up, lighting the candle and taking the bamboo chimney from her hand. "Thank God you're here," she said, as she threw herself into his arms and burst into tears. Then, brokenly, she told him about Eva.

"Don't lose hope yet," he said, stroking her hair. "Sometimes I work on the docks, loading ships going to the front. I'll go down early in the morning. There's usually at least one ship a week going out with medical supplies. There's all sorts of ways to lift a few boxes off. They do it all the time. Where do you think the black market gets everything?"

"Can you get it in time?"

"I don't know. Can you meet me here at noon tomorrow?"

"You bet. I won't go to work."

"Good. Now, what's for dinner? Want to see my lovely contribution?" he asked, pulling out a paper-wrapped package. Unwrapping it, he revealed a very ugly fish. "I've been out on a boat all week and just got in. I think he ought to make a pretty good meal. Let's get to work on it."

For the first time that day, Iris smiled. They broiled the fish over the coals, chatting and exchanging news and hope, while the rice bubbled in the pot. Bill stayed long into the night, smoking, talking, and reassuring her. In the end, he simply held Iris in his arms, warming her with his presence until she fell asleep. When she woke in the morning he was gone, but she felt a lingering warmth from knowing that he had been there and would come back by noon.

She had taken the last pumpkin saved from the season before and had a pumpkin soup simmering over the coals by noon. She was attacking the weeds in the garden when Bill arrived.

"Jackpot!" He grinned, holding out a box. "But it wasn't easy. I was supposed to be loading airplane parts. I saw a medical-supply ship being loaded on one of the other docks and waylaid one of the workers headed toward it. I convinced him that I'd gotten into a drunken brawl the night before with one of my coworkers and wanted to save face by working on the other ship. He bought it."

"Let's see the medicine," Iris said impatiently.

Laughing, Bill opened the wooden box, revealing a whole case of neatly stacked bottles. "I suppose you'd better get this right down to your doc. I'll wait here for you." He smiled. "I didn't get much sleep last night. I'll catch up on it while you're gone."

When Iris showed the doctor the heavy crate of medicine on the cart she'd commandeered, he stood looking at it in disbelief. Finally, he shook his head and murmured, "It's a miracle. If you hadn't gotten it today, your friend would have been dead in two days. Now there's some hope. And that little son of the high official will live too. Don't worry about the bill. I think you've saved two lives." He turned and hurried down the corridor, Iris following him. "She's not awake enough for you to talk to her, but you can look in."

While he went to get the injections ready, Iris went to Eva's room.

Eva was sleeping restlessly. Her complexion looked slightly yellow and waxen, her cheeks hollow. Iris allowed herself a little glimmer of hope as she went back home. Her conversation with Bill that night gave her the courage to hope openly. The following day Eva was a little better. Iris reported back to work, claiming illness for her absence of the day before. Jake seemed to have gotten worse, coughing relentlessly. It seemed as if the specter of sickness threatened Iris on all sides.

By the end of the week, the doctor held only guarded hope. He said he would release Eva, but he cautioned Iris that she would probably have recurring infections, any one of which would kill her if not treated. He recommended that they find someplace in the country, away from Tokyo, where Eva could have better food and peace and quiet. Iris said she would try to arrange it somehow. He gave her some precious vials of sulfa to take along so a local doctor could treat her when the infection recurred.

That evening over dinner, Bill asked her if she had any relatives who lived in the country. "I'll watch your house and help keep the garden going and feed the hens," he volunteered. "I have things to keep me around here for the next couple of weeks anyway. Tell the neighbors that I'm your cousin."

The next morning Iris visited her grandmother's house and talked privately to Aunt Toshiko while walking through the garden, telling her of Eva's serious illness but not the cause. "I remember my mother's sister, Aunt Suki, who lives in Shizuoka—the one I sent the insulin to right after I arrived here. Do you think it would be proper to visit her? Eva needs a rest and a change of scenery."

Aunt Toshiko reached up to pull down a branch of the blossoming cherry tree. Admiring the flowers, she said quietly, "Your mother's sister would find great joy in seeing you. And Eva would find peace there. Shizuoka is a beautiful resort area; the Suruga Bay brings warm currents in the winter and cool breezes in the summer. Your Aunt Suki lives outside the city, where she makes a small farm with her husband and two sons. I will write down the directions for you. It is a long trip."

They walked back to the house, where Grandmother was waiting with their tea. "I have thought much about the country," Aunt Toshiko continued wistfully. "They say that the children should be sent to the country when the bombs come to the big cities. They have special homes for them, you know. If it seems the bombs will come, Aunt Teiso and I will take the children to the mountains where we can live in some hidden place. If that happens, we must prevail upon you to come live with Grandmother."

"Of course," Iris agreed. "That would be best."

"But we mustn't disturb Grandmother's peace of mind by discussing this now," Aunt Toshiko murmured as they approached the room where Grandmother was sitting on her pillow, waiting for them beside the steaming teapot.

"The cherry blossoms are lovely this spring," Grandmother smiled as she poured their tea. Then she glanced at Iris and said, "You have heard, I suppose, about Sergeant Ito."

Iris felt her heart leap, but she forced herself to appear calm. "No," she said, "not since the marriage broker mentioned him here in your home."

"*Ah so desuka,*" Grandmother murmured. "That is too bad. He fell like the cherry blossoms, never knowing the withering of age. They say it was in the line of duty. His parents are very proud of him. He served the Emperor well."

Iris couldn't imagine that her grandmother would be toying with her, yet she felt as if she were under interrogation. "We each must serve in the way we feel best," she murmured, finishing her tea. "And now if you will please forgive me, I must leave." She bowed to Grandmother. "It is always a pleasure to be with you, honored Grandmother."

Aunt Toshiko wrote down the directions to Aunt Suki's farm, then as she walked with Iris to the gate she said, "I'm sure it is the kindness of Buddha which assures you that Sergeant Ito will no longer bother you." She smiled shyly. "Of all people, you have the least to grieve at his going."

Iris went home, both puzzled and relieved by the strange comments her aunt and grandmother had made. Surely they did not suspect Iris was responsible for Ito's death.

Although she was concerned about losing her job, Iris decided to take off from work even if her request for vacation time was denied. However, Jake's illness led her supervisor to agree that they both needed the rest. Since Jake was out ill that day, Iris wrote him a note, explaining that she was on vacation at her aunt's and wishing him a speedy recovery.

She began packing immediately. She would take Eva straight from the hospital to the train station. They could stay with Eva's relatives in Yokohama that evening and take the bus to Shizuoka early the next morning, breaking up the trip into two less-tiring parts. Bill came and helped her finish packing. Iris made the rounds of the neighbors, explaining that she was going to the country to help Eva recuperate, and that her cousin from Nagoya would be staying in the house during their absence.

Eva was reluctant to visit her relatives in Yokohama, but Iris insisted. Once there, however, Iris understood. Eva's grandfather, aunts, nieces, and nephews lived in a small, dingy two-room flat in the industrial section of the city. There was barely room for them to spread out their *futons*. However, the family took great joy in seeing Eva and made both her and Iris feel loved and welcome.

They left early the next morning, carrying the *o bento*, a boxed lunch of cold cooked rice, pickled plums, and tiny strips of salted fish, packed lovingly by Eva's aunts under the watchful eye of her grandfather.

Once on the smoking, charcoal-burning bus headed out of the city, Eva retreated into her silent shell, her pale face an emotionless mask. Claiming she was tired, she soon pillowed her head against Iris's shoulders and fell asleep.

Iris watched the green countryside unfolding before her.

As the noble head of Mount Fuji came into view, Iris began to feel the tight knot she'd been carrying inside slowly unwind.

The tottering bus lumbered over the winding roads, revealing neat villages, picturesque shrines, and layered terraces of rice paddies. Hours later, as they approached Shizuoka, Iris saw tea plantations and groves of mandarin orange trees weighed down with white blossoms. Eva would heal quickly in such a tranquil place, Iris thought. As they wound around the greened hillsides, Iris knew that she, too, needed this healing time.

Shizuoka was a seaside town, bustling but not frantic like Tokyo. The buildings were smaller, the streets narrower. When they got off the bus, Iris left Eva sitting on their luggage while she went to find transportation to her aunt's farm. None of the jinrickshaw drivers was willing to pedal them and their luggage such a distance, but Iris managed to find a farmer who lived not far from Aunt Suki.

Soon they were perched on the seat of the farmer's wagon, swaying up the hillside behind a patient ox. Iris had taken the last of their savings to pay for this trip. She gave the taciturn farmer some of the precious coins when he set down their luggage at the foot of a driveway that wound through a carefully tended field to a squat farmhouse with a thatched roof. The white peak of Mount Fuji rose in the distance behind purpled hills. Iris picked up their three suitcases and Eva struggled with a small case as they walked up the driveway. Eva had to stop and rest three times in that short distance. Iris didn't mind. They watched yellow butterflies dance over the new-sprung green vegetable plants as a bird warbled in the distance.

They set down their bags in front of the house and Iris rang the bell beside the door. The cool smell of moist earth filled the air and a lazy fly buzzed against the window in the sun. There was no answer. Eva was sitting listlessly on the suitcases, her eyes closed.

"I'll go around back," Iris volunteered. Eva nodded without opening her eyes.

Another field of vegetables stretched behind the house. Iris saw a lone figure at the very end. She walked down the fresh-turned rows, calling, *"Konnichi wa!"*

The woman stood up and looked in Iris's direction, shading her eyes in a gesture so familiar that Iris gasped. She then walked toward Iris, wiping her hands on her apron. Iris forgot her manners and simply stared, tears filling her eyes. It seemed as if her own mother were walking toward her. The polite, questioning look on the round, kindly face was the very look Iris's mother had when answering the door. "*Konnichi wa, Oba-san,*" Iris said, bowing low to hide her tears as much as to be polite. "I bring you loving greetings from your sister, my mother."

Aunt Suki's eyes filled with tears as she bowed to her niece. "I have waited a long time for this welcome meeting. You are received with great happiness. Thank you for the medicine you sent to me. My sister said it would be better than the insulin I could buy in Japan and she was right."

Iris could barely take her eyes from her aunt's face. Now that she was closer to her, she saw that Aunt Suki's cheekbones were broader, her mouth a bit thinner, and she was broader across the shoulders than Iris's mother. But the similarities were striking. "It was a beautiful surprise to see you," Iris murmured as she followed Aunt Suki to the back door of the house. "I thought you were my own mother. I miss her very much."

"Many people have said we are much alike," Aunt Suki said, nodding. "I can see her in your eyes. It is good to see you also. Please come in."

"I brought my friend Eva with me," Iris said. "She is waiting at the front of the house."

"Your mother wrote and said your friend came to Japan as well. She is welcome. Bring her in. Will you be living with me from now on?" she asked in a hopeful tone.

"I cannot stay more than two weeks," Iris said regretfully. "But Eva is ill and needs time to recuperate."

Aunt Suki smiled and bowed as she opened the door to Eva.

As they sat sipping tea, Aunt Suki plied Iris with questions about her family, about what she'd been doing in Tokyo, and about her grandmother, who was also Aunt Suki's cousin.

Aunt Suki's husband had died a year ago from cholera, and then her two sons had been drafted. Now she managed the small farm by herself, working from sunup to sundown in the three small fields. When she had a harvest to sell, one of the neighboring farmers would load her produce on his cart and take it to market along with his own. Aunt Suki's time was spent in solitude and long, hard work. Iris could tell that she was genuinely welcome, not only out of familial love but because she brought companionship.

They quickly settled into a pattern of pastoral living. Aunt Suki had chickens, fresh vegetables, and even a cow, which she kept in order to sell milk to a nearby tourist resort. However, Iris and Eva consumed nearly the entire milk and butter output the first week, much to Aunt Suki's amusement. Within three days Iris was milking the cow herself, hoeing the vegetables, and carefully spreading nightsoil fertilizer over the sturdy little plants.

Iris was growing strong and tan in the sunshine, and putting on weight, thanks to Aunt Suki's cooking and watchful eye. Eva was losing her sallow look and gaining weight as well. She even was able to laugh again.

Soon, Eva was helping with small household chores, cooking the rice, scrubbing clothes on a washboard in the sunshine at the back of the house, and scattering grain for the chickens.

The two weeks came to an end much too soon. Aunt Suki used every device she could think of to keep Iris from leaving. Finally, when it was clear that Iris had to return to her job, Aunt Suki insisted that Eva stay on. She needed more time to heal, and Aunt Suki desperately wanted the companionship and help. Eva looked to Iris, her eyes shining with hope.

"Of course," Iris said, laughing. She quickly pushed to the back of her mind the heavy dread she felt at the thought of living alone.

Aunt Suki insisted that Eva should stay indefinitely, and that perhaps when Iris came to get her she would decide to stay on herself. Reluctantly, Iris boarded the bus, her *monpe* filled with contraband food from her aunt's garden. She felt sad, but strong and determined. She would be alone, but she would face June 1944 with courage and good health.

The house was well tended but empty when she arrived. The late afternoon sunshine slanted across the garden and the two hens clucked contentedly around her feet as she walked down the rows of vegetables. The plants were smaller than Aunt Suki's. She'd have to get some of the nightsoil fertilizer. Gertrude pecked at Iris's *geta* persistently, so she finally went to get some chicken feed for them. Bill had left a sack on the edge of the back porch.

The sack tipped over as she turned to throw the seed to the chickens. Leaning over to pick it up, something under the porch caught her eye. She kneeled and reached under the decking, pulling a piece of cloth from under the steps.

"Oh, my God!" She sat back on her heels and stared at the moldy pair of khaki trousers. Bloodstains darkened one side. Ito's pants had been there since that fateful night. Had anyone else seen them?

Taking the scissors from her sewing box, she carefully cut them into strips, swallowing against the gagging reflex she had when cutting through the bloodstains and the fly front. Then, carefully banking her coals, she built a fire in her *konro*. One by one, she placed the strips of cloth over the coals and watched them burst into flame. With each one she wondered if anyone had seen the condemning pants under her back stoop. With each one she shivered in memory of the desperate blow she had struck with Kiyoko-san's sword. With each croaking of a frog or chirrup of an evening cricket, she jumped, fearing that someone would find her burning the evidence of her fatal crime.

The Allies were using the Hollandia airfields by April 25. Their unsuccessful bombing raids, which Iris had mocked, had lulled the Japanese into thinking they were out of reach of a real Allied air strike. Within a week hundreds of bombers and their fighter escorts darkened the sun and destroyed all Japanese equipment and troops around Hollandia.

However, the fields at Hollandia were not big enough to handle all the bomber operations that the Allied command had in mind. Fighters were based on the Hollandia fields and bold thrusts were made to gain other fields for the bombers on islands like Wakde and Biak and Owi to the north of Hollandia. Port Moresby, Woodlark Island, and even Dobodura were now considered too far south to be of much use. The Allies were on their way to Tokyo.

Cole didn't think there could be a more beautiful location for a base anywhere in the world than scenic Hollandia. There was a six-thousand-foot high mountain mass called Cyclops just to the north of Sentani Lake, separating it from the ocean. The camp was about half a mile up the slopes and looked down on the shining blue waters of the lake, which wound twenty miles back through the verdant jungled hills of

New Guinea. Cone-shaped green islands dotted the lake and stilted native houses straddled the shore. About two miles behind the camp was a spectacular five-hundred-foot waterfall springing from the brow of Cyclops Mountain, misting the dark jungle with rainbows dancing in the sunlight.

The Americans had covered the area with a new insecticide called DDT. It was so effective that they no longer had to eat their meals with the "New Guinea salute" to wave away the fat flies. The huge mosquitoes were not as persistent, either. The old joke that one of the mosquitoes landed at the end of the runway and was completely fueled up before the ground crew noticed their mistake was no longer applicable. Now, they just referred to the mosquitoes that carried away the Japanese bodies at night.

Dick leaned across the bunk and switched off the radio. Cole popped the cap off a warm bottle of beer they'd smuggled in from Australia. "I just can't figure it out," Cole said glumly. "We haven't heard Iris and Jake's Sunday program in almost two months—since the middle of April. What's happened?"

"Hard to tell. Maybe they were caught. Maybe they're sick. Maybe they just don't have anything to say. Then again, maybe the Japanese decided that the program was just too popular with the troops."

Cole drained his bottle. "That's one of the hardest things about war," he said finally. "The not knowing."

"Hey, Major Tennyson," a voice called from outside the tent. "We've got a surprise for you."

A young second lieutenant from one of Cole's commands stuck his head in the tent flap. "What is it, Daley, another of your bootlegged whiskey bottles?"

"No, sir; this one talks," he said, coming in, followed by another pilot from his group. "Thought you might like him," he said, holding out a white cockatoo. "One of the crew brought him up from down under."

The bird was perched on a wooden swing and seemed quite accustomed to attention. He turned his head almost completely around, blinked, swallowed once, then opened his beak and said, "Damn the Japs! Damn the Japs!"

"Isn't that great?" Lieutenant Daley beamed.

The bird's cry only made Cole's worries more poignant.

"Yeah," he murmured. "Thanks . . . but you'd better figure out how to feed him."

"We already worked that out, sir. There's a sack of feed from Brisbane outside the door. When you're gone, we'll just sort of pass him around the group. He'll be like our mascot."

"Does he have a name?" Cole asked, fingering the bird's feathers.

"Not that we know of. Got a suggestion?"

"How about Jake?" Dick cut in.

Cole looked at him sharply, then nodded. "Yeah. Not a bad idea. It might bring us some luck. I've always thought that was a lucky name."

"Jake it is, then," Daley said, setting the bird's stand down between the cots. "Want some beer?" he added. "We got some warm stuff just outside."

Cole shook his head and forced a smile. "Go ahead and get started, Daley. I was just on my way out. I'll join you when I get back."

He stepped out of the tent and walked up the hill behind the camp. Below, he could see the twinkling lights reflected on the lake. The stars were bright overhead. He walked to a log and sat down. The jungle was filled with the sharp trill of lizards calling to one another. The foliage rustled behind him. He knew he shouldn't be out alone at night. There were still too many stray Japanese soldiers. But he didn't care. A heavy depression was settling over him. He hadn't heard Iris's voice in almost two months. In the distance, the bird, Jake, raised his voice once more: "Damn the Japs! Damn the Japs!"

CHAPTER XXIV

Iris wasn't surprised that Bill wasn't in the house when she returned. His comings and goings were always erratic. She had been so unnerved by the discovery of Ito's trousers that

358

she couldn't eat dinner. She simply unpacked her things and took a sponge bath before going to bed. Bill would probably return in the morning, exhausted from some all-night job.

Once on her *futon*, she could only lie there listening to the distant sounds of the city, the rasp of frogs in the garden, and the movement of pine branches in the wind. A faint orange glow from the coals flickered on the white walls, reminding her of what she had just burned, haunting her. She felt helplessly alone.

Judging from the distant temple bell, it was nearly midnight, and Iris was just barely drowsy. Then she was suddenly alert, lying still and rigid as she heard the drunken singing of a man coming down their street. The voice got louder as it neared the gate. Ito had been drunk each time he'd come to the house. Were there other Kampetei officers who knew where she and Eva lived? The bell on the gate clanged and the tipsy voice reached uncertainly for a high note, then plunged back into the tavern song. He was coming up the path!

Iris slipped from under the covers and dashed to the other room. Still singing, the drunken intruder slid back the heavy wooden *amado,* then the screen in the entry. She reached up and slipped the sword from its sheath. She would not be caught like Eva, unarmed and helpless. If any drunk was coming in, he would find a surprise waiting for him. She stepped quickly into the cooking room and pressed her back against the wall.

Still singing, the man closed the *amado,* then slid the door closed behind him. Iris could see his shadow on the wall as he came into the living room. He looked big and clumsy, wearing workman's clothes. He stopped, looking at the glowing *konro*. Then, quietly taking off his coat, he slid back the door of the sleeping room. He was searching for her. She braced herself as he came out of the sleeping room and walked toward the cooking room.

"Iris?"

She stopped, the sword poised in midair. He struck a match and stooped to light a lantern. "Iris," he called, "where are you?"

Hearing the English words, she dropped the sword. "Bill?"

"What the hell are you doing?" he said, turning around and taking off his cap.

"Dammit!" she cried, tears of relief filling her eyes. "When are you going to stop scaring me half to death? Can't you let me know it's you, give me some warning or something?"

"Well, I thought bellowing at the top of my lungs all the way down the street was warning enough for you." He laughed softly. "Although now that I've seen what could happen, I think I'll throw my hat in before I come in the door next time. You're getting pretty handy with that thing. Are you bucking for samurai status?"

Iris looked at the sword at her feet and shuddered, then picked it up and gingerly put it back in its scabbard on the wall. "I thought you were one of Ito's drunken friends coming for me."

Bill shrugged. "I didn't know when you were coming back, but I figured that your cousin from Nagoya would want to paint the town red the last couple of nights he had in Tokyo. My singing was for the benefit of the neighbors. That was the second concert I've given them. You should have heard last night's."

Iris giggled. "I'm glad you're here, even though you scared me. I missed you."

"That's something I'd given up hoping for," he said softly. "If you only knew how lovely you look in that white nightgown with your hair falling loose around your shoulders, you'd forgive me for feeling the way I do." He put his hands on her shoulders. "I missed you, too," he whispered, just before his lips covered hers.

There was no question this time. He held her as a lover and she welcomed his passionate embrace. She had been so alone, so frightened for so long. The warmth of his arms surrounded her, shutting out fears, protecting her from dangers real and imagined. She clung to him, losing herself in the heat of his kisses on her lips and throat. As his hands gently caressed her, the smoldering of desire spread through her, awakening longings long frozen by fear.

As if in a dream, she felt his sure-muscled arms lift her and carry her breathlessly to her *futon*. He was gentle and strong as he covered her with his protective love, filling her with the heat of his passion. A sound of joy escaped her throat as she eagerly joined her body with his.

The throbbing song of the rain frogs swelled in the cool spring night and the deep earthy smell of the garden blended with the soft fragrance of May flowers. A light breeze slipped through the window and cooled their naked bodies as they lay on the *futon*, their legs entwined, the heat of their passion spent, the glow of their love still holding them together. A shaft of moonlight slanted across the floor, lighting the clean angles of Bill's face as he lovingly ran his fingers through her hair.

"I called you a flower before I ever met you," he whispered. "The first time I ever saw you, you came at me with a hoe and I fell helplessly in love with you right then. I've tried— God, I've tried—but I haven't been able to get you out of my mind. Who would imagine there could be a woman so brave, so smart, so beautiful . . . ?" He shook his head in wonder. "I never thought I could feel this way for someone, never thought I would want any attachments, never thought there was anyone who could understand what makes me run . . . then I found you, running too."

Iris touched his cheek with her fingertips. "We've only got each other," she murmured. "That's all there is, just we two. . . ."

She woke the next morning to see him bending over the ashes in the *konro*, the early morning sun slanting across the angle of his jaw, lighting his expression of concentration. Then, seeing her awake, he came to the *futon* and held out his hand. "Metal buttons don't burn."

Iris shuddered and pulled back in revulsion at the sight of them. "I found Ito's trousers under the porch when I came home."

"I'll throw the buttons in the harbor when I go to work. You've got to be more careful," he said sternly. "If someone had found these here, it could have meant your life."

"I guess I wasn't thinking straight. It was such a shock to find them after the long trip home."

That morning Iris properly bowed farewell as her cousin from Nagoya went down the street, carrying his luggage. The neighborhood now knew that Iris was once more alone, that all was as it should be. That night, unseen by the neighbors, Iris's lover, Bill, slipped back into the house and into her waiting arms.

Iris's life was made disgracefully pleasant by Bill's presence. Despite the deprivations of war, missing Eva, the hard work and long hours, the ration lines and poor food, she felt truly happy for the first time since she'd come to Japan.

Although his schedule was still unpredictable, Bill somehow managed to see her daily, either in some surprising disguise or by slipping into her house after dark. He became her one reason for living, the reason she left work with a light step and hurried home expectantly. In his arms, the looming shadow of starvation or burning death in an air raid seemed a mere figment of her loneliness. In his voice she found strength and reason; in his eyes she saw the love she thought she would never know again.

It was June 10, the day before she and Jake were to make their first broadcast since Jake's recovery from his long illness. They'd worked long and hard on the script. Not having any real information to convey, they'd spent their energy on keeping the propaganda messages light and as subtly humorous as they dared. The Japanese had wanted a venomous attack on the operations in the islands off the northern tip of New Guinea, where the Allies were struggling to establish a base to augment the one they'd finally obtained in Hollandia.

After much deliberation over the suggestions from Tsuneishi, Iris came up with the idea of mispronouncing the names of the islands, Noemfoor, Owi, Biak, to give a subtle message of encouragement and perhaps a laugh to the troops. With much work, she and Jake hoped she would be able to turn the script words, "The Japanese won't forget Noemfoor or Owi. You'll give Biak to the Japanese in the end," into what might sound to a Yank's ear like, "The Japanese won't forget. Know 'em for the owie you give back to the Japanese." They also were going to include a story of Japanese bravery, ending with the punch line, "The crew all returned to home base in excellent spirits, except for the fifteen dead." It was the best they could do with the script they were being forced to write and read. It was an exhausting day, practicing the lines so they could be said with just the right speed and intonation, but they finished with a feeling of accomplishment.

When she returned home, Iris was not surprised to find the house empty, but she was disappointed when it came time to go to bed and she was still alone. It was at times like this when she once more began hearing strange noises.

She crawled under the quilts, feeling the dampness of the rain in the chill of her *futon*. The coals burned in the *konro*, reflecting a thin glow onto the white screen separating the sleeping room from the main room. She closed her eyes, trying not to wonder where Bill was, trying not to worry. She had barely drifted off to sleep when a soft rustle made her awaken with a start.

"Don't worry," Bill murmured softly, "I'm just getting in." He lifted the covers and slid in next to her, his arms pulling her eagerly to him, his lips kissing her roughly. "God, I missed you," he said.

"This house can be pretty lonely without you, too," Iris answered. "What's put you in such a good mood?"

"The Allies have invaded France. They called it D-Day; thousands of troops landed on the west coast of Normandy. They're fighting their way through France, with Paris as their next stop."

"That sounds encouraging," Iris said, leaning on her elbow to watch Bill's animated face in the half-glow of the night.

"You bet. The sooner they take care of their white brothers in Europe, the sooner the Yanks will turn around and clean up the Pacific."

Iris could barely contain her rising hope. "How does Christmas back home sound?"

"Pretty good, but it might not be quite that soon. I'd settle for hearing that the Yanks are eating Thanksgiving dinner in the Philippines."

"You think we're that close?"

He shook his head. "I honestly don't know. Part is educated guessing and part is that naïve hope that seems to pop up more and more now that I'm with you." With that he pulled her to him, running his hand down the length of her body and pulling her nightgown up over her head. "For now," he said, nuzzling her breast, "I'd rather spend my time thinking about present joys."

They overslept the next morning and Iris had to hurry out into the warm rain with barely a word and a quick kiss for Bill. As she headed out the door he said, "Don't forget to tell Jake about D-Day!"

While a record of the Andrews Sisters singing "Ferryboat Serenade" played, Iris told Jake about the Allied invasion of France.

He leaned back in his chair, his thin face barely daring to take on a look of hope. "You say they're making progress?" he asked, then added with his old cynical tone, "I suppose the Hun will be taken care of within a couple of years and then they'll consider what's been going on in their own backyard."

Iris shook her head. "No. Bill says that they're making good progress. They should be able to get a German surrender within the year, surely no later than spring of forty-five."

Jake curled his lip and glanced away. "Come on," Iris pleaded. "You know the Yanks are headed straight for the Philippines right now."

"Well, they're getting there a little late for me," he said gruffly, then succumbed to another fit of coughing. Iris watched the record with a wary eye, fearful that Jake's cough would lapse into the air time when the record stopped. He was still frail from his bout with pneumonia and hadn't been able to shake the persistent cough, which weakened him. He handed her the script, indicating that she was to announce the next record in his place, while he stepped out of the broadcasting booth, closing the door on his coughs.

She lifted the needle and read Jake's lines announcing the next record. "And now for all you soldiers out there sweltering in the jungles, Jimmy Dorsey and his Orchestra will join with Bob Eberly on vocal, singing 'The Breeze and I.' "

When she'd started the record, Jake opened the door and came back in, his face pale from the exertion of the coughing. He sipped a cup of lukewarm tea and said, "Thanks for covering for me."

"I just wish I could do more to help."

"Ah, don't worry. I'm just depressed. I know the news is pretty good. Now all we have to do is hold on and see if we can last until they get here."

When Dick sent word to Cole to come down to Brisbane, Cole hitched a ride on a C-47, grateful for the chance to see Dick and get an idea of what HQ was planning next.

"What's up?" Cole asked when Dick met him at the hotel.

"Some big planning is going on at HQ. Right now they're talking about moving into Mindanao on November fifteenth, after Nimitz takes Palau at the end of September. However, there's some discussion that maybe Mindanao isn't the place for us to go. They're wondering if there's an alternative landing place in the Philippines." With a tight smile, he accepted Cole's offer of a glass of Scotch. "I got to thinking about the code you had with Jake and his pals in the Philippines. Can you think of any way of getting in contact with them?"

"Not offhand. There's sure to be someone who must have learned some of our code. At least I'd think so. But how would we get a message to them? Are there subs still taking occasional runs into the guerrillas in Leyte?"

"Yes, but those are pretty few and far between."

They were quiet, thinking through the problem for several minutes. Finally, Dick said, "You know, we have a shortwave propaganda radio program of our own. It's in English mostly, aimed at the prisoners and the people caught behind the lines. They say it reaches clear to Tokyo. What about trying that?"

"Might be worth a try."

"Well, come on then," Dick said, setting his glass down on the table by the bed. "You haven't been worth much since the Tokyo Rose broadcasts have been mostly pablum."

Cole picked up his jacket and grinned. "Yeah, but I've been worth a lot more to myself since I started hearing her voice again. I wonder what kept her quiet for so long."

Bill had been gone for a week on some mission in the countryside. Iris was exhausted and terribly lonely. She spent long hours in the garden and in the ration lines. Her hands were rough and callused from the work, her back ached, and still she couldn't sleep at night for all the sounds and imagined dangers that crowded her mind. The work at the station was getting more difficult. Besides her own program, she was given scripts to edit for other programs. Jake still had his cough, and there had been a couple of Sundays when they had not been able to broadcast because he had lost his voice. Luckily, there had been no urgent messages Bill had wanted transmitted. But if it kept up, Iris was sure that Tsuneishi would line up another announcer for her to work with.

After all, she thought as she lay in bed, listening to the rustle of the warm night breeze, it was probably best that they not fool around with the broadcasts too much anyway. The less they did, the less chance of being caught.

Just then her thoughts were interrupted by the shriek of the air-raid siren. It had been at least two weeks since they'd last had a night drill. She jumped up, threw her *yukata* on over her nightgown, and went out to the backyard air-raid shelter. The air was warm and muggy even though it was nearly midnight, typical late August heat. She'd just reached the entry of the shelter when she remembered the lantern. She wasn't about to crawl in there alone without checking first to see that she was alone. Turning around, she ran back to the house, lit the lantern, then dashed back to the shelter. The siren was still screaming. She strained her ears to listen for the dull roar of approaching planes. Nothing.

Moments after she was inside the shelter, the door opened and the warden looked in, grunted his approval, and went on his rounds. She remained there, sitting in the dark, musty earth, musing about the discomforts of war.

The door of the shelter opened suddenly and a shaft of light beamed in her face. "Do you have your hoe with you?" Bill asked.

"Get in here before you're seen!"

"Nobody's around," he said, coming in and taking her in his arms. "I watched the warden leave. Mmmm," he murmured, kissing her and nuzzling her hair. "I've missed you."

"You too," she whispered.

"How soon do you plan on going back to get Eva?" he asked, sitting down with his arm around her.

"I don't know. I know that she's probably safer out on the farm right now. I don't have enough money to take the train down to get her. Besides," she added, leaning her head on his shoulder, "I'm afraid that we wouldn't have any privacy if she comes back. Isn't that an awful thing to say?"

"Not at all. That's the biggest disadvantage. But I think you'd better leave first thing tomorrow and go get her."

"Why, what's wrong?"

"I stopped by the farmhouse of one of my contacts while I was gone," he said, lighting a cigarette. "He has a hidden radio that picks up the States and sometimes Australia. He heard a strange message from Australia two days ago. It gave some ball scores that didn't match up with what he had heard on the stateside radio and something funny about Leo Durocher. Since that station will be broadcasting the same program again within the week, I was hoping we could get Eva back at Domei to listen."

"If she's well enough to do it, I'm sure she'd try."

"Well, go down to the station tomorrow and talk to Jake. He's the one who had the code worked out. I'll be selling baskets again outside the NHK when you get off work. If it sounds like we'd better check it out, buy one from me. I'll give you your ticket money when I give you your change. You can go straight to the station from there and make it to your aunt's late tonight. You'll have two days to get back. That'll allow us a day to get Eva back at Domei."

When Iris whispered Bill's message to Jake, she knew from the expression on his face that she would be traveling that night. "Leo Durocher was the name that kept me from shooting Cole one night in Bataan." He looked at Iris's face. She was barely able to breathe. "Don't hope too much," he added. "Cole could have told Dick about that, as well as any number of other people, because we used it as a code name in my broadcasts from the Philippines."

Iris needed the train and bus ride by herself to think. She had been extremely excited since Jake had given her hope that Cole was still alive. Still, when she'd seen Bill outside the NHK Building that evening, she'd felt a wrench inside her that she couldn't explain. She felt confused, her emotions torn. Was it possible to love two men at the same time? It was something she didn't dare think about . . . yet.

The warm welcome she received from Aunt Suki was a soothing balm. However, when Aunt Suki noticed that Iris only had a small bag, she immediately began scolding her; she wanted Iris to stay there permanently.

Eva was sleeping and Aunt Suki wouldn't allow Iris to awaken her. Eva was still weak, and Aunt Suki didn't feel that she should leave her care. Iris explained that without Eva's salary, they wouldn't be able to keep their house, much less buy food. To soothe her aunt's feelings, Iris promised to stay one more night.

It was glorious to wake to the sun streaming in the window and a rooster crowing outside. Eva was already downstairs, sitting in the sunshine, drinking a glass of fresh milk. She was delighted to see Iris, but Iris was concerned the minute she saw Eva.

Eva was still frail-looking. Although the two months of country sunshine had given her pale skin a slight rosy tinge and she had put on some weight, she still didn't look strong. However, when Iris told her why she'd come, Eva insisted on going home immediately. They must do what they could to end the war.

The flash of spirit in her eyes gave Iris hope that her friend was on the road to full recovery. The following day they took the early morning bus. Eva insisted that she felt fine and didn't want to stop overnight with her grandfather in Yokohama. Even though Eva's pale face and shaky hands worried Iris, she agreed to catch the train leaving immediately for Tokyo. In just forty minutes they arrived at the Tokyo station. By that time, Iris was sufficiently worried about Eva to insist on hiring a cab with the last few yen she had.

"I don't know if she's strong enough to go back to work," Iris told Bill after Eva had immediately collapsed on her *futon* and gone to sleep.

Bill shook his head. "She doesn't look good. Maybe just a couple of days will be all she can do, but that might be all we need." He got up and looked in the bag Iris was unpacking. "I think I'd like to meet your Aunt Suki. That looks like real butter down there under those vegetables."

"And eggs and a chicken all ready for the pot." Iris laughed. "I suppose that means you have plans for dinner tomorrow night?"

"Yeah—I'll bring the wine . . . French import okay with you?"

Bill had left long before daylight and Eva slept soundly until the sun was high in the sky. Iris opened the main part of the house to allow any breezes to cool it before the heat of the day. She then went out to the garden to harvest and slice any ripened vegetables for drying. She had been working for about an hour when she heard Eva calling from the back porch.

"Now I know I'm really back home," she said with a lilt of laughter. "The only thing missing is you nagging me to get out there and do my share."

Iris stood up and brushed the dirt from her hands. "Don't be silly," she said, "you always did more than your share. I have a pot of tea ready for you on the *konro*. And Gertrude laid a large egg in celebration of your return; I'll come in and fix it for you."

Eva smiled. "You're just trying to feed me and make me strong so I can get to work at Domei today."

"Am I that obvious?" Iris laughed as she came into the

house. "Actually, it's not only the information that Bill's desperate for—we could use the money as well. I wouldn't have been able to make it on just my paycheck these past two months. Luckily, Bill's been awfully kind."

"Judging from the look on your face, I think he's been more than kind."

Iris smiled sheepishly, but her reply was interrupted by the ringing of the gate bell.

It was old Mrs. Okimoto, who did their laundry. She bowed her greeting and said, "I understand that Eva has returned home. Mr. Kawasaki saw you bringing her in late last night."

"Yes, Mrs. Okimoto," Iris said with a bow. "She will be honored to know that you noticed. Please come in and let her thank you."

Mrs. Okimoto shuffled behind Iris into the main room, where Eva was sitting sipping her morning tea.

"I came to tell you that it brings us great joy that you have returned in better health," Mrs. Okimoto said, accepting a cup of tea. "You have both always been so kind to us, bringing us our groceries and always including something for the child which we know we did not give you money for. This gift is for both of you," she said, handing Eva a package wrapped in tissue paper and tied with a red string.

Eva bowed. "*Arigato gozaimasu*," she said gratefully. "We are not worthy of such an honor."

Mrs. Okimoto bowed in return. "The present is not so much. But please, open it now."

With a smile, Eva untied the string. The glimmer of a deep emerald silk kimono, embroidered with copper and red, met her eyes. "How lovely!" Eva said, holding it up.

"The other is yours," Mrs. Okimoto said to Iris.

Iris looked down and saw the shimmering sapphire of a silk kimono with delicate embroidery of silver and green. Iris was speechless as she held it up. "Mrs. Okimoto," she said finally, "these are the most beautiful I've ever seen."

"Yes, they are lovely. They belonged to my daughter-in-law's mother. She wishes you to have them in thanks from my grandson for all the kindness you've shown us over the past two years. When you were gone, we realized the empty space you left in our lives."

She paused, looking sharply at Eva. "Now that I see you, I

know that you've been very sick. You still have a long way to go before you are completely well. I have some healthful herbs that I will send over. Perhaps they will give you strength."

Eva bowed. "Please don't worry yourself over my health. I'm not worthy of such an honor."

"You have taught many in this neighborhood a good lesson," Mrs. Okimoto said bluntly. "You have shown us the goodness to be found in all people, even those whom we've been told are our enemies. We know that Kiyoko-san was very wise in adopting you and taking you for her own. We see in Kiyoko-san's death how very much you loved her and how much she loved you. You are one of our own now."

Both Eva and Iris were deeply touched by Mrs. Okimoto's words. Their eyes were filled with tears as they bowed deeply and long. Iris finally murmured, "The honor is all ours. May we always be worthy of your trust and affection."

Mrs. Okimoto had been gone only a few minutes when the gate bell rang again. It was Mr. Kawasaki, offering to give Eva a lift to the *densha* stop in his handcart. Iris knew that Eva was still quite weak, and the ride in the handcart would save her the exhausting walk up the hill. However, she was afraid that Eva might remember the use to which they had put that same handcart that fateful evening five months ago. But Eva smiled brightly, thanked Mr. Kawasaki, and accepted his offer. Iris sighed with relief. Mercifully, Eva had forgotten.

Iris spent the afternoon standing in the ration lines, buying groceries for her neighbors and what few things she could afford for her and Eva. She caught the late bus home.

As she walked up the path, she smelled chicken cooking over charcoal. Surely Eva wasn't well enough after her first day of work to cook dinner. She'd have to have a talk with her about pushing herself too far too soon.

However, her worries were unfounded. Eva, pale and tired, was sitting on a pillow near the screen opened to the cool evening breeze from the garden. Bill was the one doing culinary magic with Aunt Suki's chicken. She put her *furoshiki* on the counter and turned to Eva. "Well, how did it go? Did they take you back?"

Eva smiled faintly. "I guess it went fine. They're always so shorthanded there, so I was put right to work. But I'm so tired, I think I'll go straight to bed without any dinner."

"You must be kidding," Iris said with disbelief.

"Sorry, kiddo," Bill said firmly, "no one's leaving this room until they've reassured me that I'm a wonderful cook."

"Couldn't I just take your word for it?" Eva pleaded.

Bill looked concerned. Eva's face had an eerie, translucent white look to it. Iris's heart sank at the realization of how ill she was.

"Here," Bill said softly, handing her a bowl of vegetable broth. "It'll give you some strength. I'll have a tender piece of this bird all ready for you in just a minute. You've got to build up your strength, Eva."

Iris looked at Bill with sudden decision. "I don't care how badly you want that information or how badly we need the money. I won't allow Eva to go back to work. She's just not strong enough."

"We don't need her to work for the message," Bill said. "She got it today. It's on that piece of paper." He gestured toward the counter.

"Fine, then I'll send word down to Domei tomorrow that Eva won't be able to work for at least another month. . . ." She stopped suddenly. "You know, maybe I could work there for two or three hours in the morning. That way, we wouldn't be so desperate for her to go back to work."

"Iris, you can't hold down two jobs," Eva protested weakly.

"I didn't say a full shift, just a couple of hours or so. Besides, I'd like the experience."

"Why don't you look at that message?" Bill cut in.

"I'm afraid that I know very little of the actual code. The part that has to do with ball scores is still in Jake's head."

"Then make sure you get it down tomorrow," he said curtly.

"Well, I don't see why you're so hot under the collar all of a sudden."

Bill lifted the chicken off the grill and put it on a lacquered tray. "I'm sorry. All I can think of is how sick Jake has been. We could lose everything if something happens to him."

"Well, nothing's going to happen to him," Iris said sharply.

"Maybe things are getting to me more than I realize," he said apologetically. Then he looked at Eva. She had fallen asleep.

Iris gently shook her. "Come on, Eva," she murmured. "Please eat with us. Eat something."

Eva shook her head mournfully. "I can't, Iris. I really can't." Tears filled her eyes. "I feel so tired. Just let me sleep, please."

Iris looked at Bill; he shook his head sorrowfully. "Sure, kid," he whispered. "I'll help get you to bed." He carried her into the sleeping room and Iris helped her undress.

When she came out, her throat was tight and she couldn't speak.

"It's too bad she couldn't eat anything," Bill said. When Iris didn't reply, he added, "She'll probably feel better in the morning. She's had a big day. We'll save some chicken for her breakfast."

Iris was too upset to eat more than a few bites. Something was very wrong, and she didn't know what to do.

The next morning when Iris looked in on Eva, she was even more concerned. Her sleep seemed sound enough, but her face had a strange yellowish look, reminiscent of when she was in the hospital. Bill offered to stay with Eva while Iris reported to work. Once she'd passed the message on to Jake, she would say she felt ill and hurry home.

Bill greeted her at the door when she hurried up the walk in mid-afternoon. "She woke up with a terrific stomachache," he said worriedly. "Mrs. Okimoto came and gave her some kind of herb tea, which seemed to help, but now she seems worse than ever. I don't know what to do."

Iris dashed into the sleeping room and found Eva curled in a tight ball, perspiration dripping from her yellowish forehead. She was kneading her stomach with her fists in a painfully familiar gesture. Iris knew immediately: she'd had another attack of the infection. "Where's the sulfa I sent with you to Aunt Suki's?" she asked Eva. "You're having another attack. We've got to get it into your system quickly."

Eva shook her head, tears flowing down the hollows of her cheeks.

"All gone? The doctor gave you a whole bunch. How could it be gone?"

"That's why I agreed to come back," she whispered. "I can't go for more than four or five days without another attack . . . hitting me. I've taken the whole supply. . . . You'll have to get some more from the doctor."

Quickly explaining to Bill, Iris left for the hospital. It took her a while to track down the overworked Dr. Higa. When she'd explained the situation, the doctor slowly shook his head. "I'm sorry," he said softly in English. "It's a miracle that she's lived this long. I have no more sulfa. The supply you found lasted barely a week. There's been no more available. I understand that they don't even have enough for the front now."

"She's in terrible pain. Can you give her something else to stop the infection?"

He shook his head again. "The fatality rate of that kind of injury is over eighty percent even with the best of facilities. It's a miracle that she survived this long. We are very low on morphine, but if you wish to bring her here to die, I will try to find enough to make her death peaceful."

"Her death?" Iris gasped. "What kind of a doctor are you? You're supposed to heal people."

He bowed his head. "I understand your anger. I feel much the same when I am made so helpless. Please try to understand. Actually, I think you might consider the fact that it would be very expensive to bring her here. She will die within a day either way. I'm sorry." He bowed politely and turned to go.

Iris stood there, stunned. Eva couldn't die. She just couldn't.

Angrily wiping away her tears, she took the *densha* home. Instead of going straight to the house, she stopped off at Mrs. Okimoto's and asked if she knew of any way to stop Eva's infection. "The herbs you gave her this morning seemed to have eased her pain," Iris said. "That's why I thought you might know of something that might actually cure her."

Mrs. Okimoto shook her head mournfully. "My herbs are old folk medicine. Sometimes they are too weak against such a *jubyo*, serious disease, as our poor Eva suffers. But we shall try." She rummaged through a wooden cupboard, then came back with two paper packets. "Take these and make a strong tea from them each. Not together. This one," she said, pointing to the larger packet, "will make her sleep without pain. The other one may or may not fight the evil of her *byoki*."

Iris bowed deeply and said, "*Arigato gozaimasu*." Then she dashed home. Bill's face was tight with concern. From the other room, Iris could hear a low groaning. "She's been like that for over an hour," he said. "She's got a raging fever and seems to be delirious."

"Let's try this," Iris said, taking out the packets of herbs.

"Mrs. Okimoto said one will help her sleep without pain and the other might help the infection."

"Where's the sulfa?"

"There's none at the hospital. Could you try to find some on the dock again?"

"There hasn't been a medical ship leaving the port for over two weeks. There's just nothing there. I'm sorry."

Iris bent over the boiling kettle, trying to hide her tears. "Then we'll just have to put our faith in Mrs. Okimoto's herbs."

"What did the doctor have to say?" Bill asked softly.

"He's a quack!" Iris snapped. "He doesn't know what he's talking about. He's a mean, stupid . . ." Her voice trailed off as she reached for the teapot handle, and then broke down in deep, gasping sobs. Bill put his arms around her and just held her, gently rocking, soothing her with his presence. Finally, Iris's sobs slowed and she heard Eva moan loudly from the other room. "He . . . he said she's going to die," she whispered. Then, reaching for the teapot once more, she filled two cups and stirred in the herbs, making a pungent broth in one cup and a sweetish grass-smelling liquid in the other. "What he didn't count on," she said, taking a deep breath, "is Mrs. Okimoto's herbs."

Iris held Eva's head while she sipped the two cups of tea. Then, still cradling her head, Iris gently wiped the perspiration from her sallow brow and brushed the moist strands of hair off her face. Eva's eyes closed and her body slowly relaxed as she drifted off to sleep. The herbs were working.

When Iris came out of the sleeping room, she had regained her self-control. Seeing Eva sleeping had given her hope and strength. Bill held out his arms and Iris sat down beside him, resting her head on his shoulder.

"War works in evil ways," she murmured. "If it wasn't for the war, Eva wouldn't be sick, Kiyoko-san would be alive, and we'd be home. Even Ito would be alive."

"Why do you think that? There's no battlefield here."

"In a way there is. It was war that brought all those awful pressures that made Ito explode into that crazy person. I never thought I'd say this, but I almost feel sorry for him. But I hate him, too. I'm glad I killed him. I hate him and the war that made him, the war that's hurting Eva right now. War makes things all twisted and evil, even when the bullets aren't flying over our heads. It makes people crazy. And the killing just keeps going on. Sometimes it's with bombs and sometimes it's with the evil corruption that war breeds. It's all the same. It's sickness, starvation, death, cruelty—everything that's evil. I feel as if it's smothering me in its evil."

Bill held her tightly. "I think you're right, my flower. At first I thought it was going to be a great adventure. Before it all began, it seemed like I could be a hero, prove my worth as an American. I thought that the nobility of America would shine through and like knights on white chargers the brave military would ride to the rescue, slaying the Japanese dragon. That's the kind of thinking that made the war in the first place. No matter what the movies or the books say, war isn't noble; it's not brave or manly; it's not even the conquest of evil. It's evil itself. And the most beautiful, true, and brave are the ones who are hurt the most."

"Like Kiyoko-san and Jake's wife . . . and . . . and maybe Eva . . . and . . ."

"And Cole," Bill said with understanding.

Iris clung to him, her tears wetting his shirt.

Iris got up once during the night and made the herb teas for Eva again. She was too weak to sit up, so Iris propped up her frighteningly light body and held the cups to her lips. Then she mercifully slipped back into her drugged sleep. Iris decided to make the rounds of all the hospitals in the city in the morning. Maybe the doctor was wrong. . . .

The next morning, she got up with the first light and made the teas for Eva. As they steeped, she went in to check on her. She was lying peacefully. In the pale blue light of morning, she didn't look quite so yellow. Iris sat down beside her, waiting for her to awaken, stroking her cool forehead softly.

Then suddenly she bent down and looked more carefully, touching Eva's throat with her fingertips.

"*Nooool*" she cried, throwing her arms around Eva's limp body.

Bill came dashing into the room, bleary-eyed from sleep.

"She's . . . she's dead!" Iris cried. Then she fell to the floor, sobbing uncontrollably.

The final thread tying Iris to her American childhood was severed. Eva died, taking with her their shared laughter, the days of dressing up in front of her mother's mirror, staying up late talking about boys, whispered secrets over Cokes and mutual awe at their budding womanhood. Eva was gone. Tender, gentle, shy, understanding Eva, killed by an invisible evil so powerful that it had the entire world gripped in its tentacles.

Bill arranged for the funeral. It was Mrs. Okimoto who suggested that Eva be placed in Kiyoko's family plot behind the little white Catholic church. The entire neighborhood mourned, but Iris couldn't remember anything for the next week. Eva's grandfather came all the way from Yokohama for the funeral, solemnly bowed to Iris, and departed without a word.

It was a fu¹ week before Iris found out that Mrs. Okimoto had given Bill some herbs to put in her tea that would act as a sedative. She was too stunned, too grief-stricken, to care. She knew she must go on, but she didn't know how.

CHAPTER XXV

The late summer heat was oppressive, making Iris's thin cotton dress stick to her skin. She stopped in the shade of an acacia tree and wiped her forehead with her wilted handkerchief, then proceeded up the street to Grandmother's house.

Bill had had to leave on one of his trips the day after the funeral. The farewell rites were over, but still Iris felt incomplete. It was not yet final. There was one more thing to do, one more rite of death: the duty of announcing that a loved one had died, the confirmation of loss in the eyes of others. Iris was turning to her family.

She opened the familiar heavy gate. The ring of the bell was muted in the hot humid air. *Asemi*, cicada, pierced the fabric of the woolen air with its stitching song. The muffled patter of midday traffic crept from beyond the neighborhood buffer, while the house was wrapped in warm, drowsy silence, mute to her announcing bell.

Finally, when still no one came, Iris called, "*Gomen kudesai*."

Aunt Toshiko answered the door. "Ah, Iris-san," she said, bowing. "How good of you to come to us."

"It is my honor, *Oba-san*," Iris said, returning the bow. She followed her aunt down the shadowed *tatami* corridor to the sitting room where Grandmother sat.

Aunt Toshiko knelt to open the screen. "Your granddaughter has come," she announced to Grandmother.

"*Subarashii wa!*" came Grandmother's voice. "Bring my *Ichihatsu no hana* in to me," she commanded, using the pet name she'd given Iris, the Japanese word for a wall iris.

Bowing to her grandmother, Iris felt a glow of love for this dear old woman whom she'd come to know and appreciate. "I wish you well, honored Grandmother," Iris murmured.

Grandmother's black hair was veined with gray and pulled back into a loose bun. As she smiled and bowed, wrinkles of pleasure pleated her eyes. A faint smell of jasmine drifted from the folds of her dark blue kimono. "Yes, you come to bring light to an old woman's darkness," she said approvingly. "You are too thin," she proclaimed as her sharp brown eyes inspected Iris. "Toshiko, bring tea and food," she commanded. "Bring *miso*. She is too thin."

Iris tried to hide the grimace she normally made when faced with bean-paste soup. "Please, just a little," she said when Aunt Toshiko brought out the bowl. "I ate lunch before coming."

Then, as she sat stoically sipping the *miso*, her aunt and grandmother chatted casually about the weather, air raids, and how the garden was doing. Beyond the back porch, Iris could see Aunt Teiso working in the garden with her seven-year-old son, Massaki, nine-year-old niece, Hanako, and six-year-old nephew, Matsuko. The children were thin, but their sun-browned skin rippled over sinewy muscles. It was a scene of tranquility, an oasis of rural peace in the middle of the city. Iris felt as if the ragged edges of her worn emotions were being gently smoothed.

Turning her attention back to the room, she replied to Grandmother's question. "*Hai, Oba-a-san*, I'm still working at NHK. They have a program each Sunday evening which I help to write and broadcast."

"You must be doing very well for them to keep you on the

same program for so very long," Grandmother said. "And what about Eva? Is she still working at Domei?"

Iris had been so lulled by the serenity of Grandmother's home that she'd blocked out the reason for her visit. Shocked back into reality by Grandmother's question, she murmured, "Eva died four days ago. She had an infection inside which wouldn't go away. There was no medicine available to help her." Iris looked into the sunlight, blinking to keep back her tears, trying desperately not to embarrass her grandmother with American emotionalism.

There was a brief silence, broken at last by Grandmother, who said simply, "It is better to be a cherry blossom than a withered winter apple." Grandmother then looked at Aunt Toshiko and nodded; Aunt Toshiko went out to the garden. When she returned, Aunt Teiso was with her.

Iris was surprised to see the red, puffy look of Aunt Teiso's thin face. She bowed her greetings and took a bowl of tea for herself.

"The fragrance of sorrow fills the air," Grandmother said to Aunt Teiso. "Eva, who helped bring Iris to us from the United States, has died."

"The flowers of summer are the most blessed," Aunt Teiso said quietly. "It is their scent filling the air. They bloom in the good times and are gone before the bitter frost." She turned to Iris. "Your grandmother's son and my husband, your uncle Kuni, has been granted such an honor. He has gloriously given his life to the honor of the Emperor by fighting valiantly on Saipan Island."

She held her head high, her face muscles taut and smooth, her hands still upon her lap. Only the unspent tears swelling her normally placid face and the bitter glint in her eye told Iris of the pain Aunt Teiso bore. Iris remembered Uncle Kuni's brusque officiousness, barely covering the gentle glance he reserved for Aunt Teiso. She remembered his children climbing over his lap, mindless of the dignity he sought to preserve, basking in his loving touch. Now he was dead, lying bloodied on the ground of some obscure island.

Iris turned her eyes to the garden. Two children, mischievous Massaki and thin, serious Mieko, were fatherless. Iris didn't know what to say, so she was silent.

"They are saying we should send the children to the countryside," Aunt Toshiko said, noting the direction of Iris's gaze. "They have schools and living quarters set up for them in several places. If we don't want that, they say we should send them to relatives in the country."

Hanako, the little girl, was singing as she pulled weeds, her reedy voice lacing the air like a playful breeze. "The house would be very quiet, if you do," Iris said softly, knowing that the children were the greatest joy of the family.

"Yes," Aunt Toshiko agreed. "Of course, Mieko-chan, who is now twelve and works most of the day in the paint factory, would have to stay. And Kibo-chan is too small to go; he too could also stay."

"Do you think there is danger of bombing?" Grandmother asked abruptly.

Iris looked down at her hands. "Yes, Grandmother, I do. The authorities are right. But then," she added quickly, noting their looks of despair, "I think we will have some warning. Maybe we can wait a little longer."

"Yes, just a little longer," Grandmother said with relief.

"But not too long," Iris added quickly, fearful that something might happen to the children. "What about my Aunt Suki?" she asked, suddenly brightening. "She's all alone on her farm and very lonely. It would make her happy to have you all go stay with her. The house is large enough and there's a big garden. When you finish your harvest here, you should take all the food and supplies you can find and go stay in Shizuoka with her."

Grandmother said quietly, "She is the sister of your mother and also the cousin of my husband. Perhaps we should send a message."

"I could never leave dear *Shutome-san*," Aunt Toshiko said, bowing respectfully to Grandmother.

"All of you must go," Iris insisted.

"I am too old and feeble to travel that distance. If I must die, it will be in my own home," Grandmother insisted. "But you have a good idea for us to consider, my granddaughter. If they all leave, you could come to live with me."

Iris paused. She would not have her privacy with Bill, but everyone's life might depend on her sacrifice. With Sergeant Ito out of the way, she could see no reason to believe that her presence would be a danger to her relatives, and obviously Grandmother felt the same. She smiled and bowed to her grandmother. "That is a pleasant circumstance to consider,

Oba-a-san. May we talk about it further when I come to visit you again?"

It would be nice to be with real family, she thought as she caught the *densha* and headed back to her empty house.

Four days later, Bill returned, tanned, hot, and weary from his travels in the countryside. He was particularly upset for some reason and Iris tried to cheer him by quickly laying out clean clothes and filling the tub in the *ofuro* with lukewarm water from the storage tank. Then, as she was scrubbing his back before he got into the tub, she asked, "What is it, Bill?"

"Nothing much," he said noncommittally. Then after a moment of reflective silence he said, "That's not true. You know, I used to be able to go for months without even wanting to talk to anyone about what was on my mind. Now I find myself thinking all the time, 'I wonder what Iris would say?' or 'I wonder what Iris would think about this?' You've spoiled me," he said, grinning over his sunburned shoulder. "Anyway, it's just one of the radio sets I have in a farmer's barn in the countryside. I'm not sure how I can recharge the battery. I don't seem to be getting through to the Philippines anymore."

"You can talk to the Philippines? Maybe I should tell Jake. It might make him feel better and you might be able to get some contacts from him."

"Don't say anything to anyone," Bill said sharply.

"I'm sorry. I wasn't thinking. You know I won't tell a soul."

Bill nodded and went on. "The other thing is a house I had on the other side of Tokyo. They're tearing down some areas they consider particularly dangerous fire hazards in potential bombing targets or strategic areas. I live in one of those neighborhoods in the guise of a part-time chauffeur for one of the army brass. Now I've got to find another place to set up my front. It's no big deal—I'm just tired of one thing after another fouling up my plans." He turned and took the sponge from her. "Here, let me scrub your back. You've been in the garden and could use a cool soak too."

"Tearing houses down . . . is it for a firebreak?" Bill nodded grimly. Iris slipped off her *yukata* and pinned up her hair. "That must be the same kind of thinking that's making them ship all the kids out to the countryside," she said. "I went to Grandmother's today; they're trying to decide if they should go along with the program."

"They'd better not wait too long," Bill warned. "The kids'll be a lot safer tucked away. Not that they'll be happy in some lousy barracks, eating thin gruel and marching goosestep up the hillsides to scour for firewood. It breaks your heart to see them. Mothers travel from the city to crouch in the bushes for just a glimpse of their children.

"C'mon, enough war talk. Let's play." He dumped the bucket over her head playfully.

A week after Eva's death, Iris received notice from Yakumo at NHK. She was to report for work the following day.

With no other choice, she reluctantly reported back to work on September 9, 1944. Jake was there, gentle and consoling when he heard about Eva. His cough was better and he said he'd missed her; but even more, he added as she handed him her lunch, he'd missed her fresh vegetables.

When they were in the booth timing and matching the records they planned to play with the script outline sent by Major Tsuneishi, Jake handed her a slip of paper. He'd figured out the code Eva had picked up from Australia at Domei News. Iris stared at it uncertainly, her heart in her throat, sensing its implications. The original message, which Iris had forgotten about until now, was written at the top of the paper:

The score from the American baseball game is:
  Dodgers 4 with 127 errors
  Yankees 3 with 128 errors
Yankee manager Leo Durocher was quoted as saying, "We'll get them next time by 4 or 6 runs. We just have to know where their weaknesses are and where to put the ball."
It sounds like the next Yankee/Dodger game will be a real thriller, especially when Leo Durocher gets his information straight.

Below the message, in Jake's handwriting was the key to its meaning:

Scores = latitude, errors = longitude
Dodgers = Japanese forces, Yankees = American forces
Leo Durocher = code name Cole and I used for identifica-

tion in the Philippines. Probably could be used now by
any others who were in on the radio net at that time.
Check map. "Leo" wants to know where to put the
Yankees next, at 4° or 6° latitude in the 127–128°
longitude area.

Iris looked up from the paper, her heart beating faster. Jake shrugged. "I don't know. It might be Cole." He turned back and picked up his script. "Not that it should matter for now. Don't think about it until this is over. Just don't get caught with that paper on you. Either memorize it or hide it. Now let's try to figure out how we can slip in whatever reply Bill tells us."

Iris folded the paper and quickly slipped it into her bra. Jake laughed. "Come on," he hooted, "that's the one place women always put things."

"It's also the last place a man will look." She reached over and took the script from Jake. "It seems we're supposed to lay on the propaganda pretty thick again this week. How're we going to avoid it this time?"

"Maybe we can't. That just might be the perfect place to slip in Bill's message."

That night Bill studied the message, then rummaged around through a parcel he'd brought with him. "I figured those numbers were something to do with maps, so I got a couple. Let's see," he said, running a slender finger across the map. "Japanese, 4° 127' means they are here, around the island south of the Philippines called Talaud. Americans 3° 128' means they're just south of the Japanese on the island of Morotai. Hm, they must be figuring on taking that soon, then." He paused. "That confirms the other information I've received. That part about four or six runs next time must mean that they want to know if they should try taking Talaud or skipping over it to Mindanao." He carefully folded his map and leaned back against the *zabuton*, lost in thought.

"Well," Iris said finally, "what should we say?"

"I'll have to check on a couple of things. I know that they have their reconnaissance flights, their guerrilla reports from the Philippines, their other spy sources. I assume that they're just asking what we see as the best route, where we've heard that the Japanese are expecting them to hit. What I'm thinking would be a surprise to everyone. I'll go out tonight and check a couple of sources. You'll have your message by tomorrow. Will that give you time to work it out?"

"I hope so. Be careful," she added as he got up and started out the door. He turned, and leaned down to give her a kiss.

"Don't worry," he said, touching her cheek. "I have a pretty good reason to come back in one piece."

But he didn't come back that night. Iris awoke with a start to see the sun streaming in the window. She spent the morning pacing and worrying about him. Finally, just before noon, he slipped in through the back garden, dirty and exhausted.

"There's a fairly big Japanese stronghold in Mindanao. And they have the advantage of having had a fully established community there in Davao since before the war," he explained as he washed his hands and face. "On the other hand, if you go farther up north, the little island of Leyte has a terrific organization of guerrillas. The Allies should consider that aspect of it. Leapfrog to where they'll be able to trap the Japanese between two enemy forces instead of just hitting them head-on. Maybe they could even form a pincer force from Palau if they effect a beachhead there in time. Whatever they do, they shouldn't fiddle around with individual islands like the navy's doing in the central Pacific. You waste time and lives doing that. Playing leapfrog—establishing a base and cutting off those Japanese bases caught behind so that they're starved out—is a tactic that makes the Japanese brass nervous as hell. They don't handle surprises well. The Allies have got to hit the Philippines somewhere, and my recommendation is Leyte."

He took the towel Iris held out to him and started drying his face. "Whatever they do, they can't skip over the Philippines. That'd be too big a nest of angry Japanese to have at their backs. Don't know how you're going to work all that into a broadcast. Do you?"

Iris laughed. "No, but give me a few minutes to think about it."

"Have you ever thought of using your name?"

"What for?"

"Well, it struck me as useful the first time I wrote it down on that envelope in Manila. I mean, not everyone has a name with military implications."

"Iris?"

"No." Bill laughed, pulling on a clean shirt. "Hashimoto. It means 'bridgehead,' you know."

"I guess I'd never thought about it. I'll mention it to Jake. But I don't see how that's going to be of much use."

"There are probably several people who have your name on file now. No matter what people come and go, military files usually stay."

Iris was quiet for a while, chewing on the end of her pencil and scribbling occasionally while Bill fixed his breakfast of rice with raw egg and soy sauce. She turned around finally. "Do you think just saying 'Leyte Good Support' would be enough about that island? I'll have to work some more on the 'hit the Philippines' idea." Bill nodded, his mouth full of rice. "Good," she said, gathering up her things. "Now I've got to get to work. Will you be here when I get back?"

"Somehow," he said, blowing her a kiss as she went out the door.

Iris and Jake had five hours before the broadcast: five hours to code the information and slip it into the patter they'd planned for that evening's show. It was 4:00 P.M. by the time they'd worked out the message.

Iris would say, "Japanese just *love* *e*ager Yanks *t*aking *e*asy gambles. *O*ne *o*ld *d*estruction *s*till *u*rges *p*itiful *p*lans *o*f *r*ecovering *t*riumph, but the Japanese are strong of spirit and will prevail."

They had forty-five minutes to practice and encode the rest of the message.

"I can't figure it out," Cole complained, looking out across the Hollandia view from the flap of his tent.

"What's there to figure?" Dick asked. "We've already decoded 'Leyte good support.' That's usually about the limit of the messages. Seems to indicate that Bill has contact with the Filipino guerrillas, which explains how some of their Japanese shipping info has been so accurate. He's probably got a line on what the Japanese are expecting. I would assume that this is just confirming the strong guerrilla support and how to surprise the Japanese. It's a gamble, but certainly not anything that's out of our range of consideration. It's beyond the support of land-based planes right now, but—"

"No, that's not it. I think there's something else in that broadcast that I'm missing. Read it to me again, from the part where Jake says something like, 'Tell me, Flower, how do you feel about the Yankee attempts at taking Japanese airfields.'"

Dick picked up the paper and read. "This is Iris: 'Japanese just love eager Yanks taking easy gambles. One old destruction still urges pitiful plans of recovering triumph, but the Japanese are strong of spirit and will prevail.' That's where the message is. Then Jake said: 'Then you have faith that they'll never get to the Philippines?' Iris answered: 'I'd give my last name to see them just try a landing in the Philippines.' Then Jake said . . ."

"That's it," Cole said. "That's got to be it. I've never heard her say anything about her name before. Why would she say it now?"

Dick shrugged. "Iris's first name means a flower in English," Dick said thoughtfully. "Do you think her last name means something in Japanese?"

Cole stared at Dick. "Where's Ted Watanabe? Is he still around here?"

"He's been helping interrogate prisoners ever since he surrendered to Sparks that day. I don't know if he's still here in Hollandia, though. They fly him all over. I'll go find out."

Within fifteen minutes Dick was back, with Ted Watanabe in tow. "Great!" Cole exclaimed, shaking his hand, "Sit down, Ted. Tell me, do Japanese names mean something?"

Ted shrugged. "Yeah, I guess you could say that some of them do. Sort of like Baker and Cook in English. Why?"

"Does Hashimoto mean anything?" Cole persisted.

Ted thought for a moment. "I guess it could if you took it apart. *Hashi* means 'bridge' and *moto* means 'source' or 'base,' like a foundation or something. Maybe the source of a bridge?"

"Or the base of a bridge," Dick speculated, "bridge base?"

"Bridgehead!" Cole shouted.

Ted answered, "I guess it could mean that. I've heard *kyotoho* used for 'bridgehead,' but there's no reason Hashimoto couldn't mean that too." He looked at Cole in bewilderment as Cole picked up the paper and read it, then laughed and slapped Dick on the back. "Is that all you needed to know, sir?" he asked finally, standing up.

"Yes, Ted," Dick said. "Thanks for your help."

"That's what she's saying," Cole said confidently after Ted had left. "We should definitely establish a bridgehead somewhere in the Philippines. It would be bad to skip over the Philippines. Leyte is recommended because of good guerrilla support and the surprise element."

"Possible support from Palau would help there, too," Dick added.

"We don't have Palau yet," Cole said.

"We will soon enough. They're landing this coming Friday."

"Well, what are we waiting for?" Cole said, heading out of the tent. "That's another reason the colonel needs our information."

The message was added to the bits and pieces the Allies were putting together, helping to tilt the scale in the direction of a Leyte landing. By September 15, 1944, when the marines were landing in Palau, MacArthur had clearance from Washington to begin plans for a landing in Leyte Gulf around October 20. The potentially disastrous plan of simply skipping the Philippines and hitting Formosa, which would have left a huge Japanese defense force surrounding the American thrust and left the fate of the Filipinos in the hands of the ruthless Japanese, was scrapped in favor of MacArthur's proposal for the invasion of Leyte.

A storm raged over the Philippines on A-Day, October 20, 1944, and Cole paced while Dick kept his ear to the radio. "I don't like it," Cole complained. "If those carriers are sunk, the planes and ground forces are stranded. What if they get nervous and pull out on us? Why didn't we get airfields closer . . ."

"Shh," he said, "MacArthur's gone ashore. They're going to broadcast his speech." He turned and looked at Cole, his gray eyes reflecting the same emotions swelling inside Cole.

Two and a half years ago, the two of them had barely escaped from the Philippines with their lives, wearing torn uniforms, half-starved and defeated. Now—

"People of the Philippines," MacArthur's voice came through the static of the broadcast, strong and resolute. "I have returned."

Cole quickly looked down to hide the tears that suddenly burned his eyes. His mind filled with a rush of memories of the languid days in their house in Manila, the gracious evenings spent with the kind Filipino people, and the lovely, gentle girl called Maria, whom Jake wanted to marry. These memories were overlaid with harsh, painful memories of an acrid smoking hell, and the bloody vision of the mangled bodies he saw on Bataan and Corregidor. He could hear in his mind the crack of menacing rifle fire that night he spent with Jake in the foxhole, eating canned salmon and ship biscuits and planning the code.

It was all so long ago—and now, through the static, through the faraway voice of their commander rising above the pops of distant gunfire, they knew that they also had returned.

Cole left the tent and went outside. Standing in the slow drizzle, he lit a cigarette.

"Did you hear?" Sparky called as he came up the path.

"Yeah," Cole said.

"I figure they'll be needing my special talents. I'm going out in the next bunch. I gotta be there to get things ready for the airfield."

Cole put his arm around Sparky's shoulder as they walked down the path. "I just wish to hell I could be there insisting that you be my crew chief again. Damn! I wish I wasn't grounded. Now of all times."

"Maybe you're not. Rumor's out that the general said he wants only crack pilots up in the first echelon. I think with nineteen victories under your belt, you'd be near the top of the list. In fact, the reason I came up here was to tell you that I'm taking it on myself to check out *King Cole* before I leave."

Cole stopped, a smug grin creasing his face. "Why don't you just go do that? Can't hurt to have my plane checked out by the best in the business. Just in case. In the meantime, I think I've got a colonel to go talk to."

Dick shipped out with the same contingent as Sparky. He was to set up intelligence coordination between the guerrillas and the regular forces. That left Cole alone. Waiting. He packed up their tent and then paced. Left to his thoughts at night, he found himself worrying about what might happen to Iris when they started bombing Japan. He stared at the picture her father had given him, and worried.

On October 26, Cole got permission to join the two squadrons of the 49th Group's P-38s staging to Morotai. On October 27, they took off from there for Leyte. As they approached the runway set up off the village of Tacloban, they could see the engineers still frantically trying to lay the last section of steel mat for the strip's surface. It was nothing more than a sand pit three hundred yards wide, reaching a little over a mile out into the ocean. They'd have to start looking for something bigger than that pretty damn quick.

All thirty-four Lightnings buzzed the runway as the ground personnel ran out to the edge of the strip, waving their arms and throwing their caps into the air. Not a bad welcome back, Cole thought as he pulled hard on the brakes, stopping just at the end of the runway behind two other P-38s.

They taxied to the edge of the runway and crawled out of their cockpits. To their surprise, they were greeted not only by American troops but by cheering Filipinos and, most surprising of all, General Kenney, whom Cole saw crawling out of a jeep with a tall, erect figure whose gold-braided field marshal's cap made his identity unmistakable—General MacArthur himself. They really had "returned."

The welcoming ceremony was brief but sincere. The navy had started pulling out their carriers for refueling in Yap. Twelve P-38s were quickly refueled and put up to cover the refueling operations of the rest. Cole was ready to go again by 5:00 P.M. It was a good thing, too. The radar told them they had ten minutes before a Japanese greeting party of five planes came over. Cole climbed into the cockpit and followed three of the Forty-ninth's best, including Dick Bong. When they returned, Cole had racked up his twentieth victory. Bong, the top ace, also came home with a victory, making his total thirty-one.

That same day, Cole witnessed one of the most senseless acts of the war. A Japanese plane roared out of the sky just before sunset and deliberately crashed into a destroyer just off shore. It was a mindless act of desperation, a futile act of hollow bravery that they would see and hear about for the rest of the war.

That night, in their tent, Cole, Dick, and Sparky celebrated their reunion and their return to the Philippines. Much to Cole's chagrin, Dick had brought the white cockatoo, Jake, along with him, maintaining that it was only right that Jake's namesake be with them when they liberated the Philippines. The bird sat perched between their bunks, periodically splitting the air with his cry of "Damn the Japs! Damn the Japs!"

Cole shuddered and said, "I wish you'd get rid of that damn bird."

"Why?" Dick said, stroking the bird's head. It closed its eyes, seeming to enjoy the attention. "He keeps us company. Sort of adds some class to our humble abode."

"He's too noisy," Cole complained as he reached for a cigarette. "They picked up two Japs in Filipino clothing right off the field tonight. There's still snipers all around."

Dick shrugged.

Cole turned to Sparky and teased, "Are you going to still keep up your flying hours?" Sparky had managed to keep up his hours while in New Guinea, but now that he was stationed in a combat zone, it would be listed as combat duty, which Sparky had maintained was injurious to the health of the best damn ground-support system they had: him.

"You know that kind of flying isn't allowed," Sparky said righteously. "But I did figure I'd test out *King Cole* personally next time I have to check out the engine."

Cole shook his head. "And just when will that be?"

"Probably tomorrow. You had a pretty long flight, then combat."

"Sparky," Cole protested, "you know the Jap snipers are all around us. The main Japanese defense is just over the hill. We aren't even supposed to go wandering around on the ground, and you're proposing to go off flying in a plane?"

"Can't hurt. I've been flying for six years now. Just because I'm a mechanic doesn't mean I'm not a pilot."

"Just because you're a pilot doesn't mean you're a combat pilot. I need you in one piece. Besides, I'd hate to lose my plane."

Sparky laughed and said good night.

It was right after the early-morning flight that Sparky started working on Cole's plane. In the early afternoon, just as Cole came out of the mess tent, he saw his plane taxiing down the runway. He didn't need anyone to tell him. Sparky was taking off alone. He watched the plane going into the sun over the mountains. He waited, pacing, from that moment on. Four hours later, the plane hadn't come back. By evening, Sparky was listed as missing in action.

Cole left early the next morning on regular patrol. His intent was to follow Sparky's course over the mountains to the west. It was his wingman, half an hour later, who came over the radio saying, "Down there, sir, off the starboard side." The partially burned wreckage of a P-38 lay protruding from the foliage. Banking, they came in low, trying to see if there was any sign of the pilot. A flutter of white birds flew from the jungle, disturbed by the roar of their engines. Cole swung around and came back across the wreckage again, just barely clearing the treetops. As he pulled back on the stick to climb back up, he felt a swelling nausea in his throat. The tip of a gold crown and the letters *ng le* were visible on the blackened fuselage. It was his plane, *King Cole*. Sparky was dead.

Probably more to get Cole's mind off Sparky than for any real help, Dick asked Cole to come with him to the village of Burauen, west of Tacloban. They would meet with some of the guerrillas there and begin compiling information. Filled with grief, Cole agreed.

They set up their headquarters in a schoolhouse. Dick planned to remain there for at least a month, but Cole was scheduled to go back to Tacloban within the week with the information they'd received by that time. They set up their tent in a clearing at the edge of the village and went to work. Of each villager, of each guerrilla they talked to, Cole asked, "Have you heard of any downed pilots?" The answers always left him more depressed than ever. "No, sir," they would say. "They're picked up right away and brought in when they're found, sir."

"You've got to stop tearing yourself apart like this," Dick told him that night in the tent. "You told him not to go out. It was all you could do."

"I should have tried harder." He lay down on his bunk, his arm over his eyes.

"Damn the Japs! Damn the Japs!" shrieked Jake, the cockatoo.

"Why the hell did you have to bring that damn bird?" Cole grumbled. "He's too damn noisy for being this close to the Japs. He'll get shot by one of those snipers just for his language."

"He's good company," Dick said, holding a nut out to the bird.

"Damn the Japs! Damn the Japs!" the bird cried as it took the nut.

Just then a burst of machine-gun fire filled the air. Cole saw a line of holes bursting through the edge of the tent just above his head. His face was warm and sticky, his arm suddenly covered with blood. Instinctively, he rolled off the bed and under the cot. Dick fell to the floor beside him. He reached out to pull him under cover with him and stopped in frozen shock. The right side of Dick's face looked mildly surprised. The left side was gone. Only white particles of bone protruded from a bloody gray pulp.

As suddenly as it had started, the shooting stopped, followed by silence, then the sound of feet running outside the tent and a sudden burst of gunfire. Cole lay under his bunk, holding Dick's lifeless hand.

"Got 'im," shouted a distant voice. "The fucker was right there in that tree, just waiting for something to shoot at. Better check the tent there."

"Oh, God," moaned a voice at the tent flap. "Call the medics!"

Cole crawled out from under the bunk. "I think it's too late for Major McDuff," he murmured quietly. "And I seem to be all right. Was anyone else hurt?" he asked absently, staring down at Dick's gory body.

"No, sir," said the infantry sergeant at the door. "He heard or saw something and just shot at it."

"Heard something," Cole muttered. White feathers were scattered over the side of the tent. Jake, the cockatoo, had been shot beyond recognition. "Yes, I imagine he heard something."

The colonel in charge of intelligence sent Cole back to Tacloban with Dick's body. In three short days he'd lost his two best friends; one to reckless adventure and one because of a damn bird's gift of gab. That seemed to be the hallmark of the war. Senselessness.

The next morning he reported in and assured the colonel that he was fit for combat. He left with the second patrol. Chalking up his twenty-first air victory, bombing Japanese shipping and strafing Japanese troops, he salved his grief with cold revenge.

Still, beyond the battle, beyond the hurried bravery, there lurked in Cole's mind an unspoken question, a gnawing inquiry that he continually pushed to the back. Yet, the gnawing grew; the unacknowledged question persisted. On the night of November 13, alone in his tent, the question made itself heard.

"Why me?" he whispered in the dark, as the tropical rains

thudded against the canvas. "Why me?" he raged into the wind. "Why have I lived? Why haven't I been killed? Why Sparky and Dick, and not me?"

He paced, crying out against the raging storm inside him, tearing pieces of guilt and confusion from his heart.

The rain dwindled and morning dawned through silvered clouds over the mountains. Cole was still walking, still smoking, pacing through the mud on the hillsides behind the airstrip.

"Major Tennyson?" came a young voice behind him. "The colonel wants you in his tent. Right now, sir."

Cole threw down his cigarette and slowly followed the private. *What now?* he thought, as his boots sucked the coagulated mud with each step.

Colonel Whiteside was waiting outside his tent. Nodding to Cole, he said, "I think there's someone in there you'd like to see."

Listlessly, Cole lifted the tent flap and looked in. A man in Filipino clothing turned around and grinned broadly at Cole's startled look. "After seventeen days, I'd at least expect a hello," he said.

Cole stood there immobilized, holding the tent flap with one hand. He couldn't quite grasp what he was seeing. "Sparky?" he whispered. *"Sparky!"*

"Hey, I'm sorry I broke your plane," Sparky said, "but there didn't seem to be much choice. You see, this Jap bumped into it with his Hamp and I didn't think it was worth much after that. I bailed out, and then figured I might as well do some ground reconnaissance while I was down there. Well, these real swell Filipinos were watching me floating down; when I landed, they were just there waiting, like a welcoming party. Turns out they're guerrillas. We had a great time. I helped them fix up some of their equipment. But then I got to thinking that maybe you needed me back here. You know, you aren't too good a mechanic, and I was sure you'd be crawling into some bird that wasn't fit for flying. Anyway, they said they'd help me come on back. So . . . hey, Cole, stop hugging me," he said, clapping Cole on the back. "It could ruin my reputation. Whatcha going to go crying for? Didn't you know I'd be coming back? I always do."

"I just . . . I just . . . I just thought you were . . . God, it's good, you son of a bitch."

"Ah, come on," Sparky said soberly. "I know. It's been rough. I heard about Dick from the colonel. It hit me pretty hard just to hear it . . . and then for you to see it, after thinking I was gone too. But don't think about that now. Things are getting better. I've got something to tell you," he said, brightening. "Did you ever know anyone named Rodrigues in Manila?"

Cole paused, looking at Sparky to see if he was kidding. "Yes," he said slowly. "That was the name of Maria's father, the girl I told you about that Jake wanted to marry. Why?"

"The guerrilla who brought me back says there's an old man named Rodrigues who's been part of their organization. He's had a thing about helping pilots who've been shot down. They're bringing him here to talk to us. Figured he might have some information about some other pilots."

He was an old man now, aged by war and grief. His clothes were tattered, his face deeply lined, but he still carried himself with the dignity Cole remembered. It was Rodrigues. His eyes shone at the sight of Cole.

Rodrigues wanted first to hear Cole's story of escape. Then, satisfied, he quietly told the story of Jake and Maria. Cole was astounded at the ingenuity of their rescue of Jake, then rejoiced when he heard of his marriage to Maria and their expected child. When he heard of Maria's violent death and Jake's subsequent capture, Cole buried his head in his hands, blinded by his tears.

Sparky quickly got up and left the tent. When Rodrigues began speaking again, Sparky returned, his eyes red.

"And your family?" Cole asked finally.

"Ah," Rodrigues said with a smile of pride. "My wife and two daughters are living with my wife's family in a tiny, isolated village in Leyte. The Japanese seldom go there. Perhaps when this war is over you will come to visit us again. And you too, Mr. Sparks."

Cole and Sparky agreed that they would want to see Jake's family before leaving the islands. Rodrigues knew of Jake's broadcasts but had not heard any. Cole invited him to come back to the camp the following Sunday. He eagerly accepted the invitation, saying, "I've not heard a radio in two and a half years."

On October 19, Rodrigues was listening to the radio with Sparky and Cole as they heard Jake and Iris broadcast their program. He noticed Cole and Sparky exchanging looks when they heard Iris's voice. He did not ask why Cole wrote down part of the conversation. When the show was over, he said, "I think that he is tricking them in the way he says those things. I think the Japanese make him say bad things about America. You are right to study his words. They don't mean anything to me because I don't know about those things in the United States. Perhaps you will see something. He is very clever, you know." With that, he took his leave, promising to keep in contact.

"Why is she talking about Alvarito's?" Sparky asked.

"Like I told you, there's usually some kind of message. Read it over again. I'm stumped this time. Dick used to be so good at this."

" 'The Americans will never be able to take the Philippines. They might as well go back to Hawaii with their assigned squadrons and celebrate surviving at Alvarito's Restaurant.' "

"We ate there about three times, didn't we?"

"Yeah," Sparky said, "but the time I remember the best was when those gobs jumped me, and you and Jake came to the rescue."

"That's probably it," Cole said. "We surprised them on both sides. They thought they had you alone and cornered you in the alley, and then Jake and I jumped in and cleaned their cans. We called it good strategy and you claimed we almost fouled you up because you were the decoy and then we took so long to come to the rescue."

"Yeah, I remember that. Do you think they're saying that might happen to us here?"

"Well, our flanks are sure as hell exposed both to Luzon and Mindanao. We'd better keep our eyes open or they'll trap us in a pincer move." Cole stopped and thought for a moment. "Do you think something is coming in on the other side of Leyte from Luzon or Mindanao?"

"Sure worth the time to tell the colonel about it," Sparky said. "Mind if I come along?"

The colonel nodded as Cole explained the information they'd just picked up from Tokyo. "There are Jap reinforcements landing across the island at Ormoc right now. Could be big trouble if we didn't know about it or if they should break through. I'll keep it in mind when we have the strategy meeting. In the meantime, go back over the notes and see if there's any more clues to what they meant."

As Cole and Sparky were going back to their tent, they were stopped by a corporal from communications. "Major Tennyson, this radio just came in for you. Thought you might want to get it right away."

Cole looked at the paper. *Rothboeck coming in with Mitchell 1700 hours Tacloban. Warm facilities requested from King Cole.*

Sparky was reading over his shoulder. "Boy, that Marta has some nerve. Imagine putting that kind of thing over the air."

"Lack of nerve is one thing we've never accused her of. Ever since you and Dick made me make peace with her back in Hollandia, she's figured I was fair game again. Nope, she's got plenty of nerve," he said ruefully. "She must be the first WASP pilot to try to bring a bomber in on this runway. It was just lengthened yesterday. What time is it?"

"We got an hour. She must have radioed after taking off from Guam."

"Well, let's go make sure there's a visitor's tent for her." He glanced at the sky and added slyly, "Weather's too warm to share my cot."

The stubby B-25 Mitchell was just circling for clearance as they got to the runway. She came in with her landing gear down in a perfect approach. It was a rough runway, but Marta barely bounced the craft as she touched down and began taxiing.

"Boy," Sparky said admiringly, "she sure can . . ." Two sharp, high-velocity rifle shots suddenly cracked through the air stopping his words. "What the hell?" he yelled as three soldiers with automatic weapons ran toward the trees at the end of the field.

Cole pushed Sparky to the ground behind a jeep. "Sniper!"

They looked at the B-25, which had drifted to the side of the runway and stopped at a peculiar angle. There was a burst of gunfire, followed by another and then a third. "Got the bastard!" called one of the soldiers coming out of the trees, holding up a Japanese cap and rifle. "All clear."

Cole got up and ran to the B-25. A Red Cross nurse was opening the door. "Get an ambulance!" she called.

Cole pulled himself into the body of the plane while Sparky ran for the ambulance. Working his way through the equipment and confused personnel to the cockpit, he had that old sinking feeling in the pit of his stomach. The copilot was a dark-haired older woman; she was gripping her right shoulder as a nurse applied a pressure bandage to her bleeding arm. Marta was slumped lifelessly over the stick. A round red patch of blood was oozing through her thick blond hair, which was pulled back in a neat bun. "She's dead," the nurse said. "The copilot was hit twice. Are you a medic, Major?"

"No," Cole murmured, "just a friend."

That night, over a bottle of Scotch Sparky had smuggled up from New Guinea, they did some serious drinking and thinking. Cole couldn't keep his old haunting question of "Why?" from filling his thoughts.

"You gotta admit one thing," Sparky said finally, toward the end of the night. "If Marta had ever told us how she wanted to die, I think she would have chosen just what happened."

"Yeah, maybe you're right."

"Or else in bed with you," Sparky added with a grim glint in his eye.

Cole looked up from the cot where he was leaning on his elbow and gave a half-laugh. "She had two things she did better than most. One of them was flying."

"If only she hadn't sent that message," Sparky said dismally.

"You think that's why there was a sniper?"

"Why else? We've had them pretty well cleared out of here for a month now. That guy was probably sent on a suicide mission to hit an important general or something."

Cole was silent for a long time, lost in thought.

As he had done when Dick was killed and when he'd thought Sparky was dead, Cole went back on the job. War didn't allow time for mourning; besides, he didn't feel that Marta would have wanted to be mourned. He and Sparky spent the next two evenings going over the notes they'd made from Iris's broadcast.

When they went in to talk with the colonel, he agreed with their assessment of the message. He also seemed to have something else on his mind. At the end of the discussion, he reached across his desk and picked up a piece of paper. "Tennyson, I'm sending you home."

"But, sir," Cole protested, "I'm in for the duration . . ."

The colonel held up his hand. "You've been out here entirely too long. I noted in your file that you haven't had any real gunnery training. Seems sort of silly after twenty-one victories, but you haven't. Probably could have had forty by now if you'd had training. After you've had some time to get to know your family again, you'll spend six weeks in gunnery."

"But, sir, you might need me before then. What about the messages? Besides, I . . ."

"Tennyson," the colonel said soberly, "I'll be frank with you. I don't think you're going to be of much use to us now. We're going to start bombing Tokyo tomorrow."

Cole swallowed the lump in his throat. "I knew that would be coming, sir."

"Common sense says you'll need some time to get things straight in your own mind, son. We'll be landing in Luzon in January. I'll make sure you're back in time for the big push, and I promise you'll be with me when we occupy Tokyo."

"Thank you, sir," Cole said with relief. "I'll hold you to that promise."

He smiled tightly and turned to Sparky. "As for you, Sparks, for pretty much the same reasons, I'm sending you home for sixty days. We'll need your, ah, special talents when we get up to Luzon and are establishing our bases. Until then, go home and rest. You've been out here a long time," he said. Then he added, "I understand that your girl is up there with Tennyson's." When Sparky nodded, his eyes wide and apprehensive, the colonel said, "Don't worry. You'll be there to go into Tokyo with us too."

Sparky smiled with relief. "How soon you want us out of here?"

"The next flight out. By the way, Sparks, if you agree, you'll be going to officers' training after fifteen days with your family. I'll need a good officer to help handle the setup of the crews in Luzon."

"Yes, sir," Sparky replied, beaming. "Seems like that would be a good time and a good place for being an officer."

"And, Tennyson, you'd better get used to being called Colonel. I'm recommending you for a Silver Star and a promotion to go with the twenty-one Japanese flags on the side of your plane."

They both left in silence. It was good news, but not

good enough to keep the colonel's words from repeating ominously in their minds: "We're going to start bombing Tokyo tomorrow."

The wind was blowing, separating the rain clouds and permitting a few glimpses of blue sky. It was going to be another bitter cold night. Iris turned to Jake with a wry smile. "It's Friday. Do you realize that back home our biggest worry would have been what's on at the movies?"

Jake started to reply just as the air-raid siren sounded. The people in the office began heading to the air-raid shelter. "Let's not go," Jake murmured. "I'm sick of these practices."

"Maybe we'd better. They said there was a real American plane overhead the first of the month. Bill says they'll be coming anytime now because Saipan is within range of the new bombers."

Jake glanced toward the door, caught the sharp look of one of the security officers, and got up slowly.

They were the last ones out of the building. Following the others by a couple of minutes had made them almost the last ones on the street. They were outside the entrance to the building that held the cellar designated as their shelter when Iris suddenly gripped Jake's arm. "Listen!" she commanded, stopping in the middle of the sidewalk.

Jake stopped and looked up. "Planes," he whispered in awe.

Just then the ground was shaken as if by an earthquake. Then the distant sound of explosions rumbled through the air, a bass to the trebled shrill of the sirens. The drone of engines increased, twining the air with a persistent growl. More explosions followed in sudden succession, shaking them as they clung to each other, looking up at the sky. Between the clouds blackened with billowing smoke they could see a patch of blue. A swarm of planes was crossing the blue, a swarm that didn't end, a death-dealing, victory-singing swarm of silver blue planes, bombing Tokyo . . . bombing them.

"They've come," Jake said, clutching Iris to him.

"And now what?" Iris asked tearfully, burying her face in his shoulder.

CHAPTER XXVI

The autumn clouds were blackened by smoke as Iris left work that night. The acrid smell of fire hung heavily over the city. She stopped briefly at her house. Seeing no sign of Bill, she left a note saying that she was going to her grandmother's.

Bewilderment and confusion filled the eyes of the people who had believed their military leaders' boasts that no enemy could touch the Japanese homeland. The myth of Nippon invincibility was revealed as a fairy tale and now the people didn't know where to turn. They struggled to maintain the facade of normalcy, stumbling as they attempted a business-like stride through their smoking city, waiting patiently for a streetcar or bus that would come behind schedule, if at all.

What was confusing to the Japanese was also ripping at Iris's heart. From the smoke and the glow of fire against the evening clouds, Iris knew that the bombing had struck an area away from Grandmother's house. What she didn't know was the location of the paint factory where Mieko and her schoolmates worked. She had to know they were all right. She was drawn to her family in this strange time. She needed them.

She had been born and raised American, yet her face and her heritage were Japanese. She had friends and family she had loved and buried here, people she'd learned to admire and enjoy. Yet, she had prayed for American victory—a victory that she knew would bring bombs on the beauty of the country, on her family, on herself.

Now that the bombs actually had come, she needed both to reach out and touch her family, reassuring herself of their safety, and to be with Bill, who had worked for the same victory she had, and whom she loved.

Iris got off the *densha* near Mieko's school where the

children returned from their enforced labor each day. Weary students were just getting off their bus. Iris stood on the corner, her eyes straining over the begrimed uniforms of the schoolchildren, searching anxiously for her little niece. Mieko saw Iris and started toward her. Iris breathed a sigh of relief and stood patiently waiting as Mieko came up to her.

She started to speak, but Mieko stopped her with a curt, *"Ikimasho."* Let's go. Following her lead, and not speaking where others might hear, Iris silently walked the five blocks to Grandmother's house. Mieko stood almost as high as Iris's shoulder, but her body was pitifully thin. Her dark braids hung down her back, thumping against her bony shoulders with each step. The middy blouse of her school uniform was soiled with ash and dirt. What had happened today? Iris wondered. Glancing at Mieko's face as they walked, Iris was stricken by her pallor and the taut lines of worry that pulled at the corners of her young mouth and eyes. In Mieko's dark eyes, Iris saw pain, fear, and desolation. What had she seen? What had aged her beyond her years? This young girl, who should have been giggling with friends, struggling over homework and jumping rope—would she ever know girlish laughter or the kiss of a lover?

They slipped in the garden gate and walked down the path in silence. As they stopped to take off their shoes, Iris whispered, "Are you all right?"

Mieko nodded solemnly. *"Hai, One-san Ichihatsu no hana,"* —yes, cousin Iris—"but please don't ask any more. I don't want to disturb Grandmother and Mother. They will be frightened enough."

Iris nodded. "But you need someone to talk to. Tell me, were you near the bombing? I was worried about your safety."

Mieko sat down on the step. "The factory was not hit. We were taken to help fight the fires and rescue people," she said, staring straight ahead, her eyes reflecting the horror of that flaming scene. "It was hopeless. We could not contain the fires. They just kept burning, leaping from building to building. I pulled a child from a burning house. She screamed and smelled like cooked meat. She died in my arms. She was the size of Kibo," she whispered, tears streaking through the soil on her cheeks. "There were many, many like that," she murmured. "We must not tell Grandmother or Mother. It will cause them fear."

Iris ached to reach out and hold Mieko, yet she knew it would be a breach of Japanese etiquette even now. Instead, she took her elbow and stood up, saying, "Come with me. I will help you wash up before anyone sees you. I was able to find some tiny oranges on the market today. They are nearly shriveled, but I think they will make a nice treat for the family. You will help me pass them out."

Mieko looked up at Iris, her eyes brimming with tears. She smiled faintly and leaned her head so that it barely touched Iris's shoulder before she turned and went into the house.

Grandmother, Aunt Teiso, and Aunt Toshiko were elated that Iris had come. They insisted that she share their meal of boiled rice and *umeboshi,* the tiny pickled plums. It was a meal said to be very patriotic, for the red plums sitting in the middle of the white rice were like the Japanese flag. It was not very nourishing, and the futility of the gesture further wrenched Iris's heart.

They talked of the bombing as if they were talking about a mere annoyance. Only after the younger children had gone to bed did they turn to a more serious subject. Now that the bombing had come, as Iris had told them it would, should they take the children and go to the countryside? Iris knew that they were reluctant to break up the family, but she feared for their safety.

Mieko was silent. Iris couldn't tell if it was from exhaustion or shock. She sat next to Iris, her knee touching hers under the *dotera,* seeking strength and comfort from Iris. If her mother and aunt and the other children went to Aunt Suki's, Mieko would have to stay behind with Grandmother and Iris because she was employed in a defense job. This fragile twelve-year-old was essential manpower for the Japanese war machine.

"Maybe it was just a bombing like the one in April of 1942," Aunt Toshiko said hopefully. "Perhaps another one won't come for a long time."

"I don't think so, *Oba-san,*" Iris said respectfully. "They are coming from a base the Americans captured from the Japanese army not too long ago, a base on Saipan, in the Marianas Islands."

She paused, suddenly remembering that that was where Uncle Kuni had been killed. Aunt Teiso's face showed a flicker of pain, then was calm.

"Go on, *Ichihatsu-chan*," Grandmother said.

"Before, they did not say where the planes came from," Iris explained. "Now they know. It is in the Japanese news this evening. The Americans are close enough now to keep on bombing. This is not the end. It is the beginning."

Grandmother nodded. "You were right before, my granddaughter. We should take your words into careful consideration when we decide."

With that the subject was dropped. Much to Iris's consternation, they were again postponing the separation of the family. She looked to Mieko to say something, but she'd fallen asleep, sitting up. From Grandmother's tired eyes, Iris could see that it was time to go. There was nothing more she could do tonight, except pray that they would leave before it was too late.

In the darkness, she returned to her house. The way was lit by the orange glow of smoldering fires against the clouds. A light rain pattered against her face, sparking the street with reflections of light, washing the smoke from the air.

The house was dark when she arrived. She slipped in the door and glanced around for a note from Bill. There was none. With disappointment, she separated out the things for Mrs. Okimoto that she had picked up for her in the ration lines that afternoon, then went to Mrs. Okimoto's house.

"Welcome, come in," Mrs. Okimoto said warmly. "The day went all right with you? You didn't have any problems?"

She led Iris into the main room of the house where her daughter-in-law sat on the *tatami* floor, throwing a ball to her son. When he saw Iris come into the room, he plopped down on his diapered bottom and began earnestly chewing his fist.

Iris bowed her greeting as she said, "No, there was not too much trouble. But there was much confusion on the streets, and not all the markets had received their goods," she explained, returning some of Mrs. Okimoto's ration papers and yen.

"It is good you got anything," Mrs. Okimoto said. "Thank you. You had no problems at your work?"

"No," Iris said, wondering why she was asking. "The bombing was on the other side of the city."

"I was worried. Since they knew where you came from they might do something to you in foolish anger."

"Oh," Iris said, with sudden understanding. "No, nothing

402

was said. You see, they use the skills I gained while growing up in the United States. While my skills are of use, I am safe."

"*Ah so desuka*," Mrs. Okimoto said with obvious relief. Then she offered Iris a cup of tea.

"Oh, thank you very much," Iris said gratefully, "but I really must go home and sleep. It's been a long day and tomorrow will also be long. But thank you for your generous offer." With that, she bowed and left.

Now that there had been bombing, the blackout rules were observed more carefully. Iris had trouble finding her way down the street and cursed herself for not bringing a lantern, even though they were of little use with a blackout shield over them. Finally, she found her gate and made her way down the walk, slipped off her shoes, and went into the darkened house.

"Where did you go?" Bill asked as she came into the sleeping room.

"Why can't you give me some kind of hint that you're here instead of scaring me half to death all the time?" Iris complained, jumping at the sound of his voice.

"I was here the first time you came in, but I didn't wake up until you were going out the door. Sorry," he smiled, "maybe next time I should leave a ribbon on the door latch."

"That would help," Iris said as she leaned down to kiss him. "Are you all right?" she asked in sudden fear, noticing a bandage on his forearm.

"Sure, I'm fine. I threw my arm up and caught a burning beam and saved a general's beauty, if not his life. Made a real hero of me. I'm more trusted than ever. It's just a burn; it'll heal. He had some doctor put some kind of mumbo-jumbo folk-medicine juice on it and I think it's actually working. Doesn't hurt anymore, anyway. Did you have any problems?"

"No, not really," she said as she began to get ready for bed. "I was worried about you. I wanted to make sure that Grandmother and all were okay. I'm pretty worried about Mieko, though."

"Was she hurt?"

"Not physically. But they were taken out of the factory to fight the fires and she saw some pretty grim things. How can they expect so much from just a child?" she asked, her anger mounting. "Why are they doing this? They're leading this whole innocent country to its death and the people are all following like a bunch of lemmings," she said, fighting back the tears.

"I know. I've been thinking the same things. It's pretty hard to look up and see the planes you've been wishing for dropping the bombs you've been waiting for, and you suddenly realize that those bombs are killing not the fools who've made this war, but the innocent women and children and everyone who didn't want the war in the first place . . . and maybe even you . . . or me."

Iris shivered in the cold as she blew out the candle and crawled in next to him. She laid her head on his shoulder and put her arms around his bare chest. "How long do you think it will be before it's over?" she whispered.

"A long time," he murmured, stroking her hair. "This is just the beginning. The bombs aren't going to stop. There was a reconnaissance plane over the city at about five this afternoon. They'll see how much damage they've done and keep coming back until there's nothing left of Tokyo. If the Nipponese won't give up after that, which you know they won't, then the Americans will start bombing each and every city and factory until there's nothing left but a smoldering ruin. Then they'll land the marines and the infantry and the tanks and they'll simply crawl up the island, wiping out every last bit of resistance they find. It'll be long and bloody."

Iris shuddered. "Won't they have the sense to surrender before then?"

She could feel him shake his head sadly. "They'll starve first. The military has a last-ditch, fight-them-off-with-old-men-and-children-wielding-bamboo-spears plan. Right now, they don't even think things are going so badly. They really believe that crap they're dishing out to everyone." His voice rose with incredulity and he leaned on one elbow, gesturing with his other hand. "They believe they'll win because they have the strongest spirit, because they're superior. They really believe that material things aren't important, that it's the spiritual which will overcome all adversity. When they hear about the huge production figures and the increasing numbers of American planes they say it doesn't matter. When they have reports of the American fleet full of the carriers they'd said they sunk way back at Midway and they now claim they're sinking again in the Philippines, they say it doesn't matter. They say their Bushido Spirit will conquer all. No, my love," he said with resignation. "You can't expect logic to surface now. It will be a long, long battle before it's over." He lay back down, wrapping his arm around her.

"And when it's over . . ."

Iris could feel his arm tighten around her. "I don't know." Then he added quietly, "I've never kidded myself about you and me. I know that what we have now is all I'll ever have. I know that if Cole comes back into the picture, riding his white charger and wearing his glittering armor, I'll be out of the picture, and quick."

"I wasn't talking about that . . ."

"I know, but I figure we've got to talk about that sometime. Now is just as good as any. Shh, don't interrupt," he said, putting his fingers over her lips as she started to protest. "I know you love me. I can see it when I come in the door. I also know that you can't love me nearly as much as I love you, because of Cole. No matter what happens, even if he doesn't come back into the picture, I'm still going to have to live with his ghost. I'm not sure I can do that. I only know that for me, for now, my love for you overwhelms my entire life. You are my life. I don't expect you to return that. You can only give that kind of love once, and you'd already done that before I ever met you. What love you give to me is all you have. For now, that's enough. When this is all over . . . I don't know."

"Bill," she cried. "I love you. I can't think about Cole. I don't know why you even brought him up. He's far away and probably dead. You and Jake have both said so. I'm here in bed with you. My life revolves around you. You're all I have. Please don't talk like this. I love you; believe me."

"I know. I'm here," he murmured, pulling her to him. "I know."

A single tear slid down Iris's cheek as she closed her eyes and kissed him. Perhaps he did know . . . maybe even more than she knew herself.

Bill had been right. The bombing continued. The air-raid sirens screamed daily, usually because of reconnaissance planes. The air was tinged with smoke, creating a blood-red moon, which rose at night to light their shivering retreat to their shelters as the planes droned overhead and the sirens howled. More and more, the air-raid shelter became like an open grave in Iris's eyes. When she hesitated to go in, Bill would put his arms around her and hold her as they went in together. No longer did the warden check each shelter; he was too busy checking the houses for sparks, watching for wild fires, and racing for shelter himself.

Food became increasingly scarce as the shipments into the city were curtailed by damaged rail lines, lack of fuel, and disrupted services of all kinds. The ration lines were longer, the faces more gaunt, and the shelves more empty. A kind of lethargy settled over the people of Tokyo. Iris and Bill felt it themselves. It was caused partly by the shock of the bombings, partly by a feeling of fear and helplessness in the face of such immense destruction, but mostly it was caused by the onset of starvation.

By the first week of January, Iris was experiencing chilblains in her feet and hands, which made movement very difficult. Bill was preparing their thin soup while she desperately tried to warm herself around the few glowing coals in the *kotatsu*. "I'm going to have to move in with Grandmother," she said finally.

"I know. I've been waiting for the time . . . dreading it," he said with a weak smile. "I've always thought that I should make my appearance as your cousin again. I don't think I've been seen coming in here by any of the neighbors. You could take me around and introduce me to everyone, tell them that I'm going to take your house because you have to move in with 'our' grandmother. That will give me someplace to stay, perhaps a place where we can be together now and then. I'll even stand in a few ration lines for your old Mrs. Okimoto. What do you think?"

"I think it sounds great. I'll go tell Grandmother tomorrow that everyone should start packing up, and then I'll move over there on Tuesday. I don't think I'm going to sleep very well until I get the children out of here," she admitted as Bill handed her a bowl of soup. "They say there's been bombing over Shizuoka too, but Grandmother got a postcard from Aunt Suki saying that she's far enough away from all the rail heads that there doesn't seem to be any danger of her house being hit. I'm going to insist that they just take Mieko with them. The authorities aren't going to chase after a twelve-year-old girl."

Bill nodded. "I've seen several children around that age and older living out in the country. Some probably have done just what you said; others have probably gone through elaborate procedures to establish a different birthdate or a doctor's form saying they're physically unable to work. There're all sorts of ways."

Iris used Bill's very words when she talked to her aunts and grandmother the next day. They listened gravely to her plans, then turned to Grandmother, who nodded wisely. "My *Ichihatsu-chan* is right again. We are gambling with the children's lives by waiting. You will all go on tomorrow's train."

Aunt Teiso accepted her decision. However, Aunt Toshiko hesitated. "If it pleases you, Mother-in-law," she said quietly, "I would like to wait until the fourteenth of the month. My husband's pay may have arrived by then, and I will be able to leave part with you after buying some goods for Cousin Suki which she will not be able to obtain in the countryside. It would not be difficult for me to travel with little Kibo-chan and a few packages."

Grandmother nodded. Clearly, Aunt Toshiko and little Kibo were her favorites and another few days with them was a pleasing idea. "You're right. It is best to take more than we had planned. You will all begin packing right away. *Ichihatsu-chan*," she said, turning to Iris, "you will sleep in the room which looks out over the garden. Teiso-san will have it cleaned and ready for you when you move your things in tomorrow." She turned to Aunt Teiso and said, "You will tell Mieko-chan tonight that she is going with you. Iris is right: they will not chase after a child. If you are asked on the train, simply say she is only ten. She is small for her age anyway."

Iris was greatly relieved that they were finally getting out with all the children. They would pick Mieko up at her school around four o'clock and go from there to the train depot.

Iris had gone with Aunt Teiso and the other children to meet Mieko at her school so Iris could say good-bye to them. The air-raid sirens caught them in the streets and they went to a shelter in the cellar of a nearby building. When they felt the rumble of the ground, they knew that this was not a practice drill. They exchanged fearful looks. When the all-clear sounded, it was after four o'clock.

The bus was not at the school, probably delayed by the air raid, so they waited. By five o'clock the bus still was not there, and Iris grew fearful. The train was to leave at six-thirty. Finally, at six-fifteen, the bus pulled up. Only a handful of children straggled out, all dirty and grimy, their faces stricken with shock. One little boy's head was bandaged. Two little girls limped out, their legs wrapped in white bandages. Mieko was not among those getting off. Aunt Teiso went to the teacher in charge, inquired about Mieko, then bowed her thanks and walked back toward Iris and the children. Suddenly her legs buckled and she fell to the ground. Iris ran to her. The teacher came up.

"She has fainted," he said matter-of-factly. "You will take care of her please. Her daughter was killed when a plane landed on the paint factory today. She cannot stay here because it will undermine the courage of the other parents." He turned and went back to the bus, where a group of worried parents were clustered around the driver.

Iris buried her face in her aunt's bosom, sobbing. "No, not my little Mieko," she cried. "She's just a little girl. Not my Mieko. She was going to be safe. . . ."

Hanako came up and shook Iris's shoulder. "Please, *Ichihatsu-san*, we must take Auntie back to Grandmother's house. We cannot catch the train now. We mustn't let others see our pain. *Dozo*, please help me with Auntie," she said, taking her aunt's arm and bravely lifting her to her feet. Aunt Teiso slowly opened her eyes and looked down at her niece. She reached out with shaking fingers and touched her thick braids, then closed her eyes and began walking slowly, leaning on Iris and Hanako.

The family huddled together that dark evening while the thin soup and small pot of rice bubbled on the *konro*. Their faces were pale and stricken in the lantern light. An insidious, unseen enemy was in their midst, slowly killing them, and they had no way to fight back, nowhere to hide. Their only hope lay in their separation, in their quick retreat to the country. They would take the midnight train. They stayed up, talking quietly, the children slumbering on the laps of the women, until it was time to go. Then, gently waking the children, Aunt Teiso gathered up their luggage and left. They all walked them to the gate, even Grandmother, who leaned on Iris's arm as they waved good-bye. Soon they would safely be in the country with Aunt Suki. Soon Aunt Toshiko and little Kibo would join them. Soon the family would be safe.

They were waiting at the station when the planes came over and the sirens wailed again. Dutifully, Teiso and the children slipped into the underground shelter at the station and waited for the all-clear. There hadn't been many people waiting for the midnight train so it was not as frightening as other air raids, with all the crush of people. Nevertheless, a bomb dropped right near the entrance. They were killed instantly.

Iris rushed to the station immediately following the all-clear signal. Amid the rubble and the rescue and fire crews, she found her family. She identified Hanako, clinging to her aunt, her long braids singed by the fire, and brave little Massaki, trying to protect his little cousin Matsuko, whose face was bloodied beyond recognition. One of the harassed rescue workers told her to leave the area; now that she'd identified four of the victims, they would take care of the rest. She got up, numb with grief, revulsed by what she'd seen, tears streaming down her cheeks. She had to go back to the house and tell Grandmother. Somehow she had to get Aunt Toshiko and little Kibo safely to Aunt Suki's.

Iris took the next two days off from work. She spent long hours in lines, waiting for the shoes, blankets, and the difficult-to-get soap and matches that Aunt Toshiko felt were necessary to take to Aunt Suki. At night they sat around the fire making a list of when the previous air raids had come. They finally decided that the safest time to travel would be between eight in the morning and noon. It also seemed that the pattern of bombings was to have one large mission, then a couple of smaller raids, and then about three days to a week of no attacks at all. That meant that Aunt Toshiko would likely be able to get to Shizuoka without too much danger.

She left with little Kibo and her precious packages early Saturday morning. Iris and Grandmother sat anxiously in the house all morning, listening for the dreaded air-raid siren. That afternoon Iris went to work, promising to pick up a newspaper on the way home. She listened to radio reports in shops as she went to and from work. No raids were reported on the main islands of Japan. The papers that night held no news of further raids.

Ten days later they received a postcard from Aunt Toshiko. They had arrived at Aunt Suki's without incident. They were safe. Little Kibo had stopped having nightmares. They hoped Iris and Grandmother would be able to join them when the weather was better. Iris looked at her grandmother, her eyes filling with tears of relief. Grandmother bowed her head, saying, "Our family is safe. From these precious seeds we will be able to grow again."

On Wednesday, Valentine's Day, Iris remembered something she could pass on through the radio program that might help the Allies to understand the situation in Tokyo. There had been no messages from Bill since Iris had moved to Grandmother's. Iris and Jake assumed that he was on some kind of mission. However, if Cole were alive, and if he heard her program and was able to interpret what she said, it might have some importance.

On Sunday, February 18, Iris broadcast: "I feel so sorry for you poor orphans out there in the Pacific, sitting there in the mud and eating your rations. Why, I just finished a wonderful Valentine's feast and thought of you. Of course, it wasn't too unusual; we eat like that all the time here, but it did make me think of how you must wish you could go back home to your families and enjoy the same thing."

When the record came on, Jake said to her, "That was a pretty big long shot, you know. There's only a slim chance that Cole was around to hear it, but if he did, will he make the connection?"

Iris shrugged. "It was the best I could come up with. I hope he remembers that time I burned the chicken on Valentine's Day. We ended up having cabbage salad and canned chicken broth. He said that it sounded like something the refugees ate during World War I. If they know we're running low on food, they might deduce that things are pretty tight and the Japanese can't hold out much longer."

Jake gave a familiar twist to his head and raised an eyebrow. "And maybe they'll be able to get the rising sun to come up in the west." Then, catching Iris's discouraged look, he added, "Then again, maybe it'll help a bit. It'll sound strange to an American ear. It's certainly better than giving up."

Iris smiled thankfully. "That's the one thing we can't do."

February 19, 1945

Dear Cole,

General (used to be Colonel) Whiteside said he'd have a courier take this letter to you at Hamilton on the next flight out. Sort of figured you might have a clue as to what I was saying this week.

Talked about a "Valentine's Feast"—at least that's the part that I thought might mean something to you. She said she was sorry for the "orphans" eating hard-tack because she's been enjoying her Valentine's feast. Said she has them all the time. Can't make heads or tails out of that one. She also said something later on about riding around as if celebrating New Years. Remember the fire engine? The courier bringing this letter to you will be coming right back through Hamilton within a day or so, so get your answer ready for him.

Some news: I'm now where you were when this all broke loose. (I'm getting pretty good at not saying things that make the censors cut holes in my letters.) I'm a 2nd Lt. just like you were. You should just see me out there bossing the noncoms around. You'd better hurry back before I pass you up.

The general says he's scheduled your return within a month. I'll bet you miss the Spam already.

That's all for now.

> Your buddy,
> Sparky

P.S. A couple of bottles of whiskey buys a lot of supplies from the navy (hint).

Hamilton Air Force Base
February 21, 1945

Dear Sparky,

Just got your letter. I'm answering it during my lunch hour. We're having pot roast and gravy. It doesn't compare to your Spam, but I'll live with it. You know, it's pretty bad when I have to wait until there's an emergency before I find out that you know how to write.

Tell the general that Valentine's Day feast must refer

411

*to a time when I. burned dinner on Valentine's Day and
the only thing we had to eat was chicken broth and
cabbage. I said then that it sounded like starvation
issue from WWI. They must be in pretty bad shape in
T. You can bet there're a lot of fire engines wailing
there, too. I try not to think about it too much—*

*I'll be back out there March 10. I expect that you've
cleaned the whole place up and haven't left much for
me to do. Have the beer cooled for my welcome and I'll
see what I can do to help those promotions keep coming.*

*Your pal,
Cole*

*P.S. Line up those naval supplies. I'm bringing Fort
Knox, navy-style.*

Sparky was there waiting when Cole's plane touched down
on Clark Field. It was a funny feeling, after three and a half
years, to see the familiar landmarks: Mount Arayat, the rolling Philippine hills, the broad verdant plain—yet all else was
obliterated. The Fifth Air Force had really bombed Clark, and
nearby Fort Stotsenburg was still a mass of blackened rubble,
despite the army's efforts to put up Quonset huts for the
men. Cole was pleased to see a P-38—*King Cole II*—sitting in a
rivetment, awaiting his use.

"I had a hell of a time getting them to keep the paint job
on that baby," Sparky said, seeing Cole's look of approval.
"They tried to tell me that you were back in the States for
good. One jerk even said you'd been killed. He apologized
when he woke up. One of your men has been flying it, taking
good care of it."

Cole laughed and pounded Sparky on the back. "Goddamn,
it's good to see a prickly bastard like you. There's too many
sops sitting around back home running things from their
armchairs. They're saying the war's over, Germany's on her
knees, and they're quitting. Hell, when I tried to tell them
what's going on in the Pacific, they looked at me like I was
crazy. Let's see if we can get into Manila and find our old
house. You'll love it, Sparks. Sits overlooking the bay." He
smiled wistfully and shook his head sadly. "Jake, Dick, and I
had some good times there."

"Manila isn't much to look at anymore," Sparky said with a

grim look, as they headed toward the general's office. "I guess you haven't heard. The bastards raped and pillaged and burned until there's only rubble left. There won't be any victory parade down Dewey Boulevard because the people that are still alive can't even find their homes, let alone clear the streets." Sparky shook his head. "You can hardly believe the stories coming out of there. They gouged out babies' eyes and smeared them on the walls like jelly. They raped every female from one to ninety, then killed them. They burned what they couldn't steal. God, it's awful."

Cole ran his hand through his hair, shaking his head in disbelief.

"Rodrigues came out of there crying his eyes out, poor guy. By the way, he's anxious to see you when you have time. I've had some pretty good meals with him. He's hoping he can bring his family back to Lubao within a month or so. Promises us a great homecoming." They had reached the general's office, where Cole had to report in. "I'll see to your things and meet you in your quarters in about an hour. I hope those cases I saw are what I think they are."

Cole learned that he was being given a split assignment similar to the one he had had before leaving. He was going to train fighter crews as they came in, go out on regular shake-down flights with the old hands to teach them what he'd learned at gunnery school, and spend the rest of his time as a G-2 with the intelligence division. The general was firm in his orders that Cole not go into combat, but Cole felt that he could live with that.

He went to meet Sparky, satisfied that he'd be there to see the end of the war. The Philippine weather was as he remembered: he was drenched with perspiration by the time he reached his quarters. Sparky greeted him with a towel and a warm beer.

"Have you heard what the next move is after the Philippines?" Sparky asked as Cole pulled out a dry uniform.

"The general said we'd have a briefing at 0700 tomorrow."

"Rumor is that we'll hit Okinawa as soon as we can, maybe by early summer, and then by fall we'll launch the main invasion of Japan."

"Sounds reasonable. Have you heard any more broadcasts?"

"Sunday had some new announcer on, ranting and raving that Roosevelt was a monster and the Germans are winning.

Iris announced three records, two of them symphonies. Probably was on the air no more than two minutes total, and said only what records were going to be played. I wonder what's the matter with Jake."

Cole shrugged as he buttoned his shirt.

"No telling. They've pulled him off sometimes for a month or more. Iris has disappeared for long times too, especially during last summer. Makes me nervous."

"That's a feeling I've got all the time these days," Sparky said.

"Hey, have you heard the latest reports?" a young lieutenant said, sticking his head in the tent flap.

"Cole, this is Lieutenant Jones. He's with communications and one of my best sources. What is it, Jones?" Sparky said, as Jones suddenly went into a starched attention at the sight of Cole. Sparky added, "This is Colonel Tennyson, but he's really a lieutenant in disguise, so don't panic."

"At ease, Jones," Cole said, grinning. "And out with it."

"Those B-29s out of the Marianas hit the Japs but good today, using a new approach. They went in at night, low level, and dropped both explosives and napalm—that new jellied gasoline that causes fires that you can't put out."

"How'd it work?"

"The first recon flight just reported in. They say that about a quarter of Tokyo is nothing but black ashes."

Sparky's face paled, but he forced a smile. "Sounds good. Thanks for the report, Jones." He turned to Cole, who was sitting on his bunk staring after the departing Jones. "Oh, God," he murmured, burying his face in his hands. "How are we going to live through it?"

"The question is," Cole whispered, "how will *they* live through it?"

Grandmother had been depressed since the first bombing, but her depression had become much worse after the terrible fire bombing of the previous night. Iris stayed home from work to be with her.

"Please, Grandmother," she pleaded that morning. "You must eat some rice. You will need your strength."

Grandmother shook her head forlornly and fingered the sleeve of her kimono. "I can still see you trying to carry me to the air-raid shelter last night. My feet don't work after the cold of this winter, and you are so frail."

"It was no problem," Iris lied. "It was my honor to have you lean on me."

"No, no," she said, still shaking her head. "When you had to run to beat out the sparks falling around the house and then kept coming back to try to carry me to the shelter again . . . The smoke and the noise were so close."

Iris shrugged. "It was no more than everyone else in the neighborhood did. I'm glad I thought of the wheelbarrow. Next time I will be able to get you there very quickly." She smiled and pushed the bowl of rice toward her grandmother once more. "I hope the wheelbarrow is not too undignified for you."

Grandmother managed a slight smile. "It is only undignified to survive when the fates do not wish it so. Here, you must take part of the rice. I heard one of the chickens clucking this morning even with all the commotion last night. Go see if she has given us an egg. We will put it in the rice with some soyu. We will enjoy our day together since you will not go to work. It is time for us to talk. Now, go look for that egg."

Iris had just handed the egg to her grandmother when she heard the gate bell ring. Going to the door, she saw Bill and ran to him. "Thank God you're all right!" she cried.

He looked down at her, his face smeared with soot. "Actually, I was worried about you," he said. "I was fine. I watched the whole show from a fishing boat about two miles out. How'd your grandmother hold up?"

Iris shook her head as she led him up the path to the door. "Not well. Ever since the chilblains this winter, she can barely walk. I tried to carry her to the shelter, then finally used the wheelbarrow to get her there." She glanced at the sack on his back. "What's that?"

"A surprise for you and your grandmother. She's been so good to me."

Iris bowed to Grandmother and announced Bill's presence. Graciously, Grandmother received him, telling Iris to bring a warm cloth for him to wash his hands and face before drinking tea with them.

"I cannot stay long," he said with a bow. "I just wanted to bring this to you." He opened the bag and revealed a large, glistening tuna. "We caught several *buri* this week. I kept this one for you. What you can't eat now, Iris can salt and dry or smoke over the coals and it will save for a long time."

Grandmother stared at the forty-pound fish. Finally, she murmured, "*Arigato gozaimasu*, dear friend. You must come to dinner tonight. It will be a celebration and Iris will prepare it for us."

"It will be my pleasure," Bill said, bowing formally despite his disheveled appearance. "Now, please forgive my hasty departure. I must report to work within the hour and I must bathe first. It will be an honor to return tonight."

Bill's appearance worked wonders for Grandmother's depression. She was determined to have everything just right and directed Iris in the careful preparation of the meal. With Grandmother leaning on her cane, watching over Iris's shoulder, Iris prepared the tuna in three ways. The rest of the large fish was carefully sliced and placed over coals to smoke dry. Shavings from these smoked pieces would make soups and delicacies for many, many meals, Grandmother assured Iris.

She then directed Iris's preparation of *sushi*—vinegared rice with tuna rolled in sheets of black *nori*, dried seaweed— and *sashimi*, sliced raw fish seasoned and served with *wasabi*, green dried horseradish moistened into a paste. She insisted that Iris take some of the few remaining dried vegetables she'd brought with her and make soup of noodles, tuna, and vegetables. It wasn't quite the meal that Grandmother might have wished, but by late afternoon she pronounced it sufficient. There were three dishes, an uneven number, and that meant good luck.

All day, as Iris worked under her direction, she talked continually, telling Iris stories of the family, secrets about where things were hidden, pointing out particular family treasures that she wanted Iris to take with her when she went back to the United States. She reminisced about Uncle Anami, expressing her hopes for his safe return even though he had not been heard from in almost two years. She now openly admitted that the United States would surely win. She also foretold that it would be a great blessing for the remnants of the family that Iris and her father were American citizens. That would make it easier for them when the conquering Americans came to Japan.

With sadness, she told of her childhood, the times of glory that Japan had known under the Meiji Empire. Iris learned more in that one afternoon about her heritage and about Japan's history than she had learned in the whole time she had been there.

Finally, just before Bill was due to arrive, Grandmother directed Iris to a cupboard in her sleeping room where she had hidden a bottle of saki. They would drink the saki tonight in solemn celebration of the *buri* and the friendship of a good man. Spring was coming and the cherry blossoms would soon scent the air. It was a time of celebration, even though smoke filled their nostrils and Tokyo burned.

The dinner was a huge success. Bill entertained them with stories, finding bits of humor and noble deeds even in the tragedy all around them. Iris warmed the saki and dutifully kept each cup filled. Grandmother laughed and told stories from olden times, enchanting Bill and Iris with her wit. At the end of the evening, as Bill was getting ready to leave, she said to Iris, "Go to the cupboard behind me on the wall there."

Following her instructions, Iris went to the cupboard and opened the doors. "Up on the top shelf," Grandmother commanded, "you will find a sword. Bring it to me."

Iris took down an ancient sword, fitted in a filigreed scabbard, and handed it to her grandmother with a puzzled look.

"This is one of the family swords," Grandmother explained. "It is not the best, but it is one of them. I know," she said with a wise look in Bill's direction, "that you are very fond of my granddaughter. You are both of the same background. That is fitting. These are not ordinary times. I will not always be here. I am going to give you this sword," she said, handing it to Bill, "because I know that you value one of my most precious treasures and will protect her with your life."

Bill took the sword and bowed to Grandmother, touching his head to the floor. "I am not worthy of this honor."

"If anyone is, you are. Take this sword along with my respect and approval. It will serve you well."

Warm tears filled Iris's eyes as she walked Bill to the door. He turned and looked at her. His eyes were also filled with tears. "I'll come to see you first thing in the morning," he said, touching her cheek and kissing her softly.

Bill was true to his word. He arrived while Iris was still

cooking the morning rice. "I didn't expect you so early," she said, kissing him in the corridor.

He seemed distracted and looked around. "Have you seen your grandmother yet?"

"No, probably too much saki last night."

Bill looked at her strangely. "Show me to her room."

"What for? You can't go wake her up. If you have something to tell her, let me go get her for you."

"No," he said firmly. "Show me to her room."

He sounded so strange, so definite. She led him down the corridor to the room where Grandmother slept. Bill slid back the door and peeked in. He motioned for Iris to stay there and went into the room. When he came out, his eyes were moist. "She's dead," he said softly.

"What? How could . . ." Iris pushed into the room. Grandmother was lying on her *futon*, dressed in her best kimono, her hair carefully arranged in the old-fashioned way. In her hand was a small sword. Her throat was cut, her blood darkening the cushion under her.

"No! Grandmother . . . why . . . ?" Iris cried, running to her.

Bill gently lifted Iris from her grandmother's body and held her as she sobbed. "She committed *seppuku* like a true samurai's daughter. I suspected that was what she was preparing for last night."

"But why?" Iris sobbed. "Why? I loved her . . . why did she do this to me?"

"Because she loved you. She considered your survival most important for the safety of the whole family, whatever part of it remains. She knew that if you had to worry about her during all these air raids that are going to keep coming, she would slow you down and maybe cause you to die. She knew that there wasn't going to be much more food, and one less mouth to feed would help you to survive. When she saw how much I loved you, she knew you would be cared for. That's why she gave me the sword. It was like a command, a sacred trust. That's when I knew she was going to do this."

Iris looked over his shoulder at her grandmother's body. She looked peaceful and calm, an image tarnished by the black clotted blood. "Why didn't you try to stop her? Why didn't you warn me?"

"I couldn't stop her. It was a noble, beautiful death in her

418

mind. How could I warn you? With your tears, you would have destroyed the harmony of her death. She couldn't have gone peacefully if she had to see you grieve. She wants me to live here with you. Is that all right? I will pretend to be your cousin again, for the sake of the neighbors."

Iris knelt and bowed low beside her grandmother's body, her forehead touching the floor, her cheeks wet with tears. "I love you, too, *Oba-a-san*," she whispered.

CHAPTER XXVII

They called it the Ring of Fire. It encircled those within its band of flame, smothering them in choking, burning death. In actuality, it wasn't a circle, but a much more efficient X. The vanguard of the B-29s came in on a new low-altitude approach, skirting under the antiaircraft fire, and dropped their napalm bombs at hundred-foot intervals, marking the target zone with a neat flaming X. The bombardiers on the B-29s following the pathfinder echelon had only to hit the burning X. For three hours they kept coming and bombing. By the time the last of the 325 B-29s reached the target, there was no longer a burning X, just miles of brilliant fires lighting up the entire sky. As the last bombers came in, the heat turbulence caused by the roaring inferno below tossed the 74,500-pound planes thousands of feet into the glowing sky.

When the drone of the last bomber faded away, nature took over. A whipping, howling wind, intensified by the spreading holocaust, carried the fire over the wood, plaster, and bamboo buildings, throwing sparks into the air, scorching more and more of the hapless city in its ravenous path.

When daybreak came, a heavy pall of smoke, like a purple shroud, hung over the city, obliterating the spring sunshine. The smoke-veiled sun hung like a gory orb in the strange sky.

Iris stayed with Grandmother's body, because the officials could not come to take care of a single old woman when the center of the city was filled with casualties. Darkness settled around her, real and imagined, and still she sat.

The night was black and silent. In the sitting room, Grandmother's pillow was empty, indented as if she'd just left it. Iris sat in the dark across from it, her face half-lit by the glow of the coals in the *kotatsu*. A light rain was sifting through the air when she finally saw Bill crossing stealthily through the back garden. His feet were heavy as he came in. With a great sigh, he sat down on the pillow beside Iris.

"There's some rice and tea," she said quietly.

"I can't eat."

"I suppose I should go back to work tomorrow. What *densha* lines are still running?"

"None."

Iris looked at his soot-blackened face. "Is it that bad?"

He closed his eyes and murmured, "Worse. I guess I'll take that tea. You'd better know what I've seen. You've got to understand."

Iris silently handed him a bowl of tea. He drained it and handed it back to her before he spoke. "You're lucky your grandmother's house is in the Meguro district. I went back to our old house. It's gone."

Bill shook his head mournfully. "I couldn't even be sure which street I was on. There's nothing left. About a quarter of Tokyo is burned flat. The buildings that were made of concrete and brick are just shells; they were ovens cooking those who hid in them."

Iris was crying silently, but Bill continued, locked in the horrifying spell of what he'd seen. "There was no hope, no shelter for anyone caught in the inferno. Corpses are piled up on the bridges. Those who sought refuge in the canals were literally boiled alive; those who jumped in the Sumida River were drowned by the mobs rushing into the water. The panic was total."

He rubbed his eyes and shook his head in disbelief. "You can't go out there. It's horrifying beyond imagination. Thousands, maybe more than a million, are homeless. Stay here, where you're relatively safe and hidden in a back street. When the trains start again, I want you to go to your aunt's. I'll stay here with you in the meantime."

Waves of nausea swept Iris as she listened. Wiping the tears from her cheeks with the back of her hand, she asked, "What about Jake? Was the area around NHK hit?"

He shook his head. "I don't know. We won't be able to get near there for days at least. Just sit and wait. If they're operating NHK, you'll hear soon enough."

Under normal circumstances, both Bill and Iris were strong, decisive people. They were survivors. But these were not normal circumstances. The disaster they faced was one they'd helped to create. Now they were worn down by constant fear. Stress had taken its toll. With death on all sides, they had lost their ability to struggle, to fight. Starvation had insidiously crept over them, covering their bodies and spirits with a blanket of lethargy, stifling their energies. It was a matter of time, of waiting. There was no way of knowing which end would come first, theirs or the war's.

For five days after Grandmother's perfunctory funeral, Iris and Bill stayed in Grandmother's house, mostly sleeping. They attended a neighborhood *tonarigumi* meeting together, announcing Grandmother's death and introducing Bill as Iris's cousin from Nagoya, who would be staying with her. The neighbors accepted the information without comment. To them she was a stranger, an interloper. Her presence made them uneasy. She had the ominous feeling that this *tonarigumi* was infiltrated by Kampetei. She and Bill decided not to go again unless summoned. They returned to the house and clung to each other through the cool spring night, listening to the patter of rain on the roof.

The dried vegetables were gone. There was only fermented cabbage and soup made from the two remaining pieces of dried fish.

"I'm going back out on the boat," Bill announced the following morning.

Iris turned her head on the pillow and opened her eyes. "Why?"

"Because we need the food, for one thing." She was silent, staring at the ceiling, frowning. He added, "And I think you'd better start planting a garden."

She was quiet for a moment, then asked quietly, "Do you think we'll be here to harvest it?"

"We'll probably be here at least until fall. I have to try to get some more information, but that's the way it looks."

"How can we last that long?" Iris whispered, her eyes filling with tears.

"The same way we've lasted this long. We've got to pull ourselves together. You can probably make it out to your aunt's, but I could use the garden myself. Don't get discouraged, but the way I see it, the Allies are just now getting the Philippines all tied up. Then they're going to have to come on up through Formosa, Okinawa, and then begin fighting their way up the Kanta Plain," he explained, tracing a map in the air with his hand. "That's going to take time—probably six months to a year."

Iris listened, calmly digesting the information. Finally, she nodded. "You're right. I'll get to work on the garden," she said with a sigh as she got up. "But I'm not going out to Aunt Suki's. First, I don't have the money. Secondly, even if I had it, I wouldn't leave you. You might find someone else to warm your *futon*."

One glance at Bill's face told Iris that her attempt at humor had hurt him deeply. She quickly went to him and put her arms around him. "I want to make sure we get through this war alive. The only way to be sure of that is for us to stay together. I hate it when you're gone," she admitted. "I know that it's necessary and that whatever it is you're doing will help in the end, but . . . I'm lost without you."

He ran his finger down her cheek and said with his old daredevil bravado, "Hey, you wouldn't want to take all the thrill out of my life, would you? There's still some cloak-and-dagger left in me, even though I do think more about gardens and pillows and a certain soft-eyed maiden. You're just afraid that you're going to have to weed that garden all by yourself."

Iris laughed and hit him with her pillow.

Bill was gone for ten days—ten days during which Iris wore herself to the point of exhaustion by putting in as much of a garden as she could find seeds for. She didn't have the strength to work for more than an hour at a time without having to sit down and rest. The rain came often, chilling her with its silvery wetness. Still she worked in the garden, afraid to face the empty house and her own imagination. Each evening she fell asleep, often so exhausted that she didn't take off her clothes or eat. Hunger pangs had been replaced by indifference.

When Bill finally returned, he had more fish for her to dry, and news from the outside world. They fed on the information as ravenously as they devoured the fish. From both they gained strength to go on. The war was going badly for Germany and well for the Allies. The Americans had well-established bases in the Philippines and were preparing for advances north. Perhaps it would all be over by Christmas.

By the middle of April, it was apparent that Iris would have to go back to work. With his erratic schedule, Bill couldn't bring in enough money. There were few enough goods on the market; they needed to be able to buy what they could when it was available. Although Iris was still afraid to go out into the bombed areas, and afraid she would find that Jake was no longer there—a loss she knew would ruin her and make her job intolerable—she knew that she was merely postponing the inevitable.

The decision was made for her on April 28, 1945. She received a postcard from NHK asking her to report back to work. Bill had gone out to the countryside again, so she stalled a few more days.

The following Monday, April 30, there was a knock on the door. A man from the American division of NHK wanted to know if she was all right. Seeing that she had been unhurt by the bombings, he reminded her that the NHK was run by the army and that, as a foreigner, she could not refuse to return to work.

Obviously he was one of the Kampetei she had heard were working at the radio station. He peered around her as she answered him, his eyes catching every detail of the house. Grateful that Bill was gone, Iris politely apologized for neglecting her work simply because her grandmother had died and she was left to live alone. She promised to report for work the following day.

The streetcars ran sporadically on the few remaining tracks and the buses had to make frequent detours to find passable streets, so Iris had to walk the last several blocks to work. As she approached the inner city, her eyes filled with horror. Black skeletons of brick buildings were outlined against the sky. Wooden window frames had burned out, leaving holes like empty eye sockets in the smoke-stained concrete walls. A heavy metal safe rested precariously on the rubble inside a hollow building, having fallen intact through the burning floors. Metal door hinges and knobs lay on a pile of ashes.

Dazed people picked their way along empty streets, stepping over blackened ruins. Beams of charcoal crosshatched the squares that once had been buildings. Ahead, where she could see across empty city blocks, Iris spotted the few remaining tall buildings. To her relief, the NHK Building was among them. Perhaps Jake was all right after all.

However, when she reached the second floor, she didn't see Jake. She went up to the third floor and approached Major Tsuneishi. Who was she to work with on her next program, she asked. He looked up from his desk and blandly said, "Why, the American POW, of course."

"But Captain Devon isn't here."

"He wasn't feeling well, and since you were still not here, he felt he couldn't work. I sent him to the doctor. He will be back tomorrow. Begin working on the script yourself. You don't need him."

"He is the professional broadcaster," Iris reminded him, fearful they might think they could eliminate Jake. "I cannot do a finished script without his guidance."

Major Tsuneishi glared at her. "I said he'd be back."

Relieved, Iris read through the news material they were to include on the program. It didn't mention Europe. But they had begun picking up local news reports from the States, writing up the worst, with ridiculously exaggerated reports of train accidents and disease outbreaks back home. Iris arranged them in such a way as to reveal their distortion.

There was one article reporting that the United States was so plagued by rampaging juvenile delinquents that they had to place curfews on children, close swimming pools, and curtail school activities. Such was the result of a decadent society. However, such closures were explained more truthfully when Iris followed the juvenile-delinquent story with one about the outbreak of infantile paralysis in two southern counties. Polio, not degenerate youth, closed swimming pools.

For once, Tsuneishi hadn't lied. Jake was there waiting for her the next day, pale and thinner than before but elated to see her still alive and unhurt. When he heard about Grandmother, Aunt Teiso, and her little cousins, he consoled her. When she told him the news that Bill had brought—that Germany was faltering—they both ached to know more.

At Jake's suggestion, Iris left work early that night to apply for a job at Domei. She hoped that maybe because she could take shorthand and type, they might use her as they'd used Eva, monitoring the overseas Allied broadcasts. She was hired immediately. They put her on a three-hour shift in the morning. The money and the news would ease their wait. Then, on May 8, 1945, she brought the news. The end was one step closer. Germany had surrendered.

Iris and Jake could barely talk about Germany's surrender for fear of revealing their joy to the rest of the office staff. However, when Bill returned the following week, he seemed distracted, more subdued than elated. Iris watched him with puzzlement as he went about getting ready for another trip to the countryside. The only genuine response she got from him that evening was when she told him about her new job at Domei.

His eyes lit up with what Iris could only call relief. "That's great," he said. "You sure could use the extra money. Besides, it isn't good for you to stay around the house half the day. Let me know if you hear anything interesting. By the way, if anyone comes by here with a message for me, just tell them that you're Hanako—that's the Japanese name for Flower," he said with a fleeting smile, "and they'll give the message to you. I'm sorry I have to leave again so soon. There's not much you should get out for the Allied information, except that the Japanese are now building their ships with wooden hulls. One well-placed torpedo or bomb and they'll sink like rocks. There's no more metal left for war purposes now that they're cut off from the southern regions of Asia. I imagine that it's the same with airplane production. The only other thing is that the Nipponese hate that new P-51 fighter plane as much as they hate the B-29 bomber. The Yanks have finally come up with some real winners." He winked. "You'll be having American turkey for Christmas at this rate."

Iris felt a strange contraction of her heart. She smiled, not trusting her voice.

"I think you should stash away whatever money you can spare," Bill continued. "Whenever you get the opportunity, buy any food that's available that will keep—you know, rice, dried goods, grains, anything that won't spoil. I'll see if I can get a few extra ration cards. When this thing comes close to ending, there's no telling what will happen. Now that their only ally has folded, the Japanese militarists are getting more fanatical about sabotage, looking for any scapegoat they can find. They really are sharpening bamboo poles for a last-ditch fight for the Emperor. When that time comes, get out to your aunt's or something. Just don't stick your pretty neck out where it will be noticed as foreign."

Puzzled by his instructions, Iris said, "When that time comes, I expect that we'll be able to find someplace to hide out together. Maybe Aunt Suki will take us both."

"It's best you know what to do now, just in case."

"Just in case what?"

"You've got to be prepared for anything."

Bill held her close to him throughout the night, softly kissing her cheek when he thought she was asleep. She lay still, feeling a deep well of emptiness opening within her, an inexplicable, hollow fear. Bill left the next morning, promising to be back by June 6.

There was a growing tension at NHK, almost as if they were braced for a final blow. Iris and Jake were allowed to include more music on their program, shortening the time they spent on propaganda. When Tsuneishi commented on this, Iris quickly smiled and said that that was their way of insuring a large listening audience among the soldiers. Now that Germany had surrendered, the American stations were bound to be filled with glowing commentary. The soldiers, bored with fighting, would turn to the station that provided them with music from home instead of long lectures. She added that that was what she thought Major Tsuneishi himself had originally intended for the program to do.

When she was done with her explanation, he pulled himself to his full height and nodded. "I was testing to see if you remembered your instructions," he said briefly, then turned and left the room.

When they were alone, Jake murmured, "You sure handled Tsuneishi. Cole would be proud of you . . . and I intend to tell him when he gets here."

Iris was stopped by a pang of sorrow. "If he's alive," she said softly, "I'm sure he'll have much more exciting things to talk about." Then she said, "What do you think about making a big joke about the P-51s? The Yanks ought to be sharp enough to pick up on the real meaning behind it." They'd used the code last week to tell about the wooden ships and were reluctant to try the code two weeks in a row.

Jake looked at her solemnly. "You don't want to count on Cole being there to pick up any private messages, do you?"

Iris said quietly, "I don't think it's realistic. I can't count on private hopes coming true." She picked up the script she'd been working on. "How's this for a lead-in?" she asked, reading from the script she'd written.

"Well, fellas, coconuts and palm trees are great for the tourists, but a change of scene wouldn't hurt your game any. I'm game, how about you? Here now we have a little number that caught our fancy. We're dedicating this to all the gang on Saipan: 'Holy Smoke, Can't You Take a Joke?' "

"That's pretty good. The change of scene tells them to keep moving on, and you even said you want to get out of here. That business about a dedication for the Saipan troops is great. Here they are bombing the hell out of us and you're playing 'Holy Smoke, Can't You Take a Joke?' for them. Now what's your idea for the P-51 encouragement program?"

Grateful that Jake didn't press her about Cole, Iris smiled and said, "What about announcing that the Americans are so hard up that they're flying flimsy P-51 fighters piloted by young girls?"

Jake laughed more heartily than Iris had seen for weeks. "That's great," he agreed. "Tsuneishi did pass on a bulletin telling about the flimsy fighters flying over Formosa. You know," he added soberly, "I'm beginning to understand what great taste in women Cole displayed when he got engaged to you."

Iris shifted uncomfortably under his gaze. "Let's get back to work," she said. "We have a program to get out."

That was May 25, 1945. That night, the B-29s returned. Showers of incendiary bombs burst into brilliant flowers of flame hundreds of feet above the ground, raining their deadly beauty on the people below. Towering spirals of flame answered from the ground, dancing into the darkness, tinging it with blood red. The sickening sweet smell of smoke and burning flesh drifted across the city, carrying the screams of fear and death on its ghostly back. The people of Tokyo called these blossoming fires of death the "Flowers of Edo," a ghoulish bit of poetry that made Iris shiver.

Alone for the first time during a big raid, Iris was directed by the fire warden not to seek shelter as usual. She had to join the fire brigade, manning buckets and watching for flying sparks that might touch off the tinder roofs of the neighborhood. She spent the entire night running from house to house, carrying buckets of sloshing water, beating falling sparks from yards and roofs. There was nowhere she could possibly go to hide from the encroaching inferno if it came any closer. Like all the others, fear sent her scurrying frantically in every direction, chasing sparks both real and imagined.

By dawn, the orange glow of the fire had darkened to an angry black. Even though the fire was still far from her neighborhood, its heavy smoke clung to the air, rasping her throat with each breath. She fell on her *futon*, her clothes torn and sooty. Exhausted, she slept the entire day, never knowing that half of Tokyo was now nothing but cinders, never knowing that the officials lacked crematorium facilities to take care of the thousands upon thousands of dead, never knowing just how close she had actually come to becoming one of those victims. She did know she would not be able to travel to work the following day. She stayed home, working the ashes into her garden soil, trying not to wonder why the smoke had a peculiar, sweet smell, trying not to worry about Bill or Jake.

By some miraculous turn of wind or fate, the NHK Building was still standing when she returned to work two days later. Jake was there, his face as ashen as the streets, but enormously relieved to see Iris alive. She was touched to notice that he was shaking and had to sit down when he saw her come in the door.

She reported to him on the horrors she'd seen, shared her skimpy lunch with him, and gave him half the bottle of vitamin-B tablets that she'd found in a pharmacy near her house. With nothing to report from Bill, they began to arrange a program heavy with long-playing semiclassical records.

When Iris returned home from work on June 6, Bill still wasn't back. Counting on his promise to have returned by this time, and praying that he was all right, Iris began getting ready for him. She was afraid that to hesitate even a little in her expectation of his return that night would be a bad omen.

With forced cheer, she prepared a dinner from dried fish and rice. Then she made a soup, using the leaves of some squash plants in the garden. She'd saved an egg, which she planned to poach in the seasoned soup as he'd taught her. When that was done, she went to get herself ready.

She had desperately missed and worried about Bill in the past two weeks. Had it not been for Jake, she thought she would have gone mad from loneliness. But her mind had been distracted by Jake's illness; whatever was wrong, it was getting worse. He put all his energy into the broadcasts—energy that he didn't really have to give.

Grandmother's was an old-style traditional Japanese house with the bathhouse away from the main dwelling. Iris slipped on her *yukata* and took her towel and a sliver of soap, then picked up the jar she used for her ersatz shampoo. She always saved whatever bits of soap she had and put them in the jar; when there was enough collected, she poured boiling water over them and the resultant jelly sufficed as a shampoo.

She stopped on her way out to the bathhouse to scatter the last bit of *awa* seed to the chickens. They were getting thin and didn't lay very well. Iris hoped that the bugs in the garden would be enough to keep them going now. Otherwise, she and Bill might have to have a chicken dinner; she shuddered to think about that as Gertrude pecked at her *geta* demanding more food.

There was no charcoal to heat the bath and Iris refused to use the public baths, communal nudity being something she'd never been able to accustom herself to. However, she'd discovered that if she opened a panel on the roof of the bathhouse, the afternoon sun would heat the water to a tolerable temperature. The long rains of June were due anytime now, and she had to enjoy what warmth the sun had to offer before then. She hummed softly as she walked down the pebbled path to the bathhouse.

She had just rinsed herself off and crawled into the old wooden tub when she heard Bill calling. Happily, she stood up and whistled loudly.

Within seconds, Bill popped his head in the door of the bathhouse. "Hey, you gonna stay here all day? I've got a hot date tonight and want to clean myself up."

"Wait! Where're you going?" Iris called as he disappeared.

"Be right back," came his muffled reply. "Just make room for one grimy guy."

Laughing with relief to see him safe and sound, Iris climbed out of the tub and dried off. She had just slipped into her *yukata* when Bill reappeared, demanding that she scrub his back before she went back into the house. Iris gave him a lingering, welcoming kiss and then complied. "I'm glad you fought off that depression," she said as she soaped his back.

"*Nanakorobiyaoki,*" he murmured.

"What's that mean?"

"It's an old Japanese saying for going against extreme adversity: Fall down seven times, get up eight." He took the sponge from her and scrubbed himself vigorously. "That's what we've got to do. We keep getting knocked down, but we've got to keep getting up until we've gotten up one more time than we've been knocked down. It's that last struggle up that wins it." He took the bucket of water and poured it over his head, rinsing off. "At least that's the lesson the Japanese army is teaching now. Somehow, it made a lot of sense to me. It's something you should practice saying to yourself."

"*Nanakorobiyaoki,*" Iris repeated. "I'll keep that in mind. But for now, my resident philosopher, I'm going to get dinner ready."

"I put a little surprise on the *shokutaku,*" he said, with a twinkle in his eye.

To her amazement, Iris found a bottle of saki on the low table where they had their meals. She carefully got out her grandmother's saki set and gently warmed the rice wine. When she lit the lantern in the kitchen, she found a sack with three large fish and four small ones. She cut a portion off one of the *buri* and filleted it. They would charcoal broil it to go with her soup. It would be a celebration of their being together, of their renewed hope.

Bill was full of stories, news, and jokes. He told her how the Americans were making headway in taking over Okinawa and that from there it was just a jump to Kyushu, the southern island of Japan. He related the devastation of the cities of Japan. But mostly he told her how pretty she was—punctuating each statement with a kiss. Iris laughed and drank the saki and told him she couldn't last without him.

"By the way," he said as he lit a cigarette after dinner, "there's a sack of *awa* for the chickens beside the back door. I bought some from a farmer who thought I was crazy. Did anyone come and leave any messages for me?"

"No. What are you expecting?"

"Someone monitoring radio messages for me. I found an old priest in a backwoods village who helps me out. I know pretty much what the message will say, but it will be good to

430

have it confirmed. You might even be able to understand it yourself, if you get it before me. If it seems to need some action and I'm not here, go ahead and use your own judgment."

That night Iris lay in Bill's arms, comforted by his steady breathing, lulled by the beat of his heart. Then in the middle of the night her contentment was dashed by a sudden foreboding. A shadow passed over her peace, extinguishing her single source of light. She turned her head and listened, trying to sort out any sound that might have caused her fear. The spring frogs were croaking. A light whisper of rain caressed the roof and murmured down the drain spout by the bedroom window.

Then the frogs were silent. There was a sudden clatter from the gate bell and the sound of heavy boots on the rock path to the house. She turned to wake Bill, but he was already sitting up, alert.

He put his hand to her lips and whispered, "Whatever you do, don't make a sound. No matter what you hear. Promise me?"

"What is it?" she whispered back in wide-eyed fear.

"Promise me," he commanded. She nodded, and he added, "Stay here." With that he slipped on his *yukata* and went to the door.

Iris could barely hear the voices above the thumping of her heart. Intuitively, she'd known the boots were those of military officials . . . or Kampetei. She strained to hear the words.

"We have reports that an American lives here," said one man.

"We will search the premises," said another. "The imperial government cannot tolerate any chance of espionage or insidious signals guiding the B-29s."

"A search won't be necessary," Bill said, his voice louder and more clear than the others, an American accent slipping into his usually perfect Japanese. "I'm the American who lives here. I came here from the Philippines after the war broke out. Figured I might—"

His words were stopped by the explosion from a gun. Iris gasped and started for the window. She could see a man in a Kampetei uniform bending over. "Get his feet," a voice said. Then they were gone.

As Iris ran to get the lantern, she heard the gate bell ring, just once this time, as if it were an afterthought. Sobbing with uncontrollable fear, she ran to the door.

There was no one there. Just a pool of blood on the *genkan*, slowly mingling with the rain, washing a pale ruby stream across the pebbles of the path.

There was nothing she could do, nowhere she could go. Iris sat alone in the darkened house, day after day, staring at the white screen leading to the entryway. She had given up.

After five days, the gate bell rang once more. Still Iris sat quietly on her pillow. Then there were footsteps going around the side of the house. With mild interest she followed their progress. The back door slid open and she found herself staring into the soft eyes of a young man.

"I am looking for Mr. Ando," he said quietly.

Iris shook her head forlornly. "He's gone."

"Then I would like to speak with Hanako."

Something stirred within her, a tiny warning signal, a remembrance, a contact from Bill beyond the barrier of death. "Do you have a message?" she asked finally. "I am Hanako."

"Then please let me to speak English," he said, smiling and bowing. "So long I cannot speak English, only to Mr. Ando-san."

Iris took a deep breath. "Mr. Ando is dead. He told me before he died that I would receive a message. He said I would know what to do with it if he wasn't here." She paused, biting her lip as she saw the hurt in the young man's eyes. Obviously, he'd cared for Bill, too. "If you will give me the message," she urged quietly.

The young man bowed his head for a moment, made the sign of the cross, then said, "I am an aspirant for Catholic priesthood. My studies stop with war. I will ask prayers for his soul. Is he in hallowed ground?"

Iris shook her head, hot tears flowing over her cheeks. "I don't know. They shot him and then took him away."

The young man was silent. Then he said, "The message today is strange. It says, 'King Cole is coming.'" He looked at her quizzically as she gasped. "This means something?"

Iris nodded. "I believe so. I will pass it on. Thank you for coming. If you have anything else, any other message, please give it to me."

"Yes, I will do that. May you go with God," he said, as he closed the screen and left Iris in the dusky light of the house.

"You also," she murmured, staring at the empty screen.

CHAPTER XXVIII

They said there were only snipers left. Okinawa, with its fine airfields and anchorages, was the final stepping stone to Japan. Now, with 12,500 Americans and 100,000 Japanese dead, it was in the "mopping up" stage. But there were more than snipers to terrorize the American troops. There were the haunting kamikaze attacks. The incomprehensible suicide dives, which materialized without warning, struck terror in the heart of every man who'd ever witnessed one. There were whispered tales of finding kamikaze pilots with feet shackled to their rudders, chilling the imagination.

Still, they fought on. Victory was inevitable. Sparky had gone out July 6 with the 35th Fighter Group, the first contingent of fighters to arrive in Okinawa. Cole had waited impatiently, chafing at any delay that kept him behind the front lines to Japan. Then, on July 10, he received orders to go out on the next transport to Okinawa, provided he was willing to take an assignment in flight intelligence only. His faithful P-38, *King Cole*, must stay behind. Cole would have agreed to anything that would put him closer to Japan.

That first night on Okinawa, he went to sleep feeling relatively safe, only to be awakened around midnight by the sound of gunfire across the field. Eight suicidal Japanese had attacked the camp and had quickly been shot. Cole settled back down. He had no sooner drifted off to sleep than he was awakened again by the sound of activity right outside his tent. Grabbing his gun, he went to the tent flap and peered out.

Silhouetted against the crescent moon was a large flatbed truck. Two bottles were handed over to the driver and the truck took off, leaving Sparky to watch after it. Cole went out

433

and stood beside him, watching the truckdriver stop across the field and begin unloading material.

"What in the hell's going on?" Cole demanded.

"Sorry if my midnight requisitioning disturbed your beauty sleep," he said, grinning. "What you see going on over there is an eight-rose mess hall being delivered by a faithful Seabee."

"Eight rows?"

"Yeah, took two bottles of Four Roses to divert it from becoming an unnecessary naval recreation hall. I sure hope the war doesn't take too much longer. I only have half a case left of that stuff you brought me. I've sheltered half the Fifth Air Force with those babies. You should get a Medal of Honor."

Cole laughed. "Well, since you've killed my sleep for such a worthy cause, why don't you come into my humble abode and help me lower the level on a nonrequisitioned bottle of Scotch?"

Sparky led the way eagerly. Cole reached into his footlocker, pulled out a bottle, and poured a generous splash into two tin cups. "Here's to Tokyo," he said, handing a cup to Sparky.

"Here's to Tokyo and getting there in time," Sparky replied, draining the cup and holding it out for a refill. Cole poured him another shot, and Sparky lit a cigarette. "You know, it all gets to you after a while. Every time I see those B-29s going over, I know they've been bombing the hell out of Japan. The odds are pretty high, you know," he added softly.

Cole nodded. "I know. You just got to fight it, that's all. Once you get down, thinking about what's the use and all that, you could do something stupid and get yourself killed. As long as we're still hearing Jake and Iris on the radio every now and then, there's hope."

Sparky put out his cigarette. "They haven't been on so regular." He swallowed the rest of his drink. "And I've never heard Eva."

"Iris mentioned her that second broadcast we heard. I'm sure that's what she meant when she said, 'Tokyo's just like the Garden of Eden, complete with Eve.'"

"A lot of explosives have gone under and over the bridge since then." He put down the cup and got up. "Ah, I'm just tired. We've made it so far. Both of us. That's a good sign."

"That's it," Cole said. "Just keep on thinking that."

Sparky stood at the tent flap, looking across the field at the rows of planes, silver in the moonlight, like great birds sleeping with their wings extended. A cool night breeze wafted in through the open tent flap. "You know," he said, "we could knock the Japanese to their knees just by bombing the hell out of those islands."

"I've been thinking the same thing," Cole said, standing beside him. "But the Joint Chiefs of Staff don't agree."

"Yeah, give the navy their due. Still, maybe it's for the best. Tokyo would be leveled the other way."

Cole was silent for a minute, then said softly, "I've seen the recon photos from the May twenty-sixth night raid. Over half of Tokyo is leveled."

Sparky turned and looked at Cole sharply, then left without saying a word.

On July 26, the Allies issued the Potsdam Declaration, demanding the unconditional surrender of Japan. It was signed by Churchill, Truman, and Chiang Kai-shek. The Japanese Diet rejected the terms, fearful that it would mean the end of the Divine Emperor. As Iris listened to the Allied broadcasts that day, she sensed that Japan had somehow condemned its islands to a terrible fate.

Depressed, she went to NHK. Jake would want to know about the latest news. Recently they had been told to soften the propaganda even more. They had been broadcasting almost nothing but music for the past two weeks. Maybe the Japanese felt that by eliminating most of the propaganda they could soften the inevitable blow of American fury. But now that the surrender had been rejected . . .

Jake listened to her report and made no comment. He seemed shakier and more weak than ever. His complexion was now clay-colored, and there was a strange blue tinge around his nose. She begged him to eat some of the fresh beans and cabbage that she'd brought from the garden. He nibbled at one bean.

She pulled out a box of records, preparing to screen some for their program that coming Sunday. Suddenly she heard the scrape of a chair and a thump. Turning, she saw Jake on the floor. "Jake?" she cried, running to him. No answer. His body was limp. His face was blue.

"*Tasukete!*" Help! she cried, opening the door.

One of the office workers came running. He stooped over

Jake and felt his chest, then called for someone to get a doctor.

"He's alive," he said, then turned Jake over and began moving his arms up and down.

Two strange men came in and carried Jake out of the room and down the stairs. Iris stood helplessly, silently watching until they were out of sight.

Going back to the record room, she sat down and tried to stop shaking. The room seemed to be spinning around her. She was shivering and drenched with perspiration.

"Here," said a voice as a hand held out a cup of water.

Iris took it wordlessly and tried to drink it. Her hands were shaking so badly that she spilled most of it on her lap. "*Arigato,*" she whispered as she handed it back. She looked up and saw her supervisor, Yakumo, standing beside her chair. He was looking at her with compassion. "Where did they take him?" she asked.

"Juntendo Hospital. You could probably go visit him tomorrow. He could tell you from his bed what to do with the broadcast."

Iris nodded numbly.

"That is, if he's still alive," Yakumo added. "Miss Hashimoto," he whispered, "I also want to tell you something. It is not safe for you to remain at NHK much longer. I am very realistic. I can see the Americans coming. I can also see the militarists in their fanaticism doing unjust things. You have served to the best of your ability, yet you have persisted in keeping your American citizenship. Maybe wisely so. However, it would not be good for you to be here when some Kampetei wants to prove his patriotism in the end. Perhaps you can do the broadcast this Sunday, but then you should not come back. I will try to have your pay ready for you."

Iris stared at him. Beads of perspiration covered his upper lip, and his face was pale. "Why are you telling me this?"

"You told me you would create a program that would bring me honor by becoming very popular with the American soldiers. You kept your word and I was honored. I will return the favor."

"Thank you for your concern, Yakumo-san."

"Perhaps when times are better, you will remember my kindness," he said awkwardly. With a jerky bow, he turned and left her sitting on the chair. Alone.

The next morning she left Domei news early, claiming that the broadcast she was assigned was too full of static to understand. It was true in part, but her real reason was that she wanted to find Jake.

Juntendo Hospital was on the edge of the bomb devastation, north of the Imperial Palace. To get there, Iris had to pass through some of the worst-hit sections of the city. Very little rubble had been removed from the streets, and no repairs had been made. It was as if the city was waiting with resignation for its inevitable fate.

There was much confusion in the hospital and only evasive answers when Iris asked to see Jake. However, after convincing a harassed doctor that she worked with Jake at NHK and needed to talk to him about her job, he acquiesced.

Jake was in a room with some other prisoners, lying in a cot in a far corner. She hurried to his side. His face was pale, but he looked peaceful. She watched his chest; then, convinced that he was still breathing and merely sleeping, she sat down on the edge of the bed.

He opened his eyes and turned to her. His face slowly lit up with a faint smile. "Hey there," he whispered, "what are you doing here?"

Tears filled her eyes, but she didn't care. She was so relieved that he was alive. "I just knew you were too ornery to really be sick. I figured I'd come down here and blow the whistle on your charade."

Jake closed his eyes for a moment. "You're going to have to go on without me. Just use the old scripts we wrote and you'll be all right," he said weakly.

Iris nodded. "That's what I've been putting together for Sunday. Jake," she said, lowering her voice, "Yakumo told me not to come back after that. Said it might not be safe."

"Believe him. The end is near. What's the news today?"

"The same. It seems as if the whole city is just braced for the next blow."

"I wonder where it will be," he mused, closing his eyes.

"Jake, did the doctor say what was wrong? Is it just exhaustion?"

He shook his head. "I'm not sure. He doesn't speak much English. I think it's the old ticker. Sort of a heart attack. That's where it hurt." He breathed deeply, swallowed, and continued, "He also said I should eat lots of vegetables."

"When Eva was in the hospital, I brought her meals. I'll ask if I can do the same thing for you, at least part of the time."

Jake nodded, his eyes closed again.

"I'll be back tomorrow. Just rest and get well." He was sleeping by the time she turned to go. Even their brief conversation had exhausted him.

Curiosity kept Iris at the Domei listening station for a week longer than she worked at NHK. She needed the money just to be able to eat, so she stayed on, despite indications from co-workers that she might be singled out for Kampeteï reprisals. During that week, she went each afternoon to the hospital, taking Jake the news of the day and rich soups cooked with fresh vegetables from her garden. She told him she would not preserve any food this summer; she just knew that it wouldn't be needed. Instead, she was eating as much as she could, drying only the few vegetables she couldn't eat immediately. Jake gained strength with each visit, although she wondered if he would ever regain the robust health he once had. She chatted with him, trying to cheer him, but he tired quickly. There was none of the familiar fighting spark left in him. *Nanakorobiyaoki*, she told herself. Fall down seven times; get up eight, she told Jake.

On August 4, 1945, she collected her last pay from Domei. Thus, she only heard the news from the Japanese sources. On August 6, 1945, Japan suddenly lost all communication with Hiroshima. They suspected that a large bomb had taken out the lines.

On August 9, she had another visit from the young man who'd brought her the message about Cole. He bowed respectfully and said, "The news is Americans drop two bombs. One on Hiroshima and today one on Nagasaki. They call these new bombs atomic. Do you know the meaning of this word *atomic*?"

Iris shook her head. "No, but it must be very bad."

He nodded mournfully. "Hiroshima and Nagasaki are gone." He made a wiping gesture with his hand. "Atomic took them. Gone. Many people dead. They say a strange fire that burns within, water not stop it." He looked at Iris with wide-eyed fear. "What can that mean?"

Iris poured him a cup of tea. "Perhaps it means it is all over," she said softly. "Perhaps it means you will have many opportunities to practice your English."

*   *   *

Iris had walked in to the rice vendor's store in hopes of finding something to eat. The store was filled with people bowing toward a radio set on the counter. Knowing that something of great importance was happening, she stood in a corner, frightened, as she listened. A high-pitched voice announced, *"We have resolved to pave the way for a grand peace for all generations to come by enduring the unendurable and suffering what is insufferable."*

What did it mean? The courtly Japanese was stilted and difficult for her to understand. Bewildered, she watched the people with their foreheads pressed to the floor, silently weeping as they heard the words. When the broadcast ended, they all remained sitting on the floor, some sobbing openly. Finally, as one woman turned, wiping her eyes, Iris said, "Please, I didn't understand. What was said?"

"Don't you know? It was the voice of our Emperor, speaking to his loyal subjects for the first time in history. In his own divine voice we have heard of the end of the war. It is over."

At her words, Iris too began to weep. Together, they shared the agony, the relief, the sense of release. It was over.

Iris immediately went to Jake. They held hands in silence as the sky darkened into night, the first night of peace. Finally, Jake whispered, "You'd better go. I'll understand if you don't come again. It's going to be a time of craziness. There are too many fanatics out there for something not to happen. You'd better stay hidden. I'll be all right here."

Iris nodded, smiling wryly. "See you at the Victory Dance."

Jake closed his eyes and smiled. Then, squeezing her hand, he waved her off.

He was right. She knew that. From all the broadcasts she heard over the store radios, pleading with everyone to lay down their arms, begging the populace to obey the Emperor and "endure the unendurable" in the name of peace, Iris knew that there was great fear of fanatics doing something to anger the Americans so that they would drop another of their terrible bombs. She didn't want to be one of the last victims of this senseless war. Not after surviving this far. She stayed inside. As the summer heat and humidity filled the air, the country waited, braced for what would come next: occupation.

Now, cut off from her last human contact, left alone in her

dead grandmother's house, Iris existed on what was left in the garden. Everything else was gone. She ate the leaves of the vegetables as well as the fruit, not having the energy even to cook them. The plums on the tree outside the door were still green; when she ate them, she suffered sharp stomach pains. She went from surviving to barely existing. She spent most of her time sleeping.

Perhaps she could go to Aunt Suki's someday, when she could find the money. Perhaps her family would be coming back to Tokyo and she would be here to see them. Perhaps when the Americans came . . . But then her mind began to swirl with terrifying images. How would they know she was an American? Would it make any difference, when her face was Japanese? The women were hiding. Dark tales were whispered of what happens when vengeful conquering troops come into a vanquished country. The government was bringing in selected young women in hopes that the Americans would slake their lust on them and not rape all the women and girls in the country.

It was all too frightening, too confusing. Iris didn't know where to turn. There was no one she could talk to. They were all dead. She didn't dare go back across the city to see Jake. Numbly, she simply turned and went back to sleep.

After Hiroshima, there was a long, tense silence from the Japanese government. America waited, holding off full-scale attack to give the Japanese time to consider. On August 8, Russia declared war on Japan. On the ninth, another awful bomb was dropped on Nagasaki. On the tenth, the Domei News Agency broadcast that Japan was willing to surrender as long as they got to keep their Emperor.

Cole and Sparky listened to the news flashes crackle across the Pacific, shaking their heads in wonder. On August 11, the United States clarified their position, their demands for Japanese surrender. Then, silence. Nothing was heard from Tokyo on August 12 or 13. Sparky and Cole, along with the rest of the Pacific forces, received orders to resume full-scale bombing attacks. Seven thousand tons of bombs would be dropped on Japan each day until they surrendered.

Cole and Sparky knew that Tokyo was sure to be the next target for the atomic bomb.

Then, on August 14, (August 15 in the Pacific) President

Truman announced the end of the war. Japan had surrendered. All pilots in the air were called back in. There would be no more bombing. That night, Cole and Sparky broke open the last bottle of their "requisition" whiskey.

Then came the long, agonizing wait, just sitting there looking at the planes parked alongside the field. It was everything Cole could do to keep from jumping into one of them and flying straight to Tokyo, with Sparky as his copilot.

On August 25 they got the good word. The general came through on his promise that Cole and Sparky would be with him when he touched Japanese ground. All the big brass, from General MacArthur on down, would land in Japan on August 30. Cole and Sparky flew in the escort group.

It was ideal flying weather, clear skies and warm sunlight. Mount Fuji, the landmark used by the B-29's, was not snow-covered like on the picture postcards, but a gray cone.

Knowing that it was all over had created a bit of a letdown. But flying into Japan with the first wave of occupation forces brought all the tension back. MacArthur believed that if the Emperor had told the populace to lay down their arms, they would. Cole and Sparky hoped MacArthur was right. Their lives had ridden on his word before, but this was somehow more of a gamble than any of the others.

There were less than five hundred infantry on the ground at Atsugi Airfield when General MacArthur's plane touched down. The fighter escort buzzed the field, then stayed aloft, creating a show of force and guarding the C-54's landing. As Cole and Sparky got out of the cockpit, the realization hit them that this handful of men was walking into a country of over seventy million people who, less than two weeks ago, had been maniacal in their determination to kill all Americans. To increase the impact, MacArthur had sent down orders that all officers were to leave their sidearms in the planes. They were to walk around unarmed, proving they were conquerors.

Cole and Sparky joined the soldiers milling around MacArthur and the Japanese greeting party. Presently, they were told to load up in a strange mélange of Japanese cars and decrepit trucks; they then set out on a long, serpentine procession to Yokohama, the nearest city. It was a tense time. The road to Yokohama was lined with Japanese soldiers, fully armed, stationed about a hundred yards apart, all with their backs turned to the procession of conquering Americans.

"What do you think about that?" Sparky muttered.

"Well, it could be a way of keeping some fanatic from breaking through and trying to stop the peace," Cole ventured.

"I don't know what they mean by it, but it sure as hell makes me nervous to see all of them with their guns drawn and me with not even a slingshot."

They were silent the rest of the ride, never taking their eyes off the strange armed guards lining their route.

Yokohama was a shock, even though they'd seen the reconnaissance photos. Seen from the ground, it was sickening. Whole blocks were burned out. Rubble filled the streets. When the procession passed by, gaunt, terrified people scurried into shelters that were no more than holes in the ground covered with rubbish. There had been an obvious attempt to clear the route for the Americans coming into the city, but it was also obvious that it would take years for the city and its people to recover. The desolation and destruction were appalling.

Sparky whistled. "They said there were more than a million people living around here. What happened to them?"

"What about Tokyo?" Cole muttered.

Strangely, the waterfront area of Yokohama was not too badly battered by the raids. The caravan pulled up in front of the New Grand Hotel, which was only a little worse for wear. Since no one but generals and important colonels were to stay there, Cole felt particularly lucky that General Whiteside claimed him as one of his aides and gave him a back room in which he could bunk Sparky on the sly. The park in front of the hotel was still clear and would serve as a bivouac area for the rest of the men. However, everywhere else, as far as the eye could see, were charred ruins. Cole shuddered as he looked out his hotel-room window across the blackened skeleton that once had been a thriving city of over a million human beings.

Sparky and Cole sweated out the wait. They checked around with the officers and found that the surrender ceremony wasn't going to take place for another two days. It would be on the battleship *Missouri*, in the middle of Tokyo Bay. That way, it would be on American property.

In the meantime, there was not much for them to do. After the first day, Cole had finished the token paperwork assigned to him and the estimates of military conditions that he had observed. By the afternoon of August 31, he had devised a plan. In order to get a clear view of the inherent military dangers to the American personnel in the Tokyo Bay region, he would have to go, with an aide, to Tokyo and scout out the area. The plan wouldn't hold water under scrutiny, but it might get them to Tokyo. He checked out a car and claimed Sparky was his aide. They knew that press correspondents had already slipped off to Tokyo, so he and Sparky wouldn't be the first. They took off, with Sparky at the wheel of a strange charcoal-burning contraption that threatened to asphyxiate them in the first ten miles.

They knew that they were among the first military to reach Tokyo, but from what they'd seen and heard there would be no problem. Word was out that the Emperor had ordered everyone to lay down their arms and make the Americans welcome. It seemed that to the Japanese, whatever that bespectacled little man said was the word of God. Cole and Sparky were fairly certain they would be safe. At least, they felt it was worth the gamble. That was why they left without telling anyone what they were up to. General Whiteside would figure it out anyway, once he noticed they weren't around.

The devastation of Yokohama had barely prepared them for what they saw on the way and in Tokyo. They'd seen the charred ruins and total destruction of a civilization, but they hadn't become immune to the sight. They were more repulsed with each additional acre of death and destruction. Human beings had systematically set out to destroy other human beings, and it was horrifying.

They didn't know where to go in Tokyo. At the hotel in Yokohama, they'd been able to get a kind of street map from the concierge. However, it was in Japanese, covered with strange crosshatchings that must have indicated streets. They had no idea what was on those streets. It seemed as if Tokyo radiated out from a central hub near the bay. Cole surmised that that hub might be the Emperor's Palace—as good a place to start as any.

They finally made it to the central part of Tokyo. People saw their uniforms and Caucasian faces and scurried away like frightened rabbits.

Cole had been right. There was a moat around a massive gray rock wall at the hub on the map. It must have been the

Emperor's Palace behind that wall. Starting at that point, they searched around and found a hotel-type building. As they pulled up in front of the marble edifice, pockmarked with bullet holes and sporting a few broken windows but otherwise in good shape, they decided to get out and ask. A little man came scampering down the steps, bowing like a woodpecker. He wore a black morning coat, a white shirt without a tie or collar, brown pants, and shoes with no socks. They stood watching his approach.

"Welcome." He bobbed. "You like stay in hotel?"

"We're considering it," Sparky said nonchalantly. "Do you have a good suite available?"

"Very good. Please follow," he said, bobbing several times more. Cole noted that although he was smiling obsequiously, his eyes were darting from side to side in panic. He felt sorry for the pathetic little man.

They followed him to a spacious suite, furnished with threadbare carpets and meticulously clean, albeit patched, bedding. There was a bath attached to the room and a window looking out over what once must have been a park. How would these people ever take care of an occupation force? Cole wondered. He was thankful that he and Sparky had had the foresight to bring along enough rations for themselves.

"You want eat?" the man asked.

"Uh, no . . . not now," Cole answered as they put down their barracks bags. "Are you the manager of this hotel?"

"Oh no," he bowed, "I'm owner."

Cole and Sparky exchanged looks. "I see. Then perhaps you can help us find some places around Tokyo."

"Most difficult," the man said, "but I will send someone to help you."

"We want to look for the radio station first," Cole said. Sparky nodded in agreement.

"Radio station?" the man repeated, obviously puzzled.

"Yes, you know, the place where they broadcast all the news to the army in the war?"

"Ah." The man bowed again. "Perhaps NHK be the place you want." He stuck his head out the door and called in Japanese. A young boy in black pants, white shirt, and wooden sandals appeared at the door. The hotel owner spoke rapidly in Japanese and the young man paled at his words. The hotel owner spoke rapidly once more, and the young man bowed.

"This is Umi-chan. He will take you to NHK. I tell him to stay with you. Bring you back here. Take you other place you say."

"Thank you very much," Cole said. "That's just what we need, a guide."

The hotel owner bowed yet again. "Please forgive him. He very frightened of American. But he know some English. He smart. He will bring you back. He my son."

Sparky looked at Umi-chan's pale face, and said, "Please tell him we don't eat people, not even Japanese."

The old man looked startled and glanced at his son. Then they smiled uneasily and bowed twice to Cole and Sparky, obviously unsure about Sparky's sense of humor. Cole found himself starting to bow back, then stopped. He nodded and said, "Well, let's go."

Umi-chan led them through the streets, over blackened blocks of lost city. He finally stopped in front of a tall building. From the antenna on the top, they assumed it was the radio station. Sparky turned to Umi-chan, who looked as if he was ready to run at any minute. "Will you come in with us?" he asked. "We do not speak Japanese."

Umi-chan silently followed them in and proceeded to ask for someone. The secretary at the desk looked at Cole and Sparky as if they were apparitions and dashed out of the room. Presently, a man with a military bearing came out. "Yes." He bowed. "What I do for you?"

"We want to talk to the Flower of the Pacific," Cole blurted out, his heart in his throat.

"She not work here anymore."

"Then give us an address where we can find her."

"She move."

"What about the announcer who was on the program with her?" Sparky put in. "He was an American POW, Jake Devon. Where is he?"

"I don't know who you mean."

"Now listen here," Sparky began, growing angry with the lie.

Cole stopped him and said, "We are American military and we are here on official business. You will cooperate with us here or at our headquarters."

The man paled and said, "I know a POW who worked here. But he is indisposed."

"What does that mean?" Sparky asked sharply.

The man backed up two steps and folded his hands behind his back. "He is ill. He is in Juntendo Hospital."

"Where is that?" Cole demanded.

"I know Juntendo," Umi-chan volunteered.

Cole and Sparky turned and followed their little guide, who now seemed to be taking some interest in their hunt.

Juntendo Hospital was a pitiful, sickening sight. People—burned, bandaged, and broken—were lying in the corridors, sleeping on mats on the floor, receiving scant care from a small, overworked staff. Relatives squatted beside beds and mats, spoon-feeding patients all sorts of vile-smelling concoctions.

It took them fifteen minutes to find someone who could answer their questions. A silence descended over each room they entered, as they searched for some kind of help. Finally, they found a man in a white coat with a stethoscope, the first sign of any medical equipment they'd seen so far. They stopped him and Umi-chan asked something in Japanese. He looked at the Americans through red-rimmed eyes and said wearily, "May I help you?"

"Thank God." Cole sighed. "You speak English."

"I went to the University of Washington. What can I do for you?"

"You have a patient here by the name of Jake Devon. He's a POW who's been working as a radio announcer. May we speak to him?"

"He's on the third floor, back room to your left. You should be able to find him. He's not strong, so don't stay long. If you're here to interrogate or arrest him, I'm going to ask that you not go up there now. He's too weak for that. It will probably be enough of a strain just seeing Americans. I don't think he did anything wrong, so don't be harsh with him."

Cole smiled. "We know he didn't do anything wrong. We're old friends of his. Can you tell us what's wrong with him?"

The doctor rubbed his eyes wearily. "As I remember, he had a light stroke. He's badly malnourished and exhausted, like everyone else in the city. He isn't my patient, but you remember these unique cases just the same. He collapsed about a month ago and has been making only slow progress since then. Your appearance might help him . . . and then again it might be a shock for his weakened state. You make the choice." He spoke briefly in Japanese to Umi-chan, pointing toward the stairs, then walked away.

Sparky hesitated and looked at Cole. "What do you think?"

Cole shook his head. "He's our only chance to find them. He's been fighting this long. I can't imagine that seeing us would make him give up. He deserves to know that we won; he's home free now."

"If I was in his spot, I'd want us to come up no matter what the risk."

Umi-chan led the way and they began searching among the many beds. Finally, in the far corner, they spotted a patient set off from the rest. They approached slowly. Cole and Sparky stared in wonder at Jake's sleeping face. He was thin beyond belief. His complexion was pale and sallow, his hair thin and lank. But the mouth was the same. Even in his sleep his eyes were the same. Cole sat on the edge of the bed and Jake opened his eyes.

He stared, unblinking, for a full minute, his eyes shifting from Sparky to Cole. Finally, he rasped, "If this is a fucking dream, it isn't funny."

Cole's eyes burned with tears as he reached out and gently held Jake's arm. "It's not a dream, buddy. We're really here."

Sparky, silenced by emotion, took Jake's other hand.

Jake started to smile but was overcome by tears. "I never . . ." His shoulders shook with great deep sobs; fearful, shaking sobs from the depths of the man who'd been through so much.

"Hey, Jake," Cole murmured, teary-eyed, "it's over now. They're signing the peace papers day after tomorrow. We're getting you out of here. You're going home."

"It's just that . . . just that I haven't had any news. Iris came up here about a week ago and said she'd heard the war was over. She'd heard the Emperor on the radio but she couldn't understand it very well because he talked in some fancy kind of Japanese." He wiped his eyes and Sparky handed him a handkerchief.

"Iris . . ." Cole barely dared to breathe. "Do you—" Cole swallowed, trying to keep his voice from breaking. "Do you know where she is?"

Jake looked puzzled. "I thought she was the one who told you where to find me."

447

"We have no idea where she is. We found you by asking at the radio station. Do you know where she is?"

"It's way out," Jake said weakly. "She's back at her grandmother's place in Meguro. I don't . . . know the address . . ." His voice began to fade and he closed his eyes.

"I have it," Cole said jubilantly, taking a slip of paper from his wallet.

"Jake," Sparky said gently, but with a note of urgency, "do you know where Eva is? Is she still . . ." He stopped. Jake had fallen asleep.

Umi-chan said he knew where the house was, when he looked at the Japanese characters Bill had written so long ago. They went back to the hotel, got the car, and chugged away through the blackened streets, following Umi-chan's repeated directions of "turn here . . . no, other way, sorry."

After forty-five minutes of driving through the dark, trying to find some landmark that Umi-chan could recognize, they gave up. Tokyo not only didn't have street names, but the house numbers were not consecutive, having been assigned according to when each house had been built rather than to its location. Umi-chan knew that they were in the right district; he just didn't know where in this maze of city blocks he could find that particular house. By this time the houses were dark and there was no sign of any human habitation. Frustrated and feeling defeated, Cole and Sparky went back to the hotel. Maybe, Umi-chan offered, it would be easier in the daylight.

As they entered the hotel lobby, Umi-chan announced to his father that they were back. He was obviously developing a proprietary feeling for "his Americans." His father bustled around nervously and began ordering people to prepare their dinner. Cole stopped him, explaining that they were too tired to enjoy a meal tonight. They went back to their room, with Umi-chan in tow. They shared their rations with Umi-chan, who brought in a bitter tea to go with their cold dinner. Much to their delight, Umi-chan ate everything in sight as if it were a rare feast. They gave him the chocolate bars from their rations and he thanked them profusely, saying he would share them with his family. He promised to take them wherever they needed to go the following morning.

Umi-chan was waiting outside their door when they got up in the morning. He cheerfully took them downstairs and led

448

them into a large room that once must have been an elegant dining room. They sat down at the only table, set with a worn, white, freshly ironed tablecloth. As soon as they were seated, a woman bustled out carrying a tray. She bowed several times as she placed dishes in front of them. Cole looked at Umi-chan and started to protest. "Umi-chan, we really want to get going. We need to find that house we were looking for last night." The woman stopped and looked at them with terror in her eyes, then looked hesitantly at Umi-chan.

"Yes, we find it," Umi-chan assured them. "It is great honor for my mother to serve you." He gestured, and she bowed again before putting down the rest of the plates.

Cole and Sparky exchanged glances. How could they take these people's food? They were so thin. Yet it was obvious that to refuse would hurt their feelings. They would eat little.

Umi-chan's mother lifted the lid from a steaming mound of white rice, poured them each a cup of that bitter tea, and then, as if revealing a masterpiece, lifted the lid from two poached eggs. Cole and Sparky smiled appreciatively and began to eat.

"I wonder where they had to go to find these eggs?" Cole whispered.

"I don't know, but they must be worth their weight in gold. God, I hope MacArthur can find some way to feed these people."

The trip to the Meguro section took twice as long in the daylight. Cole and Sparky were beginning to feel as if they'd never find Iris and Eva. Finally, Umi-chan exclaimed triumphantly that he thought he knew where they were. Jumping out of the car, he stopped a man on the street and showed him Cole's written address. The man pointed back in the direction from which they'd come. Umi-chan bowed and climbed back into the car. "We turn wrong back there," he said.

An hour later, they still had not found the house. People would willingly answer Umi-chan's questions, then glance into the car and see the Americans and slip away quickly. It was getting late. Another fruitless day was about to slip away. Iris was close by: Cole could feel it. Finally, he got an inspiration. "Umi-chan, you say we're pretty close to where we want to be. Do you think it would help to show a picture of the person we're looking for?"

Umi-chan bowed deeply. "That would be most helpful."

Cole reached into his wallet and pulled out the snapshot of Iris and her grandmother. Umi-chan took it and jumped out of the car and began asking people on the street. Presently, an old woman nodded, took Umi-chan to the corner, and gestured, waving her arms in several directions.

Umi-chan got back in the car and said, "She was a friend of the old woman in the picture. She said her friend is dead, but she told me how to get to the house."

Sparky and Cole said nothing as Umi-chan followed the directions. This time he was more confident. Within fifteen minutes they pulled up in front of a brick wall with a heavy wooden gate. Umi-chan waited in the car while Cole and Sparky shoved the gate open, causing a rusting bell to clank noisily.

Behind the gate were the remains of a lovely garden, now overgrown with weeds and baking in the summer sun. A skinny red chicken clucked and scratched in the dusty dirt beside a pebbled path. The timbered house had an arched front entrance with red paint peeling from its wooden facade. A cicada buzzed in a big tree and a dove cooed from behind the house. Another answered from the tree. Swallowing nervously, Cole went to the door and rang the bell. Silence. He rang the bell again. Still no answer.

Then there was the sound of a sliding door in the back of the house and the slow tread of feet. The door opened and a tiny, pale, thin woman stood there staring at them as if they were ghosts.

"Cole . . . is it. . ." Iris whispered.

"Hi, Posey," he said, swallowing the lump in his throat.

She put her hands to her face, tears flooding her cheeks, shaking her head in disbelief. "I never . . . you're so . . . is it . . ." Then, suddenly laughing, she self-consciously touched her hair and stepped toward him.

Cole wrapped his arms around her, afraid that he might break her. "Thank God," he murmured. He found her lips, kissing her over and over, trying to convince himself that she was really his Iris. It was all so dreamlike. Their cheeks were wet with tears of happiness. Cole felt her knees buckle and picked her up in his arms as if she were a child. "Are you all right?" he asked anxiously.

She leaned her head against his shoulder. "I guess, I just . . ." Wiping her cheeks with her hand, she smiled up at him and said, "Let's go inside and talk."

It wasn't until she'd sat down on a pillow in a room that opened to the back garden that she saw Sparky. With a cry, she put her hands to her face once more, then held out her arms. "Sparky! Oh, Sparky, you made it too! You made it too," she said, hugging him.

Sparky hugged her, looking around the room and smiling nervously. "Yeah, I made it," he said. "Where's Eva?"

"Oh, Sparky . . ." Iris said, starting to cry again. "She died last fall. I'm sorry. She was thinking about you to the very end. She loved you," she whispered, reaching out and resting her hand on his arm.

He looked out across the garden, his eyes filling with tears. "Yeah," he said hoarsely. "I figured it was that way." He got up quickly and walked out to the garden.

Cole sat down beside Iris, holding her in his eyes. "Posey, are you all right? I mean, you're beautiful, but you've lost a lot of weight . . . and you're so pale."

Iris laughed. "I'm all right. You're here, aren't you?"

The following day was the signing of the surrender on board the battleship *Missouri*. For Cole and Sparky, the war was over; they didn't need a ceremony to confirm it. At Sparky's request, they went across town to where Eva was buried next to Kiyoko in the cemetery of a small Roman Catholic church in the Shibuya district.

It sat on a slight hill overlooking the burned-out ruins of the city. The rectory had been bombed, but the church had somehow been saved. The wall that had surrounded the west side of the cemetery was gone, and part of the graveyard was beyond repair. But the far corner where Eva and Kiyoko were buried was untouched. Their headstones were under a tall pine tree. They paused by the small granite monument, inscribed: *Eva Nakamuro 2-4-20/9-4-44. Go gently, sweet friend.*

Sparky fell to his knees and buried his face in his hands.

Quietly, Cole and Iris went back to the church. There, leaning against the wall, they heard a radio playing inside.

The priest was listening to the news. They stepped to the window and heard the unmistakable tenor of General MacArthur's voice, speaking from the battleship *Missouri:*

"Today the guns are silent. A great tragedy has ended. A great victory has been won. The skies no longer rain death—the seas bear only commerce—men everywhere walk upright in the sunlight. The entire world lies quietly at Peace. . . ."

Iris turned and looked at Cole, her eyes glistening. He put his arm around her and pulled her to him. Together they listened.

"Men since the beginning of time have sought Peace. Various methods through the ages have been attempted to devise an international process to prevent or settle disputes between nations . . . all, in turn, failed, leaving the only path to be by way of the crucible of war. The utter destructiveness of war now blots out this alternative. We have had our last chance. . . ."

Iris buried her face in Cole's shirt. "You don't know what it's been like," she whispered. "So much dying . . ."

Cole stroked her hair softly, kissing her forehead. "It's over now, Posey. It's all over. We're together and we'll start from here."

"Nanakorobiyaoki," Iris whispered. "Fall down seven times, get up eight."

"My fellow countrymen," MacArthur's voice continued, *"today I report to you that your sons and daughters have served you well and faithfully. . . . They are homeward-bound—take care of them."*

ABOUT THE AUTHOR

LANA MCGRAW BOLDT was born in Oregon and attended the University of Oregon, earning a degree in English literature. She did postgraduate work in applied psychology at the University of Washington. With her husband, Darrell, she served in the Peace Corps in Micronesia. The Marshall Islands Cultural Museum is a result of some of her work there. They traveled in Asia, the Middle East, and Europe before returning to the United States.

She has worked as a teacher, a magazine correspondent, a resource writer for the Oregon Shakespearean Festival, and a volunteer in her community. She is currently at work on her second novel. She lives in Oregon with her husband and two daughters.